Neo-Victorian Fiction and Historical Narrative

Also by Louisa Hadley

THE FICTION OF A. S. BYATT
THATCHER AND AFTER: Margaret Thatcher and her Afterlife in Contemporary Culture (*edited with Elizabeth Ho*)

Neo-Victorian Fiction and Historical Narrative

The Victorians and Us

Louisa Hadley

First published 2010 by
PALGRAVE MACMILLAN

Palgrave Macmillan in the UK is an imprint of Macmillan Publishers Limited, registered in England, company number 785998, of Houndmills, Basingstoke, Hampshire RG21 6XS.

Palgrave Macmillan in the US is a division of St Martin's Press LLC, 175 Fifth Avenue, New York, NY 10010.

Palgrave Macmillan is the global academic imprint of the above companies and has companies and representatives throughout the world.

Palgrave® and Macmillan® are registered trademarks in the United States, the United Kingdom, Europe and other countries.

ISBN 978–0–230–55156–5   hardback

This book is printed on paper suitable for recycling and made from fully managed and sustained forest sources. Logging, pulping and manufacturing processes are expected to conform to the environmental regulations of the country of origin.

A catalogue record for this book is available from the British Library.

Library of Congress Cataloging-in-Publication Data

Hadley, Louisa.
  Neo-Victorian fiction and historical narrative : the Victorians and us / Louisa Hadley.
       p. cm.
  ISBN 978–0–230–55156–5 (hardback)
  1. Historical fiction, English—History and criticism. 2. English fiction—20th century—History and criticism. 3. English fiction—21st century—History and criticism. 4. Literature and history—Great Britain—History—20th century. 5. Literature and history—Great Britain—History—21st century. 6. Great Britain—History—Victoria, 1837–1901—Historiography. 7. Great Britain—Civilization—19th century—Historiography. I. Title.
  PR888.H5H33 2010
  823'.081090914—dc22

2010027519

10 9 8 7 6 5 4 3 2 1
19 18 17 16 15 14 13 12 11 10

Printed and bound in Great Britain by
CPI Antony Rowe, Chippenham and Eastbourne

Contents

Acknowledgements

This book has been in progress for a while, so thanks are due in various places. My research into neo-Victorian fiction started with my Masters and PhD dissertations at the University of Edinburgh, and I am grateful for the support of my supervisor Penny Fielding both throughout my graduate degrees and since. I am also deeply indebted to the anonymous reader who reviewed this book for Palgrave Macmillan. The insightful comments and encouraging remarks on both the initial proposal and manuscript greatly helped me to clarify my ideas. This book has been written in various cities, and with the help of various libraries. I would particularly like to thank the staff at the National Library of Scotland, the University of Edinburgh, and the University of Alberta whose patience and willingness to help have been greatly appreciated. Thanks are also due to Paula Kennedy and Benjamin Doyle at Palgrave Macmillan for their continued support and patience.

On a more personal note, I would like to thank Elizabeth Elliott who read a draft of the Introduction to this book and helped with some last-minute checking of references. Last, but by no means least, I wish to thank Gary Stewart for his patience, support and technical expertise throughout the writing of this book.

Portions of Chapter 3 and Chapter 4 appeared in 'Spectres of the Past: A. S. Byatt's Victorian Ghost Stories' and are reprinted with permission from *Victorians Institute Journal* 31 (2003): 85–99.

Introduction:
Writing the Victorians

'The history of the Victorian age will never be written. We know too much about it', or so Lytton Strachey declared in the preface to his book *Eminent Victorians* in 1918 (p. 10). Yet since the death of Queen Victoria more than 100 years ago, the history of the Victorian era has been continuously rewritten. Indeed, Strachey's *Eminent Victorians* was itself part of a Modernist rewriting that reflected an oedipal desire to emphasize the distance between the Victorians and the Modernists. As J. B. Bullen writes, 'For [Strachey], and for many of [his] contemporaries, "Victorian" was a way of distinguishing [his] own attitudes from those of [his] parents' (p. 2). Bullen recognizes that 'Victorian' here is a connotative, rather than merely denotative, term; what the Modernists sought to distance themselves from were the systems of 'repression, realism, materialism, and *laissez-faire* capitalism' that they felt characterized the Victorian period (p. 2). Confirming the oedipal nature of this relationship, Bullen suggests that the Modernist drive to assert difference from the Victorian generation was 'so strident that it now seems [...] like the nursery tantrums of children rebelling against the despotic regime of their parents' (p. 2). Although the contemporary relationship to the Victorians continues to be conceptualized in such familial terms, the Victorians, as we shall see, seem to have moved from the position of oppressive parent-figures to benign grandparents. It is not only the nature of the engagement with the Victorians that has altered over the last 100 years; both the frequency and popularity of rewritings and re-imaginings of the Victorians have increased in the second half of the twentieth, and on into the twenty-first, century.[1] The contemporary fascination with the Victorians seems to be particularly marked within the realm of fiction, where it has spawned the genre of neo-Victorian fiction. While Mark Llewellyn questions whether 'any text published after 1901 which is set in the Victorian period' should be called a neo-Victorian text (p. 175), most critics date the genre to the 1960s, which saw the publication of Jean Rhys's *Wide Sargasso Sea* (1966), a post-colonial rewriting of *Jane Eyre* (1847); and John Fowles's postmodernist experiment with the Victorians, *The French Lieutenant's Woman* (1969).[2]

Working against the desire to establish an originary narrative, Marie-Luise Kohlke, the founding editor of the online journal *Neo-Victorian Studies*, proposes that accounts of neo-Victorianism should be concerned 'not so much to locate chronological boundary markers or points of origin as crucial nodal points in neo-Victorian output and dissemination' (p. 3). The publication of A. S. Byatt's *Possession: A Romance* in 1990, and the subsequent surge in neo-Victorian fictions suggests that the period between the late 1980s and the early 2000s should be understood as one such 'crucial nodal point' in the history of Victorian re-writings. Winning both prestigious literary prizes, such as the Man Booker Prize and the *Irish Times*–Aer Lingus International Fiction Prize, and a place on the bestsellers' lists, *Possession* catapulted neo-Victorian fiction into the mainstream. A brief survey of recent Man Booker Prize shortlists reveals the continued critical success of the genre: Margaret Atwood's *Alias Grace* (1996); Matthew Kneale's *English Passengers* (2000); Sarah Waters's *Fingersmith* (2002); and Julian Barnes's *Arthur & George* (2005). Of the six books which made it to the shortlist for the 2009 Man Booker Prize, five are historical fictions: two of which are set in the Victorian or Edwardian period (A. S. Byatt's *The Children's Book*, 2009 and Adam Fould's *The Quickening Maze*, 2009), with a third, set in the 1940s, written by Sarah Waters who, Dennis suggests, is 'arguably the best-known and most widely read of the various contemporary purveyors of literary neo-Victorianism' (p. 41).[3] The Hollywood film adaptation of *Possession* in 2002 both confirmed and extended the popular appeal of Byatt's novel, and neo-Victorian fiction more generally. While television and film adaptations of Victorian fiction continue to be popular, there is an increasing market for adaptations of neo-Victorian fictions. For instance, all three of Sarah Waters's neo-Victorian novels have been adapted for television: *Tipping the Velvet* (BBC, 2002), *Fingersmith* (BBC, 2005), and *Affinity* (ITV, 2008).

In her essay 'Introduction: Speculations in and on the Neo-Victorian Encounter,' Kohlke concludes that '[m]uch as we read Victorian texts as highly revealing cultural products of their age, neo-Victorian texts will one day be read for the insights they afford into twentieth- and twenty-first century cultural history and socio-political concerns' (p. 13). As the cover image of this book indicates, neo-Victorian fictions published since the late 1980s need to be understood within the context of Margaret Thatcher's political appropriation of the Victorians. Superimposing Margaret Thatcher's face onto the iconic image of Queen Victoria as Empress of India, Peter Kennard's photomontage 'Maggie Regina: Victorian Values' (1983) hints at the cultural anxieties surrounding Thatcher's appropriation of 'Victorian values': whereas Queen Victoria ruled over an impressive empire, Margaret Thatcher came to power at a time when Britain's 'proper place' seemed to be that of 'an increasingly obscure island off the shore of north-west Europe' (Young, p. 6).[4] The neo-Victorian fictions examined in this book critically engage with this cultural context. Many of the novels explicitly address Thatcher's appropriation of the Victorians, revealing the gulf between Thatcher's ideal and the realities of Victorian life. All of the novels, however, engage with the wider issues of history and national heritage that underpin Thatcher's championing of the Victorians.

Defining neo-Victorian fiction

In her essay '(Re-)Workings of Nineteenth-Century Fiction: Definitions, Terminology, Contexts,' Andrea Kirchknopf notes the proliferation of terms for fictional rewrites of the Victorians, asking '[i]s it *Victoriana, Victoriographies, retro-, neo-* or *post-Victorian novels* we encounter when we read rewritings of the Victorian era?' (p. 59). Kirchknopf comes down in favour of *post-Victorian* because 'it connotatively blends the Victorian, the modernist and the postmodernist eras' (p. 64). Yet, as the following discussion shows, I contend that critical accounts need to understand the historical specificity of both the Victorian and contemporary/postmodern context of neo-Victorian fiction rather than blending them. For this reason, I prefer the term *neo-Victorian*, which suggests that while the Victorian era is brought into contact with a new context, it is not subsumed within that new context. Moreover, neo-Victorian seems to have gained both popular and critical currency as the term by which to designate the fictional rewritings of the Victorian era that have appeared since the 1960s.[5] The variety of terms used to describe fictional rewritings of the Victorian era reflects the variation within neo-Victorianism itself, both as a critical approach and a creative practice. As Kohlke writes, 'Neo-Victorian Studies is still in the process of crystallisation [...]; as yet its temporal and generic boundaries remain fluid and relatively open to experimentation by artists, writers and theorists alike' (p. 1). In order to encompass the range of fictional responses to the Victorians, I define neo-Victorian fiction in the broadest possible terms as contemporary fiction that engages with the Victorian era, at either the level of plot, structure, or both. Exemplifying the range of approaches neo-Victorian fiction adopts, the genre has been taken up by writers of post-colonial fiction, as in J. G. Farrell's *The Siege of Krishnapur* (1973), Margaret Atwood's *Alias Grace*, and Peter Carey's *Jack Maggs* (1997); writers of lesbian fiction, most prominently in Sarah Waters's trilogy *Tipping the Velvet* (1998), *Affinity* (1999), and *Fingersmith*; and authors of children's fiction, as in Philippa Pearce's *Tom's Midnight Garden* (1978).[6]

Although neo-Victorian fictions share a concern with the Victorian past, the way that concern enters the fictional world can vary dramatically, as can be seen by a brief summary of the texts discussed in this book. In several of the texts, the engagement with the Victorian past is explicitly mediated through Victorian literature. While some texts draw on the conventions of a Victorian genre, as in Colin Dexter's detective novel *The Wench is Dead* (1989), others position themselves in relation to a specific Victorian intertext. Even here, though, the approach can vary; Peter Carey's *Jack Maggs* re-imagines Dickens's *Great Expectations* (1860) from Magwitch's perspective while A. S. Byatt's 'The Conjugial Angel' (1992) responds to Tennyson's *In Memoriam* (1850), and James Wilson's *The Dark Clue* (2001) presents itself as a sequel to Wilkie Collins's *The Woman in White* (1860). Other texts choose to engage with historical figures from the nineteenth century: Janice Galloway's *Clara* (2002) provides a fictional account of the life of Clara Schumann, and Julian Barnes's *Arthur & George* follows the real-life figures of Arthur Conan Doyle and George Edalji. Michèle Roberts's *In the Red Kitchen* (1990) creates a fictional protagonist based on the historical figure of Flora Cook. Then there are those novels that create fictional characters and events as a way to explore issues that were central to Victorian culture. Thus, Sarah Waters's *Affinity* follows the exploits of an imprisoned fictional medium to explore the issue of spiritualism and the position of women within Victorian society. Both Graham Swift's *Ever After* (1992) and A. S. Byatt's *Possession: A Romance* similarly create fictional Victorians, and their own textual worlds, to explore Victorian issues. In their adoption of a dual plot structure, which depicts twentieth-century academics engaging with the textual remains of the fictional Victorians, these novels explicitly dramatize the relationship between the present and the past.

Dana Shiller, one of the first critics to define the genre, identified two strategies within neo-Victorian fiction:

[1] Some of these texts imitate Victorian literary conventions, either by creating altogether new stories or by reimagining specific Victorian novels from a new angle ... [2] while others are more overtly 'postmodern' in style and tone, but concern themselves with Victorian subjects. (p. 1)

According to Shiller's definition, *The Dark Clue* and *Jack Maggs* would both belong to the first category of 'imitat[ing] Victorian literary conventions' and 'reimagining specific Victorian novels from a new angle'. Yet they are equally concerned with exploring 'Victorian subjects' in their concern with biographical narratives. This concern with biographical narratives also occurs at the level of literary conventions since both texts explore the forms of biographical narratives. These novels, then, collapse Shiller's distinction between Victorian conventions and Victorian subjects, revealing that these two strategies can co-exist within a single text. Despite this, Shiller's definition remains useful for my purposes. Most importantly, she recognizes that neo-Victorian fictions can be 'overtly "postmodern" in style and tone,' while resisting the urge to conflate neo-Victorian fiction with postmodernism. Critical accounts of neo-Victorian fiction often understand the genre in relation to wider trends in postmodern, post-war or contemporary fiction, or, alternatively, as merely a continuation of Victorian literature rather than a genre in its own right.[7] In the last few years, however, there has been a shift towards recognizing neo-Victorian fiction as a distinct creative practice requiring its own critical assessment.[8] In this book, I position neo-Victorian fiction in relation to historical fiction, arguing that both its Victorian and postmodern context impacts its engagement with historical narratives.

Written in one period, but evoking another, historical novels always occupy a complex position in relation to the present and the past. Critical accounts of historical fiction tend to prioritize the moment of production over the era that is revived within the novels. For instance, Avrom Fleishman's *The English Historical Novel: Walter Scott to Virginia Woolf* (1971) examines 'the late Victorian historical novel' and considers Woolf's fiction alongside that of fellow modernist Conrad (p. 149). Diana Wallace's *The Woman's Historical Novel: British Women Writers, 1900–2000* (2005) similarly adopts a chronological approach, with a chapter devoted to the historical fictions produced in each of the decades of the twentieth century. In adopting an historical and chronological approach to the genre, such accounts align diverse texts on the grounds of historical proximity. Historical fiction, however, is defined as much by the period it evokes as by the period it is written in. All historical novels, therefore, adopt a dual approach which combines a concern with the past and a concern with the present. This dual approach is most apparent in novels which adopt a dual plot structure, with events occurring in both the historical period being evoked and the contemporary era of the novel itself. As a consequence of this dual approach, historical fictions written around the same time will vary according to the era they evoke.[9] For instance, the current trend for historical novels set in the Tudor period is marked by a concern with gender roles as in Philippa Gregory's novel *The Queen's Fool* (2004).[10] By contrast, the neo-Victorian fiction produced since the 1980s is marked by a concern with history and historical narratives; it is not only concerned with reinserting the Victorians into historical narrative, but also with exploring the ways in which historical narratives affect responses to the past. As I have suggested, this interest in historical narratives is prompted by these novels' engagement with the Thatcherite context of the 1980s and 1990s. Yet it is also prompted by the historical location of these narratives as the nineteenth century was intensely interested in history, both in terms of its valuation of the past and its consciousness of its own position within history.

Given its focus on the forms of historical narratives, this book necessarily emphasizes the importance of the Victorian context in neo-Victorian fiction. Yet, as I have said, neo-Victorian fiction adopts a dual approach. Consequently, critical accounts need to be aware of both its contemporary and Victorian contexts. Neo-Victorian fiction coincides with a wider cultural fascination with the Victorians, a fascination which often results in the erasure of the historical specificity of the Victorians. Rather than merely being another manifestation of that cultural fascination, though, neo-Victorian fictions seek to both reinsert the Victorians into their particular historical context and engage with contemporary uses of the Victorians which efface that historical context.

Why the Victorians? Why now?

At the most fundamental level, the Victorians hold a central place in the contemporary cultural imagination because of the position they occupy in relation to the twentieth century. Close enough for us to be aware that we have descended from them and yet far enough away for there to be significant differences in life-styles, the Victorians occupy a similar place to our grandparents.[11] Removed by a generation, we escape the 'anxiety of influence' that characterized the Modernists' reaction to the Victorians and prompted the disparagement of writers like Lytton Strachey and Virginia Woolf. Thus, contemporary writers are perhaps more sympathetic to the Victorians than the preceding generation.[12] Moreover, the physical presence of the Victorians in British society makes them hard to ignore: numerous buildings, structures and institutions remain from the Victorian era.[13] It is not just at the level of public edifices that the Victorians maintain a presence, however; the development of new techniques for documenting individuals in the nineteenth century means that there is a vast array of information preserved about the Victorians. In particular, the establishment of regular censuses and registers of births, deaths and marriages have made it possible for everyone to trace their family lineage back at least as far as the start of the nineteenth century. As E. A. Wrigley remarks, 'The Victorian age was not the first period in English history of which it can be said that there remains written evidence about every man who then lived. [...] But in the Victorian age the volume of information compiled for every individual mounted fast' (p. 6). The development of such practices, then, extended the opportunities for the Victorians to leave behind physical records of their time and at least partly accounts for their continued presence in the contemporary cultural consciousness.

While these remains provide vivid illustrations of the Victorian past, they also prompt a recognition of the immense differences between the Victorian way of life and our own. This is particularly marked in the case of photography. The development of photographic techniques in the nineteenth century means that more images abound of the Victorian era than of any previous period in history. While these photographs bring the Victorians into the present moment, they also remind the viewer that the subjects are dead and gone. As Roland Barthes theorized, the indexical nature of a photograph 'certifies, so to speak, that the corpse is alive, as *corpse*: it is the living image of a dead thing' (pp. 78–9). The physical conditions of photography in the nineteenth century reinforce this connection with death as subjects had to be clamped into position and retain a fixed look for the long exposure times. In fact, many of the photographs of babies and animals from the Victorian era would have been taken post-mortem because of the difficulties of photographing such subjects while alive.[14] The formality surrounding portrait photography in the nineteenth century clearly distances these images from our own 'point and shoot' generation. Photographs, then, both affirm and yet undermine the closeness of the Victorians to us. Jennifer Green-Lewis addresses this paradox in her essay 'At Home in the Nineteenth Century: Photography, Nostalgia, and the Will to Authenticity' (2000): 'The Victorians continue to exist in the absolute and paradoxical present of the photograph, always there yet gone forever; both in, and out, of history; always already dead – yet still alive' (p. 31).[15] The idea that the Victorians are both 'in and out of history' is fundamental to understanding the contemporary return to the Victorians. Clearly the Victorians are 'in history', not only by virtue of being dead and gone, but also because of their position within historical narratives. The Victorians occupy an instrumental role in the history of modernity and, particularly within Britain, are central to a narrative of national development. Yet the Victorians are also 'out of history'; within the contemporary imagination, there is a tendency to remove the Victorians from their specific historical context. This paradoxical position of the Victorians underpins attempts to explain the contemporary fascination with them, which highlight either the distance between the Victorians and us – their strangeness and the discontinuities between the present and the past – or their proximity to us – their familiarity and the continuities between the present and the past.

Accounts which point to the strangeness of the Victorians as the source of contemporary interest suggest that the return to the Victorian era is prompted by an awareness of its difference from our own period. Such accounts are often motivated by a nostalgic impulse which positions the Victorian era as a 'golden age' from which the present has dropped off. This appeal to a past era of 'greatness' is particularly prone to political appropriation and the Victorians were made to serve just such a purpose by the Conservative Prime Minister Margaret Thatcher (in office 1979–1990). In the run up to the 1983 General Election, Thatcher invoked 'Victorian values' in an attempt to capitalize on the cultural value of the Victorians and to assert a direct lineage between the values of the Victorian era and her own political values. Although 'Victorian' had become a pejorative term at the turn of the twentieth century, Thatcher turned it into a positive term that had visible political effects. As Raphael Samuel puts it 'Mrs Thatcher annexed "Victorian values" to her Party's platform and turned them into a talisman for lost stabilities' (p. 9). The term 'Victorian' was ripe for reassessment and Thatcher's political use of the term was no doubt aided by the cultural reclamation of the Victorian era that was being undertaken by the Heritage Industry and the 'Laura Ashley look' in the 1980s (Samuel, p. 14). As Samuel notes, these cultural practices 'had the effect, so far as popular taste was concerned, of rehabilitating the notion of the Victorian and associating it not with squalor and grime, but on the contrary with goodness and beauty, purity and truth' (p. 14).

These values of 'goodness and beauty, purity and truth' are the very values that Thatcher sought to evoke in her adoption of the phrase 'Victorian values'. In a speech delivered to the Glasgow Chamber of Commerce in 1983, Thatcher defined her idea of 'Victorian values' as 'honesty and thrift and reliability and hard work and a sense of responsibility for your fellow men [...]'. When asked to clarify what she meant by 'Victorian values' in a radio interview a few months later, Thatcher drew attention to the position of the Victorians as our grandparents, and implicitly identified them as the moral standard against which we should be measured:

> I was brought up by a Victorian grandmother. You were taught to work jolly hard, you were taught to improve yourself, you were taught self-reliance, you were taught to live within your income, you were taught that cleanliness was next to godliness. You were taught self-respect, you were taught always to give a hand to your neigbour [*sic*], you were taught tremendous pride in your country, you were taught to be a good member of your community. All of these things are Victorian values. (*The Decision Markers*)

Thatcher's promotion of the Victorian era was part of a wider attempt to stir up patriotic pride in Britain's past. In an interview for *Weekend World* in January 1983, Brian Walden put it to Mrs Thatcher that 'what you seem to be looking for is a more self-reliant Britain, a thriftier Britain, a Britain where people are free to act, where they get less assistance from the State, where they're less burdened by the State' and that these values amounted to 'Victorian values'. Thatcher wholeheartedly agreed with Walden's assessment of her values, responding with patriotic pride that '[t]hose were the values when our country became great' (*Weekend World*). Such patriotic sentiments are clearly overlaid with nostalgia, which presents a selectively positive view of the past. Walden hinted at this process of selection when he drew attention to the other side of Victorian values, claiming that '[i]f we are going to have these sorts of values we're going to have a more unequal, or at least an equally unequal society than the one we've got at the moment' (*Weekend World*).

In emphasizing the elements of the Victorian past that are occluded in Thatcher's evocation of 'Victorian values', Walden reveals the extent to which Thatcher's political appropriation of the Victorians divorces them from their historical context.

The discrepancy between Thatcher's ideal of 'Victorian values' and the reality of the Victorian era has been highlighted by many commentators. Much has been made of the irony that Margaret Thatcher pursued a policy of decreasing state intervention whilst evoking the era which saw the first movements toward the establishment of the Welfare State.[16] Thus, Thatcher's espousal of 'Victorian values' rejects the historical reality of the Victorian era in favour of contemporary stereotypes about the Victorians. Thatcher further removes the Victorians from their historical context in eliding the very historical specificity she claims for 'Victorian values'. To return to the Glasgow Chamber of Commerce speech, Thatcher claimed that the values she promotes 'are not simply Victorian values. They do not go out of date. They are not tied to any particular place or century. [...] they are part of the enduring principles of the Western world. And if we just write them off and wave them goodbye, we are destroying the best of our heritage'. While Thatcher seems eager to identify with and revive a particular era of Britain's past, the Victorian era, she simultaneously erases historical distinctions by declaring Victorian values timeless values. What began as a nostalgic lament for a lost golden age, a lament which implicitly asserts the distance between the present and the past, becomes an assertion of continuity between the present and the past. In evoking the figure of her Victorian grandmother, Thatcher sought to remind the British public of their affinity with the Victorians and encourage the return of those values that the Victorians had promoted.

In other fields, the strangeness of the Victorians is not merely nostalgically mourned, but rather exoticized and fetishized. The recent BBC adaptations of Victorian novels, which have become an almost obligatory feature of the Sunday evening, autumn schedule, continue the aestheticization of the Victorians that began with the Merchant-Ivory productions of the 1980s and other such 'heritage' films. These films were part of a wider 'heritage culture' in Britain during the 1980s which sought to bolster a sense of a fixed national identity;[17] they offer a visual feast in their sumptuous display of Britain's cultural heritage as encoded in both its landscapes and properties, particularly the country house estates, and the furnishings and costumes. As Andrew Higson's insightful analysis of the heritage film has shown, these films revel in the visual display of the past, lingering over shots of the landscape and 'period details' often at the expense of depicting the interactions between characters. Higson's essay 'Re-presenting the National Past: Nostalgia and Pastiche in the Heritage Film' (1993) argues that in these films 'the past is displayed as visually spectacular pastiche, inviting a nostalgic gaze' (p. 109). By focusing on the reproduction of the style of the Victorian era, rather than the substance, this aestheticization of the Victorian past clearly removes it from history. The extent to which heritage films efface the historical context of the Victorian era is evident in the conflation of the Victorian era and the 'long nineteenth-century' in such productions, so that adaptations of Austen and Forster novels are absorbed into discussions of the return to the Victorians.[18]

Many recent adaptations have relinquished the visual nostalgia for the country house in favour of a more realistic portrayal which reinserts the Victorians within their historical context. Yet even while depicting the squalor of Victorian life, such adaptations are prone to nostalgia. For example, the BBC's 2005 serialization of Elizabeth Gaskell's *North and South* seems to be countering the aestheticization of the Victorian era in heritage films in its focus on the grim reality of life in the Manchester cotton factories. In the first episode, Margaret gets her first glimpse of life inside the cotton factory; however, in this scene the gritty reality is overlaid with nostalgia. Before entering the work room, Margaret coughs from the cotton fibres, but once the doors are open the scene switches to slow motion to show the fibres drifting languorously through the air and the noise of the machinery is overlaid with orchestral string music. Moreover, the scene's concern with the historical and social realities of life in the Manchester cotton mills is overtaken by the burgeoning love story as it also depicts Margaret's first glimpse of John Hale. The attempt to return the Victorians to a place within history, then, is ultimately undermined; by shifting the viewer's attention to the love story, the scene emphasizes the universality of the experience of love and thus removes the Victorian characters from their specific historical context.

Although love is presented as a universal, the Victorians' attitude towards sex and sexuality is more frequently cited as evidence of the gulf between the Victorians and us. Victorian attitudes towards sex are seen to be grounded in the historical context of the Victorian era and the equation between 'Victorian' and prudery in contemporary parlance reveals the assumption that we are more liberated than our Victorian ancestors.[19] Despite this, Victorian attitudes retain a nostalgic appeal which screen adaptations of Victorian novels are quick to capitalize on. Viewers' comments on episodes of *North and South* indicate the appeal of Victorian attitudes towards sex; comments such as 'Alas, we no longer live in a time of such raw and powerfully evoked emotions. We can but dream!' and 'As for the romance – how much more impact does it have than the "in your face whether you like it or not" modern screenplays of today' reveal the assumption that the Victorians experienced sexual desire more keenly because it was repressed.[20] Although Michel Foucault's *The History of Sexuality* (1976) highlighted the proliferation of Victorian discourses about sex and sexuality, the 'repressive hypothesis' has retained its force in the popular imagination (p. 10). The Victorian era is nostalgically reconstructed as a time of sexual innocence, a time far removed from our own culture of permissive sexuality. Yet there is also a contradictory desire that underpins such adaptations; viewers want to witness the eruption of the passion and emotion believed to be barely contained beneath the high-collars and stiff petticoats, an eruption which positions the Victorians as 'just like us'. In pandering to these desires, screen adaptations of Victorian novels erase the historical distance between the Victorians and us, placing the Victorians 'out of history'. To return to *North and South*, the ending of the BBC serialization, in which Margaret and John share a public kiss on a railway platform, not only rewrites the ending of Gaskell's novel but also writes the historical and social context out of the love story. The passionate and public nature of the kiss, as well as the fact that Margaret travels back to Milton with John unchaperoned, transgress the social and moral mores of the day.

The frequency with which Victorian novels are adapted for the big and small screen is not only a consequence of the attractions of Victorian romances but also a reflection of the position of the Victorian novel in contemporary society. Since the turn of the millennium, the BBC alone have presented new versions of *Daniel Deronda* (2002), *He Knew He Was Right* (2004), *North and South* (2004), *Bleak House* (2005), *Jane Eyre* (2006), *Cranford* (2007), *Oliver Twist* (2007), *Lark Rise to Candleford* (2008), *Tess of the D'Urbervilles* (2008), and *Little Dorrit* (2008). One viewer's comment on *Jane Eyre* reveals the cultural currency that Victorian 'classics' continue to have in contemporary society: 'It makes such a pleasant change having something with substance to watch over the weekend'.[21] This desire to return to 'traditional' values of literature reveals the extent to which the perception of the novel genre is grounded in the nineteenth-century form of 'classic realism'.[22] Victorian ideas about the importance of plot and character have become so dominant that in adopting these elements Byatt's *Possession* is judged to have 'all the earmarks of a Victorian "good read"' (Janik, p. 162). Victorian novels are felt to fulfil the desire for plot, rounded characters and narrative interest in a way that postmodern fictions apparently cannot.[23] Sarah Waters makes this point in an interview with Abigail Dennis, arguing that nineteenth-century fiction allows for a 'celebration of narrativity' that was denied in the 'arid' 'mainstream literary fictions in this country [...] in the 90s' (p. 46). This argument understands the present return to the Victorians as a backlash against the cultural fragmentation which accompanies postmodernism. In this incarnation, the Victorian era is constructed as a period when faith was possible and there was a confident belief in the progress of human society, in contrast to contemporary society, which is characterized by division and fragmentation, a loss of faith in the certainties of grand narratives. Such accounts of Victorian literature position it as naive and simplistic in comparison to the more intelligent and self-reflexive texts of postmodern literature. Thus, while this approach explicitly positions the Victorian era as a 'golden age' of literature, it also implicitly positions it as inferior. The Victorian novel, then, is simultaneously confined to its historical position, which renders it more naive than contemporary texts, and taken out of its historical context in its embodiment of the supposedly universal characteristics of 'good reads'.[24]

Although the political and cultural uses of the Victorians outlined thus far serve different purposes, they all stem from a perception of the Victorians as different from us. Reactions to that difference range from nostalgic lamentation, to a desire to recuperate the past and re-establish its connection to the present, to an implicit sense of superiority over the Victorians. There is another set of narratives, however, that take as their starting point the idea that the Victorians are not so different from us. Such accounts posit the nineteenth century as a moment of transition, marking the advent of the modern society we now inhabit; they interpret the current return to the Victorian era as prompted by a sense of recognition and familiarity. Rather than a 'them' vs. 'us' mentality, then, these narratives take the familiarity of the Victorians as their point of departure and explore the connections between the present and the past.

In the introduction to his book *Inventing the Victorians* (2001) Matthew Sweet suggests that contemporary culture propagates a mis-perception of the Victorians, one that is designed to make us seem liberated by comparison. Sweet's book seeks to contest this narrative of disjunction between the Victorian past and the present, but in doing so he establishes another narrative – one that implicitly positions the Victorian era as the beginning of the modern world.[25] The idea that modern Britain developed out of the Victorian era similarly underpins the

BBC's documentary series *What the Victorians Did for Us* (2001), presented by Adam Hart-Davis. As the title suggests, this series, and the accompanying book which was published in 2002, sought to explore those Victorian innovations that have had a continuing impact in the present.[26] Although this approach positions the Victorians within history, it is susceptible to a teleological bias which reconstructs the Victorian period as the inevitable forerunner of modern society. Such accounts position the Victorian era as 'a time of unprecedented cultural, scientific and technological change – a time extraordinarily like our own' (Hart-Davis, *blurb*).

As these examples show, the appeal of the Victorians is a result of the complex combination of their historical proximity to and distance from the contemporary era. Sarah Waters, author of three neo-Victorian novels to date, alluded to this dual appeal of the Victorians in her interview with Abigail Dennis. Explaining her choice of the 1890s as the location for her first lesbian historical novel, Waters claims that it was a time when 'things were changing, but they were foreign enough to be interesting' (p. 44).[27] Sally Shuttleworth's essay on the appearance of Darwinian ideas in contemporary fiction similarly highlights the dual appeal of the Victorians: 'For the Victorians there was a decisive crisis of faith, a sense that the world was shaking under them, an ecstatic agony of indecision. For the post-modern era no such form of crisis seems possible, for there are no fixed boundaries of belief' (p. 260). Shuttleworth's assessment, then, seems to conflate the two narratives I have been tracing: it positions the Victorians as the moment of transition for the modern world – the moment of the 'decisive crisis of faith' – yet it also betrays a sense of nostalgia for the Victorians since even the possibility of such a crisis has been lost in the modern world.

Neo-Victorian fictions reinsert the Victorians into their historical context and thus avoid a purely nostalgic or aesthetic approach to the Victorian past. Yet they remain aware that the present moment has emerged out of the Victorian context. Consequently, these novels reveal both the continuities and discontinuities between the Victorian past and the present. Neo-Victorian fictions, then, are not merely part of the contemporary fascination with the Victorian past; they are aware of the purposes the Victorians are made to serve and in returning to the Victorians self-consciously comment on the political and cultural uses of the Victorians in the present. For instance, many of the neo-Victorian texts written since the 1980s engage with Margaret Thatcher's political appropriation of the Victorians and their values. In their commitment to historical specificity, they often seek to highlight the underside of the Victorian era that Thatcher effectively wrote out of her political rhetoric. This aspect of neo-Victorian fiction is particularly drawn out in the discussion of Dexter's *The Wench is Dead* and Roberts's *In the Red Kitchen* in Chapters 2 and 3 respectively.

The bi-directionality of neo-Victorian fiction, pointing to both the Victorian past and the contemporary present, is explicitly dramatized in novels that adopt a dual plot. Of the texts discussed in this book, four of them – *The Wench is Dead, Possession, Ever After* and *In the Red Kitchen* – adopt a plot structure which sees the action of the novel split between a nineteenth-century plot and a twentieth-century one, although Roberts's novel also includes a third plot set in Ancient Egypt. With one foot in the nineteenth century and one in the twentieth, these texts highlight the need to understand neo-Victorian fiction within both its contemporary and its Victorian context. Even those novels that are located wholly in the nineteenth century, however, incorporate an awareness of the contemporary position of the writer and reader since as historical fictions neo-Victorian novels necessarily adopt a dual relationship to the past.

Neo-Victorian fiction as historical fiction

Critical accounts of neo-Victorian fiction tend to focus on its moment of production and thus discuss it in terms of the categories of postmodern, post-war, or contemporary fiction. While some reviewers and critics draw attention to the genre's relationship to Victorian literature, this usually remains at the level of identifying intertextual allusions. Aligning these texts with the category of postmodernism precludes an extended consideration of the impact of the Victorian context. Whether it is seen as an extension of or departure from modernism, postmodernism is always understood in relation to modernism. My approach to neo-Victorian fiction does not seek to deny its connections to postmodernism; indeed, several of the novels discussed in this book are written by authors that are considered exemplars of postmodern fiction: Julian Barnes's *Arthur & George*, Peter Carey's *Jack Maggs*, Janice Galloway's *Clara*, Michèle Roberts's *In the Red Kitchen*, and Graham Swift's *Ever After*. Rather, I adopt a dual approach that seeks to understand neo-Victorian fiction in relation to both its contemporary and its Victorian context. My approach, then, mirrors the dual approach of neo-Victorian fiction which, I have suggested, is characteristic of all historical fiction.

According to Georg Lukács, whose *The Historical Novel* (1962) remains the standard critical account of the genre, the historical novel 'arose at the beginning of the nineteenth century at about the time of Napoleon's collapse' (p. 19). As a Marxist critic, it is unsurprising that Lukács establishes such a direct relationship between historical context and fictional conventions. Indeed, he argues that the 'French Revolution, the revolutionary wars, and the rise and fall of Napoleon' altered the way in which individuals understood their position in relation to historical forces: 'for the first time [...] history [became] a *mass experience*, and moreover on a European scale' (p. 23). He goes on to suggest that these events 'strengthen[ed] the feeling first that there is such a thing as history, that it is an uninterrupted process of changes and finally that it has a direct effect upon the life of every individual' (p. 23). It was as a reaction to this lived experience of history that the historical novel, with its focus on a fictional character caught up in the forces of history, developed. Although Lukács recognizes that fictions concerned with history can be found in earlier time periods, he dismisses them, claiming that these 'so-called historical novels [...] are historical only as regards their purely external choice of theme and costume. Not only the psychology of the characters, but the manners depicted are entirely those of the writer's own day' (p. 19). It was only with the novels of Sir Walter Scott in the early nineteenth century that the historical novel truly emerged. Scott's novels remain the benchmark against which all historical fiction must be measured since they achieve the 'specifically historical' in their 'derivation of the individuality of characters from the historical peculiarity of their age' (p. 19). For Lukács, then, historical fiction is intimately connected to historical context, both in terms of the genre's development and the incorporation of history within the text.

Although the historical novel developed at the beginning of the nineteenth century, the Victorians are not particularly known for their historical novels. John Bowen's assessment of Victorian historical fiction is fairly typical: 'for all that it was produced in such a propitious climate, much historical fiction of the period can only be judged to fail, often quite spectacularly' (p. 245). This perception of Victorian historical fiction seems to be borne out in the contemporary revival of the Victorians. Of all the BBC adaptations undertaken in the last decade, none have been of Victorian historical fictions, despite the abundance of possible sources. It seems that the cultural currency of Victorian classics does not extend to Victorian historical novels.

It is not just that recent critics have failed to appreciate the Victorian historical novel, even contemporary commentators disparaged the historical fictions of the day. As George Henry Lewes wryly commented: 'To write a good historical romance is no easy task; to write such as are published [...] is, we believe, one of the easiest of all literary tasks' (p. 34). Lewes's criticism focused in particular on the incorporation of historical details into historical fiction: 'The writers of this bastard species are of two kinds: the one kind has a mere surface-knowledge of history, picked up from other novels [...]. The other has "crammed" for the occasion: knows much, but knows it ill [...]' (p. 35). A more frequent criticism levelled against Victorian historical fiction, however, was its tendency to assimilate the past into the present. For instance, George Eliot's *Romola* (1862–3) depicts a heroine whose opinions and attitudes correlate more closely to the nineteenth-century world in which the novel was written than the fifteenth-century world in which it was set. This presentist approach, however, corresponded to the Victorian view of history. As A. Dwight Culler argues, the Victorians looked into the past in order to find analogues for their present situation; 'they agreed that the mirror of history provided a perspective glass which enabled one to see through contemporary controversy to more lasting truth' (p. 3).

In condemning Victorian historical fiction, however, such assessments overlook the importance of what Avrom Fleishman terms 'novels of the recent past' in Victorian literature. According to Fleishman, in order to qualify as historical, a novel must be set 'beyond an arbitrary number of years, say 40–60 (two generations)' (p. 3). If the category of historical fiction is expanded to incorporate 'novels of the recent past', which would include that exemplar of the classic realist novel George Eliot's *Middlemarch* (1871–2), then Victorian historical fiction can hardly be judged a failure. Indeed, the Victorians' commitment to realism presupposes a commitment to the historical reality of the world being depicted. In setting their texts in the recent past, Victorian novelists sought to understand the dramatic changes that had been wrought on their society and to delineate how the past had become the present. Consequently, such novels adhere to Lukács's belief that historical fiction should reflect the 'specifically historical'.

Neo-Victorian fictions similarly work within the conventions of the 'classic historical novel' as defined by Lukács; they are marked by a commitment to the historical specificity of the Victorian era. In using the term historical specificity, I draw on the characteristics of historical fiction outlined by Lukács and, although less directly, the commentators on Victorian historical fiction discussed above. As we have seen, Lukács suggests that in historical fictions the characters' psychology should derive from their historical period, not that of the writer. By locating their characters within the 'historical peculiarity of their age' (Lukács, p. 19), neo-Victorian writers avoid the charge of presentism that has often been levelled at Victorian historical fictions. Presentism implicitly validates the idea of universal values that transcend historical boundaries and, therefore, is prone to (mis)appropriation for political ends. As we shall see in Chapter 1, when neo-Victorian fictions incorporate historical figures, they remain committed to the historical specificity of that figure; they do not simplistically establish Victorian 'types' but rather question the very processes by which an historical individual becomes an exemplar of an age. Although establishing the specific historical context is important, there are, as Lewes' comments pointed out, pitfalls. The incorporation of too much historical detail can actually detract from the verisimilitude of the historical context. Similarly, while neo-Victorian fictions seek to establish the historical specificity of their nineteenth-century contexts, they do not present 'mere surface-knowledge of history' (Lewes, p. 35). The Victorian context does not merely function as backdrop, or costume; rather it is integral to the plot and thematic concerns explored in the novels.

Neo-Victorian fiction, however, is rarely understood in relation to Victorian and pre-Victorian forms of the historical novel. Rather, it is usually aligned with postmodern fiction's engagement with history. For instance, Sally Shuttleworth argues that retro-Victorian texts adopt 'an informed post-modern self-consciousness in their interrogation of the relationship between fiction and history' (p. 253). Although she identifies 'an absolute, non-ironic, fascination with the details of the period, and with our relations to it', her use of the term 'retro' aligns these texts with a nostalgic appeal to the aesthetics of the past (p. 253). Shuttleworth positions neo-Victorian fiction within Frederic Jameson's account of 'the appetite for "retro" [...] where styles of the past swiftly replace one another, without any sense of the cultural and social baggage they had previously carried' (p. 255). As this suggests, for Jameson, the 'retro' is divorced from its specific historical context. Shiller, however, contends Jameson's criticism, claiming that neo-Victorian fiction 'present[s] a historicity that is indeed concerned with recuperating the substance of bygone eras, and not merely their styles' (1997, pp. 539–40). Similarly, I argue that the historical specificity which is central to neo-Victorian fiction prevents it from being subsumed within the ahistoricism of postmodernism.

Not all accounts of postmodern fiction, however, subscribe to Jameson's assessment of its ahistoricism. Linda Hutcheon's *A Poetics of Postmodernism* (1988) identifies a concern with history in postmodern fiction, designating such texts 'historiographic metafiction'. As the term implies there are two, apparently paradoxical, impulses present within historiographic metafiction. The term historiographic signals its commitment to both the social and historical world and to epistemological questions regarding the nature of history, while metafiction highlights its fascination with the workings of literature. For Hutcheon, historiographic metafiction is the characteristic genre of postmodern literature, not only because of its proliferation but also because it encapsulates the very contradictions at work in postmodernism itself. In making the category of historiographic metafiction synonymous with postmodernism, however, Hutcheon renders it too inclusive. While neo-Victorian fiction is historically contemporaneous with postmodernism, and indeed several 'postmodern' authors have turned their hand to the genre, most neo-Victorian texts eschew the conclusions of postmodernism.[28] The singularity of the Victorian context distinguishes neo-Victorian fiction from other postmodern historiographic metafictions.[29]

Although neo-Victorian fictions engage with 'postmodern' questions about the possibility of narrating of the past, they move beyond the self-reflexivity of postmodern fiction to consider specifically Victorian forms of historical narratives. Thus, Hutcheon's category of historiographic metafiction needs to be refined. Hutcheon asserts that 'There is no dialectic in the postmodern: the self-reflexive remains distinct from its traditionally accepted contrary – the historico-political context in which it is embedded' (1988, p. x). In the case of neo-Victorian fiction, however, these two elements are intrinsically interrelated. The adoption of metafictional strategies in neo-Victorian fiction is deeply implicated in the historical location of the Victorian era. The metafictional aspects of neo-Victorian texts are inflected with a self-conscious questioning of the possibilities of narrating the past, read in relation to Victorian forms of historical narrative. Indeed, I argue that the Victorian context of these novels demands such a self-reflexive approach to historical narratives since the Victorians were intensely self-conscious about their position in history.

History in the nineteenth century

In the popular imagination, the Victorian era is thought to have been dominated by the ideology of progress, by a focus on the present that seems at odds with a concern with history and historical narratives. Yet the nineteenth century was intensely interested in history, both in terms of its valuation of the past and its consciousness of its own position within history. The proliferation of historical romances after Scott attests to a strong antiquarian interest in the fashion and manners of the past. Despite the dominance of the novel in contemporary conceptions of Victorian literary output, historical narratives, which included but were not limited to historical fiction, formed an important part of Victorian cultural life. According to Richard D. Altick, the completion of the 'monumental *Dictionary of National Biography*' in 1900 was 'a fitting climax to a hundred years of incessant biographical writing' (p. 78).

This concern with history and historical narratives is not antithetical to the ideology of progress, but rather an integral part of it. The study of history enabled the Victorians to understand their own position in a wider historical narrative, and specifically the differences between the present and the past: 'in the course of looking to the past [the Victorians] became conscious of the distinctive characteristics of the present' (Culler, p. 284). Often, this resulted in viewing the past with the self-satisfied assurance that progress had been made and that human history had reached an advanced stage of its development. Frederic Harrison expresses this view in only slightly less confident tones:

> We *are* on the threshold of a great time, even if our time is not great itself. In science, in religion, in social organisation, we all know that great things are in the air. 'We shall see it, but not *now*' – or rather our children and our children's children will see it. [...] It is the age of great expectation and unwearied striving after better things. (p. 425)

This confident belief that the Victorian era was moving toward a better future at least partly accounts for the documentary impulse that characterized Victorian social and political life. The introduction of new forms of documentation, such as census taking and registers of births, deaths and marriages, can be read as a response to the present situation: recording the present for the purposes of social policy. Yet the process of documenting individuals also served the ideology of progress since it enabled the Victorians to identify and quantify the effect of their improvements and to leave a record of their achievements for future generations to assess. As I have suggested, the immense documentation surrounding the Victorian era is at least partly responsible for the contemporary fascination with the Victorians since it enables the Victorians to have a physical presence in the present.

I have suggested that the Victorian context of neo-Victorian fiction prompts its concern with historical narratives, that the Victorians' self-consciousness about their own position within history requires a parallel self-consciousness from neo-Victorian fiction. In the neo-Victorian texts discussed in this book, this self-consciousness manifests as a concern with the modes of narrating the past and indeed the very possibility of narrating the past. This concern often prompts an exploration of the boundary between history and fiction, a process that is generally considered a feature of postmodern fiction. Yet in neo-Victorian fiction, this concern is intimately connected to the engagement with the Victorian era. As Linda Hutcheon has suggested, the boundary between history and fiction only became formalized in the nineteenth century; prior to that history and literature were 'considered branches of the same tree of learning' (1988, p. 105). Neo-Victorian fiction's commitment to the historical specificity of the Victorian era, then, necessarily affects its exploration of the relationship between history and literature. This is most obvious in those novels which deal with biographical narratives since, as I will show, biography was instrumental in asserting the division between history and literature. In all of the neo-Victorian novels discussed in this book, however, the exploration of the boundary between history and literature occurs within a historically specific Victorian context, reminding the reader that these concerns are not unique to the postmodern era.

The separation of history and literature in the nineteenth century is often understood as part of a wider movement toward specialization in Victorian culture. With the development of university courses in both literature and history there was an increasing need to identify the respective qualities and methods of the disciplines. To assert its independent status, history sought to distance itself from literature and align itself with science through the adoption of scientific principles such as objectivity, reliability and a commitment to factual evidence. This aspiration towards science can be seen in the opinion of a Victorian history professor that 'History was merely a branch of biology. The doings of human beings in the past were to be studied and recorded as cold-bloodedly as the wriggling of insects under the microscope' (qtd. in Sofer, p. 128). This movement towards a scientific approach in history was influenced by the theories and methodologies of the German historian Leopold Von Ranke. Often referred to as the 'father of historical science', Ranke is generally credited with promoting a commitment to documentary evidence and scientific methodologies in nineteenth-century historiography (qtd. in Iggers and von Moltke, p. xv). According to Ranke, the past should be approached with objectivity and understood in its own terms, not as an analogue for the present: 'It is not up to us to judge about error and truth as such. We merely observe one figure (*Gestalt*) arising side by side with another figure [...]. Our task is to penetrate them to the bottom of their existence and to portray them with complete objectivity' (p. 42). Thus, the historian should not distort the narrative of the past to accommodate his own partisan interests or preconceived notions about the period he is depicting.

According to David Amigoni, the popular genre of biography played a crucial role in the separation of history and literature in the nineteenth century. Amigoni's account, put forward in his influential study *Victorian Biography: Intellectuals and the Ordering of Discourse* (1993), turns on the dual meaning of his central term 'discipline'. He argues that biography was not only instrumental in establishing history as an academic discipline by appealing to a mass audience, but also in disciplining that audience in the emerging scientific modes of historical thinking and so granting legitimacy to the new, scientific, historical methodology. The reliance on documentary evidence and the attempt to remove the biographer as much as possible from the narrative are the two most obvious ways in which biographical narratives adopted a scientific approach to the past. As we shall see in Chapter 1, this approach reached its apex in the 'Life and Letters' mode which became the dominant form of the biographical narrative in the nineteenth century.

In its attempts to present a purely objective reflection of the life as lived, Victorian biography strives to make the mode of representation, the narrative itself, invisible. Reviews of biographies generally focused on whether the portrait presented was a 'true' likeness of its subject, rather than the techniques used to present that subject. In this respect, biography can be understood as imitating the process of photography which had emerged in the mid-nineteenth century. According to Stephen Bann, photography is connected to developments in the 'historical-mindedness' of the nineteenth century, which he argues is concerned with 'the mythic aim of narrowing the gap between history as it happened, and history as it is written' (p. 165). Photography, for Bann, represents the achievement of this aim since 'the crucial relevance of photography to historical representation lies in the fact that it gradually converts the otherness of *space* [...] into an otherness of *time*, which is guaranteed by the indexical nature [...] of the photographic process' (p. 134). As with photography, the value of a biography resides in its indexical relationship to its subject. The importance of this indexical relationship between the narrative and its subject is evident in the emphasis placed on truth in biographical narratives. As Carlyle remarked in his 1832 essay 'Biography', the memorableness of events in biography 'depends on the object; on its being *real*, on its being really *seen*' (p. 76).

Despite its connections to scientific methodology and developments, biography maintained literary elements thus revealing history's own proximity to literature. Indeed, it is often these literary elements that are emphasized in accounts of biography's popularity: 'With less stateliness than history, biography throws more light on political and social affairs, than its elder sister; [...] and imparts a breathing, life-like spirit to what would, otherwise, be the dull record of chronology' (Mansfield, p. 17). While biography has less authority than history, it clearly has more dramatic interest as a result of the 'life-like spirit', a spirit which aligns it with literature and the imagination. Similarly, despite asserting the importance of truth, Carlyle recognized that biographical narratives should do more than present 'tombstone-information' about its subject, information such as 'when and also where they came into this world, received office or promotion, died and were buried' ('Boswell's Life of Johnson', p. 3). Carlyle's judgement of Boswell's *Life of Johnson*, therefore, diverged from the opinions of many Victorian critics, who criticized Boswell for recording Johnson's conversations because of the act of imagination necessarily involved. By contrast, Carlyle finds no fault with this aspect of the work; rather, he recognizes the importance of imagination and empathy for an understanding of the past. He asks, 'What things have we to forget, what to fancy and remember before we, from such distance, can put ourselves in Johnson's *place*; and so, in the full sense of the term, *understand* him, his sayings and his doings?' ('Boswell's Life of Johnson', p. 3). Carlyle's approach to history involves a combination of factual knowledge of the past with the ability to vividly depict the *life* of the past, an ability that requires the use of the imagination and, in particular, the historian's empathy. History, Carlyle implies, needs to incorporate both its scientific and literary impulses in order to provide the fullest possible account of the past. The issue of how to achieve this combination has always been a central concern in historical fiction, which by its very nature combines historical and literary approaches to the past. Given the dual approach of historical fiction, neo-Victorian fiction's engagement with this issue needs to be understood not only in relation to nineteenth-century views on history, but also twentieth-century ones where, as we shall see, questions about the role of the imagination in historical narratives become implicated in political discourses about the role of history.

History in the twentieth century

As I have indicated, the explosion of neo-Victorian fiction in the 1980s and 1990s coincided with Margaret Thatcher's time as Prime Minister and her adoption of Victorian values. Thatcher's call for a return to Victorian values was part of a wider appropriation, and manipulation, of the past for present political purposes. This political appropriation of the past was most evident in the debates surrounding the National Curriculum for history, which, as Suzanne Keen has argued, was 'underpinned by a Conservative nationalist agenda' (p. 101). The Victorians came to occupy a central place in the National Curriculum, with more than 20 per cent of the examples used for the Statements of Attainment taken from the Victorian era.[30] In particular, the curriculum focuses on the success stories of Victorian developments in industry, trade, and science and so confirms Thatcher's nostalgic view of the Victorian era as a period of uncomplicated belief structures and unprecedented progress.[31]

Among both educators and politicians there seemed to be agreement about the importance of history as a subject, and its purposes. History was thought to be 'an essential ingredient in our civilization, and an essential attribute of an educated person' (qtd. in Tytler, p. 4b). An awareness of our national past was considered crucial for an understanding of our present national situation since, to quote one commentator, 'who we were constitutes such an important part of who we are – or think we are' ('Who we were', p. 17). It is precisely for these reasons that history became the battleground for the fiercest debates, with Margaret Thatcher herself entering into the debate during a session of Prime Minister's Question Time. The debate centred on the questions of *what* and *how* history should be taught and was broadly divided into two camps – the traditionalists who prioritized a facts-based approach and the 'new history' camp which favoured a skills-based approach. In this division, nineteenth-century debates about history's position in relation to science and literature resurface. The traditionalist camp recalls attempts to align history with scientific methodologies in its focus on facts and adoption of an evidential approach to the past. By contrast, the 'new history' camp emphasizes skills such as interpretation and empathy that, as we shall see, align history with a more imaginative, and therefore literary, approach to the past.

The approach of the so-called traditionalists was based on the belief that it is possible to recuperate the past through a detailed knowledge of its facts: 'history *is* the knowledge of what happened in the past' (Arkin, p. B7). Consequently, the emphasis for teaching and assessment is placed on chronology and facts; since students should be accumulating knowledge, assessments should be designed to specifically test their knowledge. This approach was legitimized through its alignment with science; it was claimed that it promoted 'neutrality and intellectual rigour' in opposition to the supposedly more subjective approach of the new history (Norris, p. 10). The vehement support for this approach from both educators and politicians can be seen as a backlash against the cultural relativism of postmodernism and its contention that since the past is only ever knowable through texts there can be no 'true' or accurate version of the past. As Suzanne Keen notes, the demands for a return to 'traditional' approaches to history teaching 'owed [...] much to a memory of traditional history' (p. 105). This memory of traditional history can be traced back to the Victorian era, which is perceived as a time of lost stabilities, a time when facts were facts. Such a view draws on the portrait of Mr Gradgrind in Charles Dickens's *Hard Times* (1854), who insists that 'Facts alone are wanted in life', yet it fails to recognize Dickens's parodic intent and the novel's conclusion that facts alone are not enough (p. 9).[32]

The traditionalist, facts-based approach became intimately connected to history's role in preserving a sense of national identity and, as such, was favoured by Margaret Thatcher. At Prime Minister's Question Time on 29 March 1990 Sir John Stokes asked 'Why cannot we go back to the good old days when we learnt by heart the names of the Kings and Queens of England, the names of our warriors and battles and the glorious deeds of our past?' Thatcher's response left no doubt as to which side of the debate she favoured: 'Children should know the great landmarks of British history and should be taught them at school'. This exchange implies that Britain's national identity was in some way threatened by the proposed movement away from a facts-based history towards a skills-based approach. Clearly, then, the issue of how to teach history had become inextricably intertwined with the issue of what history to teach. This association between a need for a rigorous, facts-based approach to history and a desire to reinstate Britain at the forefront of history teaching had already been articulated by Norman Stone in an article in *The Sunday Times*, where he wrote 'We should require a sound knowledge of British history rather than a rag-bag of "empathy" about countries far away' (p. B8). In Stone's rhetoric, British history is promoted by its association with factual learning, 'sound knowledge', whereas empathy is attacked for being a 'rag-bag' approach that detracts from the teaching of the more important British history.

As these comments indicate, a skills-based approach is associated with a shift in focus away from both a factual history and a version of history based on the actions of kings and important historical figures. This approach is more inclined towards social history since it encourages students to think about ordinary people's responses to key historical events. The approach of the 'new history' was based less on knowledge and more on interpretation of the past, at least in its characterization by Conservative politicians; teaching focused on the analysis of documents to uncover the covert biases in supposedly neutral, factual accounts of the past. Thus, the new history problematized the reliance on facts in traditional history. Consequently, the methods of assessment also differed; rather than testing a student's knowledge of the past, essentially a memory-exercise, the emphasis was on testing the student's ability to find out about the past, to interpret it and construct a narrative of it from the documents and information available.

The element of the new history that provoked most controversy was the use of empathy: a mode of understanding the past that encouraged students to use their imagination in order to think themselves back into the lived experience of the people in the past. Consequently, assessment of history in this model was based not so much on students' knowledge of the past but rather on their ability to understand and connect with the past. Since this connection with the past occurred at the level of the imagination, the 'new history' was seen as closer to a literary than scientific model of history. As Anne Sofer comments, empathy is 'an imaginative dimension to history which brings it closer to literature and drama than to science and analytical theory' (p. 128). It is precisely this imaginative dimension that prompts such criticism from the traditionalists, who argue that empathy is in fact an unhistorical method of approaching the past since it assumes the existence of universal values and erases the historical specificity of the past.[33] Rather, it approaches the past from the perspective of the present and judges it on the basis of current values. Norman Stone provides a damning assessment of the empathy approach on precisely these grounds: 'Students of history need to understand that people in the past had different beliefs and values, and should not be judged from the point of view of a fifteen-year-old in 1988' (p. B8). As we saw, Victorian historical narratives were often condemned for just such a presentist approach to the past. Neo-Victorian fiction, however, seeks to avoid such charges. Its concern with historical narratives is connected to both the Victorian context that it evokes and the contemporary context in which it was written. Consequently, neo-Victorian novels hold out the possibility of establishing an empathic connection to the past without resulting in presentism.

Chapter review

In exploring various forms of historical narratives, neo-Victorian fictions not only attempt to narrate the Victorian past but also explore the ways in which that past has been narrated in the present. Each of the following chapters examines a different approach in narrating the past, and the analysis of the neo-Victorian novels reveals the extent to which their engagement with those narratives is grounded in the context of the Victorian era. For instance, Chapter 1 considers the adoption of bio-graphical narratives in Peter Carey's *Jack Maggs*, James Wilson's *The Dark Clue*, and Janice Galloway's *Clara*. While other contemporary texts have engaged with the role of biographical narratives in narrating the past, these neo-Victorian texts are inherently grounded in Victorian forms of biography.[34] Focusing on the 'Lives and Letters' mode of biography, which dominated the nineteenth-century genre, these texts explore the discourses of truth and decency that surrounded Victorian conceptions of biographical narratives. They also examine the role that Victorian individuals play in our perception of the Victorian era and question the position of individuals as types in historical narratives, both biographi-cal and fictional. Chapter 2 turns to consider two novels which adopt the conventions of detective fiction, a genre that emerged during the nineteenth century. Both Julian Barnes's *Arthur & George* and Colin Dexter's *The Wench is Dead* evoke that most famous of all literary detec-tives, Sherlock Holmes. In examining the idea of 'evidence', Barnes's and Dexter's novels explore issues surrounding historical narratives, issues to do with the possibility of accessing and narrating the past. The three texts discussed in Chapter 3 – A. S. Byatt's 'The Conjugial Angel', Sarah Waters's *Affinity* and Michèle Roberts's *In the Red Kitchen* – exam-ine the haunting of the present by the past. While ghosts have become a fairly frequent mechanism for exploring the relationship between the present and the past, in these neo-Victorian fictions this literary trope is explicitly connected to the nineteenth-century phenomenon of spiritualism. Written by women, all three of these texts engage with the gender politics of spiritualism and the nineteenth century more generally. Yet alongside this political motivation, they also reveal the tension between scepticism and belief that accompanied spiritualist activities in the Victorian era. The final chapter turns to A. S. Byatt's *Possession: A Romance* and Graham Swift's *Ever After* to explore models of reading the past. Both novels adopt a dual plot which follows the quest of an academic researcher to uncover the past in its literary remains. In doing so, they examine the ways in which reading can establish a posi-tive connection between the present and the past, a connection that in some instances can even bring the past to life.

In exploring different forms of historical narratives, these neo-Victorian texts also self-consciously reflect upon their own position as historical narratives and the function of the historical novelist. Each of the texts discussed in the following chapters raises issues that are central to the writing of historical fiction and each narrative presents a figure that provides an analogue for the historical novelist. This is perhaps most obvious in relation to biographical narratives, which are clearly constructed by a biographer figure. As I suggest, neo-Victorian fiction's concern with biographical narratives explores issues of truth and decency, which clearly have implications for the historical novelist: How far is it permissible to delve into the private lives of individuals in the name of history? And does the relationship between biographers and their subject provide an analogue for the relationship between the present and the past? The idea of the detective as a figure for the historian has been proposed before; as I explain in Chapter 2, the detective undertakes an explicitly historical process in solving crimes since they retrospectively construct events to make sense of the past.[35] While there are affinities between the processes of the detective and the historian, I argue that neo-Victorian detective fictions also establish a connection between the detective and the writer of historical fictions. Most obviously, the idea of evidence connects to the role of historical fact in historical fictions, but the retrospective nature of detective fiction, which reconstructs the past from a present perspective, also raises questions about the relationship between the present and the past in historical fiction. Neo-Victorian detective novels, then, explore the idea that the present needs to do justice to the past and thus implicitly question whether the historical novelist can 'right the wrongs' of the past. In those neo-Victorian texts which examine spiritualism's role in establishing a connection with the past, it is the medium figure who becomes the representative of the historical novelist. While the connection between the medium and the novelist has been made before, Chapter 3 reveals that in neo-Victorian fictions that connection is affected by their treatment of Victorian spiritualism.[36] The complex systems of scepticism and belief that surrounded nineteenth-century spiritualism are explored in the ambiguous positions occupied by the medium figures in Byatt's 'The Conjugial Angel', Roberts's *In the Red Kitchen*, and Waters's *Affinity*. Through their complex medium figures, all three authors explore the opposition between fact and imagination in historical fiction. The final chapter focuses on the role of textual remains in establishing a connection between the present and the past. In comparing academic readers with family readers, these novels imply that an ideal reading of the past is one that combines a scholarly engagement with the past and an emotional connection to the past.

The Coda moves from a consideration of historical narratives to explore these texts' engagement with Victorian literary narratives. Yet neo-Victorian fiction's engagement with Victorian literary narratives remains explicitly connected to their concern with historical narratives. The Coda examines the various ways in which neo-Victorian texts engage with Victorian literary narratives, from writing sequels or responses to individual Victorian texts, to adopting Victorian genre conventions, to engaging with Victorian realism. Whatever strategy is adopted, all of these novels understand Victorian literary conventions within their specific Victorian historical context. As a result of their dual approach, neo-Victorian fictions are acutely aware of the distance between the Victorian past and the present. Consequently, they do not naively adopt these Victorian forms, nor do they attempt to pass as Victorian novels. Rather, they recognize the need to transform the Victorian conventions within their contemporary narratives.

[Handwritten notes:]

Postmodernist
The French Lieutenant's Woman
The Crimson Petal & the White.

Artifice
Productive to point of parody.
Imbuing victorian w/ drawing
attention to artifice.
Fiction attacks realism
Fault pulled realism away.
Ways of reading Barthes.
death of author.

Theorist

1
Narrating the Victorians

Biographical narratives intimately shape our perception of the Victorian era; we know the Victorian past through its principal 'characters', both historical and fictional. The very designation of the period as the 'Victorian era' reveals the extent to which such individual characters determine our perception of the period; the Victorian era is unmistakably the era of Queen Victoria. In part, this is due to both the longevity of her reign and the fact that her death in 1901 neatly marked the transition from the Victorian to the 'modern' period. But Queen Victoria's prominence in the contemporary imagination stems from more than just dates; she exemplifies the characteristics we have come to think of as 'Victorian'. Queen Victoria's reign was marked by her excessive mourning for her husband, Prince Albert, which lasted from his death in 1861 until her own death in 1901. The cult of mourning that Queen Victoria inspired is at least partly responsible for the popular perception of the Victorians as serious and straight-laced, a perception encapsulated in the attribution to Queen Victoria of the saying 'We are not amused'. Similarly, Queen Victoria seems to epitomize 'Victorian' attitudes towards sex. She is commonly credited with dispensing the advice that married women should 'lie back and think of England' and claiming that lesbianism did not exist. While the attribution of these opinions to Queen Victorian has been debunked in scholarly circles, as indeed has the more general perception of the Victorians as prudish and repressed, these anecdotes neatly fit the contemporary perception of the Victorian era, and confirm Queen Victoria's position as the representative of the age to which she gave her name.[1]

In contrast to this positioning of Queen Victorian as the epitome of the Victorian 'type', there have been recent attempts to consider her as an individual. The 1997 film *Mrs Brown* sought to counter the narrative of Queen Victoria as a grieving widow by focusing on rumours of her relationship with John Brown, a servant at her Balmoral estate, and a possible secret marriage. As the title suggests, the film is concerned with the personal, private figure of Victoria, rather than her public roles as Queen of England and Empress of India. Similarly, the more recent film *The Young Victoria* (2009) focuses on the period leading up to Victoria's coronation and her early relationship with Prince Albert. Both of these films participate in the wider cultural fascination with the Victorian era outlined in the Introduction. By focusing on the personal dimensions of the most public figure from the Victorian age, they can be seen as attempting to render the Victorians 'just like us'. Indeed, the tagline to *The Young Victoria*, 'Love rules all', highlights the film's concern with the 'universal' theme of love, despite its very specific historical location.

It is not merely that the Victorian era is defined by its personalities, there also seems to be a sense that Victorian figures are more interesting subjects than contemporary figures. In 2002, the BBC ran a poll, with accompanying television programmes, to find the British nation's 'Great Britons'. Unsurprisingly, most of the figures that made the short-list came from the past. There seems to be an implicit assumption that the term 'great Briton', and the related term 'hero', applies more readily to figures from the past than from the present. In part, this is due to the belief that greatness can only be judged retrospectively; it requires historical distance from the subject. Yet there is also a suggestion that such greatness is no longer possible in the contemporary age. The presence of two Victorian figures in the top ten – Isambard Kingdom Brunel and Charles Darwin were voted second and fourth respectively – implies that the Victorian period was particularly suited to the creation of 'heroes'.[2] Phineas G. Nanson, the protagonist of A. S. Byatt's *The Biographer's Tale* (2000), explicitly subscribes to this view, claiming that the fictional Victorian 'Bole [...] crammed more action into one life than would be available to three or four puny moderns' (p. 8). The frequency with which Victorian figures are the subjects of contemporary biographies seems to confirm this perception. Of the winning biographies for the past decade of the James Tait Black Memorial Prize, four have had Victorian subjects: George Eliot, Charles Darwin, John Clare, and a joint biography of Ellen Terry and Henry Irving.[3] The 'celebrity' status of such Victorian figures is apparent in the number of contemporary narratives that return to their lives, such as the recent film *Creation* (2009) which focuses on Charles Darwin and was released shortly after the 150th anniversary of the publication of Darwin's *On the Origin of Species*. Despite such historical significance, the film seems to focus on

the relationship between Darwin and his wife, played by real-life husband and wife Paul Bettany and Jennifer Connelly. Unsurprisingly, the
trend for reviving historical Victorians has also found its way into neo-
Victorian fictions. For instance, Janice Galloway's *Clara* (2002) provides
a fictional biography of the nineteenth-century pianist and composer
Clara Schumann. As with *Mrs Brown* and *The Young Victoria*, the title
of Galloway's novel signals its focus on the private individual, rather
than the public figure. Yet while such films emphasize the 'universal'
elements of the narrative, *Clara* remains grounded in the historically
specific context of the Victorian era.

It is not only historical Victorians who continue to fascinate, but also
fictional Victorians. There is a prevalent conception that characters in
Victorian novels are in some sense more real than those in postmodern
fiction. In 2005, a thread on the Victoria research discussion forum,
composed of academics and graduate students in Victorian studies,
asked contributors to identify the characters they empathized with from
Victorian fiction. One contributor revealed that her identification with
Esther Summerson, the heroine of Charles Dickens's *Bleak House* (1852–3)
was so great that 'I still count her among my friends in my mental
universe.'[4] It is hard to imagine a similar discussion about characters from
postmodern novels. The sense that characters in Victorian novels have,
in some way, an existence beyond the confines of the novel spurs the
desire for adaptations and sequels of classic Victorian texts.[5]

The popularity of contemporary sequels, or prequels, of Victorian
novels, however, can not be dismissed as merely a backlash against postmodernism or a nostalgic urge to revive the Victorians. Part of the appeal
of such sequels is simply the massive readership Victorian novels have
enjoyed through their position as 'classic novels' that are often taught at
schools and the more recent proliferation of television and screen adaptations. Victorian fictional characters have become part of the contemporary image of the Victorian era. Two of the neo-Victorian novels discussed
in this chapter provide an 'afterlife' for characters from Victorian novels.
As a sequel to Wilkie Collins's *The Woman in White*, James Wilson's *The
Dark Clue* (2001) provides the reader with an account of what happened
to Walter Hartright and Marian Halcombe after Collins's narrative ended.
Peter Carey's *Jack Maggs* (1997) is not so much a sequel as a 'reimagining'
of a Victorian novel. In rewriting Charles Dickens's *Great Expectations*
from the perspective of Magwitch, whom he renames Jack Maggs, Carey
provides a fuller biographical account of Magwitch's life.[6]

In these texts, the return to the Victorian era is grounded in a concern with historical narratives. In resurrecting Victorian figures then, be

they historical or fictional, neo-Victorian authors do not merely participate in the contemporary nostalgia for the Victorian era. Rather, they
engage with questions that are central to the way in which we narrate
the Victorian past, questions such as the relationship between the past
as lived and the past as narrated and the extent to which individuals
can be understood as 'representatives' of an historical age. These issues
converge in the novels' concern with the forms of biographical narratives in the nineteenth century.

Nineteenth-century biography

According to Cora Kaplan, biography is enjoying a renaissance at
present. She argues that the current 'triumphal moment' of biography
'might seem [...] like the crude revenge of nineteenth-century realism
on the cool ironies, unfixed identities and skewed temporalities of the
postmodern' (p. 37). Kaplan's account suggests that the current popularity of biographies is at least partly prompted by a nostalgic desire for
the lost certainties of self-hood, and implicitly positions the Victorian
era and its forms of realism as more simplistic than 'the cool ironies [...]
of the postmodern' (p. 37). While postmodern literature frequently
rejects the principles of Victorian realism, contemporary biographies
continue to adopt nineteenth-century narrative forms. Indeed, the
multi-volume biographies that characterized the genre in the nineteenth
century seem to be the particular locus for the recent biographical renaissance. Peter Ackroyd's *Dickens* (1990), rightly referred to by Kaplan
as 'monumental,' is only the most notable example of such 'weighty'
biographies (p. 50).

Although the Victorian era is generally thought of as the 'age of
the novel', biography was an equally important and popular genre.
Numerous large-scale biographical projects, which proved to be both
popular and profitable, were undertaken in the nineteenth century,
such as *Lives of Eminent British Statesmen* (1836–9), the *English Men of
Letters* series (1878–1970), and Samuel Smiles's 3-volume work, *Lives of
the Engineers* (1861–2). Trumping these, was Leslie Stephen's mammoth
project of the *Dictionary of National Biography* which was begun in 1882
and completed in 1900. As Alan Shelston suggests, the completion of
the DNB marked 'an appropriate culmination to both the genre, and the
taste which fed it' (p. 17).

The 'taste which fed' biography in the Victorian era was a concern with
character, a concern that was equally important in Victorian fictions. As
George Levine notes, '[t]he nineteenth-century novel tended to place

character at the center of meaning' (p. 8). Indeed, he suggests that the nineteenth-century novel 'takes the shape of fictional autobiography, or, if it is narrated in the third person, biography' (p. 13). The importance of character in the Victorian novel accounts for the prominence of the *Bildungsroman*, a genre which traces the educational, spiritual or moral development of an individual, often following their progress from childhood, or early youth, into adulthood. A cursory list of the titles of some of the most famous Victorian novels reveals this focus on the development of the individual: *Oliver Twist* (1838), *Jane Eyre* (1847), *David Copperfield* (1849), and *Tess of the D'Urbervilles* (1891).

The concern with character in both fictional and biographical narratives of the nineteenth century is, as Levine notes, 'a moral preoccupation' (p. 8). Although biography and fiction shared this moral preoccupation, biography was felt to have the advantage because of its grounding in truth. According to Levine, 'for the Victorians a moral impulse was not necessarily incompatible with fidelity to the "real"' (p. 13). Indeed, moral examples were felt to be most effective when they were true. This commitment to truth was lauded as an ideal for biography by many nineteenth-century thinkers, most famously Thomas Carlyle. In his 1832 essay 'Biography', Carlyle claims that the memorableness of events in biography 'depends on the object; on its being *real*, on its being really *seen*' (p. 76). The increasing social mobility of the Victorian era highlighted the need for moral examples and models of conduct, yet it had also rendered traditional models, such as Plutarch's *Lives of the Noble Greeks and Romans*, outdated. Samuel Smiles responded to this need with the publication of *Self help; with illustrations of character and conduct* in 1859. The book, originally delivered as a series of lectures addressed to the Leeds Mutual Improvement Society on 'The Education of the Working Classes', presented a series of brief biographical sketches of individuals who had achieved success through perseverance and hard work.

Horatio Mansfield's 1854 article 'The Biographical Mania' accepts that biography should have a moral purpose, but laments that this purpose is not being met in the 'tide' of contemporary biographies (p. 16). Mansfield implies that there is an inverse relationship between the number of biographies produced and the 'quality' of their subjects: 'biography, instead of confining itself, as was once the case, to the apex of the pyramid, now nestles itself at the base, and really, on some occasions, it grubs at the foundations of the edifice' (p. 16). The image of a pyramid might suggest that Mansfield's ideas about worthy biographical subjects are inflected with a class bias. Yet, as his later comments reveal,

Mansfield believes that the choice of subject should be determined by the type of life the person has led, rather than their station in life: 'no man or woman, be they high or low [...] should have his or her "life" taken, unless they walked through the world with visible stamp and brand of being true to some great principle, of having done some good work, of having resisted some arch temptation, of having held up a distinct light to the world' (p. 18). Mansfield's views on the appropriate biographical subject, then, are underpinned by the assumption that biography should fulfil a moral purpose; it should provide its readers with a model of a 'good life'.

One of the criticisms Mansfield levels at contemporary biographies is that the choice of biographical subject is often motivated by 'the notoriety of the deceased' (p. 17). Returning to the image of the biographical tide, Mansfield suggests that such biographies are 'not biography, but rather its scum' (p. 17). In contrast, he asserts that 'real biography is a matter of time, and when the man can be seen in his just proportions, the biographical tribute is or is not duly paid, according to circumstances' (p. 17). In making this recommendation, Mansfield clearly positions biography as an historical pursuit, implying that to present a true biography there needs to be a temporal distance between the biographer and their subject. As we have seen, the belief in the necessity of historical distance continues to hold sway in contemporary evaluations of individuals.

This ideal of a temporal distance between the biographer and biographee is connected to the belief that biography should provide a moral example; Mansfield states that '[i]n the moral as well as in the natural world, there is a certain focal distance to be observed, if we are to see things in their relative proportions' (p. 21). In establishing a connection between the natural and moral worlds, Mansfield aligns the desired objectivity of the biographer with the objectivity of the scientist. He rejects the idea that the best biographer is someone who knew the subject intimately; indeed, he positively abhors the trend for biographies written by a friend or relative of the biographical subject, declaring that 'it is next to impossible that consanguineous or very "friendly" biography should be truthful' (p. 21). For Mansfield, then, truth is understood in terms of scientific objectivity. Mansfield explicitly declares the importance of truth, saying that 'Biography is useful in the direct proportion that it is truthful' (p. 21).

Although the commitment to truth is central to Mansfield's conception of biography, he recognizes that it is by no means easy to maintain. Indeed, Mansfield implicitly accepts that there should be limitations to biographical truth. He suggests that biography should be guided by the principle of discretion when he says that '[w]e may not tear down the curtain of domestic privacy' (p. 22). In his article, Mansfield implicitly sets up an opposition between truth and decency, an opposition which became central in nineteenth-century discussions of biography. Indeed, the question of biographical discretion was raised several times in the course of the nineteenth century. Elizabeth Gaskell's *The Life of Charlotte Brontë* (1857) was felt to have transgressed the boundaries of decorum with the revelation that Charlotte's brother, Branwell, had had an affair with a married woman, a revelation which brought the author the 'threat of legal proceedings' (Shelston, p. 28). Interestingly, Gaskell is more frequently criticized by contemporary commentators for failing to reveal the true nature of Charlotte's feelings for M. Heger.[7]

The tension between the opposing impulses of truth and discretion in biography became most contentious in the scandal prompted by the publication of J. A. Froude's biographical series on Carlyle. As part of this project, Froude published the private writings of Jane Welsh Carlyle, which revealed that her marriage to the great Victorian thinker was far from happy. In publishing *The Letters and Memorials of Jane Welsh Carlyle* (1883), Froude was working within the accepted mode of 'Life and Letters' biography, which compiled documentary evidence to present a complete life of the biographical subject. However, the personal nature of these documents, and in this instance the negative portrayal they contained of a public figure, opened up questions concerning the role of the biographer. As Trev Broughton has commented, the Froude–Carlyle debate raised wider questions about biographical methodology: '[it] was as much about questions of biographical "evidence" and "proof" as about the Carlyle's love-life, or lack of it' (p. 553). At the heart of the Froude–Carlyle scandal was the tension between truth and decency, a tension that also raised the question of who the biographer was accountable to: should the biographer's commitment to presenting the reader with a full and truthful picture of the biographical subject outweigh a concern for discretion and loyalty to the subject?

Mansfield's views on the 'Life and Letters' mode of biography engage with precisely this question of how much truth the biographer should reveal. The 'Life and Letters' approach, which became the dominant biographical mode in the nineteenth-century, was underpinned by a commitment to truth. The form was predicated on the belief that the biographical subject could be known most fully through their own words; it sought to give the reader direct access to the biographical subject through the presentation of as much documentary evidence as possible. In their attempt to present a complete life, these biographies clearly operated within the ideology of realism that dominated the Victorian novel. This approach positions the biographer as a recorder, rather than interpreter, of the life – a position that parallels the supposedly objective stance of both the omniscient narrator of nineteenth-century fiction and the scientist.

Although Mansfield accepts biography's commitment to truth, he rejects the principle of total inclusion on which 'Life and Letters' biographies were based. Instead, he favours the principle of selection, saying that 'the biographer must not attempt to float reams of diary and correspondence down his pages – he must only give the cream of these' (p. 22). Moreover, he notes an interesting consequence of the biographical mania, and particularly the prominence of the 'Life and Letters' mode of biography, when he remarks that 'not a few individuals now in the land of the living write letters [and] keep diaries [...] all for the modest purpose of accumulating materials and saving trouble to their historical eulogist' (p. 22). Normally, a biographical project is undertaken because an individual's life is considered to have been noteworthy in some way, but here the process seems to be reversed: the individual keeps records on the assumption that their life will prove to be noteworthy. Mansfield clearly disapproves of this reversal of the biographical project; his use of the phrase 'historical eulogist' implies there is an element of self-censorship in the process, which undermines the biography's claims to truth.

Although Mansfield implicitly criticizes biographies that attempt to allow the subject to speak for themselves, he adheres to the belief that the biographer should be absent from the biography. He notes that 'last but not least' of the ideals upon which biography should be written, is the idea that 'the writer should keep himself in the background as much as possible' (p. 22). Such an ideal implies that the mode of representation, or even the fact of representation, should be effaced so that all the reader sees is the subject. Like a portrait, a biography is judged in terms of whether it presents 'a correct likeness' of the subject (p. 22). In this respect, biography seems similar to photography, which was advancing at a rapid rate at the mid-point of the nineteenth century.[8] Indeed, Mansfield's rhetoric implicitly makes this connection when he talks of figures having 'his or her "life" taken' (p. 18). Despite the theatrical air that frequently surrounded photography in the Victorian era, the Victorians came to recognize the indexical relationship between the photographic image and the object or person represented in that image. A photographic portrait validates an individual's existence by providing a trace of them; it records the subject's presence in a particular place at a particular time. This indexical role of photography became most apparent with the Police Force's decision to establish a photographic database of criminals.[9] Biography similarly establishes an indexical relationship to its subject since, as Carlyle said, it 'depends on the object; on its being *real*, on its being really *seen*' ('Biography', p. 76).

Despite the numerous criticisms he levels at the current state of biography, Mansfield clearly believes that, in the right hands, it can be a worthwhile pursuit. He hints at the qualities of biography that may account for its popularity when he says that 'with less stateliness than history, biography throws more light on political and social affairs, than its elder sister; [...] and imparts a breathing, life-like spirit to what would, otherwise, be the dull record of chronology' (p. 17). In reviving Victorian characters and Victorian forms of biographical narratives, the neo-Victorian novels discussed in this chapter similarly bring a 'life-like spirit' to the Victorian age. Yet they also engage with Victorian forms of biographical narratives and the issues that, as we have seen, dominated nineteenth-century discourses of the genre.

Neo-Victorian biographical novels

The three novels discussed in this chapter all reveal their concern with biographical narratives in their choice of subject. Janice Galloway's *Clara* provides a fictional biography of a historical figure, the nineteenth-century pianist and composer Clara Schumann, and in doing so incorporates numerous figures from the nineteenth-century musical world who constituted her circle. By contrast, Peter Carey's *Jack Maggs* and James Wilson's *The Dark Clue* both revive characters from Victorian fiction, Abel Magwitch from *Great Expectations* and Marian Halcombe and Walter Hartright from *The Woman in White* respectively. Yet these novels also include historical figures within their narratives. In *The Dark Clue*, Wilson has the fictional Marian and Walter encounter such historical Victorians as John Ruskin, Elizabeth Eastlake, and Henry Mayhew. In Carey's *Jack Maggs*, Dickens himself is brought into the novel, although he is fictionalized as the character Tobias Oates.

The concern with biographical narratives is also evident in these texts' narrative forms. This is most obvious in Wilson's *The Dark Clue*, which follows Marian and Walter as they research a biography of the painter J. M. W. Turner. In depicting such a biographical quest, Wilson's novel belongs to what John F. Keener categorizes as 'biographer-hero' novels (p. 216). Keener understands such novels as part of the wider postmodern project within fiction and suggests that they self-consciously 'target biographical form as well as content': 'they try not only to *narrate* biography in progress, but to *enact* it' (p. 216). Wilson's narrative technique, which sees the entirety of the novel narrated through a series of letters and diary entries, clearly aligns *The Dark Clue* with this intention to 'enact' biography.

This narrative technique, however, is not merely a postmodern strategy; rather, it is intimately connected to the novel's position as a neo-Victorian novel and, more specifically, its relationship to its Victorian intertext. The 'original' on which *The Dark Clue* is based, Wilkie Collins's *The Woman in White* adopts a similar narrative technique. Walter Hartright's narrative, which opens Collins's novel, sets out his purpose to imitate the proceedings of a court, which has implications for the narrative structure: 'The story [...] will be told by more than one pen, as the story of an offence against the laws is told in Court by more than one witness' (p. 5). The subsequent narrative is composed of various texts that acquire the status of evidence; these various accounts combine to provide the reader with a complete version of events. Collins's fictional approach recalls the totalizing impulse behind the 'Life and Letters' form of biography. In adopting this technique in his neo-Victorian novel, then, Wilson not only establishes an intertextual relationship to Collins's novel, but also highlights his concern with Victorian forms of biographical narrative.

Although not 'biographer-hero' novels, Galloway's and Carey's novels also 'enact' their concern with biographical narratives through their narrative techniques. The titles of both novels indicate their focus on the narrative of the individual. As I suggested earlier, the trend for eponymous fiction in the Victorian era was connected to the concern with character that motivated both fictional and biographical narratives. Although the tradition of eponymous fiction seems to have almost entirely died out in contemporary literature, Galloway's and Carey's neo-Victorian novels are notable exceptions. The fact that these novels revive Victorian figures confirms the idea that Victorian characters are considered as more real than those in contemporary fictions.

The decision to fictionalize the life of a Victorian figure, however, is also connected to these novels' engagement with Victorian forms of biographical narratives. By using only Clara's Christian name as the title to her novel, Galloway immediately signals that she is less concerned with the public life of Clara the pianist than with her emotional and domestic life. Beginning with Clara's childhood and moving through her adolescence to her married life with Robert Schumann, *Clara* follows the pattern of a nineteenth-century *Bildungsroman* which, as we have seen, was the typical pattern for eponymous fiction in the Victorian era. In tracing the movement of Clara's life from childhood to motherhood, Galloway clearly engages with feminist ideas about women's life narratives. Indeed, Galloway's novel participates in a feminist interrogation of the forms of biographical narratives that challenges the 'Great Man' approach to biography, which focuses on the public achievement of famous men. In using only Clara's Christian name, Galloway disassociates her subject from the men in her life who, as we discover, attempt to control and determine her biographical narrative. The novel similarly questions the 'Great Man' approach to history at a structural level; it juxtaposes official records of Clara's life, specifically her childhood diaries and the marriage diary she later shares with her husband, with her thoughts and impressions on her role as a wife and a mother. Interestingly, although Galloway contests the appropriation of Clara's narrative by the men in her life, the novel ends with Robert Schumann's death in an asylum. Given that Clara outlived Robert by 40 years, during which time she continued to be a prolific performer and composer, this suggestion that Clara's life ended with Robert's seems to go against the feminist impulses of the novel. However, it is more a consequence of Galloway's decision to focus on the private and emotional, rather than public, life of Clara.

Carey's novel is similarly underpinned by a political concern with the individual, although it is the post-colonial subject that is his focus. *Jack Maggs* is a direct transformation of Charles Dickens's *Great Expectations*; it presents a fictional biography of the fictional character Abel Magwitch. As a *Bildungsroman*, *Great Expectations* is clearly connected to the biographical impulses of the nineteenth century, and particularly the belief that biographical narratives should provide a moral example. This is evident in the narrative technique of Dickens's novel, which adopts the confessional tone of an autobiographical narrative. The position of Pip's narrative voice at a point in the future enables him to pass judgement on his former actions and so reassures the reader that he will eventually develop into the model of a 'good character' that was expected from a *Bildungsroman*. In rewriting Dickens's novel, Carey counters the *Bildungsroman* form of the classic Victorian novel and shifts its focus to a marginalized figure.

In Dickens's version, we only know as much of Magwitch's story as is relevant to Pip's life; Magwitch is only permitted one chapter in which to narrate his life and even then the account is far from complete. Indeed, Magwitch opens his account by denying the biographical impulse: 'I am not a going fur to tell you my story, like a song or a story-book' (p. 316).

Rather, his life is reduced to the repeated phrase 'in jail and out of jail' (p. 316). Although Magwitch rejects the biographical impulse, he appears to have adopted the principles of decorum and discretion that, as we have seen, influenced Victorian biographical practices. Magwitch assures Pip that 'I'm getting low, and I know what's due. Dear boy and Pip's comrade, don't you be afeerd of me being low' (p. 317), and this sense of decency prevents him from revealing further details on his criminal career. In contrast to the sparse account of Abel Magwitch's life provided in *Great Expectations*, Carey allows Maggs to provide an account of his own life, in his own words. Throughout Carey's novel, Maggs is shown to be self-consciously involved in the process of narrating his life in the letters he obsessively writes to Phipps, the Pip character in Carey's version. *Jack Maggs* does not solely rely on Maggs's account of his life, though. Rather, the novel juxtaposes the various accounts that Maggs gives of his life: his letters to Phipps, the account he provides to his employer, Percy Buckle, and the narrative pieced together from his mesmerism sessions with Tobias Oates. It is only by piecing together the information from these various accounts that the reader is able to understand Maggs's biography. Although Carey's novel gives Maggs a voice of his own, then, the narrative technique still suggests that this account needs to be supplemented by other narratives.

The concern with marginalized figures in both Galloway's and Carey's novels is implicitly connected to the ethical dimensions of biography; both novels explore the ethics of appropriating another's life for narrative purposes. This exploration of the ethics of biography connects to an examination of the relationship between the biographer and biographee, which, as we shall see, provides an analogue for the position of the historical novelist towards the Victorian past. The ethical issues surrounding biography also prompt a consideration of the conflict between truth and decency that, as we saw in the previous section, came to dominate nineteenth-century discussions of the genre. In exploring the nature of biographical truth, these novels also self-consciously question the possibility of accurately narrating the past.

Textual lives

While the textualization of the past is a common concern in postmodern fiction, in these neo-Victorian novels, it is explicitly grounded in an examination of the Victorian forms of biography. Biography, as a genre, is characterized by secondariness: the biographical subject is always mediated to the reader through the perspective of the biographer. Even the 'Life and Letters' form, which seems to provide direct access to the biographical subject, can only provide access to the textual remains of those subjects. In their reliance on diaries, letters, and notebooks to narrate their novels, these authors all explore the relationship between the lived life and the written account of that life and, by extension, raise questions about the possibility of accessing the past.

As a biographer-hero novel, Wilson's *The Dark Clue* self-consciously examines the role of textual remains in biographical narratives through the figure of Marian. Coming across the correspondence of Kitty Driver, Marian reflects that while letters seem to promise direct access to the writer, in reality, they merely reinforce the writer's absence since they are only written when the writer and addressee are physically separated. The writing of a biography is similarly predicated upon absence since it is usually prompted by the death of the subject and thus serves as a testament to their death, as much as to their life. *The Dark Clue* implicitly reveals that the biographer's access to their subject depends on whether the textual remains were deemed important enough to preserve. Yet even if all documents are preserved, there is no guarantee that they will provide the truth of the individual's life. As Marian's comments on letters reveal, such texts are written in particular circumstances and, especially with letters, usually for a specific addressee. Consequently, they are determined by questions about what is important, relevant and appropriate to be recorded. The principle of inclusion on which the 'Life and Letters' mode of biography is based, then, is undermined by the process of selection undertaken by the biographical subject. The narrative structure of *The Dark Clue* itself highlights this point. Narrated solely through diaries, letters, and notebook entries, the reader's knowledge of events relies on the accounts provided by the characters themselves. Towards the end of the novel, Marian discovers a notebook kept by Walter under lock and key which reveals experiences and thoughts not recorded in his diary. The discovery that even diaries, that supposedly most revelatory of genres, are subject to self-censorship emphasizes for the reader the limitations of biographical accounts based on the textual remains of the past.

The Dark Clue also engages with the question of whether factual accounts of an individual can provide enough material to recreate their life in a biographical narrative. The role of facts is explored through an analogy with photography. As an artist, Walter rejects the practice of photography, suggesting that it is too bound by its relationship to the real to be able to reflect the truth of things. Conversely, though, in his writing he seems to prefer a photographic approach. Indeed, he understands his role in the narrative of *The Woman in White* as being merely to bring together the various accounts to reflect what happened, rather than to offer any interpretation of events. This analogy initially seems entirely appropriate since biography, like photography, is meant to efface the mode of representation. Yet, Walter's opposition between facts and truth hints at the inadequacy of photography and, by extension, biography to capture the fullness of an individual's life. Walter's opinions echo those expressed by the historical Elizabeth Eastlake in an article for the *Quarterly Review* in 1857. Eastlake's stated aim in the article is 'to decide how far the sun may be considered an artist' (p. 445), but she concludes by lamenting that 'the more photography advances in the execution of parts, the less does it give the idea of completeness' (p. 464).[10] While the inadequacy of representation to capture the world is often considered a postmodern concern, here it is explicitly connected to the specific discourses surrounding biography and photography in the nineteenth century.[11]

Galloway's *Clara* similarly explores the opposition between factual and emotional accounts of the past. The first entry in Clara's diary 'begins with dates: the wherefores and whens of birth, what house, which town – pack drill' (p. 61). Such 'tombstone information', to borrow Carlyle's phrase, does not do justice to Clara's life ('Boswell's Life of Johnson', p. 3). Indeed, the early accounts are actually written by Clara's father, Herr Wieck, whose commitment to facts prevents him from perceiving or comprehending the thoughts and feelings of his daughter. The novel, then, sets up a conflict between the official version recorded in Clara's diary and Clara's experience of events. The narrative voice allows the reader to see a different account of events, one that appears more 'authentic' to Clara's experience than the written accounts recorded by her father. Clearly, then, this narrative approach is connected to Galloway's feminist impulses in *Clara*; Galloway suggests that the emotional aspects of a life are often dismissed in historical accounts, such as biographies, which are supposed to be concerned with facts.

In *Jack Maggs*, the letters that Maggs writes to Phipps appear to provide the reader with access to the past of Maggs, and indeed at several stages seem to conjure that past to reality for Maggs himself, yet they also point to the limitations of such written accounts. The letters are written in an unconventional way: backwards and in violet ink, which gradually disappears from the page. The idea of reversal in Maggs's letters connects to the post-colonial project that Carey is undertaking. In presenting a new perspective on a Victorian classic, Carey forces the reader to see a different story, one that is obscured in the original. Paradoxically, though, the letters that Maggs writes as a testament to his life are not granted a permanent existence. Indeed, the only account which remains of Maggs's life at the end of the novel is Tobias Oates's fictional version *The Death of Maggs*.

Although biography is a textually mediated form, the 'Life and Letters' mode of biography that dominated in the nineteenth century sought to remove the figure of the biographer and allow the reader direct access to the biographical subject through their textual remains. Such an approach is predicated upon the belief that diaries and letters provide access to the 'inner' lives of their subjects and so are essential for any attempt to entirely understand an individual. Despite their narrative structure, all three novels incorporate moments which seem to promise such full and direct access to the past.

In Wilson's novel, this direct connection with the past is prompted by an encounter with the textual remains of the past. For the majority of the novel, Walter's connection to Turner is mediated through the letters and journals of those who had known him. Yet, at one point in the novel, Walter is lucky enough to find a textual fragment written by Turner himself. Mrs Bennett, who had known Turner as a young man, produces a fragment of one of his poems which she had found discarded after an outing and treasured over the years. With the discovery of this fragment, Walter seems to feel that he has gained direct access to his biographical subject. Walter's distracted response when handed the fragment, and his subsequent silence, reveals his assumption that the poem has granted him access to the 'soul' of the artist. According to Altick, literary biography of the nineteenth century was predicated on the assumption that 'there is an essential connection between person and artist [...] Individual traits and circumstances, in other words, are the key to art' (p. 11). If the artist's personality can provide the key to understanding their art, it could equally be argued that the opposite is true, that art can reveal the artist's personality. The fact that the fragment is an early draft of a poem, containing several crossed-out lines, reveals the fascination with manuscripts and with texts in the handwriting of the past that, as we shall see in Chapter 4, prevailed in the nineteenth century. It is clearly this encounter with the supposedly unmediated soul of Turner which prompts Walter's subsequent declaration of Turner as the greatest artist of all time. The novel itself reinforces Walter's belief that art can provide access to the soul as Marian, like many other characters in the novel, comes to believe that Turner's art holds the answer to the dark clue of his life. Indeed, it is while looking at one of his paintings that Marian has the epiphany which reveals the secret of Turner's life to her.

Galloway's *Clara* similarly suggests that art can provide access to the soul of the artist. Before the narrative even begins, Galloway incorporates a contents page which resembles a musical programme. The title of the main musical piece, 'Frauen Liebe und -Leben Op. 42: Woman's Life and Love', suggests the movement of the life to follow and hints at the intimate connection between Clara's life and her music (p. 3). Interestingly, though, there are very few excerpts from Clara's music incorporated into the novel. Rather than the music, it is the narrative voice of the novel which seems to promise direct access to Clara's thoughts and feelings. For instance, Clara's experience of her first period is narrated to the reader not through any textual account, but through the direct narrative voice. There is a clear suggestion that such events were not considered important enough to be recorded in textual accounts. Clara recognizes that '[n]one of this had much to do with what people wanted to hear [...], but it was what made the deepest ridges in her memory. Applause and performance she took for granted, yet they were triumph, success, the real story' (96). In interspersing textual accounts with direct narration, Galloway's *Clara* highlights the inability of biographical accounts to capture the emotional reality of the past. By contrast, she explores how the realist narrator of Victorian fiction can be used to give the illusion of direct access to the individual and the past.

In Carey's *Jack Maggs*, it is Jack's oral rather than written account which seems to promise access to his inner soul. The account that Jack gives of his past to his employer is contradicted by the version of his history he reveals during his mesmeric sessions with Tobias Oates. Mesmerism is part of a wider group of 'sciences of the mind' that developed during the Victorian era and which attempted to understand the 'character' of an individual. Usually, this involved reading external signs in the facial features (physiognomy) or cranial bumps (phrenology) to determine the individual's underlying nature, but in the case of mesmerism the assumption was that an individual's character and actions are determined by the movement of unseen magnetic forces. In this sense, then, mesmerism connects to the biographical impulse to establish the true character of the subject.

This interest in accessing the private recesses of the individual's mind or soul is central to the biographical project. In using the personal letters and diaries of their subjects, the 'Life and Letters' mode of biography promises to take the reader beyond the public persona to the inner individual. Although this impulse was justified by the realist motivation which underpinned such biographies, it also raised the issue of decency which, as we have seen, became particularly fraught in nineteenth-century biography. The very private nature of the documents used in biographies renders the biographical subject vulnerable; they reveal things that the writer might not wish to be made public. In *The Dark Clue*, Marian reveals the ethical dilemma facing the Victorian biographer when she contemplates reading Walter's notebook. Marian notes the cultural belief in the sanctity of personal texts, but justifies her intrusion by distinguishing between letters and diaries, which deal with private feelings, and notebooks, which record facts. Although privacy has come to be thought of as a universal concept, as Kaplan notes, it is a 'historically constructed idea' (p. 47). In its engagement with the 'Life and Letters' biographical mode, Wilson's *The Dark Clue* specifically addresses Victorian attitudes toward privacy and decency.

Biographical decency

The concern with the private accounts of an individual's life in these texts signals a wider concern with their private lives. Living in a post-Freudian world, this interest in the inner life of an individual usually focuses on sexuality and sexual desires, and this seems to be particularly true for the Victorians. The perception of the Victorians as 'prudish' and 'repressed' has prompted what Kaplan terms a 'prurient curiosity about the period' (p. 86). As we saw in the Introduction, this interest in Victorian sexuality is based on both a nostalgic perception of the Victorian past as a time of sexual innocence and a paradoxical belief that the Victorians were 'just like us' beneath their repressed exteriors. While the treatment of sexuality in these novels is informed by these contradictory impulses, it is also explicitly connected to the novels' concern with biographical narratives and participates in Victorian debates concerning the 'proper' sphere of investigation for a biographer.

Galloway's novel narrates Clara's first period, her experiences in the marriage-bed, and her miscarriage. While these events are treated with a certain amount of reticence, they are more explicitly dealt with than in Victorian fiction or biography. The presentation of Clara and Robert's sex life reveals the dual impulse that underpins the contemporary interest in the Victorians: the impulse to render them both strange and familiar. The Schumann's sex life is recorded in the household diary, where Robert enters 'his secret sign for the occasions on which they had sexual congress' (p. 359). The very fact that Robert records these occasions chimes with the popular perception of the Victorian attitude towards sex: that it was a duty to be undertaken seriously and regularly, almost like the winding up of a clock. These encounters are recorded by the letter 'F', yet while a contemporary audience might be inclined to interpret this as shorthand for *fucked*, it is more likely to stand for *fornicated* which corresponds to the Victorian context (p. 359).[12] Despite this, the novel does hint at a more open, and supposedly modern, attitude towards sex in Robert and Clara's relationship; the observation that '[a] new pregnancy alert for once wasn't more than a scare, thank the Lord' suggests that for the Schumanns sex was not merely about procreation (p. 358). Robert and Clara's marriage, then, confirms the view that the Victorians treated sex as a serious matter while also revealing the pleasure they took in it – a pleasure usually reserved for us more liberated moderns.

Carey's novel similarly treats sexuality in a more frank way than its Victorian predecessor would have, although it is still couched in a semblance of Victorian propriety. For example, the novel narrates an episode in which Mercy Larkin is prostituted out to a stranger by her mother. Although the actual rape is only glancingly referred to, Mercy distinctly recalls the physical sensation left by the residue of her encounter, a detail which Victorian novels tended to omit, or at least couch in euphemism.[13] It is not only in its presentation of sex that *Jack Maggs* is more frank than Victorian fiction, but also in its treatment of issues such as homosexuality, abortion, and contraception that would have been considered taboo in Victorian fiction. In *Jack Maggs*, Carey seems to be partly motivated by a desire to shock the reader into a recognition that the Victorians are not so different from us, or at the very least a recognition that the etiquette of middle-class Victorian society did not apply across the social spectrum. Although the incorporation of such elements is part of these novels' engagement with biographical narratives, it is also connected to neo-Victorian fiction's engagement with Victorian forms of realism, which is explored further in the Coda.

The Dark Clue is also more frank in its depiction of sexual desires and sexual acts than Victorian fiction as it narrates Walter's encounters with prostitutes and his rape of his sister-in-law Marian in her own bed. As with the sexual scenes in *Clara* and *Jack Maggs*, *The Dark Clue* adopts a measure of reticence in narrating this latter event. While the events leading up to the rape, including Walter's touching and undressing of Marian, are explicitly narrated, the account does not record the moment of rape itself. Given that the account is taken from Marian's diary, it is perhaps not surprising that she chooses to omit the terrifying moment and instead ponder Walter's mental state as he committed the act. The incorporation of such events, however, is not merely prompted by a desire to 'sex up' the Victorians, but rather is a result of the

Victorian context; specifically, it is part of *The Dark Clue*'s position as a sequel to *The Woman in White*. It could be argued that Wilson's novel depicts the consequences of the *ménage à trois* that, as John Sutherland points out, is hinted at in the closing pages of Collins's novel (p. ix). Moreover, Wilson is clearly drawing on the sensation genre which *The Woman in White* inaugurated. Such novels were intended to produce a physical reaction in their readers by depicting shocking events within the domestic sphere. In this respect, the sensation novel seems to follow the biographical urge to reveal the private individual behind the public façade. Clearly, in our post-Victorian, and post-Freudian, world, the definition of 'shocking' has changed drastically and so Wilson has to push the boundaries, to the extent of depicting a sexual encounter with a child prostitute. Indeed, the fact that *The Dark Clue* is subtitled 'A novel of suspense' hints at the inability for contemporary writers to be truly shocking.[14]

The biographer and the biographee

Wilson's treatment of sexuality is also explicitly connected to the novel's concern with biographical narratives; the alteration in Walter's behaviour comes as a direct result of his biographical researches and so is part of the novel's exploration of the relationship between the biographer and their subject. As we saw in the preceding discussion, Mansfield felt that too close a relationship between the biographer and biographee marred the resultant biography; rather, he advocated for objective distance between the biographer and their subject. Indeed, one of his ideals for nineteenth-century biography was that it should provide direct access to the subject; the biographer should be absent from the biography. The 'Life and Letters' mode of biography attempts to fulfil this purpose by presenting the subject in their own words, with the biographer reduced to the role of editor. Despite this ideal of biographical objectivity, however, the 'Life and Letters' mode actually blurs the line between biography and autobiography since it uses the letters and diaries of the subject, which are essentially autobiographical accounts, in order to construct the biographical portrait.

In *The Dark Clue*, however, the process seems to be reversed: as the novel progresses, it becomes less concerned with Turner than with the lives of his biographers, Marian and Walter. Thus, *The Dark Clue* moves from a biographical project to an autobiographical project. Marian's discoveries concerning the repressed elements of Turner's life are simultaneous with the realization of her own repressed desires for Walter. Contemplating the *Bay of Baiae* Marian realizes that it is actually two paintings; it shows Sybil and Apollo at the outset of their narrative, but also depicts their subsequent destruction and desolation (p. 273). Marian applies this observation to Turner's life to account for what initially appear to be contradictions in the dates of important events. She concludes that Turner's life mirrors his art; he led two lives and almost invariably kept two houses. As Marian uncovers the dark clue of Turner's life, she similarly acknowledges the dark clue in her own life. Eventually, the realization dawns on Marian that she too is leading two lives: her public life as the devoted half-sister to Laura and her private desires for Laura's husband Walter. The biographical process, then, prompts Marian to make sense of her own autobiographical narrative.

Although the revelations about Turner provide Marian with useful insights into her own psyche, the dangers of too close an identification between the biographer and biographee are explored through Walter's relationship to his biographical subject. As his investigations into Turner progress, Walter's identity begins to merge with Turner's as he takes on first Turner's pseudonym Jenkinson and later Turner's personality. Walter subsequently begins to re-enact scenes from Turner's life when he engages in sexual relations with a prostitute in the manner that, apparently, Turner himself had liked. Walter's own personality seems to entirely disappear after this event, culminating in him raping his sister-in-law Marian. A psychoanalytical explanation of these events might suggest that the adoption of Turner's pseudonym distances Walter from his innermost desires; it is only through this persona that he is able to realize those desires. Thus in renouncing his identity Walter is actually able to uncover his 'true self'. Yet the characters themselves reject such a conclusion; rather, they interpret Walter's behaviour as the result of a sickness or a demonic possession.

Whereas *The Dark Clue* reveals the dangers that the biographical project poses for the biographer, *Clara* and *Jack Maggs* explore the problems for the biographical subject. Both novels reveal the extent to which the biographical subject's narrative can be taken over by the biographer or, in the case of *Jack Maggs*, the novelist, an issue which is explicitly connected to their political projects. In light of the post-structuralist deconstruction of the subject, biographical narratives provide an important space for reasserting the subject, a space that is politically important for movements such as feminism and post-colonialism which assert the rights of a unified and identifiable group of subjects. According to Linda Hutcheon, 'the current post-structuralist/post-modern challenges to the coherent, autonomous subject have to be put on hold in feminist and post-colonial discourses, for both must work first to assert and affirm a denied or alienated subjectivity: those radical post-modern challenges are in many ways the luxury of the dominant order which can afford to challenge that which it securely possesses' (1989, p. 168). These novels, however, do not naively seek to recuperate a lost sense of subjectivity, but rather reveal the extent to which identity is constituted in political terms.

Galloway's *Clara* demonstrates the extent to which Clara's narrative is determined by the men in her life and the narratives they impose on her. This appropriation of Clara's narrative is most extreme in the case of her father, Wieck, who constructs a narrative for Clara from the moment of her birth. Rewriting the family narrative to overlook Adelheid, who had died in infancy, Clara becomes 'His true first-born' (p. 23). Prior to this revelation of Wieck's views on his daughter, the narrative presents two commonplace predictions about children. The first prediction strives to understand children's future temperament and position in life in relation to their position within the family: 'First-borns, they say, make solid citizens: prepared for, fussed over; complicity with the adult world is assured. Second-borns are rebels, dissenters. The near miss, it seems, grates' (p. 22). In repositioning Clara as his first-born, then, Wieck tries to determine her future and initially it seems to have succeeded. Yet in marrying Robert Schumann against her father's wishes, Clara's second-born traits resurface. Implicitly, then, Clara resists the narrative imposed on her by her father and society. The most damaging instance of Wieck's imposition of a narrative onto Clara's life is his stubborn refusal to understand her as a woman. For Wieck, Clara's gender is incompatible with the narrative he has constructed of her as a great musician and so he rigorously ignores it, to the extent of refusing to comment on her very obvious, and numerous, pregnancies.

Wieck does not merely impose his own patterns on Clara's narrative, but actually becomes the author of it. The first excerpt from Clara's diary reveals that it is not merely kept at the behest of her father but is initially written by him: 'My diary. His own hand. *Mine*' (p. 61). The shifting pronouns in this sentence reveal the contradictions between biography and autobiography and the different purposes they serve. Indeed, Clara's diary is not intended as a private document, but rather as 'durable proof' of her life (p. 61). Wieck's view of the diary's role suggests that the biographical process has been reversed: 'impressions are not enough, but names, places, facts must be detailed enough to look back upon, reuse when needed for verification, classification, durable proof' (p. 61). This commitment to proof reveals that rather than serving as a record of the lived life, the written account becomes the proof of existence. The novel explicitly explores the diary's role as proof in relation to a farewell concert held in Leipzig: 'Had he [Joachim] really played for them? and on the same violin he would use all his life? Her diary says so, but Clara can't recall' (p. 280). Although in this instance the narrative account provides the truth of the past, the novel highlights that such self-authored accounts as diaries can be subject to the caprices of memory.

The reversal of the relationship between the narrative account and the lived life in *Clara* recalls Mansfield's condemnation of 'The Biographical Mania', which he claims resulted in the situation whereby 'not a few individuals now in the land of the living write letters [and] keep diaries [...] for the modest purpose of accumulating materials and saving trouble to their historical eulogist' (p. 22). Clara's diary clearly belongs to this category: 'Now the decisions have been made that this life will be remarkable, someone must record it' (p. 61). Thus, rather than the written record serving to *verify* the life, it seems as if Clara's identity is *constructed* through such narrative accounts. And, lest we needed reminding, those narrative accounts are constructed by her father: 'the *Diaries* are *Posterity's*, which is to say an Authorized Version, and his, without saying, is the authority that applies' (p. 62).

In *Jack Maggs*, for all his attempts at control, Maggs's narrative is ultimately taken out of his hands: through the processes of mesmerism, Tobias Oates gains access to Maggs's 'inner soul' and appropriates his narrative for his own fictional purposes. Carey skilfully interweaves the mesmerism sessions with the letters that Maggs writes to Phipps so that certain events of Maggs's past are revealed to the reader prior to Maggs's narration of them to Phipps. The most forceful example of this is the revelation that Maggs's child died, which the reader discovers through one of Oates's mesmerism sessions several chapters before the letter in which Maggs reveals the nature of his relationship with Sophina. Although Carey employs the mesmerism sessions to dramatic effect in his narrative, they also function as an analogy for the biographical process and so raise concerns about the ethical dimensions of biographical narratives.

While under Oates's mesmeric influence, Maggs is entirely vulnerable; he reveals aspects of his history that he is desperate to keep hidden, both because they are private and because the revelation of his true identity and his position in England would mean death. Understandably concerned about these dangers, Maggs agrees to participate on the condition that Oates keeps the records of the sessions under lock and key and shows them to him afterwards. Oates, however, falsifies the accounts and so Maggs remains unaware of the secrets he has disclosed. Like the biographical subject, who is usually dead when their biography is written, Maggs has no right of reply. In Oates's hands, mesmerism becomes an entirely unethical practice which establishes a parasitic relationship between him and Maggs. Oates's reaction to the revelation that Maggs is a convict from New South Wales, achieved while Maggs is in a mesmeric trance, is entirely devoid of human feelings; while Percy Buckle expresses sympathy for Maggs's ordeal, Oates merely sees the opportunities for his fiction.

Since Oates uses the information gathered from his mesmerism sessions to form the basis of his novel *The Death of Jack Maggs*, Carey's concern with the ethical dimensions of mesmerism extends into a broader concern with the ethics of turning a life into a narrative, be it fictional or biographical. On discovering that Oates is writing about him and, more importantly, Sophina, Maggs accuses Oates of being a thief. Initially, Oates tries to pacify Maggs by claiming that his novel is a testament to Sophina, a way to preserve her memory. In trying to justify his actions, Oates implicitly connects his fictional project to biographical projects, which frequently had such a memorial function in the Victorian era. Oates tries to further justify his actions by reasserting the distinction between fact and fiction. When Maggs accuses him of plotting his death, Oates distinguishes between the fictional Jack in his novel and the real Jack Maggs. Indeed, he claims that the use of Maggs's name is only a temporary measure. Yet Oates never changes the name; he publishes his novel as *The Death of Jack Maggs* and makes his own name on the back of Maggs's life story. Oates's appropriation of Maggs's life, then, takes on sinister dimensions. Indeed, Oates's narrative usurps Maggs's own account as by the end of the novel *The Death of Maggs* is the only written testimony to Maggs's life that remains. The reader, however, is provided with another account of the final days of Maggs's life back in Australia with Mercy and their children, which contests the fiery ending Oates conceives for Maggs.

The ethics of appropriating a life for narrative purposes is explored not only through Oates's dealings with Maggs but also in the very presence of Oates in the novel. Tobias Oates is a fictional version of Magwitch's original creator, Charles Dickens. Like Dickens, Oates began his professional life as a 'hack' journalist and a writer of short sketches before becoming an acclaimed novelist. Dickens is known to have drawn on contemporary events and, in the case of *David Copperfield*, events from his own life to furnish his fiction. Similarly, Tobias Oates draws his characters from life. Although Carey adopts the name Tobias Oates, the main elements of Oates's life history remain recognizable as the biography of Dickens. In basing Oates on Dickens, then, Carey could be considered guilty of the same crimes that Maggs accuses Oates of. Although he changes the name, the correspondences are plain enough and the portrait of Oates/Dickens is not entirely flattering. While Carey questions the ethics of fictionalizing real people, then, he remains implicated in this process. The close correspondence between the figures of Oates and Dickens connects Carey to his Victorian predecessor and raises questions about the relationship between the two authors and, more broadly, the relationship between neo-Victorian fictions and their Victorian 'originals' that will be addressed in the Coda.

In *Jack Maggs*, the correspondence between Oates and Dickens explicitly highlights the connections between biography and fiction and, consequently, the role of the biographer and that of the novelist. While Galloway's and Wilson's novels do not make such explicit connections, their exploration of the relationship between the biographer and the biographee similarly provides an analogue for the relationship between the historical novelist and the past they bring to life. Both *Clara* and *Jack Maggs* reveal the dangers of approaches that appropriate biographical subjects and deny them an individual existence. In particular, the negative example of Oates in Carey's novel reveals the importance for novelists to engage with the past with empathy and sympathy, rather than merely appropriating it for their own purposes. By contrast, Wilson's *The Dark Clue* reveals the dangers of too close an identification between the biographer and biographee. Walter's loss of identity suggests that biographers need to maintain a 'safe' distance from their subjects. This distance supposedly guarantees objectivity which, as we have seen, was highly prized in Mansfield's conception of the ideal form of biography. In *The Dark Clue* we see the terrible consequences that result when identification with the biographical subject takes over the biographer's own identity. Taken together, then, these three novels seem to advocate a relationship with the past which maintains an objective distance while being sensitive to the lived reality of the past.

Types vs. individuals

In these neo-Victorian fictions, the engagement with Victorian forms of biographical narratives is connected to a wider consideration of their own position as historical fiction. Thus, the three novels discussed in this chapter not only explore the forms and ethics of biographical narratives but also consider the role of individuals in historical narratives. As I suggested in the introduction to this chapter, the contemporary perception of the Victorian era is largely determined by its 'characters', both historical and fictional. Biographical narratives tend to position the individual either as a 'type', a representative of larger cultural issues, or as an 'exceptional' figure. Interestingly, though, narratives that centre around an exceptional figure often end up confirming the type since it is only in contrast to the stereotype that such figures become exceptional. In terms of the Victorians, the process by which the exceptional figure confirms the stereotype is particularly pronounced in accounts of the Victorians' sex lives and encapsulates the dual impulse of positioning the Victorians as 'strange yet familiar' that underlines many contemporary responses to the Victorian era. The revelation of the passionate nature of Robert and Clara's marriage in *Clara* is an example of this. In their very un-Victorian attitude to sex, Robert and Clara confirm the common perception of the Victorians as prudish and reserved. As I have shown, the treatment of sexuality in *Clara* is rooted in the novel's concern with nineteenth-century biographical narratives and ideas surrounding the 'proper' sphere of investigation.

It is not only biographical narratives that position historical figures as a 'type' or an 'exceptional' figure, however, but also historical fiction. Georg Lukács's theory of historical fiction prioritizes Scott's historical fictions, which he claims 'give living human embodiment to historical-social types' (p. 35). In Lukács's formulation, then, the historical novel should portray the individual as a 'type' or 'representative' of an historical era. He claims that 'what is lacking in the so-called historical novel before Sir Walter Scott is precisely the specifically historical, that is, derivation of the individuality of characters from the historical peculiarity of their age' (p. 19). Interestingly, this commitment to historical specificity seems to apply more to fictional figures than historical figures. Lukács argues that '[d]etail for Scott is only a means for achieving [...] historical faithfulness [which derives from] the authenticity of the historical psychology of his characters' (pp. 59–60). Although neo-Victorian fiction retains Scott's commitment to the 'historical psychology' of its fictional characters, the treatment of historical Victorians is more than merely a way to add 'authenticity' to the historical world they recreate. The depiction of historical Victorians in neo-Victorian fiction is explicitly connected to the concern with historical narratives, specifically biographical narratives in the case of the novels discussed in this chapter.

In contrast to Lukács's account, Linda Hutcheon argues that 'the protagonists of historiographic metafiction are anything but proper types: they are the ex-centrics, the marginalized, the peripheral figures of fictional history' (1988, pp. 113–14). She suggests that this rejection of 'types' extends to the treatment of historical figures in postmodern fiction, who 'take on a different, particularized, and ultimately ex-centric status' (1988, p. 114). For Hutcheon, this concern with 'ex-centric' figures is part of a 'postmodern ideology of plurality' which undermines any 'sense of cultural universality' (1988, p. 114). Moreover, she claims that the process of incorporating historical figures differs in postmodern fictions. While traditional historical novels incorporate historical data 'to hide the joins between fiction and history in a formal and ontological sleight of hand', postmodern novels highlight the separation between fiction and history: '[h]istoriographic metafiction incorporates, but rarely assimilates such [historical] data. More often, the process of *attempting* to assimilate is what is foregrounded [...]' (1988, p. 114). Indeed, Hutcheon suggests that historical details have become almost unimportant in historiographic metafictions, which adopt a playful attitude towards the known facts of history: 'certain known historical details are deliberately falsified in order to foreground the possible mnemonic failures of recorded history' (1988, p. 114).

As I have argued from the outset, neo-Victorian fiction cannot be understood solely in relation to postmodern forms of historical fiction. While historiographic metafictions gleefully embrace the slippage between history and fiction, neo-Victorian fictions remain committed to the attempt to recover the past, even as they accept the limitations of such a project. Moreover, their concern with the possibility of knowing the past is explicitly rooted in an engagement with particular forms of historical narratives in the nineteenth century. As we have seen, the three novels discussed in this chapter examine the relationship between the past and its textual remains in terms of the specific forms of Victorian biographical narratives. Similarly, the treatment of historical figures in these novels is intimately connected to their interrogation of biographical narratives.

By incorporating the figure of Ruskin into *The Dark Clue*, Wilson explicitly explores the temptations, and limitations, of treating historical figures as 'types'. The details surrounding Ruskin's failed marriage with Euphemia Chalmers Gray are fairly well known and have determined the contemporary perception of Ruskin as an example of the Victorian 'type', which seems to have become synonymous with sexual hypocrisy.[15] The resonance that Ruskin's name bears is explicitly commented on by Walter who reflects on the process by which the image associated with the name of a famous person ultimately becomes that person. Walter's observation could be seen as a comment on the incorporation of historical figures in fiction, where the depiction of the historical figure often depends on the associations conjured up by their name.

Wilson himself seems to adopt this approach in the incorporation of the figure of Mayhew at the end of the novel. As a minor character, Mayhew's presence could be said to add 'authenticity' to the Victorian setting of the novel. Yet Mayhew's presence draws on his historical position as a social researcher who circulated among the lower classes of Victorian society. Similarly, the incorporation of Ruskin diverges from the strategy of incorporating famous names to authenticate the fictional world. As Walter recognizes, the image conjured up by Ruskin's name is based on false perceptions. Wilson resists the temptation to use Ruskin as a type; rather, his portrait of Ruskin relies on his historically specific position as an art critic in the Victorian era. Thus, while aware of the stereotypes about Ruskin, Wilson's commitment to the historical specificity of the Victorian era prevents him from merely perpetuating those stereotypes. Wilson's portrayal of Ruskin is intimately connected to the novel's concern with biographical issues as Walter's comments draw attention to the way in which 'personalities' are created and implicitly questions the role such figures play in our understanding of the Victorian era.

Given the political motivations of *Clara* and *Jack Maggs*, it is unsurprising that they focus on figures that Hutcheon would deem 'ex-centrics'. As we have seen, however, this concern with ex-centric figures is explicitly connected to the novels' concern with biographical narratives since they explore the ethical dimensions of the appropriation of the 'other'. Galloway's novel seems to be concerned with the 'ex-centric' in its decision to narrate the life of the female pianist Clara Schumann. Indeed, the political impulse behind Galloway's novel seems to connect it to the 'postmodern ideology of plurality' that Hutcheon identified as central to historiographic metafiction (1988, p. 114). Yet the depiction of Clara is grounded in the historical specificity of the Victorian era; as an 'ex-centric' she brings more sharply into focus the 'type' of the nineteenth-century woman. In *Clara*, Galloway explores the ways in which Clara's life is shaped by the pre-determined patterns imposed on it by her father. Clara's father seeks to deny her femininity since it is incompatible with his narrative of her as a great musician: as he retorts to a neighbour who criticizes Clara's repertoire, 'My daughter is an artist, Mademoiselle, not a woman of any sort' (p. 130). Despite Wieck's stubborn denial of Clara's femininity, her exceptional position actually serves to highlight the conditions for 'normal' nineteenth-century women. For instance, the reaction of Clara's step-mother to the revelation that Clara was to have only 'one corset [...] and that just for special' indicates the extent to which women's lives were constrained by social expectations of femininity (p. 109).

Jack Maggs most obviously engages with the 'ex-centric' in its narration of the life of a marginal figure from Dickens's *Great Expectations*. In Dickens's canonical text, Magwitch functions more as a plot mechanism than a character in his own right. Throughout Carey's novel, Maggs resists such side-lining in his insistence on narrating his own life story. Carey's novel, then, can be seen as part of the impulse of the post-colonial writer to, in Salman Rushdie's phrase, 'write back'. Although Maggs initially seems to have escaped the influence of Dickens's narrative, Carey implicitly reveals the extent to which Maggs's sense of self has been determined by such literary narratives as *Great Expectations*. Despite being deported to the colonies, Jack Maggs explicitly conceives of himself as an Englishman and it is this identity which motivates his return to England. Maggs's idea of an Englishman is implicitly constructed through literary narratives; *Great Expectations* traces Pip's transformation from an orphan with limited prospects to a man of 'expectations' and so forms part of the discourse surrounding the ideology of 'self-help' in the mid-Victorian era. Interestingly, it is not Pip who is the model of the 'self-made man' in Dickens's novel, but rather Magwitch. Yet Carey's novel suggests that there are underlying prejudices in Dickens's novel which prevent the elevation of Magwitch to the position of 'gentleman'. In contrast, in *Jack Maggs* Maggs returns to Australia and continues to be not only financially successful but also honoured as a pillar of the community. In rewriting Dickens's *Great Expectations*, Carey reveals the extent to which English narratives, and particularly Victorian narratives, have shaped post-colonial identity. In an interview with Eleanor Wachtel, he hinted at this connection between Victorian narratives and post-colonial identity, claiming that 'Australia kept on being Victorian long after the British stopped being Victorian' (104).

Conclusion

Located wholly in the nineteenth century, the neo-Victorian novels discussed in this chapter initially seem to efface their own position as a historical novel, instead presenting a 'correct likeness' of the Victorian era and its narrative forms (Mansfield, p. 22). Although they do not have an explicit twentieth-century frame, however, these novels do incorporate elements that implicitly reveal their distance from the

Victorian era. The political impulse that at least partly motivates *Clara* and *Jack Maggs* is just one of the ways in which these authors highlight the distance between the nineteenth and twentieth centuries. This positioning can be understood as part of these novels' concern with biographical narratives. As we have seen, nineteenth-century biography similarly seeks to present a 'correct likeness' of the subject and thus efface the mode of representation. Yet biography is also characterized by secondariness. Although a biography promises direct access to its subject, the biographee is always mediated to the reader through the biographer.

The condition of secondariness is fundamental to neo-Victorian fiction. In his article 'What is Neo-Victorian Studies', Mark Llewellyn frames neo-Victorianism in the context of the 'notion of belatedness that dogged Victorianism and the Victorian period itself' (2008, p. 167). Taking Isobel Armstrong's assessment that Victorian poetry 'is on the way somewhere' as applicable to the whole idea of the 'Victorian', Llewellyn asks '[a]t the height of out (post)modernity, why do we continually mark and stage a return to a period that was caught between two "bigger" notions?' (2008, p. 167). Given that the very condition of secondariness seems to derive from the Victorian era itself, the issues of originality and authenticity become problematic in relation to neo-Victorian fiction. The question arises as to whether these novels can be said to exist in their own right, as independent and unique works of art, or whether they are merely parasitic on their predecessors' texts.

Neo-Victorian fiction is clearly aware of the legacy of Victorian literature and culture, a legacy it seeks to incorporate rather than efface. This is most apparent in the case of Wilson's *The Dark Clue* and Carey's *Jack Maggs*, since both novels directly engage with a Victorian predecessor.[16] Both Wilson and Carey point up the silences and omissions in Victorian texts, although Carey does it to more political effect in *Jack Maggs*. These novels, then, transform their Victorian intertexts. As we saw earlier, this transformation is part of these novels' examination of the notion of decency in Victorian biographical narratives. Yet it is also part of their position as neo-Victorian novels. Neo-Victorian fictions do not seek to collapse the distance between the Victorians and us; rather, their depictions of the Victorian past remain aware of the position of the twentieth-century author and reader and are self-conscious about how the Victorian past is narrated in the present. As we shall see in the Coda, this approach is central to neo-Victorian fiction's engagement with Victorian literary narratives.

2
Detecting the Victorians

Neo-Victorian fiction presents the process of recovering the Victorian past as similar to that of a detective solving a case; 'clues' from the past need to be interpreted in order to make sense of 'what really happened'. Many neo-Victorian texts adopt the trope of detective fiction, most obviously in encouraging the reader to identify the intertextual traces of Victorian fictions. In A. S. Byatt's *Possession*, the reader is further encouraged to take on the role of the detective as they, like the questing academics within the novel, interpret the textual remains of the past in order to uncover what happened between the two nineteenth-century poets. In dealing with how we can know and narrate the Victorian past, most neo-Victorian fictions adopt the analogy of the historian as a detective, but in those novels that explicitly adopt the forms and conventions of detective fiction, an analogy is also drawn between the detective and the historical novelist.[1] Colin Dexter's *The Wench is Dead* (1989) and Julian Barnes's *Arthur & George* (2005) both work within the established conventions of detective fiction, although their approaches to the genre differ, as do the nature of the crimes they investigate. Detective fiction provides a way for these neo-Victorian novelists to explore questions not only of the possibility of knowing the past but also of the responsibility that the present owes to the past.

Detective fiction is characterized by epistemological concerns; indeed, Brian McHale goes so far as to claim that it is 'the epistemological genre *par excellence*' (p. 6). Raising questions of what we know about the world and the systems by which we acquire that knowledge, detective fiction connects to neo-Victorian fiction's concern with how we can know, and narrate, the Victorian past. In neo-Victorian detective fiction, this interest in the narratives of the past particularly focuses on the issues of evidence, truth and judgement about the past. In *Postmodernist*

Fiction (1996), McHale characterizes the transition from modernism to postmodernism as a shift from an epistemological to an ontological dominant, from a concern with questions about modes of knowing to a concern with questions about modes of being. In this account, then, detective fiction would seem to be a modernist mode of writing.

In recent years, however, there has been an upsurge in novels adopting the conventions of detective fiction, not only in genre fiction, where detective fiction has remained popular since its inception, but also in literary fictions and especially in postmodern fiction. The emergence of the postmodern detective novel seems to counter McHale's implication that detective fiction is a modernist genre. Perhaps the most famous example of the postmodern detective novel is Umberto Eco's *The Name of the Rose* (1980), which centres around a series of murders that take place in an Italian monastery in the fourteenth century. In an explicit allusion to the most famous of all literary detectives, Eco's detective is named William of Baskerville. Although Eco's novel sparked a renewed interest in historical detective fictions, not all such texts adopt the attitude of postmodern play that characterized his engagement with history. This is particularly true of neo-Victorian detective fictions.

As I argue throughout this book, neo-Victorian fiction is contemporaneous with but cannot be reduced to the category of postmodernism; it is distinguished from postmodernism by its Victorian setting. While all detective fictions implicitly recall their nineteenth-century roots, most often in the creation of a Holmesian or anti-Holmesian detective figure, neo-Victorian fictions engage with the specific historical context out of which detective fiction emerged. This concern with historical specificity is perhaps most obvious in the tendency for neo-Victorian detective fictions to be based on real nineteenth-century crimes. Both of the novels discussed in this chapter draw on true crimes: Julian Barnes's *Arthur & George* is based on the Great Wyrley Outrages of 1903 while Colin Dexter's *The Wench is Dead* fictionalizes the murder of Christine Collins in 1839.

The popularity of historical detective fictions may be in part because the very structure of detective fiction implies a concern with history. Whereas most fictions are teleological in orientation, working towards the end-point of the narrative, detective fiction looks backwards and attempts to account for and reconstruct the past. The events and objects of the detective story only acquire meaning at the end of the story, when the detective reconstructs the events of the narrative and reveals them as 'clues'. Detective fiction, then, engages in a process of historical recovery. The temporal direction of detective fiction can be explained using Tzvetan Todorov's essay 'The Typology of Detective Fiction' (1971). A Russian critic of the Formalist school, Todorov defines the different types of detective fiction in terms of their structural organization. He takes as his starting point '[t]he classic detective fiction which reached its peak between the two world wars and is often called the whodunit' (p. 44). Drabble suggests that in the hands of the 'Golden Age writers' the detective novel was characterized by 'artifice [and an] insistence on murder as a game' (p. 276). Although Drabble identifies the Golden Age as the 1920s, the idea of the detective genre as a puzzle or a game emerged in the late-nineteenth century and was popularized by the phenomenon of Sherlock Holmes, who is as often concerned with the question of 'howdunit' as with 'whodunit'.

Todorov asserts that the 'whodunit' detective novel contains 'not one but two stories: the story of the crime and the story of the investigation' (p. 44). He continues, saying that '[i]n their purest form, those two stories have no point in common'; there is no temporal overlap between the two stories since '[t]he first story, that of the crime, ends before the second begins' (p. 44). The second story, that of the investigation, starts at the end of the first story and works backwards to reconstruct the events of the first story. Todorov understands this duality of stories in terms of the Russian Formalist distinction between *fable* (story) and *suzjet* (plot): while the crime provides the story, it is the investigation which provides the plot of the detective novel (p. 45). Indeed, Todorov claims that the first story, that of the crime, 'is in fact the story of an absence: its most accurate characteriztic is that it cannot be immediately present in the book' (p. 46). Although the investigation story is present, Todorov argues that 'it is a story which has no importance in itself, which serves only as a mediator between the reader and the story of the crime' (p. 46). He further elaborates on this distinction: 'the first – the story of the crime – tells "what really happened," whereas the second – the story of the investigation – explains "how the reader (or the narrator) has come to know about it"' (p. 45).

The terms in which Todorov conceives of this difference between the two stories correlates to the distinction that is often made between history and historiography. Whereas history is 'what really happened in the past', historical narratives concern 'how the historian has come to know about the past'. Like the crime story, the past is characterized by an 'absence'; it can never wholly be recovered in the present. Yet whereas Todorov suggests that the investigation plot has 'no importance in itself', neo-Victorian fictions reveal the importance of the narratives of the past and the extent to which those narratives can determine our view of the past. In positing two types of interest in detective fiction, *curiosity* and *suspense*, Todorov again raises issues that pertain to historical narratives. He suggests that the whodunit is characterized by curiosity, which 'proceeds from effect to cause' (p. 47). This approach corresponds to that of historical writing since it necessarily starts in the present and works backwards to the past. Similarly, neo-Victorian fictions start in the present, if only because of the position of the author, and work backwards. As we will see in Chapter 4, several neo-Victorian novels dramatize this process in the adoption of a dual plot which sees the twentieth-century characters 'investigating' the nineteenth-century past. In Dexter's *The Wench is Dead*, this is not merely a trope; the novel presents a twentieth-century detective figure investigating a nineteenth-century crime. However, not all neo-Victorian fictions adopt such a retrospective approach to the past. In their exploration of the relationship between the present and the past, many neo-Victorian novels work forward from the past to establish continuities with the present.

Engaging with detective fiction is part of neo-Victorian fictions' wider concerns with historical narratives. The temporal structure of detective fiction provokes a consideration of the relationship between the present and the past, and its epistemological concerns raise questions about the possibility of knowing the past, the role of evidence in establishing a connection to the past and the nature of our responsibility towards the past. This sense of responsibility to the past is evident in the commitment to the historical specificity of detective fiction. Neo-Victorian detective novels are intimately aware of the historical conditions surrounding the emergence of detective fiction in the nineteenth century.

Nineteenth-century detection

Although detective fiction's 'Golden Age' occurred in the 1920s and 1930s, making it contemporaneous with modernism, it first emerged as a separate and identifiable genre in the nineteenth century (Drabble). Moreover, Conan Doyle's creation of Sherlock Holmes at the end of the nineteenth century has become the touchstone for all subsequent fictional detectives. Indeed, as Stephen Knight notes, the name of Sherlock Holmes has become 'a synonym for a detective' (p. 67).

Detective fiction did not spring up out of nowhere, however, but had roots in other forms of nineteenth-century writing. Stephen Knight's *Form and Ideology in Crime Fiction* (1980) traces the development of the genre from its pre-Victorian roots, through Poe's Dupin stories, to the emergence of the fully-fledged detective novel in England and the subsequent creation of Sherlock Holmes at the end of the nineteenth century. Knight positions *The Newgate Calendar* as an important precursor to the detective story; he claims that *The Newgate Calendar*, like other pre-Victorian crime narratives, was based on 'the basic notion, and hope, that the all-pervasive, inescapable Christian reality provides a protection against crime' (p. 12). The narrator in *The Newgate Calendar*, then, 'can do no more than watch, listen, record reports and apply "normal", shared evaluative reactions. This gives the impression of an unmediated, direct form of narration which responds to the underlying idea that society needs no special mediation to restore itself' (p. 17). In contrast, the emergence of detective fiction was based around the notion that an intelligent individual is needed to make sense of the irrational world of crime. As Knight notes, the model for the 'intellectual, infallible, isolated hero' of much subsequent detective fiction was created by Edgar Allan Poe in the figure of Auguste C. Dupin (p. 39). Poe wrote a series of stories in the 1840s that involved Dupin in various criminal cases, including a contemporary criminal case which had remained unsolved. Knight argues that 'Poe's masterly illusion is to make Dupin move from and through the scientific to the special authority of the visionary' (p. 43). As we shall see, this apparent conflict between a scientific and speculative approach to detection is central to Barnes's novel *Arthur & George*.

The development of the English detective novel is usually dated to Wilkie Collins's *The Moonstone* (1868), although some critics have argued that his earlier sensation novel *The Woman in White* (1860) also contributed to the formation of the detective genre.[2] Sensation and detective fiction adopt a similar plot structure: both genres hinge on the discovery of a secret from the past that threatens the social order in the present. Scott McCracken relates the development of the detective genre to the establishment of the 'modern legal process' based on evidence, a relationship which is clearly evident in Collins's *The Woman in White* (p. 51). In the opening to Collins's novel, Walter Hartright explicitly connects the narrative approach to the legal system:

> the story here presented will be told by more than one pen, as the story of an offence against the laws is told in Court by more than one witness – with the same object, in both cases, to present the truth always in its most intelligible aspect [...]. (p. 5)[3]

In this instance, sensation fiction seems concerned with both the sensational events and the possibility of narrating those events, a concern which, as we have seen, is inherent in the two plots of detective fiction.

Conan Doyle's creation of Sherlock Holmes in his stories of the late 1880s formalized the genre conventions of detective fiction, most obviously as related to the figure of the detective. Holmes clearly follows in the footsteps of Dupin as a rational, emotionally detached detective; his detective process is grounded in empirical observation of the minute details of the world around him.[4] Yet his conclusions are actually the result of deductive reasoning; he reads the empirical evidence as signs of social relationships.[5] The popular appeal of Sherlock Holmes has ensured that this has remained the model of the detective for much subsequent detective fiction. Almost as soon as Holmes appeared he became the standard against which all subsequent fictional detectives were measured, and usually found wanting. Indeed, he became the model not only for fictional detection, but also for the processes of detection in the historical world of the Victorian and Edwardian eras. An article in the *Penny Illustrated Paper* in April 1912 announced the opening of a 'special technical police school' in Paris which it claims locals have dubbed 'Sherlock Holmes College' ('Romance of the World's News,' p. 261). Similarly, an article covering the retirement of Frank Froest from Scotland Yard in September 1912 was titled 'A Sherlock Holmes in Real Life'.

The relationship between fictional and real detection, however, was not one way. Rather, the emergence of detective fiction in the nineteenth century and the specific characteristics that were favoured for the detective figure need to be understood in terms of the social and intellectual context of the Victorian era. As a result of the population increase and urban migration that occurred in the nineteenth century, the model of Christian reality presupposed by *The Newgate Calendar* began to break down; in a society where people no longer know their neighbours, the detection of crime becomes more difficult. The city, in particular, becomes shrouded by a sense of unknowability and anonymity. The establishment of the Metropolitan Police Force in 1829 can be understood as a response to the fear and anxiety caused by the anonymity of the city, and from 1842 onwards there was a specific 'Detective Department', which was later renamed to Criminal Investigations Department.[6]

The emergence of the detective figure in real life may go some way to accounting for its appearance in fiction during the latter half of the nineteenth century. Although detective fiction did not appear in its own right until the late 1860s, Charles Dickens's *Bleak House*, published between 1852 and 1853, included a detective figure in the character of Inspector Bucket. While he was among the first detectives in English fiction, Inspector Bucket was not the model for subsequent fictional detectives. From Sherlock Holmes on, detective fictions have tended to centre on an amateur detective whose ability to solve crimes indicates the inadequacies of the official police force. The portrait of the official police force as at worst incompetent or at best too closely bound by rules and regulations hints at anxieties surrounding the newly established force in the nineteenth century. This preference for the amateur detective in detective fiction continued until the 1960s, when there seemed to be a move towards the professional detective.[7]

It was not only the real life figure of the detective that affected the emergence of detective fiction, but also the processes of detection that developed in the nineteenth century. The Holmesian model of ratiocination was derived as much from actual nineteenth-century practices as it was from the model of Dupin. As I said in the Introduction, the nineteenth century saw the introduction of numerous state practices for identifying and documenting the individual. The most significant of these developments was the establishment of the census in 1801, but the impulse also led to the passing of bills that required the registration of births, deaths and marriages.[8] As with the establishment of the Metropolitan Police Force, these practices can be understood as a response to the increasing urban population in Britain, which made it both increasingly necessary and increasingly difficult for the state to account for its citizens.[9] These two activities, documenting the individual and monitoring criminality, converged in the adoption of technological advances such as photography and fingerprinting by the police force. During the late nineteenth century Francis Galton developed the technique of composite photography and one of the uses to which he put this technique was to try to identify if there was such a thing as a criminal 'type'. More directly applicable to the police force was the creation of a photographic file of convicted criminals, a 'Rogues Gallery', in 1862; the establishment of an official police photographer in 1901; and the formation of the Fingerprint Bureau at the turn of the century.[10] Such technological advances seem to presuppose the possibility of knowing and classifying the criminal world, an assumption which similarly underpins most detective fictions. Indeed, as Walter Benjamin indicates, '[t]he detective story came into being when this most decisive conquest of a person's incognito had been accomplished [through photography]' (p. 79).

While such technological procedures have become a staple of contemporary detective fiction, nowhere more so than in the procedural detective show *Crime Scene Investigation*, the impact on nineteenth-century detective fiction was a result of a more pervasive shift in attitudes towards evidence in the Victorian era.[11] As Scott McCracken argues, the detective novel appeared 'at a time when the collection of evidence and the presentation of a case were replacing the extraction of a confession by torture' (p. 51). In Conan Doyle's stories, Holmes is clearly preoccupied with the accumulation of evidence, but not necessarily for the purposes of justice. Indeed, at times, as in 'The Adventure of the Blue Carbuncle' (1892), Holmes allows the criminal to escape justice once he has 'extracted' the confession that satisfies his inquiring mind. This confession is not acquired through torture, though, but rather through a display of his intelligence; since Holmes already seems to know 'what really happened', the criminal is not so much confessing as merely confirming his reconstructed version of events. Interestingly, in this story Holmes allows the criminal to escape, even though an innocent man is being held under suspicion of committing the crime. The role of justice in the detective story is particularly pertinent to the neo-Victorian novels discussed in this chapter since both present cases that have already been through the judicial process. This concern with the processes of justice can be seen as one of the ways in which these novels transform the conventions of nineteenth-century detective fiction.

The movement towards a more scientific, empiricist approach to evidence was part of a wider intellectual trend which favoured objective rationality.[12] The emergence of various disciplines in the nineteenth century that sought to understand and categorize the individual can clearly be seen as contributing to the development of detective processes both in fiction and within the Metropolitan Police Force itself. While disciplines such as phrenology and physiognomy might now be considered pseudo-sciences, they were based on the assumption that a person's character could be interpreted through 'reading' the physical traces of their cranium or face.

The idea of paying attention to minute details to draw wider inferences is clearly evident in Holmes's favourite detective technique. Many of the stories open with Holmes encountering an unidentified object and reading the object to draw conclusions about the owner. For instance, in 'The Adventure of the Blue Carbuncle' Holmes reads a hat to deduce that the owner is intellectual, no longer as rich as he once was, and no longer loved by his wife (pp. 149–50). The deductions that Holmes makes about the hat serve to reinstate its owner into the network of social relations that have been removed by the city and thus render both the object and its owner 'knowable'.

Detective fiction is ultimately based on a confident belief that the world is 'knowable'; what is mysterious in detective fiction is only so because it awaits proper interpretation. Keyman remarks that in detective fiction 'if narrative is fundamentally epistemological, so too is mystery – not an absolute unknown but precisely something that is known to someone who is not telling it to others' (p. 11). Although the events are originally shrouded in mystery, then, the mystery belongs to the realm of the knowable, rather than the supernatural. This confidence in the ability to know the social world connects to the realist project of much Victorian fiction. According to Knight, 'the subtly developed, perfectly controlled response of one pair of authorial eyes and ears fictionally creates the myth [...] that a single individual, if clever and patient enough, can unravel the world of experience' (p. 23). In their adoption of an omniscient narrator, then, realist narratives suggest that the world is ultimately knowable, if only through the mediation of particularly gifted individuals.

Knight, however, recognizes that this idea of omniscience can extend to 'include a first person narrator' (p. 24). This is most obvious in detective fiction, where the detective performs a similar function to that of the omniscient narrator as they elucidate the connections between seemingly random characters and events to present a coherent and contained world. Detective fiction, then, is not only allied to the realist project, but could also be seen as metafictionally reproducing the situation of realist fiction. The detective character replicates the position of the narrator within the text as he interprets the clues and provides the information he has uncovered to the reader. In neo-Victorian detective fiction, the detective figure not only metafictionally replicates the position of the narrator, but also that of the historical novelist. In exploring the relationship between the past and the present, then, neo-Victorian fictions not only consider the forms of historical narratives, but also examine their own position as historical narratives.

Neo-Victorian detective fictions

Colin Dexter's *The Wench is Dead* and Julian Barnes's *Arthur & George* explore the possibilities of narrating the past through their position as detective fictions. Dexter's novel is the eighth in his hugely popular Inspector Morse Mystery series, although it departs from the usual format of a Morse mystery in its concern with a nineteenth-century crime. The novel, however, opens not with the crime, but with the hospitalization of the detective hero. It is while recuperating in hospital that Morse reads an account of a nineteenth-century murder on the canals and begins to question the conviction of two boatmen for the murder. With the help of his trusty sidekick Sergeant Lewis, clearly a Watson figure to Morse's Holmes, and the daughter of another patient in his ward, Morse conducts historical research to uncover 'what really happened'.

Barnes's *Arthur & George* is less immediately identifiable as a detective novel. Barnes is often considered an exemplar of postmodern writing and several of his novels have come to be considered 'canonical' texts of postmodernism because of their exploration of the boundary between history and fiction. With *Arthur & George*, Barnes has taken his concern with history and identity into the nineteenth century, but he is also, as the summary on the back cover indicates, concerned with 'the fateful differences between what we believe, what we know and what we can prove'. As both the creator of the most rational detective in fictional history and an ardent believer in spiritualism, Arthur Conan Doyle, the 'Arthur' of the title, proves an interesting figure through whom to consider these issues. While this interest in epistemological issues aligns the novel with the concerns of detective fiction, its connection to the detective genre is established even more explicitly.

The narrative structure of *Arthur & George* requires the reader to adopt the role of detective. Using only the protagonists' first names, both the title and the cover blurb refuse to reveal the identities of the novel's subjects. Moving back and forth between 'Arthur' and 'George', the narrative involves the reader in a process of detection; they are invited to decode the identities of the protagonists as well as the relationship between them. George's identity is explicitly revealed to the reader during the 'Beginnings' section as he is questioned by a local police officer and, despite the fact that the officer knows who he is, required to give his full name. By contrast, Arthur's identity has to be deduced by the reader, which is not too difficult given his status as a prominent figure in Victorian history and culture. Towards the end of the first chapter, 'Arthur' is unequivocally identified by the revelation that he created a character called 'Sherlock Holmes' (p. 61).

Whereas Barnes's previous novels tended to emphasize the fictional nature of history, as a neo-Victorian novel, *Arthur & George* is very much grounded in historical fact. The protagonists of the novel, Sir Arthur Conan Doyle and George Edjali, are verifiable Victorian figures, and the events that bring them into contact are known historical facts. While Arthur is a famous Victorian, the details of whose life are fairly well-known, George is a more obscure historical figure, whose life and impact on Victorian culture are little-known outside the spheres of local and judicial history. The divergent positions of these figures is reflected in the different narrative techniques Barnes adopts in dealing with them. *Arthur & George* follows each of the protagonists independently from childhood, interleaving episodes from Arthur's life with those from George's life until the point at which their stories converge. Interestingly, Barnes adopts the past tense for the early 'Arthur' episodes whereas all of the 'George' episodes are narrated in the present tense. As a prominent Victorian, the details of Arthur's life are relatively well known; in a sense, his history is closed off since we already know the end. In contrast, George is a little-known Victorian figure and so Barnes has greater imaginative license to invent and bring this figure to life.

Dexter's novel is also grounded in historical fact as he draws from the annals of nineteenth-century crimes for his novel: the murder of Joanna Franks is based on the real-life murder of Christine Collins on the Oxford canal in 1839. Although he maintains certain historical details, such as the surname of one of the boatmen convicted of Collins's murder, Dexter alters both the name of the victim and the date of the crime, transposing it to 1859. Similarly, there is nothing in the original accounts of the murder to suggest the surprising solution Morse provides to the crime. In rewriting the known facts of the past, Dexter goes against the commitment to historical specificity that I have argued characterizes neo-Victorian fiction. Although *The Wench is Dead* addresses many neo-Victorian concerns, most obviously in its adoption of a dual plot structure which dramatizes the relationship between the present and the past, its position as a detective novel is more important. The alterations to the known facts of the case, then, allow Dexter to present a typical Morse mystery in which which the detective uncovers an unusual and unlooked for solution to the crimes he encounters.

The concern with historical crimes also has implications for the detective process since both novels deal with crimes that have already been through the judicial system. In both cases, however, the initial resolution to the crime is revealed to be wrong. *Arthur & George* follows the prosecution of George Edjali for the Great Wyrley Outrages, his subsequent release and the campaign mounted by Arthur Conan Doyle to clear his name. Although George's innocence is implied by his release from prison before his term had ended, it is not until Arthur becomes involved in the case that his innocence is proved sufficiently for him to receive a full pardon from the Home Office and resume his career as a solicitor. Despite the involvement of Arthur, though, the case remains unsolved. Equally, the case which *The Wench is Dead* centres on, the murder of Joanna Franks, has supposedly already been solved and the perpetrators convicted and hung for their crime. Morse's investigations into the nineteenth-century case, however, propose a radically different solution; he deduces that the murder of Joanna Franks was staged by the victim and her husband in order to make a claim on the life insurance policy. In contrast to *Arthur & George*, however, justice is never served for the men wrongfully convicted of the crime.

In centring on the issue of justice, these novels raise questions about the responsibility that the present owes to the past and whether it is possible to right the wrongs of the past. Although both novels raise similar questions, the answers differ greatly, in large part because of the different approaches taken by the authors. Barnes's *Arthur & George* adopts an omniscient narrative perspective which switches between the two protagonists. Although the novel has a dual plot, both plots occupy the same temporal plane: the novel is set wholly in the late-nineteenth and early-twentieth centuries. While *Arthur & George* does not explicitly dramatize an opposition between the present and the past, its dual concern with detective fiction and spiritualism raises questions about the possibility of connecting with the past.[13]

By contrast, *The Wench is Dead* moves between the nineteenth and twentieth centuries in its narration.[14] While the majority of the Joanna Franks case is presented to the reader through the mediation of Wilfrid M. Deniston's account, the narrative does at one point take the reader directly to the nineteenth-century events. Juxtaposing the nineteenth and twentieth centuries in this way, Dexter explicitly considers the continuities and discontinuities between the Victorians and us. Moreover, the dual plot also draws attention to the connection between the detective and the historian, to the idea that knowing the past is a process of detection. There is always a sense in detective fiction that the mystery can only be penetrated by the superior intellect of the detective figure, but in *The Wench is Dead* this narrative structure has particular implications for the relationship between the present and the past. In adopting a dual plot in which a twentieth-century detective solves a nineteenth-century crime, *The Wench is Dead* implies that the contemporary detective is in a position to correct the mistaken conclusions of his nineteenth-century predecessors. This evolutionist approach is perhaps a consequence of the detective genre which, as we have seen, adopts a retrospective narrative approach. Written in the present, neo-Victorian fictions necessarily adopt a retrospective approach to the Victorian past. Yet, not all neo-Victorian fictions adopt such a teleological or evolutionist approach which prioritizes the present over the past. By contrast, Barnes's *Arthur & George* starts from the past and moves forwards to explore the connections between the Victorians and us.

The detective figure

The detective figures in both *Arthur & George* and *The Wench is Dead* are clearly modelled on Holmes. Given that Arthur Conan Doyle was responsible for creating the most famous detective of all time, it is unsurprising that Barnes's Arthur self-consciously understands his involvement in the Edalji case in terms of his proximity to Holmes. Prior to his involvement in the case, Arthur seems persistently keen to distance himself from Holmes and eventually kills off his fictional creation. Yet, once he becomes involved in George's case he eagerly adopts some of the qualities of Holmes and frequently places his secretary, Woodie, in the role of Watson. For instance, Holmes often adopted disguise to gain access to places; similarly, when first travelling to Wyrley, Arthur decides that it is important to travel incognito and 'insist[s] upon disguise; first material, then psychological' (p. 312).

As the eighth novel in a successful series, *The Wench is Dead* clearly asserts the importance of the detective figure, Inspector Morse. Dexter's novel opens with Morse, but whereas the Sherlock Holmes stories usually opened with a display of the detective's superior intellect, *The Wench is Dead* opens with the consequences of Morse's ageing body as he is suffering with a stomach ulcer. The novel sets up a clear opposition between the limitations of Morse's body and the capacities of his mind as he is hospitalized for much of the novel. Despite this, Morse is a detective figure very much in the mould of Holmes: he is a confirmed bachelor with few emotional connections, although he comes to form a close bond with his 'Watson', Sergeant Lewis. Like Holmes, Morse is an educated man with refined tastes which include Wagner and A. E. Housman. Both Holmes and Morse have a 'vice' which, while frowned upon by polite society, is justified by their superior intellect. Holmes has a narcotic addiction which he indulges when he is without a case, the suggestion being that Holmes's superior intellect requires constant stimulation. Interestingly, in *Arthur & George*, Barnes suggests that Holmes's vice was an 'indulgence his creator was nowadays embarrassed to have awarded him' (p. 334). Morse's 'vice', by contrast, is alcohol, a much more socially acceptable vice in the twentieth century. Indeed, he claims that alcohol actually aids his thought processes; it is 'a necessary stimulant to his brain cells!' (p. 71).

It is not only in terms of his personality that Morse is modelled on Holmes; his approach to detection similarly follows the model of ratiocination enshrined by that most famous of all fictional detectives. As explained earlier, this process of detection was characterized by intellectual, emotionally detached observation. Morse's passion for crossword puzzles hints at his view that crimes are puzzles to be solved by the application of rational thought. Indeed, it is an anagram which prompts Morse to resolve the final puzzle of the crime. The idea of crimes as puzzles suggests they are unimportant and have no implications for the social world. Indeed, Morse himself expresses this opinion in relation to the Franks case: '[t]he theoretical problem which his mind had suddenly seized upon was no more than a bit of harmless, quite inconsequential amusement' (p. 66). In this instance, Morse's lack of concern with the social implications of the crime can be justified by the temporal distance between the crime and the investigation since there is no hope of him righting the injustice of the past.

Although Morse's attitude might seem cavalier, it is important to remember that he encounters Deniston's account while recuperating in hospital. Yet, rather than an amateur who solves crime for diversion, Morse is part of the new generation of fictional detectives who is a detective by profession. Most nineteenth- and early twentieth-century detective fictions present an amateur-detective figure as the hero who works alongside, or more often in opposition to, the police force and points up their inadequacies in solving crimes. The shift towards the professional detective began with Ruth Rendell's first Inspector Wexford novel, *From Doom to Death*, published in 1964.[15] While the professional detective of the mid- to late-twentieth century works within the established police force, with all of its forensic and other apparatuses at their disposal, they are usually an outsider or 'rogue' figure who frequently disregards the rules and procedures of the police force. Although Morse's interest in the Franks case begins when he is off duty, he soon enlists the help of his sergeant and makes use of the official resources of the Police Force. Yet Morse never entirely adheres to official channels; he knows how to work with and around the rules and procedures that govern the officers of the Police Force. For instance, Morse successfully arranges the exhumation of a grave in Ireland for the price of three bottles of whisky.

By contrast, *Arthur & George* initially seems to recall the approach of nineteenth- and early-twentieth-century detective fiction in pitting an amateur detective, Arthur, against the official police force and judicial system. Although *Arthur & George* does reveal the inadequacies and prejudices of several members of the local police force in dealing with George's case, however, it does not entirely dismiss the police force as inept. While Captain Anson might seem to fit the model of the inefficient professional police officer, his concern with 'the how and the when and the what' aligns him with Holmes's own rationalist approach to detection (p. 125).

Uncovering the evidence of the past

Although both Morse and Arthur adopt a rational, empirical, Holmesian approach to solving the crimes they are presented with, the differing positions of these detectives affect their relationship to the evidence of the crimes. As I have said, Arthur exists in the same historical moment as George and so is able to make direct inquiries of the people involved in the crime he investigates. By contrast, Morse investigates a case which took place over 100 years earlier and so is hindered by his inability to directly access those involved in the crime; instead, he has to rely on a textual account which was itself written more than 100 years after the events it describes. Consequently, *The Wench is Dead* explicitly muses on the nature of the evidence of the past and the possibility of ever uncovering 'what really happened'. This is most evident in the multiple levels of textual mediation between the detective and the crime he investigates, and by extension between the reader and the crime.

The nineteenth-century murder case is distanced from both Morse and the reader by several layers of textual mediation: Morse encounters the Joanna Franks case through Deniston's account of the trial, which is itself compiled from a variety of textual sources. As with the novels discussed in Chapter 4, Dexter incorporates the textual accounts into his narrative so that the reader has access to them. The reader, then, is brought into direct contact with the 'clues' of the crime and encouraged to participate in the process of deduction alongside the detective figure. While reading Deniston's account, Morse notices and questions its assumptions and discrepancies, and it is this that prompts him to undertake his own investigation into the crime. Although the reader is explicitly told of some of the queries Morse has regarding Deniston's account, the revelation of others is delayed, confirming the traditional approach of placing the detective in a superior position to the reader. This hierarchy goes against the approach of much historical fiction in which the reader shares the novelist's privileged access to the past.

Given his temporal distance from the crime, most of Morse's investigations take the form of historical research, carried out for Morse by the ever-faithful Sergeant Lewis and Christine Greenaway, the daughter of another patient on his ward who happens to be a senior librarian at the Bodleian. Their efforts provide Morse with documents, such as a table of insurance premium costs in the 1850s, that help him formulate and test his theory of the case. Morse explicitly figures this 'research' in terms of the debates in history teaching that, as we saw in the Introduction, dominated discussions of the National Curriculum in the late 1980s: 'The documents which Morse now handled were just the thing (he had little doubt) for satisfying the original-source-material philosophy which was just then swamping the GCSE and A-Level syllabuses' (p. 84). Although this comment appears to betray a scepticism about the value of such an approach to the past, Morse's delight in the original texts is subsequently revealed: 'And for Morse, whose School Certificate in History (Credit) had demanded little more than semi-familiarity with the earliest models of seed-drills and similar agricultural adjuncts of the late eighteenth century, the reading of them was fascinating' (p. 84). The implication is that these texts grant the reader a fuller access to the past than can be achieved through the rote-learning of dates and inventions that characterized Morse's historical education. The narrator reflects that even as a boy 'it had been the written word, rather than the tangible artefact, which had pricked [Morse's] curiosity' (p. 147). In confirming the important role texts play in both preserving the past and enabling a connection between the present and the past, Dexter's novel adopts a similar approach to A. S. Byatt's *Possession* and Graham Swift's *Ever After*, which are discussed in Chapter 4.

Despite this textual mediation, Dexter's novel does display a confidence in the ability of the detective to uncover 'what really happened in the past'. Indeed the novel implies that this very distance is what allows Morse to solve the crime. Initially, Morse seems to have trouble grasping 'the real problems raised by this narrative' (p. 69). He comes to recognize that he is 'Too near the picture. He was standing where the coloured paints on the narrow-boat's sides had little chance of imposing any pattern on his eye. What he really needed was to stand that bit further back from the picture; to get a more synoptic view of things' (p. 69). Despite the limitations, Morse ultimately manages to achieve this 'synoptic' view and solve the case. There is a sense that such a 'synoptic' view is only possible because of Morse's position in the twentieth-century; it is only with distance, and by implication perspective, that the 'pattern' of events can be seen. The idea that distance provides perspective is a familiar one in historical narratives, which often suggest that those living through the events could not perceive their significance in the way that the historian can. Dexter's novel actually takes this conclusion further by implying that the nineteenth-century judicial system is inept, or at the very least gullible. What the nineteenth century had treated as a murder, Morse reveals to have been an insurance fraud. Moreover, Morse's conclusion about Joanna Franks's supposed murder prompts him to uncover a further insurance scam, in the death of Joanna's first husband F. T. Donovan. The novel, then, suggests that we have to wait until the twentieth century for the true crime to be brought to light.

As I have suggested, this evolutionist perspective results from the novel's position as a detective fiction which works retrospectively. While many neo-Victorian fictions adopt a retrospective approach to the past, they frequently reject such a naive assumption that the present has improved upon the past.

Although Morse's encounter with the past is mainly mediated through its textual remains, his investigation into the case also uncovers physical artefacts of the past. Sergeant Lewis's visit to the local police station archives unearths the box that Joanna Franks had with her during her fateful trip. Inside the box, Lewis finds the shoes that had belonged to Joanna and that had featured so prominently in Deniston's account of her murder. The frequent references to Joanna walking along the towpath without her shoes on and her claims that the boatmen had taken her shoes were at least partly responsible for the niggling feelings of doubt Morse had after reading the account. The fortuitousness of this find indicates the difficulty of accessing the past. In the police archive, Lewis is surrounded by boxes, only some of which are labelled and none of which correspond to the year in which the original trial took place, 1860. Despite this, he determines to look quickly through the rest of the boxes and, 'after what had proved to be a long look' comes across Joanna's box, which contains her shoes (p. 128). Lewis's patience in searching through the disorganized remnants of the past suggests that the past is accessible to the present, though it requires perseverance, hard work, and an element of luck.

The narrative similarly rewards the reader's perseverance with the remains of the past by granting them direct access to the events of the nineteenth century. In Chapter 26, Morse imagines himself presenting his theory of the case before a judge and jury, ending with the declaration that 'All theory, all reconstruction, all probability are as nothing compared with *the simple, physical truth of what actually happened at the time*' (p. 156). Morse then promises to tell the judge and jury exactly what happened and indeed the following chapter transports the reader back to the nineteenth century to provide access to that '*physical truth*'. The events of that night are narrated directly to the reader in Chapter 27, but at the end of the chapter it is revealed that Morse has been dreaming. Despite this, the events are subsequently confirmed by the account from the surviving boatmen, although Morse had been wrong about one minor detail. The novel, then, confirms the convention that the detective's superior knowledge grants them privileged access to the past, which in the case of Morse even extends to his dreams. Moreover, the novel seems to suggest that an imaginative recreation of the past can provide a way to access the past. This prioritization of the imagination connects the detective figure to the historical novelist, who similarly uses the imagination to access the past.

In adopting a dual plot, Dexter's novel highlights differences between nineteenth- and twentieth-century attitudes towards evidence. In particular, Morse acknowledges the impact of technological advances in the twentieth century on the detective process. Pondering why the original charge of rape had been dropped during the early stages of the trial, Morse recognizes that the lack of 'DNA biological fingerprinting' in the nineteenth century was a hindrance (p. 67). Yet he remarks that 'even in that era, the charge of rape could often be made to stick without too much difficulty' (p. 67). He continues, however, by commenting on the differences in attitudes towards rape and rape victims between the nineteenth and twentieth centuries. Morse suspects that attitudes towards rape in the 1850s 'would be a few leagues less sympathetic than that reflected in [his] morning copy of *The Times*' (p. 67). These comments suggest that the contemporary era has moved beyond the nineteenth century, both in terms of procedures and attitudes: we are both more scientific and more sympathetic than the nineteenth century. This idea that the contemporary era has improved upon the Victorian past seems to be borne out by the structure of the novel as a whole. The resolution of the nineteenth-century crime by the twentieth-century detective seems to confirm such an evolutionist approach to the past. As I have suggested, this approach is in part a consequence of the retrospective nature of detective fiction which is emphasized by the dual plot structure of *The Wench is Dead*.

Unlike Morse, who investigates a crime from the past, Arthur occupies the same temporal moment as the Great Wyrley Outrages. Whereas Morse's engagement with the evidence of the past was mediated through textual remains, for Arthur such evidence is directly accessible to him. The novel replicates this situation by immersing the reader in the nineteenth-century world the protagonists occupy. While historical documents relating to the crime are incorporated into the novel, they are not the only way the reader engages with the events surrounding the crime. The events surrounding the forged letters are narrated directly to the reader in the early 'George' episodes, while the first horse-maiming is narrated directly in the first 'Arthur & George' episode. Although the evidence of the past is more directly accessible to both the detective figure and the reader, *Arthur & George* explicitly meditates on the nature of evidence and the possibility of knowing the past.

In its dual concern with detective fiction and spiritualism, Barnes's novel raises the question of the difference between knowing and believing. During his trial, George's solicitor, Mr Meek, emphasizes the role that belief, rather than evidence, plays in the judicial process: 'It's a question of belief. What we believe, why we believe it. From a purely legal point of view, the best witnesses are those whom the jury believes most' (p. 193). Part of the difficulty of George's case, derives from his failure to believe the impact that his racial origin might have on the jury's perception of him. When Arthur raises this possibility, George dismisses it saying 'if you are proposing that my ordeal has been caused by race prejudice, then I must ask you for your evidence' (p. 301). Requiring evidence before he is willing to believe in something, George here betrays his training as a lawyer, yet, as Arthur replies, '[t]he fact that no evidence of a phenomenon can be adduced does not mean that it does not exist' (p. 301).

Despite this assertion, Arthur's approach to detection is grounded in his confidence in observable fact. As we have seen, Holmes instituted the idea of 'deductive reasoning' as the best means of detection, a method which relies on empirical observation of the world around him. Fittingly, in *Arthur & George*, it is sight which resolves for Arthur the question of George's innocence. When he first goes to meet George, Arthur observes him from a distance and it is these observations that confirm his initial belief that George is innocent of the crimes for which he has been committed. Arthur notes that George 'holds the paper preternaturally close, and also a touch sideways, setting his head at an angle to the page' (p. 294), and concludes that George has 'Myopia, possibly of quite a high degree. And who knows, perhaps a touch of astigmatism too' (p. 294). It is this diagnosis, which George confirms by producing the spectacles he generally forgets to wear, that for Arthur provides indisputable proof of George's innocence. As a 'former ophthalmologist' (p. 294), Arthur concludes that George's eyesight is so bad that he could not have committed the crimes, all of which took place at night. More importantly, Arthur suggests that sight provides not only the proof of George's innocence but also the clue to why he was wrongfully convicted. Arthur notes the 'false moral inferences the general public is inclined to draw from ocular singularity' and implies that this at least partly explains why George was convicted of the crimes (p. 294). George's eyesight, then, not only provides the knowledge of his innocence, to those who know how to 'interpret' the evidence correctly, but also reveals how belief in his guilt occurred.

Based on his empirical observations, and his diagnosis of George's vision, Arthur concludes their initial interview with the declaration: 'No, I do not think you are innocent. No, I do not believe you are innocent. I *know* you are innocent' (p. 306). Arthur sets up a clear distinction between thinking, believing, and knowing something and the increasingly assertive tone reveals that it is knowledge which is above all prioritized. While 'thinking' and 'believing' imply an element of speculation and faith respectively, 'knowing' is aligned with fact and truth. Unsurprisingly, then, it is knowledge that the detective aims for. Arthur takes a similar approach in his researches into spiritualism, but he is careful to temper his desire for knowledge with a healthy scepticism which asks 'what was the minimum, not the maximum, that could be deduced?' (p. 55). Despite this scepticism, Arthur believes that with a sufficient accumulation of facts, it is possible to confidently know the truth about both the crimes and what happens after death. When Arthur visits Anson to present his theory of George's innocence, he asks 'What, in your opinion, really happened?', to which Anson replies: 'That, I'm afraid, is a question from detective fiction. It is what your readers beg, and what you so winningly provide. *Tell us what really happened*' (p. 381). Anson goes on to explain that most crimes happen without witnesses and so the possibility of knowing *what really happened* slips out of reach. Rather, he accepts the limitations of knowledge, commenting that 'What we know, what we end up knowing, is – enough to secure a conviction' (p. 382). He suggests, then, that a confident assertion to knowledge is only possible in a fictional world; in the real world, knowledge has its limits. The novel similarly seems to suggest that there are limits to what observation and knowledge can reveal about a crime and the past. This opposition between Anson's and Arthur's approaches is dramatized in the novel's narrative approach. The historical novelist frequently works within the gaps of known history, and Barnes adopts this approach when he provides a narrative account of the first horse-maiming, an event 'without witnesses'. Yet he also respects Anson's recognition of the limits of historical knowledge by refusing to identify the unknown criminal and thus provide a fictional resolution to the unsolved crime.

Juxtaposed with the limits of detective fiction is the practice of spiritualism which, for its believers, holds out answers about life's greatest mystery: what happens after death. While spiritualism is, as we shall see in the following chapter, a common theme in neo-Victorian fiction, it seems incongruous with the detective genre and its emphasis on rationality. Indeed, Conan Doyle's dual position as the creator of the most rational and empirical detective and champion of spiritualism has long troubled scholars and fans of his work. Although Barnes makes connections between the detective and clairvoyant, however, he does not seek to resolve this tension away.

At the end of the novel, George attends a public spiritualist meeting at which it is hoped Arthur will manifest. George's reaction to the events he witnesses remains sceptical, 'He does not know whether he has seen truth, lies, or a mixture of both' (p. 500). The culmination of the meeting, in which the medium transmits a message from Arthur to his widow, is drowned out for George, and the rest of the audience, by an organ. Despite previous displays of omniscience, the narrator does not allow the reader to overhear the spiritualist's message. The narrative voice thus refuses to pass judgement on the veracity of spiritualism, instead maintaining an attitude that combines scepticism and belief concerning 'the space where Sir Arthur has, just possibly, been' (p. 501).

This combination of scepticism and belief is in part due to the fraught position spiritualism occupies in relation to the issue of evidence. As we saw earlier, Arthur asserted that 'The fact that no evidence of a phenomenon can be adduced does not mean that it does not exist', an opinion which can be read as a justification for spiritualism (p. 301). The difficulty of applying standard notions of empirical evidence to spiritualist phenomena is brought home to George at the public meeting. Because of his poor eyesight, George uses binoculars to try and see the stage, prompting another member of the audience to explain to him 'You cannot see him that way. [...] You will only see him with the eyes of faith' (p. 499). This connection between sight, evidence and spiritualism is particularly significant given that 'clairvoyance' means the ability to see into the future or to see things that are beyond the perception of the normal senses. Spiritualism, then, adopts a different narrative trajectory from detective fiction; whereas detective fiction operates retrospectively, using clues in the present to reconstruct the events of the past, spiritualism works prospectively, going from the past and moving towards the future. As I have suggested, the dual approach of neo-Victorian fiction combines these two approaches to the past: in its commitment to the historical specificity of both the Victorian and contemporary moment, neo-Victorian fiction both works backwards from the present to the past and forwards from the past to the present.

Solving the past

The nature of historical narratives is explicitly addressed in the resolutions of these novels. Detective fiction is characterized by its neat and fixed ending, what Frank defines as 'the requisite coda'; it demands 'the summing up of the case in a coherent narrative organized chrono-logically and causally with no apparent omissions – with no enigmas, conundrums, or hieroglyphic puzzles unresolved' (p. 202). The very plot structure of detective fiction depends on the resolution of the crime. As Grossvogel notes, '[a]s a genre, the detective story is optimistic and self-destructing. [...] the intensity of the "mystery" is voided by our awareness of the mystery's transitoriness' (p. 15). It is this commitment to providing closure that has led many critics to identify detective fiction as a conservative genre. While detective fiction demands closure, the possibility of conclusively knowing something about the past is less likely in historical narratives. Despite this, neo-Victorian fictions often provide a resolution that conforms to the reader's desire for such closure. Suzanne Keen remarks that 'romances of the archive' frequently provide 'strong finishes', 'revealing with a certainty rarely exposed to sceptical questioning *which* truth lies permanently inaccessible, beyond the reach of the fallible questioner' (p. 43). These comments are applicable to neo-Victorian fiction where such neat resolutions are part of a desire to revive the past.

Given the different historical positions of the detectives in relation to their respective crimes, it is perhaps not surprising that *Arthur & George* and *The Wench is Dead* adopt different perspectives on the possibility of resolution. It might be expected that Arthur's temporal proximity to the case would make a resolution more likely, yet the question of who committed the Great Wyrley Outrages remains unanswered, even as George is cleared of all involvement in the crime. In his 'Author's note', Barnes quotes 'the last public statement on the case,' in which George states that '[t]he great mystery [...] remains unsolved' (p. 504). In refusing to provide a neat resolution to the mystery, then, Barnes displays his commitment to historical specificity.

The fact that the mystery remains unsolved, however, is not merely part of Barnes's commitment to historical specificity; it is also part of his transformation of the detective genre. *Arthur & George* diverges from the two-story formula that Todorov argued characterized the 'whodunit' detective novel. According to Todorov, the crime story is anterior to and absent from the novel, which instead focuses on the investigation story. In Barnes's novel, however, the crime story is integrated into the novel itself. In fact, one of the horse-maimings is narrated directly to the reader. Moreover, the investigation story comes much later in the novel, rather than at the start.

It is not only in its structural organization that Barnes's novel transforms the detective genre; the nature of the investigation story also differs from the traditional approach of the detective novel. Drabble suggests that 'The point of a mystery is that the culprit is revealed to general surprise, not that vengeance is exacted for his crime.' By contrast, Barnes's narrative focuses less on the process of deduction and more on the processes of justice: George's treatment in the courts and the representations of the case against him. Although Arthur does not solve the case, in that he fails to uncover the real perpetrator, he does resolve the issue of George's involvement in the case. This clearly diverges from the approach in several of the Holmes stories, where there is a sense that official justice is less important than the knowledge of who committed the crime and how. It is almost as if Holmes views crime aesthetically; he is motivated less by the idea of social justice than by the idea of completion and neatness in the resolution. Arthur, however, is more concerned with the processes of justice, which are shown to have real effects on the lives of George and his family. By insisting on the processes of justice, Barnes transforms the conventions of nineteenth-century detective fiction. This transformation, however, is not motivated by a desire to correct the nineteenth-century form; rather, it stems from Barnes's neo-Victorian concern with the relationship between the present and the past. In focusing on the issue of justice, *Arthur & George* implicitly reveals how the past can impact on the present by drawing out the repercussions George's case had on the English judicial system, specifically in highlighting the need for a Court of Appeals. In this instance, then, the novel rejects the retrospective approach of detective fiction; it begins with the events of the past and works forward to draw out the connections between the past and the present.

In contrast to Barnes's novel, Dexter's *The Wench is Dead* follows the traditional mandates of detective fiction in providing a neat resolution to the crime. As I have said, this could be understood as a comment on the ability of the present to interpret and explain the past. The resolution of the crime is brought about by both the textual and tangible evidence Morse uncovers, the final piece of which is found at Joanna Franks's parental home. Under the layers of wallpaper, Morse and Lewis uncover the markings recording Joanna's and her brother's heights over the years. The markings indicate that Joanna was only 4' 9" when she had been married whereas the woman pulled out of the canal several years later was 5' 3¾". Morse and Lewis agree that it is highly unlikely that Joanna 'had grown those seven inches between the ages of twenty-one and thirty-eight' (p. 228). While not conclusive, the evidence does suggest, '[b]eyond any reasonable doubt', that the murdered woman found in the canal was not Joanna Franks (p. 228). This evidence reveals the fragility of the connection between the present and the past; when Morse and Lewis arrive at Joanna's family home, the street is in the process of being demolished to make way for the 'Derby Development Complex' (p. 218). Moreover, the discovery is only made because the house prompts Lewis to recollect his own childhood and the practice of measuring the children's heights against the wall. The resolution of the crime, then, seems to depend on chance, timing and an empathetic engagement with the past.

Although it is this tangible 'finger-tip of contact' with the past that resolves the case in Morse's mind, it is not until a few weeks later that the final piece of the puzzle comes to him, prompted by a consideration of textual documents (p. 211). Riding a train on his way to a conference, Morse notices the name of Favant among the list of delegates, a name that he remembers from the case as a possible witness who could never be traced. Staring out of the window, 'his brain tidying up a few scattered thoughts,' Morse has the sudden realization that Don Favant is an anagram of F. T. Donovan, the name of Joanna's first husband who Morse had already established had not died earlier but, he suspects, remarried Joanna under the pseudonym Charles Franks (p. 236). Morse's revelation unequivocally removes for him the 'one per cent of doubt' that had remained about the case (p. 228).

Although Dexter's novel is aware of the textual mediation of the past, then, it maintains a confident belief in the possibility of accessing the past. The incidents with the shoes and the measurements at Joanna's parental home indicate that the past remains just beneath the surface of the present; it is accessible as long as you have the patience, intelligence, and empathy to uncover it. As I have suggested, detective fiction works on the assumption that the past is knowable and that the detective figure will ultimately resolve the mystery that was the occasion for the novel. Although it engages with questions about the possibilities of historical narration, neo-Victorian fiction similarly remains committed to the possibility of reviving the past in the present. It uses the imagination to recreate those elements of the past that remain unknown, but this imaginative process remains grounded in the historical specificity of the Victorian era.

Morse's investigation into the murder of Joanna Franks raises questions about the debt that we owe the past. Morse frequently comments that his involvement in the case is merely a diversion, 'a bit of harmless, quite inconsequential amusement' (p. 66). Although by the end of the novel it is clear that Morse's frequent declarations that '[i]t doesn't matter' are disingenuous, there is still never a sense that Morse is trying to seek justice for the wrongly hanged men (p. 218). Oddly, the lack of such an imperative might well explain Morse's continued interest in the case, even after he has been discharged from the hospital ward. The epigraph to chapter 2, taken from Albert Camus's *The Fall*, asks 'Do you know why we are more fair and just towards the dead?' and answers it is because 'We are not obliged to them' (p. 10). The idea that the present is not *obliged* to the Victorian past is perhaps a result of their position as our grandparents. As discussed in the Introduction, we are far enough removed from the Victorians to avoid the 'anxiety of influence' that characterized the modernists' response to them. Morse's investigation, then, is spurred on more by the sense of being bested by Joanna Franks and by his long-standing desire to have all the ends neatly tied up than by a desire for justice.

The temporal distance between the crime and Morse's investigation eliminates the imperative for justice since the boatmen wrongly convicted of Joanna's murder have already been hung for the crime. Despite this, the novel does suggest that the past has repercussions for the present and therefore we have a responsibility towards the past not merely for its own sake but also for ours. Because of its dual plot structure, the continuities between the Victorian past and the present are foregrounded in *The Wench is Dead*. The plot of Dexter's novel seems to privilege the twentieth century over the Victorian era since it is the twentieth-century detective who resolves the nineteenth-century crime. Yet Dexter also uses the dual plot structure to draw out the connections between the two periods and to criticize the present. Pondering the original charge of theft in the Franks case, Morse suggests that the motives for such crimes are not bound by historical context: 'But there was surely one thing, above all, that thieves went for, whether in 1859 or 1989: money' (p. 148). In drawing out the similarities between the 1980s and the Victorian era, Dexter subtly criticizes the state of contemporary society. Indeed, the particular point of connection, money, hints at the aspect of contemporary society that is the target of his criticism: Thatcherism. As I discussed in the Introduction, the upsurge of neo-Victorian fictions in the 1980s and 1990s is at least partly a response to Thatcher's appropriation of 'Victorian values' during the 1983 General Election. Dexter implicitly criticizes Thatcherism for its paradoxical attitude to the Victorian past: despite nostalgically invoking 'Victorian values', Thatcherism oversaw the destruction of the physical legacy of the Victorian era in the tearing down of public buildings. The resolution of the crime reveals the dangers of destroying such physical connections with the past; Morse is only able to solve the Franks case because he reaches her family home before it is torn down by developers.

Conclusion

While Dexter uses his dual plot to comment on the connections between the present and the past, both novels are more concerned with the responsibility that the present owes to the past. This sense of responsibility clearly has implications for the historical novelist and the project of reviving the past. The historical novelist has a commitment to establishing the connections between the past and the present in a way that respects the reality of the past, the needs of the present, and the historical specificity of both. In neo-Victorian fictions, this is achieved through the commitment to historical specificity; their imaginative engagements with the past remain grounded in the known facts of the past. The two novels discussed in this chapter take different approaches to reviving the past. In *The Wench is Dead*, the past is mostly mediated to the reader through its textual remains and the one instance where it is directly revived turns out to have been dreamt by Morse. It might be expected, then, that the novel highlights the inaccessibility of the past. Yet Morse's dream turns out to be true, if not in every detail then at least in its broad understanding of events. Dexter's novel, therefore, implies that an imaginative approach to the past can provide a way to access the truth of the past. By contrast, *Arthur & George* adopts an omniscient narrator who grants the reader direct access to the pasts of Arthur and George, as well as narrating events at which neither was present. While such an approach confidently revives the past for the reader, Barnes grounds his imaginative license in the historical details of the case, and thus leaves the Great Wyrley Outrages unsolved.

Although both novels are concerned with the processes of justice, Morse's approach tends to position the past as an intellectual puzzle to be solved whereas Arthur is driven more by a sense of justice and a desire to correct the wrongs of the past. These different approaches are reflected in the novel's conclusions; while *The Wench is Dead* confidently holds out the possibility of solving the crimes of the past, *Arthur & George* recognizes that the past, and justice, is not always so neat.

3
Resurrecting the Victorians

The Victorian era and its narrative structures continue to haunt contemporary culture, and many neo-Victorian writers seek to understand that relationship between the present and the past through an explicit engagement with ghosts.[1] While other historical fictions use ghosts to explore the relationship between the present and the past, most notably Toni Morrison's *Beloved* (1987) and Pat Barker's *Regeneration Trilogy* (1990, 1993, 1995), in neo-Victorian fictions the engagement with ghosts is usually connected to the specific context of nineteenth-century spiritualism. Therefore, these fictions tend to incorporate not only ghosts, but also medium figures. Writing about the usefulness of the tropes of haunting and spectrality for thinking about 'the contemporary novel's sense of the Victorian', O'Gorman notes that ghosts are, for the most part, passive' (p. 3). By adopting the figure of the medium, then, the neo-Victorian novels discussed in this chapter seek to establish a more active engagement with the Victorian past. Neo-Victorian authors also use the figure of the medium as a means to explore the forms of historical narratives, including that of historical fiction itself. While there have been several neo-Victorian novels that deal with spiritualism, the discussion in this chapter focuses on just three: Michèle Roberts's *In the Red Kitchen* (1990), A. S. Byatt's 'The Conjugial Angel' (1992) and Sarah Waters's *Affinity* (1999).

'The Conjugial Angel' (1992) continues Byatt's interest in reviving the Victorian era that was established with her more famous, because Booker prize-winning, novel *Possession: A Romance* (1990). The novella positions itself as a response to Tennyson's *In Memoriam* (1850), which was written in response to Arthur Hallam's death. Emily Jesse, Tennyson's sister, had been engaged to Hallam when he died, yet Tennyson's poem appropriates and displaces Emily's grief. Initially, Tennyson merely aligns himself with Emily, but as the poem progresses his grief overtakes Emily's and he usurps her position as Arthur's widow:

> Two partners of a married life –
> I look'd on these and thought of thee
> In vastness and in mystery,
> And of my spirit as of a wife. (97, l. 5–8)

Paradoxically, though, in omitting the troublesome matter of Emily's subsequent marriage to Captain Jesse and replacing it with the marriage of another sister, *In Memoriam* also denies Emily a life after Arthur and so traps her in the role of grieving widow. Byatt's novella seeks to imagine an afterlife for Emily Jesse and understand her involvement in spiritualism. The title of Byatt's novella, which incorporates several layers of meaning, indicates her dual concern with spiritualism and gender. King notes that it evokes 'the image of the angel in the house', an image that became central to Victorian conceptions of femininity, as well as Emanuel Swedenborg's concept of an angel as 'a "conjugial" being because it contains both sexes, signifying the marriage of goodness and wisdom' (p. 105). Moreover, the proximity of 'conjugial' to 'conjugal' points to the way in which nineteenth-century spiritualism enabled the exploration of desires forbidden in the rest of Victorian society, which Byatt explores through the figures of Emily Jesse and Lilias Papagay in the novella.

As with Byatt's novella, the title of Waters's *Affinity* reveals its concern with the interaction of spiritualism and transgressive desire. The term 'affinity' has both a spiritualist and a sexual meaning, both of which are drawn upon in the novel. Waters's novel explores nineteenth-century spiritualism through the figure of Margaret Prior. The narrative follows the middle-class Margaret and the effects of her visits to Millbank ladies' prison, where she encounters the spiritualist medium Selina Dawes. Like Byatt's and Waters's texts, Roberts's *In the Red Kitchen* includes a nineteenth-century spiritualist; however, whereas Byatt's and Waters's texts are set wholly in the nineteenth century, Roberts's novel explicitly incorporates alternative time-frames. Spanning three historical periods and two geographical locations, *In the Red Kitchen* intertwines the narratives of five different women who are all connected in some way to the nineteenth-century medium Flora Milk, whom Roberts bases on the historical figure of Florence Cook.[2] In its engagement with ghosts and spiritualism, *In the Red Kitchen* draws on the genre of Gothic fiction, which Roberts claims is 'connected to femininity in some weird way' since 'the haunted house is a body, a maternal body, a sexual body, a dead body' (Newman, p. 131). Roberts's spiritualist novel, then, explores the opposition between the material and the spiritual which was so fundamental to nineteenth-century society in general and particularly its gender ideologies.

The fact that these texts are all by women is no coincidence; nineteenth-century spiritualism challenged Victorian ideologies of gender by providing a space in which women could earn a living. In light of this, it is not surprising that critical interpretations of neo-Victorian fiction's engagement with spiritualism focuses on the issue of gender. Jeanette King's study *The Victorian Woman Question in Contemporary Feminist Fiction* (2005) argues that contemporary women writers return to the Victorian era because it 'provides an opportunity to challenge the answers which nineteenth-century society produced in response to "the Woman Question"' (p. 6).[3] She suggests that spiritualism holds a particular appeal for these writers because they 'recognize that the ambivalence surrounding female mediumship is symptomatic of the contradictions arising out of both religious and scientific discourse about gender in this period' (p. 93). For King, then, these contemporary novels are part of a political approach to the past that seeks to 'rewrit[e] history from a feminist perspective, and recover [...] the lives of women who have been excluded or marginalised' (pp. 3–4).

In focusing on women who were involved in nineteenth-century spiritualism, these texts participate in such a recuperative, political project. The three texts examined in this chapter, then, belong to a strand of neo-Victorian fiction which engages with the Victorian era in specifically political terms. Indeed, Byatt and Roberts explicitly identify the work of Alex Owen, who wrote the feminist study of spiritualism *The Darkened Room: Women, Power and Spiritualism in Late Victorian England* (1989), as a source for their fictions.[4] Owen's account of nineteenth-century spiritualism recognizes its subversive potential and indeed implicitly understands it as a response, whether conscious or unconscious, to the limited position of women in Victorian society. She notes the temporal correspondence between spiritualism and the woman's movement in the nineteenth century, remarking both that '[s]piritualism emerged contemporaneously with the consideration of woman's proper role and sphere which became known as "the woman question"' (p. 1) and that '[t]he flagrant aspects of female mediumship slowly lessened as women's prospects improved' (p. 234).[5] Yet Owen also recognizes the extent to which spiritualism was complicit with Victorian ideals of femininity; she argues that 'passivity became, in the spiritualist vocabulary, synonymous with power. And here lay the crux of the dilemma' (p. 10). As Owen goes on to explain, spiritualism granted women freedom only by confirming the definition of women as passive and weak constructed by patriarchal Victorian society. The qualities that Victorian gender ideology defined as feminine – passivity, 'a moral and spiritual sensibility,' and a 'de-eroticised sexuality' (p. 7) – were precisely the qualities that were considered essential for mediumship. Indeed, spiritualists themselves argued that mediumship did not represent a transgression of the feminine norm but rather was the 'epitome of femininity' (p. 202).

Although all three texts contain a feminist revisionist impulse in their approach towards the Victorian era, the authors write from very different positions in relation to feminism. In imagining a narrative for Emily Jesse beyond that allowed for in *In Memoriam*, Byatt's 'The Conjugial Angel' has an explicit feminist revisionist impulse. Byatt's relationship to feminism and the idea of 'women's writing', however, is problematic. In interviews and essays she consistently rejects attempts to categorize her fiction saying 'my temperament is agnostic, and I am a non-believer and non-belonger to schools of thought' (Byatt, *Passions*, p. xiv). She seems especially resistant to being categorized, and perhaps dismissed, as a 'woman's writer' and does not particularly consider herself a feminist.

Unlike Byatt, Michèle Roberts embraces her position as a 'woman writer': 'I'm quite happy to say that I'm a woman writer' (Newman, pp. 125–6). Roberts is avowedly feminist and her writing is clearly influenced by the French feminist theories of Julia Kristeva, Luce Irigaray and Hélène Cixous. Her fiction is frequently concerned with the relationship between women, particularly mothers and daughters, and often stages an overtly political project of 'trying to find and invent stories of people who haven't been seen as important' (Roberts in Newman, p. 121). These ideas come together in the novel *In the Red Kitchen*, which explores the dark side of maternity and the ways in which patriarchy determines women's relationships to other women. The theoretical interests of Roberts's works are evident in her exploration of the intersection between nineteenth-century spiritualist discourse and the emerging medical discourses of psychology and psychoanalysis.[6]

Sarah Waters's approach to feminist issues clearly differs from that of Byatt and Roberts since her writing engages not only with the position of women but also that of the lesbian in the Victorian past. Her three neo-Victorian novels, *Tipping the Velvet* (1998), *Affinity* (1999) and *Fingersmith* (2002), all explore relationships between women who may or may not explicitly identify themselves as lesbians. Waters's recuperation of the past in these fictions is explicitly politically motivated; she seeks to 'queer' official versions of history by incorporating those figures who have previously been excluded. This recuperative approach to the past is not confined to women; Waters also adopts a Marxist perspective by drawing attention to the position of the lower classes. As Mark Llewellyn notes, however, 'the one voice we never hear [is] that of the maidservant Ruth Vigers' (2007, p. 199). Rather, it is 'the very act of revealing the voices of the past [which] draws attention to our failure to recognize the other class-marginalized individuals' (2007, p. 199). The historical situation of spiritualism in the nineteenth century, practised as it was by many lower-class women and allowing for the exploration of transgressive desires, makes it a particularly fertile theme for Waters's exploration of the position of women, lesbians and the lower classes in the Victorian era.

The feminist concerns of these three texts are intimately connected to their engagement with the forms of historical narratives; they explicitly raise questions about whose past gets written and how. Where King's analysis focuses on the issue of *whose* past gets written, the question of *how* the past is written is equally important in neo-Victorian fiction. Indeed, King's focus on the gender aspects of spiritualism downplays the importance of history, both in terms of setting and its narrative forms, in these novels. While King suggests that the texts she discusses 'engage fully with the discourses of nineteenth-century scientific and cultural life', her argument ultimately prioritizes the contemporary, rather than Victorian, context of these texts: 'Their interest is, I believe, in what the Victorian period can add to the modern reader's understanding of gender' (p. 5, 6). Such a presentist approach to the past is, as I shall show, at odds with the way in which the texts themselves conceive of the relationship between the present and the past. All three of these authors dramatize the interpenetration of the present and the past; they are sensitive to both the pastness of the past and its influence in the present. King implicitly positions such feminist fictions in opposition to postmodern historical fiction, declaring that they 'satisfied the appetite for knowledge of the past' (p. 3). The treatment of the past in these neo-Victorian novels, however, is as self-reflexive as in postmodern historical fictions; the engagement with spiritualism becomes a medium through which to examine the relationship between the present and the past and the role of facts and imagination in historical narratives. Yet the authors do not lose sight of the historical context of nineteenth-century spiritualism and the challenges it posed to gender ideologies.

In her study *The Woman's Historical Novel: British Women Writers, 1900–2000* (2005), Diana Wallace has suggested that historical fiction allows women to 'cross-write as men', to transgress the boundaries of what are considered appropriate subjects for women to write about (p. 209). The historical novelist, therefore, challenges gender conventions in a similar way to the nineteenth-century medium; indeed, Wallace argues that 'the female medium becomes a suggestive figure for the historical novelist herself, ventriloquizing the voices of the past' (p. 208). She notes that historical fiction of the 1990s is characterized by the frequent presence of the medium figure, a figure which enables writers to construct 'a "dialogue" between past and present' (p. 209). Wallace aligns these texts with postmodern concerns about 'the ways in which representations of history change over time and their relation to the structures of power, not least those of gender' (p. 204). Indeed, her over-arching argument that historical fiction reveals much about the time in which it was written adopts a presentist approach to the past. Moreover, the structural organization of her study, which devotes a chapter to historical fiction written in each of the decades of the twentieth-century, prioritizes the moment of production over the location of historical fictions. Thus, alongside the neo-Victorian texts of Byatt, Roberts and Waters, Wallace examines the forms of haunting in Pat Barker's World War One trilogy *Regeneration*. I argue, however, that in neo-Victorian fiction the historical location affects the type of historical novel that is written, that the engagement with historical narratives is intimately affected by the nineteenth-century setting of the texts. Consequently, the exploration of spiritualism and haunting in neo-Victorian fiction differs from that in Barker's novels, as does the nature of the relationship between the present and the past. In Barker's novel, the treatment of spiritualism is explicitly connected to discourses surrounding shell-shock and examines the ways in which war emasculates men. Although these neo-Victorian novels are concerned with gender issues, this is only part of their wider consideration of the role of spiritualism in nineteenth-century society.

In his study *Death and the Future Life in Victorian Literature and Theology* (1990), Wheeler notes that spiritualism has often been dismissed as 'a somewhat quaint aspect of the Victorian culture of death' (p. 121). Such an approach constructs an implicit opposition between nineteenth-century belief and twentieth-century scepticism, in which modern subjects are seen as superior to their Victorian predecessors, having surpassed their superstitious beliefs. The dual approach of neo-Victorian fiction forestalls such an approach. The question of authenticity, however, remains central in these texts. Alex Owen's influential study *The Darkened Room* suggests that this question is a preoccupation in all accounts of spiritualism, and categorizes the responses into three groups. The first possible explanation dismisses spiritualist activity as the result of a deliberate fraud on the part of the mediums. Owen suggests that this perspective has dominated historical and biographical accounts of nineteenth-century spiritualism and mediums and has 'had the effect of closing down the discussion' (p. xviii). The second explanation posits spiritual activity as the result of an 'unconscious production' by the medium (p. xiv). The third possible explanation that Owen posits is that the spiritualist activity is 'genuine' (p. xiv). In their commitment to historical specificity, the neo-Victorian texts discussed in this chapter reveal how these three categories collapse in the complexity of nineteenth-century responses to spiritualism. In returning spiritualism to its historical context, these texts suggest that it needs to be understood in terms of the function it served in Victorian culture and its relationship to other nineteenth-century religious, scientific and historical narratives.

Nineteenth-century spiritualism

The nineteenth-century phenomenon of spiritualism first emerged in America in 1848 with the infamous table-rapping in the home of two young girls, Kate and Maggie Fox (Owen, p. 18). It soon crossed the Atlantic to Britain, however, where it became a popular cultural force for the remainder of the nineteenth and on into the early twentieth century. Spiritualism's popularity was both attested to and extended by the involvement of many public figures in its practices. As we saw in the previous chapter, Sir Arthur Conan Doyle became interested in spiritualism towards the end of the century and, as Owen notes, '[e]ven Queen Victoria and Gladstone were known to have dabbled' (p. 19). By the 1870s, spiritualism had become firmly established within Victorian society and in 1874 the British National Association of Spiritualists was established in London (Owen, p. 25).

As I suggested earlier, nineteenth-century spiritualism challenged Victorian gender ideologies by granting women power within the spiritual world. Although there were several prominent male mediums in the nineteenth century, most famously Daniel Dunglas Home (1833–1886), the majority of mediums were female. R. Laurence Moore's account of the female medium in nineteenth-century America cites the census of spirit mediums conducted in 1859, which revealed that there were

110 male mediums to 121 female mediums. While the difference is not large, the mere fact that women outnumbered men at all is remarkable given the limited access that women had to education and professions in the Victorian era. This would seem to suggest that spiritualism subverted the Victorian ideal of femininity, the 'Angel in the House' image popularized by Coventry Patmore's poem (1863), by bringing women into the public realm and allowing them to engage in a profession. As Owen's account reveals, however, women's position within spiritualism remained constrained by traditional gender hierarchies.

In Western civilization, women have usually been tied to the body and the material world, whereas men are connected with the higher world of the spirit and the mind. Such gender hierarchies are evident in the debates surrounding the issue of spirit clothes in the Victorian era. Drawing on Ruth Brandon's research, Spooner argues that the issue of clothing was a 'major source of anxiety circulating around spirit appearances' (p. 355). The question of 'how [...] the authentic spirit [should] be dressed' was frequently raised and the preference seemed to be for 'one form or another of classical white drapery, a garment presumed universal and free from historical association' (p. 356). It is interesting that the preference should be for clothing 'free from historical association' since establishing a connection with the past is precisely the point of spiritualism. Yet Spooner notes that this preference was not equally applied to male and female spirits; rather, male spirits 'seemed permitted more variety' (p. 357). In contrast, female spirits almost invariably appeared in drapery, which Spooner argues was a result of women's fashions being '"marked" as feminine' and 'their greater association with the historically datable and unavoidably material world of conspicuous consumption' (p. 357). Although Owen has noted the temporal coincidence between spiritualism and women's movements in the nineteenth century, the emergence of spiritualism was not only connected to ideology, but also to the material conditions surrounding death in the Victorian era.

Given the high mortality rate in Victorian Britain, particularly among the young, it is not surprising that spiritualism became popular as a way of offering solace and consolation to the bereaved. In his sociological study of the rituals surrounding death and mourning in the Victorian era, *Death, Heaven and the Victorians* (1971), John Morley notes the high mortality rate among the urban working-classes that was a direct consequence of the rapid speed of industrialization (p. 7). In particular, the infant mortality rate was so high in the Victorian era that '[t]he empty cradle [...] was a reality in many homes,' and not just among the working classes (7). The particular crisis of faith prompted by the death of a child recurs in several neo-Victorian texts, including Byatt's *Possession: A Romance* and Graham Swift's *Ever After*, both of which are discussed in the following chapter. In incorporating grieving mothers who turn to spiritualism for comfort, the three texts considered here combine their engagement with the material conditions that prompted spiritualism's popularity in the nineteenth century with their feminist concerns.

The material conditions surrounding death in the Victorian era were very different from those in our own sanitized world. On the one hand, death was a prominent feature of life for all Victorians since deaths often occurred at home and the body was usually 'laid out' there prior to the funeral. On the other hand, the passing of legislation such as the Metropolitan Interments Act in 1850 sought to keep the living and the dead separate. According to Morley, the Act 'marks the beginning of the great change' in attitudes towards funerals and, by extension, death (p. 51). The 1850 Act responded to the 'scenes of revolting desecration and profanation of the graves and remains of the dead which were frequently witnessed in the crowded burial grounds of London [...]' (Glen, p. iii). The key provision of the act was the requirement that 'public burial grounds be provided at a suitable distance from the metropolis; that, with a view to prevent the near approach of the population to such burial grounds, no new dwelling-houses be permitted within a distance proportioned to the size of the cemetery and the number of interments for which it is calculated' (Glen, pp. iv–v). Consequently, the physical presence of the dead became more removed from the living, a distance which spiritualism sought to diminish by promising to connect the living with the spirits of the dead.

As Owen remarks, spiritualism was caught in a tension between matter and spirit: '[s]piritualists opposed what they regarded as the gross materialism of an age in which things of the spirit no longer had relevance, but proposed a new metaphysical cosmology based upon an (albeit rarefied) form of matter' (p. xvii). The materiality of Victorian death is evident in the various paraphernalia of mourning that came to hold so much significance. Foremost among these mourning rituals were jewellery items made from the hair of the deceased, which Morley claims were '[t]he jewelry of sentiment *par excellence*' since 'symbolic allusions were supplemented by the use of an actual part of the body' of the deceased (p. 66). Thus, the jewellery not only served as a memorial for the deceased but also preserved a trace of them in the present. The development of photographic techniques in the nineteenth century similarly fulfilled this desire for a trace of the individual, and they too became part of the memorial process surrounding death. This was particularly true of infants since the long exposure times made it difficult to photograph such subjects while they were still alive. Thus, it became a common practice to have photographs taken of a dead child; indeed, such photographs were often the only photographic evidence of the child.[7] Spiritualism appropriated this function and produced spirit-photographs as evidence of an afterlife. The importance that spirit-photographs came to have in the spiritualist movement can be seen as part of an attempt to gain legitimacy by aligning it with science. Yet photography itself occupied an uneasy position in relation to science as some felt that it was more properly an art. While spirit-photographs were supposed to guarantee spiritualism's claims, they could also undermine photography's claims to mimesis. The idea of spirit-photographs, then, points up the paradoxical relationship of spiritualism to the opposition between matter and spirit. It also suggests the uneasy position that spiritualism occupied in relation to discourses of science and technology in the nineteenth century.[8]

The British National Association of Spiritualists sought to align spiritualism with science and rationalism. In an attempt to legitimize spiritualism, it was 'dedicated to carrying out and publicising carefully documented scientific research into spiritualist phenomena' (Owen, p. 25). Many contemporary commentators drew analogies between spiritualist phenomena and the technological advances of the day. In an anonymous article published in *Blackwood's Edinburgh Magazine* in 1853, W. E. Ayton sought to account for spiritualist phenomena by an appeal to rational, materialist causes: 'is it not possible that some of these phenomena may be attributable to natural agencies, such as magnetism, electricity & c., though their operation is not yet understood?' (p. 640). In aligning spiritualist phenomena with science, however, the author of this article did not seek to legitimize spiritualism; rather, he denies the otherworldly source of such phenomena. Paradoxically, then, while suggesting that spiritualist activity is genuine, such a rational explanation undermines its pretensions as a religious phenomenon. Indeed, of the many scientific experiments that were carried out into spiritualism, at least as many were intended to prove the fraudulence of spiritualism as were intended to vouch for its veracity. In response to these experiments, many mediums claimed that spiritualist activity could not occur in the hostile environment fostered by a sceptical scientific experiment.[9] Rather, they positioned spiritualism as a religious activity that required faith without material proofs.

In an anonymous article for *The Quarterly Review* in 1863, H. L. Mansel captures the conflict between scepticism and belief that such claims induced:

> Doubtless there may be spiritual reasons, of which we know nothing, why darkness should be preferred to light; but unhappily, those sceptical materialists, who are the very persons who most need to be convinced, will persist in saying that the same darkness, which is indispensable to the true manifestation, is also favourable to the false. ('Modern Spiritualism', p. 191)

Although Mansel concedes that spiritualism might be true, he is unable to entirely rid himself of scepticism. Mansel's ambivalent response to spiritualism is evident throughout the article, and indeed he opens by stating that he does not 'profess absolute unbelief; our state of mind rather approaches to that "honest doubt" which theologians of advanced views are never weary of telling us, after Tennyson, contains more faith than half the creeds' (p. 179). Mansel's approach of 'honest doubt' prompts him to be sceptical of spiritualist phenomena that occurs during séances, noting that: 'People go to these meetings with their expectations raised, and their imaginations excited; they come prepared to see, and desiring to see, something wonderful [...]' (p. 190). This explanation of spiritualist phenomena, then, seems close to Owen's idea of an 'unconscious fraud', although Mansel implies that it can be prompted by the 'audience' as much as by the medium.[10] Despite this scepticism, Mansel does seem to believe that genuine spiritualist phenomena is possible since he states that 'phenomena taking place at a séance should be received with more suspicion than those which present themselves without any such preparation' (p. 190). Interestingly, all three of the neo-Victorian texts discussed in this chapter incorporate spiritual manifestations that take place outside the confines of a séance. While this might imply that the reader should credit such manifestations as genuine spiritual phenomena, the texts undermine such an easy position of belief.

Mansel's notion of 'honest doubt' explicitly draws on the sentiments expressed in Tennyson's *In Memoriam*. Written over a period of seventeen years, *In Memoriam* expressed Tennyson's grief at the death of his friend, Arthur Hallam, and his ensuing crisis of faith. In lyric 96, Tennyson addresses the claim that 'doubt is Devil-born' (l. 4) and retorts 'There lives more faith in honest doubt, / Believe me, than in half the creeds' (l. 11–12). Articulating the spiritual anxiety that many Victorians experienced as a result of scientific developments, Tennyson's poem became a mouthpiece for the age. Begun in 1833, Tennyson's poem responded to Charles Lyell's *Principles on Geology*, which appeared in three volumes between 1830 and 1833. Lyell's theory argued that the earth had undergone a series of geological transformations that occurred gradually, over vast expanses of time, and so challenged the biblical account of history which, as James Usher had calculated, dated the earth as only 4,000 years old. By framing his comments in relation to Tennyson's poem, then, Mansel seems to align spiritualism with religion, suggesting that scientific investigation into spiritualist phenomena has rendered absolute belief difficult. Yet later in the article Mansel opposes spiritualism to religion. He states that, in trying to claim spiritualist phenomena 'a rank [...] of the same kind [...] with the miracles of Christ and His Apostles,' spiritualists have denigrated religion: 'the effect [...] is, not to raise the modern manifestations to the rank of the Scripture miracles, but rather to sink the latter to the level of a common ghost-story' (p. 181).

Within a decade of the publication of Tennyson's poem, Darwin's *On the Origin of Species* (1859) appeared. Darwin's theory of gradual evolution over successive generations was only possible in a world with an immeasurable history, such as had been established by Lyell. Together, these theories challenged the centrality of human history in the history of the earth and prompted anxiety over human origins in Victorian culture. As Gilmartin notes: '[t]raditionally, the further back a pedigree can be traced, the more noble it is considered to be. Part of the anxiety over pedigree after Darwin was a haunting sense that a pedigree could possibly be traced back too far' (pp. 17–18). These theories also prompted a related anxiety concerning endings. By challenging the comforts of religion, these scientific theories undermined the idea of an afterlife, and thus can be seen as contributing to the popularity of spiritualism, which held out the promise of proof of an existence beyond the earthly.

Neo-Victorian ghost stories

In engaging with spiritualism, neo-Victorian authors are clearly aware of the multiple functions that it served in nineteenth-century society. In particular, the possibilities that spiritualism opened up for women in the Victorian era partly explains its attraction for contemporary women writers and accounts for the tendency of such authors to adopt female mediums as the protagonists for their fictions. In the fictions of Byatt, Waters and Roberts, however, this interest in spiritualism is also intimately connected to their concern with historical narratives, and so, therefore, is the position of the medium figure. Wallace's idea that the medium is a metaphor for the historical novelist is a potent one, as is her suggestion that in these fictions, '[t]he question of authenticity – of history and of fiction – is [...] focused through the suspicions that the medium herself is fraudulent' (p. 209). As the subsequent discussion will show, the question of authenticity and the position of the mediums in these novels connects to the opposition between fact and imagination in historical fiction. The position of the medium in these texts goes beyond an opposition between authenticity and fraudulence to encode the tension between scepticism and belief that, as we have seen, characterized nineteenth-century responses to spiritualism. The texts not only interrogate the systems of belief and scepticism through the position of the medium, but also adopt numerous strategies to complicate the position of the reader in relation to the spiritualist phenomena they depict.

Encoding scepticism and belief

While Byatt's previous foray into neo-Victorian fiction, *Possession*, adopted a dual plot to dramatize the relationship between the past and the present, 'The Conjugial Angel' is located entirely in the nineteenth century. As a feminist response to *In Memoriam*, Byatt's novella incorporates intertextual references to Tennyson's poem, which contribute to the reader's immersion in the nineteenth century. Yet Byatt does subtly incorporate a twentieth-century narrative perspective at times, particularly in the discussion of the physical materiality of Emily's dog, Pug. Waters's *Affinity* is similarly located entirely in the nineteenth century, although she, like Byatt, occasionally incorporates a twentieth-century perspective. For instance, Waters's description of Millbank prison and its regime of punishment seems to be influenced by Foucault's theories on the operations of surveillance and power.[11] Despite incorporating twentieth-century perspectives at times, both novels are committed to the historical specificity of the Victorian era and Victorian attitudes towards spiritualism. This is most evident in the texts' temporal location: both are set in the mid-1870s, when spiritualism was striving for legitimacy through the establishment of the National Association of Spiritualists in 1874.[12]

By locating their texts entirely in the nineteenth century, it might be expected that Byatt and Waters reject a sceptical twentieth-century approach to spiritualism. Yet neither text encourages absolute belief in spiritualism; rather, they reveal the complex interaction between scepticism and belief within the nineteenth-century itself. By contrast, Roberts's novel includes not only a contemporary setting, which is a recurrent feature of much neo-Victorian fiction, but also ancient Egypt, and so explicitly dramatizes the dialogue between the present and the past that the medium and the historical novelist create. Again, though, there is not a simplistic opposition between nineteenth-century belief and twentieth-century scepticism; rather the novel reveals the complexity of belief systems in both the nineteenth and twentieth centuries and addresses the psychological and emotional functions of spiritualism.

The narrative approaches of these texts further encourage the reader to adopt an ambivalent position towards spiritualism. Both *In the Red Kitchen* and *Affinity* adopt first-person narrative voices which immerse the reader in the world of nineteenth-century spiritualism, yet these accounts do not necessarily encourage belief. By relying on first-person narratives, the reader is made aware of the subjective nature of what is being presented to them. This is reinforced by the fact that both novels present multiple, conflicting first-person accounts, none of which are privileged as the truth. This layering of narrative voices prevents any easy opposition between scepticism and belief in the spiritualist phenomena depicted in the novel. Indeed, it could be argued that in presenting such competing voices the narratives of these novels replicate the role of the medium, who channels a myriad of spirit voices.

In the Red Kitchen presents the reader with the narratives of five different women as recounted through diaries, letters and direct narration. The conflict between these accounts is most apparent in the three versions from the nineteenth century, although the narratives of the twentieth century and ancient Egypt also call into question the status of the events of the nineteenth-century plot. The novel opens with a letter from an unidentified narrator vehemently denouncing Flora as a fraud. The letter comes before the reader encounters Flora and so clearly seeks to frame the reader's response to her. In acknowledging that '[e]veryone falls for [Flora's tricks] at first,' the letter pre-empts the reader's desire to credit Flora as genuine (p. 1). Furthermore, the description of Flora as 'a monster in silk skirts' prompts the reader to question the relationship between appearance and reality and encourages them to read Flora as a fraud (p. 1). At the same time, though, it encourages the reader to adopt the same approach to the letter itself. Halfway through the letter something of the writer's true motivations are revealed in the declaration that 'I could have been a good medium [...] but she wouldn't let me take my chance' (p. 1). This recognition of the writer's jealousy undermines the letter's credibility and so forces the reader to revise their conclusions about Flora.

As the novel progresses, it becomes clear that this unidentified narrator is Rosina, Flora's sister. This revelation gives the reader further cause to suspect the writer's motivations and so doubt the letter's accusations. The narrative frequently demonstrates the sibling rivalry between Rosina and Flora, a rivalry which is only intensified by Flora's relationship with George, originally Rosina's beau. Moreover, the revelation of Rosina's identity actually implicates her in the very tricks she denounces as the narrative hints that she may be the 'accomplice' identified in the initial letter (p. 1). Towards the end of the novel, we discover that Rosina subsequently married the man to whom her letters are addressed and so her actions are again revealed to have ulterior motives. In her final letter she writes: 'How humbly moved I am that, you having suffered so much at the hands of the *one* sister, the *other* should be allowed to heal and restore you!' (p. 147). This healing process is a result of Rosina's 'mediumistic gifts' which allow Mr Redburn to contact his late wife. Yet Flora's account indicates that Rosina does not have spiritualist powers: 'Knowing that she hasn't got it in her makes her furious' (p. 42). In the case of both Flora and Rosina, then, the interweaving of narrative threads makes it impossible to say whether their spiritualist powers are genuine or not.

Waters's *Affinity* is narrated through two interlocking diaries: that of Margaret Prior, covering the period between September 1874 and January 1875 when she makes frequent visits to Millbank women's prison, and that of Selina Dawes, a prisoner Margaret befriends and a spiritualist medium. In providing diary accounts from both Margaret and Selina, the novel draws the reader in with the promise of personal revelations. Although first-person accounts are subjective, and therefore possibly suspect, diaries are commonly believed to contain the secrets of the inner self. Consequently, it might be expected that Selina's diary entries would unequivocally answer the question of the veracity of her spiritualist powers, yet this is not the case. Early on, Selina copies into her diary excerpts from a spiritualist book she has been given by Mr Vincy. Although the entry incorporates 'tricks of the trade', it is not clear whether these are taken from the book, are told to Selina by Mr Vincy or are Selina's own tips (p. 74). Interestingly, the clearest indication of Selina's fraudulence comes in Margaret's diary, after Selina performs a 'trick' to make a word appear on her arm. Selina confesses to Margaret that she used a knitting needle and salt to make the word appear, yet she questions 'Did it make the spirits less true, if she sometimes passed a piece of salt across her flesh' (p. 168). Given that the word she materializes is 'truth', this instance clearly indicates Selina's paradoxical position in relation to truth and lies (p. 168).

The narrative structure of the novel, which intersperses short extracts from Selina's diary with longer accounts from Margaret's narrating her encounters with Selina in the present, similarly encodes ambiguity concerning the veracity of Selina's powers. Although Margaret is initially sceptical, she gradually comes to believe in Selina's spiritualist powers. While the early displays of Selina's powers can be explained away as the result of coincidence or emotional empathy, when objects start to materialize in her bedroom, Margaret can no longer dismiss them in this way. The narrative structure encourages the reader to identify with Margaret and adopt her opinions, so they too shift from scepticism to belief in Selina's powers. As the narrative progresses, however, the reader discovers that Margaret's diary does not present a purely objective account. Although she claims that the diary will be a disinterested account of the facts of her visits to Millbank, Margaret unconsciously reveals her emotions. As the reader becomes aware of the true nature of Margaret's feelings for her brother's wife, Helen, they recognize that her unquestioning belief in Selina's powers stems from a similar, unacknowledged, desire. Consequently, Margaret's judgement on Selina's powers is shown to be based in subjective opinion rather than objective fact.

In contrast to the first-person accounts of *Affinity* and *In the Red Kitchen*, 'The Conjugial Angel' adopts a third-person omniscient narrative voice reminiscent of Victorian realist fiction. Since the spiritualist phenomena are presented directly to the reader, the narrator's objectivity grants the events a degree of authenticity. Sophy's spiritual powers are presented as indisputable facts: she 'saw with her eyes, and heard in her ears, the unearthly visitors' (p. 163). Yet the novella does not encourage absolute belief in spiritualism. Indeed, Byatt explores the attractions of spiritualism, focusing on the role it served in many women's lives in the nineteenth century. In drawing out such emotional aspects, the novella prevents the reader from adopting an objective and distanced perspective on spiritualism.

Lilias's interest in spiritualism stems from her constrained position within Victorian society; as a middle-class widow her sphere is limited to the domestic realm and 'the eternal servant problem' (p. 171). Although she initially attends the séances for news about her lost husband, presumed drowned at sea, it soon becomes apparent that she continues her interest in spiritualism for the contact it brings her with the living. It is not just Lilias who attends the séances for social reasons, however; the descriptions of the two séances that occur in 'The Conjugial Angel' reveal the extent to which spiritualism had become a bourgeois entertainment by the 1870s. At the first séance, Mr Hawke organizes the seating arrangements in 'a kind of parody of dinner-party placement when there were insufficient men' (p. 187). The fact that women outnumber men at the séance hints at the attractions spiritualism held for Victorian women because of the social freedoms it granted. The entertaining elements of the séance are even more apparent in the second instance. Sophy's attempt to describe the apparition she sees leads to a discussion of angels and wings and prompts Mrs Jesse's recollection of an observation that 'Angels are only a clumsy form of poultry' (p. 202). As this irreverent levity shows, '[t]he séance, even at its most intense, visionary and tragic, retained elements of the parlour game' (p. 202). The narrator accounts for such irreverence by claiming it as a defence mechanism: 'there were all sorts of pockets of disbelief, scepticism, comfortable and comforting unacknowledged animal un*awareness* of the unseen, which acted as checks and encouraged a kind of cautious normalness' (pp. 202–3). This comment equally refers to the narrator's uneasy positioning in relation to nineteenth-century spiritualism. The distancing of the narrator from absolute credulity in spiritualism seems to imply an objective stance from which the phenomenon can be interrogated. Yet, such objectivity is counteracted by an awareness of the emotional nature of spiritualism, which was fundamental to its predominance in the nineteenth century.

The emotional needs that underpinned spiritualism are most forcibly demonstrated in the figure of Mrs Hearnshaw, who attends the séances in an attempt to come to terms with the loss of five infant daughters. In an age when infant mortality was high, the grief of losing a child was a common problem and, indeed, each of the texts discussed in this chapter reflects this historical situation by incorporating mothers who have lost children. The narrative that Lilias constructs about the Hearnshaws suggests that women such as Mrs Hearnshaw were trapped within an ideological system that foregrounded their role as wives and mothers while the social conditions of Victorian life undermined that role through infant mortality. As Mrs Hearnshaw laments 'I give birth to death' (p. 180). The connection of women with both birth and death has long been a feature of western society and can account, at least in part, for the prevalence of women mediums in the nineteenth century. This connection is given a darker treatment in Michele Roberts's *In the Red Kitchen* where the suggestion of maternal infanticide is made apparent in the linguistic closeness of the words '*Mother*' and '*Smother*' (p. 94). In 'The Conjugial Angel,' the presence of Mrs Hearnshaw serves to remind the reader of the emotional element to spiritualism which a purely objective approach fails to take into account. The imaginative elements of the novella, then, allow Byatt the freedom to explore the emotional truth that is obscured by official history's concern with the question of authenticity.

In her discussion of the novella, Wallace focuses on the position of Sophy, arguing that 'Byatt's medium [...] is genuine (despite the suspicions of those who attend her séances)' (p. 209). 'The Conjugial Angel', however, includes another medium figure, Lilias Papagay. In adopting two medium figures, Byatt further complicates the reader's position towards spiritualism. She sets up an opposition between Sophy Sheekhy and Lilias Papagay to interrogate the conflict between belief and scepticism towards spiritualism. 'The Conjugial Angel' opens by introducing, and contrasting, these two figures: while Lilias is described as 'of imagination all compact', Sophy is 'apparently more phlegmatic and matter-of-fact' (p. 163). This initially seems to construct an opposition in which Sophy is privileged by her association with fact, and by implication truth, yet the novella resists any easy categorization of Lilias as a false and Sophy as a true medium. The reader is prompted to question the veracity of Sophy's spiritualist powers through the use of the qualifying word 'apparently'. While this might seem to distance the twentieth-century reader from the spiritual beliefs of the nineteenth-century characters, such objective scepticism is equally undermined. The description of Lilias's imagination as a 'suspect, if necessary, quality' (p. 163) suggests that we need to move beyond a simplistic opposition between belief and scepticism to consider the emotional function that spiritualism served in nineteenth-century society.

As the novella continues, the idea of a simple opposition between scepticism and belief is continually undermined. By foregrounding Lilias's imagination in the opening sentence of the novella, Byatt prepares the reader to question the status of the spiritualist message she later transmits, via passive writing, to Mrs Hearnshaw. The idea that Lilias's imagination is a 'necessary, quality' raises the possibility that Lilias strains her imagination to provide a comforting message to the grieving Mrs Hearnshaw. Indeed, Lilias's preference for 'tactfully ambiguous' messages implies that she engages in fraud, either consciously or unconsciously (p. 199). King's interpretation of this message implicitly positions it as an unconscious fraud; she claims that 'although this language has qualities appropriate to a child, it betrays its origins in Mrs Papagay through the inclusion of one of Captain Papagay's pet words, "pudy"' (p. 114). The novella, however, prevents any such easy positioning of Lilias as a false medium, whether engaged in conscious or unconscious fraud. The message that Lilias transmits from Mrs Hearnshaw's dead children, that she is expecting another child, transpires to be true. The fact that Lilias had no prior knowledge of the expected arrival undermines the possibility of an unconscious fraud in this message. The prophecy is only partially confirmed, however, as the narrative does not reveal the gender of the unborn child, which the spiritualist message had identified as female. Even if we interpret Lilias as a false medium, however, the novella refuses to condemn her by highlighting the emotional truth that motivates her actions. Lilias is more aware of the need for séances to offer consolation, irrespective of the hard truth of the message, than Sophy.

Sophy's spiritual powers are similarly brought into question in the novella, although less directly. The most vivid spiritual manifestation occurs outside the confines of a formal séance, when Sophy is visited by the ghost of Arthur Hallam in her bedroom. Although Sophy's experience is entirely individual, it is not presented subjectively. Rather, the omniscient narrative technique of the novella means this manifestation is presented directly to the reader. Moreover, as discussed above, Mansel's article reveals a suspicion that séances were 'staged' performances and so the private nature of this manifestation can actually be seen as a guarantee of its veracity. As King points out, however, the message that Sophy transmits to Emily Jesse in the final séance of the novella directly contradicts the message she had received from Hallam when he manifested in her bedroom. King suggests that 'Sophy may have simply misread Emily's endless attempts to communicate with Hallam as a desire for just such a message', thus raising the possibility that Sophy engages in a conscious fraud (p. 116). Whether or not the vision is genuine, Sophy's motivations are called into question by this deceit.

As we have seen, in Roberts's novel, Rosina's accusations against Flora are revealed to be personally motivated. Yet there is some corroborating evidence for her claims. Although Rosina claims that Mr Andrews will verify her accusations, the reader is never presented with Mr Andrews's testimony and so is torn between the differing versions of two women who both have adequate motivation for lying. According to King, the novel's structure ultimately prioritizes Flora's account. She states that, while the novel gives Rosina the last word, 'the power of Flora's narrative is such that its credibility survives this final attack' (p. 126). Yet Flora's own account raises questions about the veracity of her spiritual powers.

After meeting with her mentor, Flora notes 'no dawdling: I need all my spare time for practising' (p. 44). While 'practising' does not necessarily mean that her powers are faked, the novel later reveals that this same mentor, Mr Potson, was subsequently exposed as a fake. On another occasion, Flora hints that her mediumistic powers are faked, at least some of the time. She comments that 'any slips with the coffee cups can be forgiven just so long as I make sure to go into a trance afterwards', although it is not clear if this trance is fake or merely artificially induced (p. 74). Immediately after this comment, though, Flora remarks that 'the spirits aren't to be treated that way. I can't turn Hattie on and off like a tap. She comes to me when *she* chooses [...]' (p. 74). Paradoxically, then, Flora's admission of fraud is turned into a guarantee of the authenticity of the spiritual manifestations of Hat and Hattie. Yet the reader here is caught in the paradox; it becomes almost impossible to determine which aspects of Flora's narrative should be credited as genuine, and which dismissed as fake. Thus, while the novel does not entirely close down the possibility that Flora's spiritualist gifts are genuine, neither does it close down the possibility that Rosina's accusations are true.

Susan Rowland's account of *In the Red Kitchen* suggests that the novel dissuades the reader from judging between the various accounts by 'expos[ing] the power structures involved in defining one narrative as "history" and the rest as fiction' (p. 207). Rather, she suggests, the novel 'encourages hysterical reading', which refuses to privilege one account over the others (p. 208). This idea of a 'hysterical reading' is clearly connected to the novel's concern with psychoanalysis, which attempts to provide a rational, scientific explanation for Flora's spiritualist powers. During the course of the narrative, William takes Flora to La Salpetrière hospital and Dr Charcot, supposedly because he thinks her spiritualist powers are actually a result of hysteria. Accepting this explanation would not necessarily position Flora as a 'fraud', it would merely locate the source of her mediumistic visions in her unconscious. Yet the narrative structure of the novel discourages the reader from accepting this explanation since science and medicine are clearly aligned with the male doctors in the novel. As Rowland comments, in order to accept this explanation, the reader would have to 'side with the male doctors against Flora, and hence adopt the masculine gaze of theory (here of hysteria) that objectifies woman as Other' (p. 208). As we shall see, this denial of the authoritative voices of male scientists is part of the novel's exploration of the role of facts and imagination in historical narratives.

Sarah Waters's *Affinity* differs from Byatt's and Roberts's texts in that there is only one figure that is identified as a medium: Selina Dawes. The ending of Waters's novel seems to unequivocally position Selina as a fraud in the revelation that her spirit guide 'Peter Quick' and the supposed spiritual manifestations that Margaret has received were produced through the very real agency of Ruth Vigers. Waters skilfully intersperses the diary entries so that this twist in the story comes as a shock to both Margaret and the reader. As Llewellyn points out, by the novel's end we 'realize that we have been duped' (2007, p. 199). Although he recognizes the importance of the 'one voice we never hear', he claims that 'we have been duped not by the narrative but by our romanticization of the characters and the situations described to us' (2007, p. 199). However, it is precisely the narrative structure of the novel, which encourages the reader to adopt Margaret's middle-class perspective and silences Ruth Vigers, that prevents the reader from recognizing Ruth Vigers as the primary agent behind the events.

The novel, however, actually encodes ambiguity about Selina's powers and the ending itself is not as decisive as it might first appear. While Selina's knowledge of Margaret's feelings about her dead father can be traced back to Ruth's reading of her diary, no such rational explanation is given for Selina's knowledge of Mrs Jelf's grief. Selina claims to be in contact with Mrs Jelf's dead son and uses this information to manipulate Mrs Jelf, who is a warden at Millbank prison, into passing letters between her and Ruth, and facilitating her eventual escape from the prison. Despite the fact that no one at Millbank knew that Mrs Jelf had lost a child, Selina's knowledge could be attributed to a skill in reading people's emotions. Yet, her ability to locate the precise cause of Mrs Jelf's sadness, and to correctly surmise the gender of the deceased child, leaves open the possibility that Selina's powers are genuine.

Fact vs. imagination

As we have seen, all three of these novels encode ambiguity towards spiritualism; they never let the reader occupy an easy position of outright scepticism, or even outright belief. Given the tension between scepticism and belief that characterized nineteenth-century responses to spiritualism, this ambiguity is clearly part of these texts' commitment to historical specificity. Yet, it is also connected to their exploration of the forms of historical narrative. In their ambivalent presentation of medium figures, these texts reveal the complex interaction between fact and fiction in the construction of historical fictions. The opposition between a factual and an imaginative approach to the past is implicitly figured in gender terms. Traditionally, history, with its emphasis on facts and truth, has been understood as masculine, while literature and other imaginative pursuits have been seen as feminine. Historical fiction, then, occupies an uneasy position because of its combination of historical fact and imaginative license. Yet, as Wallace has argued, it has frequently been seen as a feminine genre. Tracing the development of the genre, Wallace explains that 'Women writers turned to the historical novel at the beginning of the [twentieth] century, at the moment when male writers were moving away from the genre, with the result that it has come to be seen as a "feminine" form' (p. 3). All of the novelists discussed in this chapter are involved in a feminist project of recuperating the history of women who have been excluded from official versions of the past. Writing in the gaps of recorded history, they necessarily adopt an imaginative approach to the past which enables an emotional connection between the present and the past. Yet this does not mean privileging an imaginative approach to the past at the expense of a factual approach. Rather, these authors recognize the need for a combination of the two approaches.

Waters's *Affinity* is the most obviously fictional of the three texts discussed here since the characters in the novel are entirely fictional inventions and no historical sources are cited.[13] This prioritization of the imaginative aspects of historical fiction seems to correlate to the position of the medium in *Affinity*. Despite hints towards her genuineness, it is possible to read the ending of the novel as revealing Selina as a 'fake' medium. Given the association between the medium figure and the historical novelist, the positioning of Selina as a fake medium has important implications for Waters's own fictional project. Drawing explicitly on Wallace's analogy between the medium and the historical novelist, Llewellyn argues that 'Selina's duplicity must do something to call into question the role of such "ventriloquizing" itself' (2007, p. 201).[14] Indeed, he concludes that whereas in 'The Conjugial Angel' 'the metaphor can draw comfort from the fact that not all mediums are portrayed as "dishonest",' the situation is more 'disquieting' in *Affinity* since 'Waters's medium is a fake' (2007, p. 201). As I have suggested, however, the novel does not unequivocally position Selina as a fake medium. Moreover, Waters questions the very concept of 'fake' and thus deconstructs the opposition between true and fake. She implies that what is designated as fake is merely that which does not conform to a socially acceptable norm. This idea is explored most explicitly in Margaret's exchange with Agnes Nash, who is incarcerated in Millbank for 'passing bad coins' (p. 106). Margaret's question that 'It could never be right, could it, to be a counterfeiter?' betrays uncertainty about whether counterfeiting is really a crime. Agnes goes on to explain the workings of the 'thieves economy', in which the bad coins are passed amongst themselves: 'It is quite a family business, and no harm done to no-one' (p. 107). Margaret concedes that 'her defence of it was terribly persuasive' (p. 107).

Agnes's use of the term 'queer' to refer to counterfeit coins is particularly appropriate in light of Waters's exploration of the position of the Victorian lesbian in *Affinity*. Waters simultaneously draws on the nineteenth-century meaning of *queer* as 'counterfeit or forged' and the twentieth-century meaning of 'homosexual' (Ayto and Simpson, p. 182). Although initially a derogatory term for homosexuals, 'queer' was reclaimed in the later decades of the twentieth century as a positive political statement by gay rights' movements. Waters's novel explores the idea that, in the sexual economy of Victorian Britain, lesbians and spinsters are designated as 'fake' or 'counterfeit' because they do not fulfil the normal roles of wife and mother expected of a woman. Margaret hints at this connection when she aligns spinsters with ghosts: 'Perhaps [...] it is the same with spinsters as with ghosts; and one has to be of their ranks in order to see them at all' (p. 58). The narrative suggests that lesbians occupied a similar position within Victorian society; indeed, in focusing on Margaret, Waters implies that many Victorian spinsters may have had unacknowledged lesbian desires.

This questioning of the concept of fake has implications for Waters's engagement with historical fiction. Waters seems to suggest that imaginative accounts of the past are seen as 'fictional', or 'fake', because they do not conform to a socially established norm of history as fact. Waters's novel implies that this is particularly true of women-centred accounts of the past which tend to focus on the emotional aspects of women's lives. Thus, while the narrative suggests that Selina is a fraud, this does not necessarily undermine the fictional project Waters undertakes in this and her other neo-Victorian novels. Rather, it points up the way in which the category of history is policed by designating those accounts that do not conform to it 'fake' or 'fictional', merely stories. The suggestion seems to be that women writers need to undertake such imaginative approaches to the past in order to redress the balance of factual history which excludes women's narratives.

In using diaries to convey the narrative, Waters indicates that her 'history' is concerned with the emotional aspects of the past that have not been recorded in official documents. Margaret's diary opens with a consideration of the role of facts in the narration of history, which is explicitly figured in relation to the masculine authority of her father: 'Pa used to say that any piece of history might be made into a tale: it was only a question of deciding where the tale began and where it ended' (p. 7). After dismissing several possibilities, Margaret settles on the gates of Millbank as the starting point for her tale. The possibilities that she dismisses reveal the biases of history and the problems women encounter when trying to write historical accounts: 'he might begin it at seven this morning when Ellis first brought me my grey suit and my coat – no, of course he would not start the story there, with a lady and her servant, and petticoats and loose hair' (p. 7). As this implies, the problem for women is that the realities of their historical existence are deemed unimportant for traditional histories. Similarly, what is considered important in traditional histories is irrelevant for Margaret. She notes that 'though I was told the date of [the building of the prison] this morning I have forgotten it now' (p. 7). Although Margaret strives to present a purely factual account of her visits to Millbank, she eventually comes to realize that her emotions have entered into her account: 'I thought that I could make my life into a book that had no life or love in it – a book that was only a catalogue, a kind of list. Now I can see that my heart has crept across these pages, after all' (p. 241).

Roberts's novel is more obviously rooted in the realities of nineteenth-century history than Waters's as the central characters are based on historical figures: Flora Milk is based on the nineteenth-century medium Florence Cook and Sir William Preston is based on the spiritualist investigator William Crookes, who is thought to have had sexual relationships with the mediums he investigated.[15] Moreover, King Hat could be a version of Hatshepsut who was the fifth Pharaoh of the eighteenth dynasty of ancient Egypt.[16] Interestingly, while it is Flora who is based on the nineteenth-century medium Florence Cook, it is Rosina who achieves the materialization of Florence Cook's spirit-guide, Katy King (p. 147). This further complicates the ambiguous positions of these two figures as true or false mediums.

In terms of historical writing, *In the Red Kitchen* similarly explores the opposition between factual and emotional accounts of the past that, as we have seen, is present in *Affinity*. As I have said, the novel's narrative structure presents interlocking accounts from five different women; these accounts are taken from diaries and letters, which have traditionally been seen as feminine forms that are more concerned with the trivial and emotional aspects of everyday life than the grand movements of history. This tension is most apparent in the opposing explanations for the spiritualist phenomena in the novel. The women's accounts focus on the emotional role of spiritualism, which is juxtaposed with the scientific explanation proposed by William Preston and Dr Charcot. Interestingly, though, *In the Red Kitchen* does not allow these men a narrative voice in the novel. Consequently, the scientific explanation is not granted the status of truth, as might be expected. Moreover, Roberts reveals how such supposedly rational and objective explanations are shaped by prevailing stereotypes and power structures. Rowland claims that *In the Red Kitchen* 'offers a cultural critique of the scientific claims of [Freudian and Jungian theory] by imagining the genesis of theory as historically constituted through culture, not scientifically transcendent of it' (p. 211). The most compelling example she cites of this is Roberts's approach of writing the real sexual abuse of women back into Freud's theory of hysteria. Similarly, the novel suggests that William Preston takes Flora to La Salpetrière to remove himself from an emotional entanglement with her.

Byatt's 'The Conjugial Angel' is the most explicitly factual in its incorporation of the historical figures of Emily Jesse, Arthur Hallam and Alfred Tennyson. In the numerous intertextual connections she establishes with Tennyson's *In Memoriam*, Byatt indicates the extent to which Emily's experience has been written out of history. Her novella, then, rewrites history by presenting an imaginative account of Emily Jesse's response to Arthur Hallam's death. By bringing Emily Jesse into contact with fictional characters, Byatt is able to bring Emily to life and give her an existence independent of Tennyson's *In Memoriam*. Interestingly, while 'The Conjugial Angel' is often positioned as a feminist response to Tennyson's poem, it is actually Lilias and, to a lesser extent, Sophy, who provide the emotional core to the story.

The figure of Lilias clearly draws out the connection between gender and historical narratives. Lilias's interest in story-telling prompted her to try to make a living as a writer when she was widowed, yet we are told that 'her skills in language were unequal to it, or the movement of the pen in purposeful public writing inhibited her [...]' (p. 168). Byatt implicitly draws attention to the fact that 'purposeful public writing,' such as history, has traditionally been written by men and so excluded women. Spiritualism seems to provide an outlet for Lilias's desire to write; specifically, automatic writing grants Lilias a degree of linguistic freedom as 'her respectable fingers wrote out imprecations in various languages she knew nothing of' (p. 169). Despite not knowing the language, Lilias recognizes these words, 'with their fs and cons and cuns, [as] Arturo's little words of fury, Arturo's little words, also, of intense pleasure' (p. 169). The linguistic freedom that automatic writing grants Lilias, then, transpires to be a limited freedom since it can only be gained through appropriating the voice of her husband. This is clearly part of the more general paradoxical position that spiritualism occupied in relation to nineteenth-century gender ideologies, but it also reflects the position of the historical novelist. As we have seen, Wallace suggests that historical fiction has allowed women to 'cross-write as men' (209), yet Byatt's novella implicitly reveals the limitations that such an approach imposes on women's writing. In contrast, all three novelists are concerned not with writing about those experiences that have usually been considered men's subjects, but rather in repositioning women's concerns within historical narratives.

The contrast the novella sets up between the two mediums also has implications for the project of writing historical fiction undertaken by Byatt herself. It might be expected that Lilias's imaginative approach to the past is privileged; Byatt is, after all, writing historical *fiction*. Yet the novella refuses such a simplistic opposition between a factual and an imaginative approach to the past. The initial description of Lilias's imagination as 'a suspect, if necessary quality' reveals the complex position of the imagination in historical fiction (p. 163). The identification of Lilias's powers as 'suspect' might suggest that an imaginative approach to the past is fraudulent in contrast to the 'matter-of-fact' approach favoured by Sophy (p. 163). Yet, as I have shown, the novella resists positioning Lilias as a 'fake' medium and Sophy as a genuine one. Similarly, Byatt resists privileging a facts-based approach to historical narrative over an imaginative approach. While imagination might be 'suspect', Byatt acknowledges that it is also 'necessary', preventing any easy condemnation. Lilias's interest in the inner lives of the people she associates with and her propensity to create stories about them highlights the role of the imagination in constructing an empathetic and emotional engagement with the past. The presence of Sophy within the novella reveals the need to combine an imaginative approach to the past with a factual approach. The one instance in which Sophy strays from her commitment to the facts and alters the message she transmits from Hallam to Emily Jesse ends in disaster.

These novels suggest that any attempt to write the past needs to balance the demands of history and literature, to ground the imagination in historical specificity. This connects to the feminist motivation which underpins these novels; they all seek to provide alternative narratives to official history. This is most explicit in Byatt's rewriting of Tennyson's narrative, but it is also apparent in the adoption of such 'feminine' genres as diaries in the narratives of *Affinity* and *In the Red Kitchen*. Yet this fictional approach is also a result of these texts' position as neo-Victorian fictions which are committed to both resurrecting the Victorian past in the present and respecting the historical specificity of the past.

Victorian ghopsts

The role of facts and imagination in narrating the past also has implications for the relationship between the present and the past that is presented in these texts. A factual approach to the past would seem to petrify the past, rendering it unequivocally past. Such an approach can encourage a nostalgic perspective towards the past, which laments the loss of what has gone before. Conversely, though, a factual approach understands the past on its own terms and respects its historical specificity. By contrast, an imaginative approach to the past might seem positive in that it can bring the past to life, yet the potential pitfall of such an approach is that it can refashion the past to address the emotional needs of the present. The narrative structures of *In the Red Kitchen* and *Affinity* explicitly dramatize the relationship between the present and the past in their presentation of multiple time-frames. Although Byatt's text adopts a single time-frame, all three texts use the theme of spiritualism and specifically the position of ghosts to explore the relationship between the present and the past.

In Waters's novel, most of the spiritualist phenomena that is narrated occurs outwith the formal confines of the séance. The conditions of the prison in which Selina is incarcerated, with its locked doors and barred windows, resemble the precautions that were taken by scientists seeking to prove the veracity, or otherwise, of spiritualist phenomena. For much of the novel, these conditions serve to guarantee the spiritualist phenomena that Margaret experiences, such as the unexplained appearance of flowers in her bedroom. Yet the end of the novel reveals these phenomena to have been the result of human intervention.

Although there are no actual ghosts in *Affinity*, Waters explores the relationship between the present and the past through the narrative technique of interlocking diary entries. By interweaving entries from Selina's and Margaret's diaries, Waters's undercuts the traditional approach to historical writing. The diary accounts not only switch between Margaret's visits to the prison and Selina's life before her incarceration, but Selina's diary itself is presented out of order. While this certainly aids the creation of suspense in the novel, allowing Waters to postpone the revelation of the power hierarchy in Ruth and Selina's relationship until the final entry of the novel, it also disrupts the usual linear approach of historical accounts. By refusing to adhere to a strict chronological sequence, *Affinity* questions the idea that historical narratives present a progressive account whereby the present builds on and extends the past. As we have seen in the previous chapters, neo-Victorian fiction similarly rejects such a progressive approach to the past. The narrative structure of *Affinity* provides an alternative model for the relationship between the present and the past, one which reveals the interpenetration of the present and the past. Again, this correlates to the dual approach of neo-Victorian fiction, which seeks to understand the present and the past in their own historical moments, while also drawing out the connections between them.

Despite this, Waters presents an example of a negative and damaging relationship to the past in the figure of Margaret. Although she keeps a diary in which she records her thoughts and feelings, Margaret is eager to distance herself from, and thus deny the importance of, the past. Indeed, her trips to Millbank, which are the occasion for her diary, are undertaken in an attempt to seal herself off from the past and she imagines the wardens 'fastening my own past shut, with a strap and a buckle' (p. 29). Her previous diary, which had recorded her relationship with Helen, has been burnt and the end of the novel suggests that the current diary will meet the same fate. In refusing to return to and remember the past, Margaret fails to learn from it and move on. Indeed, Margaret's relationship with Selina already seems to have followed the pattern of her relationship with Helen. This aversion to revisiting the past is made explicit in her final diary entry, for which, interestingly, no date is given: 'But I must write, while I still breathe. I only cannot bear to read again what I set down *before*' (p. 348). The final words of Margaret's entry hint that it is not only the end to the diary, but also to Margaret's life; her inability to learn from the past, clearly has damaging effects in the present.[17]

Although 'The Conjugial Angel' is located wholly in the nineteenth century, it dramatizes the relationship between the present and the past through the ghost of Arthur Hallam. The two mediums in Byatt's novella represent different approaches to the relationship between the present and the past. Lilias's interest in spiritualism stems from her desire to connect with the living and thus suggests that the treatment of the past in fiction needs to be connected to the concerns of the present, that historical fiction cannot merely indulge in escapist nostalgia. Sophy's vision of Arthur Hallam, however, highlights the pitfalls of such an approach. When Hallam manifests to Sophy in her bedroom, he does not appear as an ethereal spirit but rather as 'a dead man' (p. 249). The narrative dwells on the physical description of Hallam's body as 'purple-veined, with staring blue eyes and parched thin lips' (p. 249). Hallam implies that he remains trapped in his material state because of the excessive mourning of those he left behind. When Sophy tells him that he is 'much mourned, much missed' she notices '[a] spasm of anguish' (p. 250). This encounter, then, implies that our relationship with the past should not appropriate it for our own needs, but rather respect its historical specificity and thus allow the past to remain in the past.

The novella also incorporates another possible spirit manifestation in the appearance of Tennyson in the text. While most critics accept that Arthur appears to Sophy, the ontological status of Tennyson in the novella is not so secure. Ann Marie Adams argues that, given the historical detail surrounding his presence in the novella, Tennyson should be read not as a result of Sophy's spiritualist mind, but rather as an independent individual. She suggests that 'the only thing the young medium creates is a link to the aging poet's mind' (p. 27).[18] Yet, the presence of Tennyson in the novella has a certain ghostly quality. For most of the novella, Tennyson is present only through his poetry and Emily Jesse's recollections of their childhood; in chapter 10, however, Tennyson is granted a physical presence in the narrative. This chapter is framed by Sophy's spiritual vision of Arthur Hallam and so achieves the spiritual connection longed for in Tennyson's *In Memoriam*: 'So word by word, and line by line, / The dead man touch'd me from the past' (95 l.33). The novella, then, suggests that literature can provide a way to connect with the past. Indeed, the novella specifically resurrects the ghosts of authors, Hallam and Tennyson. Moreover, Sophy uses poetry to induce her trances: Hallam's ghost appears to her while she is reciting John Keats's poem 'The Eve of St. Agnes' (p. 248). Although Hallam's appearance in the novella suggests the need to respect the pastness of the past, the figures of Hallam and Tennyson reveal that the past has an afterlife in the present through its literary remains. This mutual relationship between the present and the past clearly connects to neo-Victorian fiction's dual impulse, its commitment to both the moment of its production and its historical location.

The interpenetration of the present and the past is even more explicit in Roberts's *In the Red Kitchen* since the action of the novel takes place in three distinct temporal locations: the narratives of Flora, Hattie, and Hat occur in Victorian London, 1980s London, and Ancient Egypt respectively. Roberts, like both Byatt and Waters, seems to suggest that we need to understand the connections between the present and the past without prioritizing one time period over another. The incorporation of a twentieth-century plot is a recurrent feature of neo-Victorian fiction and is at least partly a response to the political appropriation of the Victorians by Thatcher's Conservative government. Hattie's narrative serves as an implicit indictment of the Thatcher era with the stark revelation that she 'went on the game' to afford the deposit for her house, and the even starker admission that she knew 'several other women [...] who drifted in and out of prostitution depending on the state of their finances' (p. 14). The harsh socio-economic realities of life for the 'homeless poor' (p. 13) in Hattie's London undercuts the idealized version of 'Victorian values' touted by Thatcher in the run up to the 1983 General Election by emphasizing the dichotomy between the 'haves' and the 'have nots' that underpinned Victorian society. This critique is furthered by the nineteenth-century plot of the novel, which points up the class divisions between Flora and Rosina Milk on the one hand and the Prestons on the other. Thatcher's revival of 'Victorian values' was based on a nostalgic assumption that the past was better than the present, which is clearly grounded in the assumption of a disconnection between the present and the past. In juxtaposing the nineteenth and twentieth centuries in her novel, Roberts not only undermines the nostalgic version of the past by drawing attention to the historical realities, but also re-establishes the connections between the present and the past.

This connection between the present and the past also occurs at a spiritual level in the novel. Despite the uncertainty over Flora's mediumistic powers, *In the Red Kitchen* seems to corroborate some of the spirit manifestations narrated in the novel. For example, in the first few chapters of the novel, Flora recounts seeing a figure at her father's funeral and remembers as a child being rescued from a cabinet by someone she had assumed was a neighbour. As the novel continues, the reader comes to identify these figures as King Hat and Hattie King respectively. The position of these three characters in the novel, however, is not straightforward. The narrative structure deliberately fosters uncertainty about the ontological status of its protagonists. Rowland proposes three ways of defining the relationship between the three central characters; they 'could be mediums, women in touch with a creative unconscious, or fiction writers' (p. 206). Rowland goes on to say that 'they operate in an ontological field which includes all three possibilities in a continuum, not one to the exclusion of the others' (p. 206). Yet the situation is even more complicated. Within the first explanation, it is unclear which of the three characters is the medium and which the ghost. Indeed, even the characters themselves seem unsure of the ontological status of their visions. While this uncertainty might seem to promote scepticism towards the spiritual manifestations in the novel, there are certain elements that are hard to ignore. For example, while Flora is in the hospital at La Salpetrière it is the vision of Hattie that helps her escape. Clearly, then, Roberts is highlighting the emotional function that these apparitions serve. It is possible to adopt a psychological interpretation of the connection between these three figures. In the twentieth-century plot, Hattie has visions of Flora as a child and King Hat could be part of the fantasy world that Hattie creates to escape from the trauma of abuse. Such a reading, however, prioritizes the twentieth-century Hattie, a presentist approach that the novel's narrative structure prevents since Hattie's visions of Flora seem to be reciprocal. Unlike most texts that incorporate ghosts, then, Roberts's novel does not construct a one-way haunting. Rather, the 'ghosts' in *In the Red Kitchen* travel forwards as well as backwards and all three time periods are interconnected.

The interpenetration of the present and the past is signalled in the novel not only through the literal hauntings but also through the recurrence of certain sights, sounds and smells. The three central characters seem to be connected by their sensory experiences. For instance, the 'scent of lilies' (p. 7) recorded in Hat's first narrative recalls Flora's first narrative, with the remembered 'stench of lilies' from her father's death-room (p. 3). In establishing such sensory connections across historical locations, Roberts seems to be privileging an emotional engagement with the past. That this is associated with a feminine approach to history is evident in the importance of the eponymous red kitchen in such connections.[19]

The extent to which emotional responses can determine our relationship to the past is explored through the figure of Hattie. Initially, she denies the past; for instance, she admits that she has never written a diary before since 'The past, my own past, has not mattered to me' (p. 17). As the narrative progresses, the reader discovers that Hattie was abused as a child, and thus her disengagement from her own past can be understood as a defence mechanism against her traumatic experiences. Eventually, though, she has come to recognize the need to 'give myself a history' and accept that although 'the past leaps away in a trail of silver; yet I need to go on trying to hold it' (p. 17). It is through the process of keeping a diary that Hattie is able to integrate the past with the present and then move on from it. This need to establish a connection with the past, while refusing to let it dominate the present, culminates in her decision to name her unborn child Flora, after coming across the gravestone of Flora Milk in the local cemetery. Hattie, then, ultimately demonstrates a positive connection with the past similar to that which neo-Victorian fiction tries to establish.

Conclusion

The concern with spiritualism in these three novels is part of their interest in recuperating female histories, an interest which is highlighted
by the importance of the domestic locale in *In the Red Kitchen*. As
I have shown, spiritualism provides a space for these writers to explore
not only the position of women in the nineteenth century, but also
the nature of the relationship between the present and the past. The
complex nature of the opposition between 'genuine' and 'fake' in these
novels reveals the extent to which the historical novelist is implicated
in both an imaginative and a factual approach to the past. Given the
association of factual history with masculine history, this concern with
the role of facts and imagination in historical narratives is clearly part of
these texts' concerns with feminist issues. Indeed, these texts imply that
an imaginative approach to the past is necessary to recuperate the narratives of women who have been written out of official accounts of the
past. Yet this engagement with the role of the imagination in historical
narrative is not only a consequence of these authors' position as women
writers, but also their position as neo-Victorian authors. Neo-Victorian
fictions clearly present an imaginative engagement with the past, but
one that remains grounded in the historical specificity of the Victorian
era. Moreover, the position of the medium figure has implications for
the role of the neo-Victorian novelist. As we have seen, the medium
provides an analogue for exploring the roles and responsibilities of the
historical novelist: their job is to establish a living connection with
the past, but one that does not usurp the past merely for the needs
of the present. This approach to the past corresponds to that of neo-
Victorian fiction, which in its dual approach respects the historical
specificity of the past and present while also establishing connections
between the two periods.

4
Reading the Victorians

Contemporary society's engagement with the Victorian era is often mediated through texts, not only the texts of Victorian novels (and their numerous film and television adaptations) but also the neo-Victorian texts with which this book is concerned. It is unsurprising, then, that a common concern in neo-Victorian fiction is the way in which the Victorian past is mediated to the present through its textual remains. This concern is most evident in the recurring plot in which a twentieth-century figure encounters the textual archive of the nineteenth century, usually uncovering some hitherto unknown information about the Victorian past. In their adoption of a dual plot structure, with events in both the nineteenth and twentieth centuries, such novels dramatize questions about the nature of the relationship between the present and the past, and the possibility of accessing the past that, as we have seen, are central to neo-Victorian fiction. This chapter examines two such novels: Graham Swift's *Ever After* (1992) and A. S. Byatt's *Possession: A Romance* (1990). Byatt's novel is not only the most famous example of this approach, but also the most wide-ranging, incorporating as it does the textual remains of almost all of its nineteenth-century characters.[1]

For Suzanne Keen, concern with the textual archives of the past is a recurring feature of contemporary British fiction, which she designates as 'romances of the archive' (p. 3). Using Byatt's *Possession* as the touchstone for the subgenre, Keen defines 'romances of the archive' as 'adventure stories, in which "research" features as a kernel plot action' (p. 35). These novels, she argues, follow the structure of a quest narrative: the protagonist is a quester, often an amateur or if an academic then one on the fringes of the intellectual community, who encounters and overcomes various obstacles before ultimately uncovering a 'truth' about the past. 'Buil[t] on a foundation of "documentarism",' Keen argues, romances of the archive '[answer] the postmodern critique of history with invented records full of hard facts' (p. 3). *Possession* and *Ever After* both fit within Keen's model of the 'romance of the archive' as they depict the central plot situation of twentieth-century characters encountering the textual remains of nineteenth-century predecessors. Although the questers in the archive are academics, they are marginalized within that community either because of their lowly status, as is the case with *Possession's* Roland who is a post-doctoral research assistant, or because their academic credentials are called into question, as with Bill Unwin, the narrator-protagonist of *Ever After*.

In her definition, Keen distinguishes between 'romances of the archive' and 'the traditional kind of novel consisting entirely of a wholly imaginary archive or collection' which 'expects the reader to play the role of the researcher in the archive' (p. 10) and so 'eliminates the representation of active scholarship' (p. 30). In privileging the '*representation* of active scholarship', however, Keen overlooks the ways in which this representation can encourage an active engagement with the past on the part of the reader. *Possession* clearly depicts such 'active scholarship' as the research into the past becomes part of a literary detective game that draws in all of the twentieth-century characters, yet the incorporation of the textual remains of Ash and LaMotte allows the reader to engage in the process of detection as well, and constitutes an imaginary archive.[2] Similarly, although the archive in Swift's novel is not subject to as much speculation as that in Byatt's, the textual remains of Matthew Pearce are incorporated for the reader's benefit. Thus, both novels not only depict scholars involved in researching the past but also encourage their readers to establish a connection with the past through the incorporation of textual remains. The reader does not merely *passively* watch the questers engage with the texts of the past but also *actively* engages with those texts themselves. In these novels, then, reading becomes more than just a metaphor for the relationship between the present and the past; it becomes the active process by which the past is brought to life for the reader.

For Keen, 'romances of the archive' 'enact and criticize their culture's fascination with the uses of the past' and thus engage with contemporary debates concerning the function and value of history and heritage. She suggests that despite this critical stance these novels remain complicit with heritage in their 'attempt[ ] to recuperate heritage sensations from periods rendered inert or shameful by academicians' (p. 109). The version of the past presented in these novels, then, is often 'conservative, nostalgic, defensive, [and] insufficiently sceptical about finding the truth' (p. 5), an assessment that, as we saw in the Introduction, also applied to the version of history promoted in the Conservative's National Curriculum. Keen argues that both the version of history presented in 'romances of the archive' and the patriotic view of history promoted by Thatcher's Conservative government are responses to Britain's post-imperial condition. She suggests that since archives 'serve as repositories of memory' (p. 14) they are 'an especially vivid emblem of what remains when the Empire is no more' (p. 15). Keen's analysis aligns 'romances of the archive' with a heritage approach to the past that seeks to establish a 'usable past' appropriate to Britain's post-imperial position (p. 5). According to Keen, the fact that 'romances of the archive' respond to Britain's state of post-imperial decline is most apparent in the choice of historical periods to which they return, periods in which 'the British (oft English) national story is central and influential' (p. 4). This seems particularly true of neo-Victorian texts which, in returning to the Victorian era, revive a period whose 'developments in government, industry, transport and technology imply a tale of progress' (p. 107). Again, as we saw in the Introduction, the Victorians featured prominently in the Conservative's nationalist National Curriculum for history since they fit into a patriotic, and nostalgic, narrative of Britain's past accomplishments.

Despite recognizing the importance of the historical location of the archives, Keen's definition of the 'romance of the archive' centres on its position within contemporary British fiction and so, unsurprisingly, focuses on the contemporary rather than historical context of these novels. Although she recognizes the connection between archives and imperialism, Keen overlooks the fact that this connection was established during the nineteenth century. Consequently, then, while she acknowledges *Possession*'s position within the subgenre of neo-Victorian fiction, she does not engage with the historical specificity that characterizes such fictions. Indeed, Keen claims that Dana Shiller's conclusions about 'the seemingly antithetical attitudes towards the Victorian past' in neo-Victorian fiction 'can be extended to include all the other times reached and reinterpreted in romances of the archive' (p. 34). Although she acknowledges that neo-Victorian fiction 'cannot be explained away as mere period nostalgia', she suggests that '*Possession* uses the past for the pleasure of evoking a vanished world and time, [...] and for the dress-up fun of imitating the Victorians' (p. 34). As this book argues, however, the return to the Victorian era in contemporary fiction cannot be understood simply as a postmodern appropriation of the styles of the past; rather neo-Victorian fiction adopts the specific historical narratives of the nineteenth century to explore questions about the role and function of history. In the case of neo-Victorian 'romances of the archive', such as Byatt's *Possession* and Swift's *Ever After*, the engagement with the documents of the past needs to be understood in terms of the role and function of documents in the nineteenth century.

Nineteenth-century documents

As we saw in the Introduction, the Victorian era became increasingly concerned with maintaining a documentary record of the time, a drive which affected all spheres of Victorian life. Since knowledge is an important part of the process of control, particularly control from a distance, this documentary urge became a central feature in the imperialist drive of the nineteenth century. As Thomas Richards notes in *The Imperial Archive* (1993), 'An empire is partly a fiction. No nation can close its hand around the world' (p. 1). He goes on to argue that '[t]he British may not have created the longest-lived empire in history, but it was certainly one of the most data-intensive' and suggests that 'knowledge-producing institutions' formed the 'administrative core of the Empire' (p. 4). Such institutions included the British Museum and its associated library, which had been established in 1753. The connection between the archival impulse and nationalism was revealed in the notion that the British Museum should be a point of patriotic pride, a notion which was widely expressed in the nineteenth century. As a commentator in *The New Monthly Magazine* noted in 1850, 'In proportion to the enterprise, wealth, and power of a nation will a museum be perfect' ('The British Museum', p. 197).

This connection between patriotism and the remains of the past is also evident in the antiquarian book clubs that emerged in the early nineteenth century. As Ina Ferris has argued, Sir Walter Scott's Bannatyne Club 'understood itself from the start as a civic and national institution' and as such was committed to reprinting texts of importance to Scottish history, often in the original Scots' language (p. 145). Such book clubs exemplified the shift in attitudes towards documents and their relationship to the past that took place during the nineteenth century. Ferris's article 'Printing the Past: Walter Scott's Bannatyne Club and the Antiquarian Document' (2005) claims that the emergence of bookclubs in the early nineteenth century marked 'the turn whereby the value of the past no longer inheres in its intelligibility [...] but in an illegibility that was the sign of its authenticity' (p. 144). Yet Ferris distinguishes the purposes of the London-based Roxburghe Club, which reprinted books on aesthetic grounds and valued them solely in terms of their rarity, from those of Scott's Edinburgh-based Bannatyne Club, which she suggests was '[i]nterested more in the printing of old texts than in the production of fine books' (p. 145).

This distinction between 'texts' and 'books' is part of a wider intellectual turn in the nineteenth century regarding the position of the texts of the past. Ferris argues that the Bannatyne Club understood the texts of the past as 'documents'. Drawing on John Guillory's conception of the 'document', Ferris argues that 'the document as a category makes central the axis of reception rather than production: a piece of writing achieves status as a document (i.e. a piece of information) only insofar as it answers a question of interest to a reader' (p. 149). Thus, the document is 'a category pertaining to the afterlife of texts, privileging a later moment of reading over the initial moment of writing' (p. 150). It is this which prompts Ferris to talk of the 'peculiar temporality of the antiquarian document' (p. 144). While such antiquarian book projects as Scott's Bannatyne Club were thought to 'represent regressive energies in a progressive world' (Ferris, p. 148), this view is complicated by the very category of the document. Ferris claims that 'Antiquaries [...] inhabited a more gothic modality in which the past could always return through its traces to disturb the clarity of linear flow' (p. 148). This gothic modality is most obvious in the position of texts as documents: 'when texts of the past turn into documents, they no longer inhabit either the past or the present but the space of their intersection' (p. 155). This 'inter-space' between the present and the past opens up 'an active cognitive space for readers on the terrain of historical knowledge' by bringing 'the reader closer to the actual words of the past' (p. 150). The importance of the 'actual words of the past' is once again evident in the shift from text to document. With texts, it is the '*message*, moving readily across historical time and hence available for translation' that is prioritized and valued (p. 155; my emphasis). By contrast, the category of document 'underst[ands texts] as the *trace* of another time requiring presentation rather than translation' (p. 155; my emphasis).

This movement towards understanding the texts of the past as documents which provide a *trace* of the past is evident in the establishment of the Royal Commission of Historical Manuscripts in 1869. The commission was established with the purpose of 'ascertain[ing] what manuscripts calculated to throw light upon subjects connected with the Civil, Ecclesiastical, Literary or Scientific history of this country, are extant in the collections of private persons and in corporate and other institutions' ('The Royal Commission', p. 629). Private texts of the past became public records only insofar as they contributed to a national history, and it was only if they contributed to that national history that they were considered worth safeguarding from 'those casualties to which valuable collections of manuscripts are liable from various causes' ('The Royal Commission', p. 632). It was not only the Royal Commission of Historical Manuscripts, however, which sought to compile and preserve the documentary remains of the past; the British Museum, and in particular its associated library, was involved in a similar project.

In an anonymous article published in *Blackwood's Edinburgh Magazine* in 1884, entitled 'The British Museum and the People who go there', R. K. Douglas suggests that material remains bring the past to life, allowing the visitor to 'see', 'witness' and 'follow' the events of the past (p. 197). Of all the remains collected in the museum, Douglas implies that the collection of manuscripts promises the best chance of accessing the past since they contain 'materials for the history of the whole civilised world, in the handwritings of those who have made history' (p. 205). In particular, then, it is documents in the 'handwritings' of figures from the past which seem to promise the fullest possible access to the past. This fascination with manuscripts of the past was a central feature in the biographical mania that, as discussed in Chapter 1, overtook the nineteenth century. Indeed, many of the documents preserved for the purposes of national history are equally those that would have been incorporated into biographical accounts. This overlap is evident in neo-Victorian archive novels which often centre around private texts that reveal a secret about the author's life.

In bringing the past imaginatively to life, such documents seem to collapse both history and geography, enabling a visitor to become 'a denizen of every clime and a contemporary of every age' (Douglas, p. 197). Although this might initially seem like an example of the presentist approach for which school history and heritage movements were so berated in the 1980s and 1990s, Douglas explicitly disparages those visitors who '[b]eing ignorant of history, [...] reduce everything to the level of the present time' (p. 212). Rather than bringing the past into the present, then, there is a suggestion that the collected materials enable the visitor to move backwards into the past. Douglas suggests that the materials collected in the Museum provide 'uncorrupted evidence' which allows the visitor to 'start almost from the cradle of the human race [... and] trace the history of the world through all succeeding centuries' (p. 197). In this respect, the British Museum seems to partake in a similar gothic modality to that which Ferris identified in the antiquarian book projects of the early nineteenth century. The material remains of the past occupy a similar 'inter-space' between past and present and thus seem to enable an active engagement between the present and the past.

The textual archives of *Possession* and *Ever After* similarly occupy an 'inter-space' between the present and the past. In exploring the idea of reading as both a metaphor and method for engaging with the past, however, they do not privilege the moment of reception over the moment of production, the present over the past. Rather the model of reading that these novels promote is one that acknowledges the past on its own terms, while also establishing a positive connection between the present and the past. It is not just the textual archives that occupy this 'inter-space', however; the dual approach of neo-Victorian fiction, its commitment to historical specificity combined with its awareness of its contemporary moment of production, aligns the genre itself with the gothic modality of the antiquarian document.

Neo-Victorian archive novels

The dual approach of neo-Victorian fiction is most explicitly drama-tized in those novels which adopt a dual plot. As I have said, both A. S. Byatt's *Possession* and Graham Swift's *Ever After* present a narrative in which the twentieth-century figures encounter the textual remains of the nineteenth-century figures. This structure seems to construct a clear division between the present and the past, a division which also indi-cates the nature of the relationship between the present and the past: the past is dead and gone and is only accessible to the present through its textual remains. As we have seen, however, the conception of the document in the nineteenth-century antiquarian movement allows for a more complicated temporality; the past is recognized to have an 'afterlife' which can 'disturb the clarity of linear flow' (Ferris, p. 148). In *Possession* and *Ever After*, the afterlife of the texts of the past is achieved through the process of reading texts, a process which brings the past imaginatively to life in the present. Reading does not always have such positive effects, however; there are readings that seek to possess the past and in doing so deny it an afterlife in the present. Conversely, there are readings which seek to appropriate the texts of the past for the pur-poses of the present. Both *Possession* and *Ever After* provide examples of these negative approaches to reading the past, but they also present examples of readers who adopt a more positive approach to the past. Byatt and Swift do not merely provide positive models of reading, but rather encourage the reader to adopt a similar approach in reading their novels. By embedding the nineteenth-century texts within their narrative structures these novels open up a similarly 'active cognitive space for readers' to that which Ferris identified within the antiquarian book projects of the early nineteenth century (p. 150).

Textual remains

The dual plot of Byatt's *Possession* initially constructs a hierarchical relationship between the present and the past, but rather than privileging the present, as might be expected, it seems to privilege the past.[3] The position and function of the nineteenth-century texts incorporated into the novel make this hierarchical relationship explicit: the nineteenth-century texts are used as epigraphs to the chapters, which, for the most part, describe the adventures of the twentieth-century characters. The nineteenth-century texts, then, literally frame the twentieth-century events of the novel. Indeed, in several instances, these texts provide the key to interpreting the events that follow. The most important example of this process is also the first: in the opening chapter, Roland Michell comes across two previously undiscovered drafts of a personal letter written by the nineteenth-century poet Randolph Henry Ash to an unidentified female recipient. Drawn by their vitality and mystery, Roland removes the letters from the London Library. This removal transgresses the boundaries of a scholarly engagement with the past, and thus is often read as a theft. Yet Roland's actions are not censured by the novel. The epigraph, taken from one of Ash's poems, provides a different framework within which to interpret Roland's actions. The epigraph opens with the line 'These things are there' and continues 'They are and were there' (p. 1), suggesting the vital relationship that literary remains can establish with the past. This recognition of the vitality of the past is clearly mirrored in Roland's response to the letters. While the epigraph suggests the need to respect the historical specificity of such literary remains, 'They [...] were there', it also affirms the living presence of the past in the present. It is this vitality of the past that makes Roland's 'theft' of the letters understandable and excusable: 'It was suddenly quite impossible to put these living words back into page 300 of Vico and return them to Safe 5' (p. 8). While a safe does exactly what its name implies, keeps things safe, it also locks them away from sight and prevents them from having an existence in the present. In using Ash's poem as the epigraph to the chapter, Byatt guides the reader's response to the twentieth-century events the chapter depicts. Moreover, the epigraph's message asserts the role that the past has in understanding the present. It would seem, then, that the Victorian past explains the present.

It is not merely that the past explains the present in *Possession*; it comes to dominate it. As I have argued elsewhere, the very names of the twentieth-century protagonists Roland and Maud, taken from a Robert Browning and Tennyson poem respectively, indicate their ghostly position in relation to the nineteenth century (Hadley, 2003, p. 94).[4] As the novel progresses, the past comes to seem more alive and more vital than the present. The nineteenth-century plot comes to wholly determine the twentieth-century one as the protagonists Roland and Maud not only embark on a literary quest to determine the nature of the relationship between Ash and LaMotte but their own relationship comes to match the patterns of their nineteenth-century precursors. Thus, the twentieth-century figures come to seem the more ghostly in the novel as their plot becomes entirely connected to that of the Victorians. Prompted by clues they find in the letters, Maud and Roland travel to Yorkshire, where they suspect Ash and LaMotte had stayed together. Roland and Maud do more than just follow in the footsteps of Ash and LaMotte, however, they replicate them. Of Roland and Maud we are told 'They paced well together, though they didn't notice that; both were energetic striders' (p. 251). The subsequent description of Ash and LaMotte recalls this description, connecting the twentieth-century characters to the nineteenth-century ones: 'They both walked very quickly. "We walk well together," he told her. "Our paces suit"' (p. 280). Ironically, it is when Maud and Roland decide to escape their Victorian predecessors that they are closest to them. Roland proposes to Maud that they go to Boggle Hole since 'It's a nice word' and 'There's no Boggle Hole in Cropper or the Ash letters' (p. 268). As the reader later discovers, however, Ash and LaMotte had also spent a day at Boggle Hole, 'where they had gone because they liked the word' (p. 286). In *Possession*, then, the afterlife of the past threatens to take over the present; the Victorians seem to have moved out of their position in the past and taken up residence in the present.

Maud explicitly considers the relationship between the present and the past in such vampiric terms. After the first day spent reading LaMotte's side of the correspondence at Seal Court, Maud reflects that '[t]his thickened forest, her own humming metal car, her prying curiosity about whatever had been Christabel's life, seemed suddenly to be the ghostly things, feeding on, living through, the young vitality of the past' (p. 136). The lack of vitality in the present is apparent in Byatt's characterization: there is a clear opposition between the nineteenth-century characters, who are mostly writers, and the twentieth-century characters, who are readers or critics. Thus, whereas Ash and LaMotte are represented

by an abundance of texts in the novel, the twentieth-century protagonists, Roland and Maud, are represented by no texts. By implication,
then, the present appears but a shadow of the past, unable to produce
original literature itself and living off the textual productions of the
nineteenth-century.

Despite seeming to privilege the nineteenth-century past over the
twentieth-century present, for the most part the nineteenth century is
mediated to the reader through the twentieth-century characters. While
the nineteenth-century texts appear as epigraphs to the chapters, the
chapters themselves often incorporate images of the twentieth-century
academics reading, and more importantly analysing, those texts. So,
while the nineteenth-century texts frame the twentieth-century plot
of the novel, they are also framed by the twentieth-century readings
of them. This is most obvious in the case of LaMotte's poem 'The Fairy
Melusine' which is presented to the reader in its entirety just over halfway through the novel. Although the poem is given a chapter in its own
right, by the time the reader reaches it, he/she has already discovered
some of the details of LaMotte and Ash's affair, biographical information which can influence a reader's response to the text. Moreover,
prior to reaching the text of LaMotte's poem, the reader has read the
interpretations, or 'readings', of the poem forwarded by two of the
twentieth-century academics. Fergus Wolff's psychoanalytic interpretation is presented early on in the novel (p. 33) when he summarizes his
knowledge of LaMotte and her writing for Roland, but Leonora Sterne's
feminist interpretation is presented much closer to LaMotte's poem,
ensuring that it is fresh in the reader's mind when they are finally presented with the poem in its entirety (pp. 244–6). Byatt, then, seems to
be suggesting the difficulty of accessing the texts of the past in isolation
from the interpretations of the present, a difficulty that is particularly
pronounced in the case of nineteenth-century texts, given the prominence of the era, and its literature, within contemporary society.[5]

Whereas Byatt's *Possession* opens with the words of one of its nineteenth-
century protagonists, the opening chapters of Graham Swift's *Ever After*
are solely concerned with the narrative of its twentieth-century protagonist Bill Unwin. The first extract from Matthew Pearce's Notebooks does
not come until Chapter 5; set off in a separate chapter, the placement of
the nineteenth-century text suggests the distance between the present
and the past. Yet, as the narrative progresses, Bill begins to incorporate
shorter extracts and frames Matthew's accounts with his own interpretation. The position of the nineteenth-century texts in the novel, then,

replicates the role of the past which, as we shall see, eventually becomes appropriated by Bill for his present needs.

Models of reading

The twentieth-century academics in *Possession* not only provide a framework for reading the nineteenth-century texts incorporated into the novel, but also more general models of the process of reading the past. As academics, the twentieth-century characters are obviously professional readers whose encounters with the past take place within the institutional contexts of universities and libraries. Given the prominence of academics within the twentieth-century plot of the novel, it might be expected that *Possession* prioritizes a scholarly engagement with the past. Yet, in the tradition of British campus fiction, Byatt satirizes academia. Byatt directs her most biting satire at Fergus Wolff and Leonora Sterne, academics who read the texts of the past through the lens of psychoanalytic theory. These theoretical readings are revealed to be reductive in their focus on a single concern, usually sexuality. Moreover, the novel suggests that these approaches are motivated more by contemporary concerns; consequently, such readings wrench the nineteenth-century texts out of their historical context and impose present structures of understanding onto them.

Despite the academic setting of the novel, then, Byatt does not prioritize a purely scholarly engagement with the past. Indeed, the textual remains of the nineteenth-century poets soon break out of their institutional contexts – Roland removes the letters from the London Library because of their vitality. The vitality of these letters is in part due to their personal nature: they are addressed to a woman, not his wife, with whom Ash clearly had an intense connection. The personal nature of these letters, and the possible scandal that they hint at, is only part of what contributes to their vitality. The letters also seem more vital and alive because they never reached their destination: they have remained unread since they were written. It is this unfinished element of the documents which prompts the literary detective quest that drives the plot of *Possession* as Roland seeks to first identify the woman the letters were addressed to and then to uncover proof of the relationship between Ash and LaMotte. As this quest progresses, Roland's engagement with the documents of the past moves even further from a scholarly, purely intellectual engagement – both literally, as the quest takes him to Seal Court, Yorkshire and Brittany, and metaphorically as Roland comes to connect on an emotional level with the nineteenth-century poets.

Although Byatt validates Roland's emotional engagement with the past, she cautions against an emotional approach which is grounded in the ego of the individual. Cropper's engagement with the remains of Ash stems from entirely personal motivations and, as such, he comes to represent the model of a negative approach to the texts of the past. Although he holds an official position as an academic, Cropper's scholarly concerns with the past are outweighed by his position as a collector. Cropper prides himself on having the 'the largest and finest collection of Randolph Henry Ash's correspondence anywhere in the world' (p. 96) and the chapter which introduces him is prefaced by an epigraph from Ash's poem *The Great Collector*. As with Roland, then, the nineteenth-century text directs the reader's response to the twentieth-century character. Ash's poem describes the 'gaze' of the collector as the objects of his desire are 'extracted one by one' (p. 92). The use of the verb 'extracted' suggests removal of a thing, by force, from its natural environment. A similar fate seems to await the letters Cropper is trying to acquire from Mrs Wapshott as he illicitly copies them in the dead of night, 'perched' on a toilet seat (p. 93).

As a collector, Cropper is more concerned with the preservation of the texts as *objects* of the past, rather than *documents*; his interest in Ash's remains stems from a desire to possess *all* of his remains and bring them together in a single collection. In this respect, Cropper recalls the approach of many early Victorian book clubs, such as the Roxburghe, which were concerned with 'the production of fine books' and the preservation of 'aesthetic rather than scholarly collectibles' (Ferris, p. 145). Cropper claims that while the *message* of the texts will remain accessible to scholars, the documents themselves, as *traces* of the past, will be 'preserved where the air is best, where breath cannot harm them' (p. 386). Cropper's image of the ideal museum would remove the past from its original context and seal it off from the present, adopting a synchronous approach to the past. In *On Longing* (1993), Susan Stewart argues that such synchronicity is inherent in all collections: '[t]he collection replaces history with *classification*, with order beyond the realm of temporality. [... A]ll time is made simultaneous or synchronous within the collection's world' (p. 151).

If the collection is disconnected from the past, it is equally disconnected from the present. Cropper's museum prevents any direct, physical connection between the documents of the past and the researchers in the present and in doing so removes those objects from the historical process. To return to Stewart, the collection 'replace[s] the narrative of history with the narrative of the individual subject – that is, the collector himself' (p. 156). Cropper's approach to Ash's remains certainly seems to prioritize his own identity as a collector. The first scene in which we encounter Cropper reveals his appropriation of Ash's past. Cropper has acquired Ash's signet ring, stripped it of its historical specificity and appropriated it for his own needs in the present. The only point of connection between the present and the past, then, is Cropper himself. Cropper's position as a collector has come to dominant his entire identity. Imaginatively writing his autobiography, Cropper usually abandons the project after his first encounter with Ash's remains, 'almost [...] as though he had no existence, no separate existence of his own after that first contact' (p. 105). Contrary to Stewart's argument, then, it is not the collector who gives a coherent identity to the collection, but rather the collection which gives an identity to the collector. Even so, Cropper's relationship to the past is firmly rejected by the novel as a negative relationship; it both removes texts from their original historical context and denies them a *real* afterlife in the present by fixing them within the collection.

In contrast to Cropper's negative relationship with the past, the protagonists of the novel, Roland Michell and Maud Bailey, serve as examples of a positive engagement with the past. Identified as 'old-fashioned textual critic[s]' (p. 50), Roland and Maud combine a scholarly approach that is committed to the historical specificity of the past with an emotional response to the past that stems from the past itself, rather than from the present. This commitment to historical and textual research is rewarded in the novel as Roland and Maud triumph over the more theoretically-minded academics. Roland clearly seeks to understand Ash's remains within their historical context and indeed his first steps after acquiring the letters are to try and ascertain, through textual and historical research, the identity of the addressee. Justifying his actions to Maud, Roland remarks that he took the letters because '[he] wanted them to be a secret. Private. And to do the work' (p. 50). For Roland, then, the personal motivations are underpinned by a scholarly commitment to the letters; as an academic, he is drawn to the research involved in tracking down the mysterious woman to whom the letters are addressed. It is this combination of scholarly and personal motivations that validates Roland's engagement with the past. Roland seeks to understand the past on its own terms and connect it to the present – not through an act of appropriation but rather by placing it in a wider narrative of personal, familial, and national identity.

Although Roland's approach to the past is valued by Byatt, it is Maud who represents the ideal reader in the novel. As I have argued elsewhere, the ending of the novel brings together all of the twentieth-century academics for the reading of LaMotte's final, unopened letter to Ash; the ensuing 'circle of readers' implies that 'the ideal reading would be comprised of a composite of the various models of reading (biographical, scholarly, theoretical and personal) that are represented' (Hadley, 2003, p. 98). Combining as she does a scholarly and personal, familial relationship to the past, Maud represents the ideal reader. Maud's initial interest in LaMotte was prompted by the family connection and by a desire to recuperate the 'silly fairy poetess' (p. 86) from a familial narrative that diminishes her achievements. Maud's engagement with the past, then, is clearly prompted by genealogy. Yet she remains unaware of her true family connection to Ash and LaMotte until the very end of the novel. Consequently, she does not place herself at the centre of her genealogical investigations. Unlike Cropper, whose engagement with the past is dominated by his ego, Maud's encounter with the past focuses on LaMotte. She encounters the past on its own terms and, as a consequence, uncovers the connection between the past and the present. These connections are made explicit in the final scene of reading in the novel; the letter that the academics exhume from Ash's grave reveals not only that LaMotte and Ash's illegitimate child survived, but also that Maud is a direct descendant of that child. In having Maud read this letter to the gathered circle of academics, Byatt reinforces the idea that any reading of the past needs to balance a scholarly and an emotional approach, a commitment to the historical context of the documents of the past with a concern for their afterlife in the present.

In Graham Swift's *Ever After* a similar opposition is constructed between an academic, scholarly approach to the past and an emotional, familial one. Yet, whereas *Possession* reconciled these dual impulses in the single figure of Maud Bailey, there is no single figure in Swift's novel who can reconcile these impulses. In part, this is a consequence of the presentist approach of the family reader, Bill Unwin, whose engagement with the textual remains of his ancestor, Matthew Pearce, is explicitly determined by his genealogical narrative. Bill's interest in Pearce's Notebooks is prompted by his present anxieties, in particular the vexed question of his paternity. Although not strictly a genealogical investigation, then, Bill's engagement with the past is prompted by a desire to understand his own origins. As the narrative progresses, however, it becomes obvious that Bill's engagement with the past is less part of an attempt to understand his present situation than to escape it. That Bill has entirely dissociated himself from the present is evident in the startling declaration with which he opens his narrative: 'These are,

I should warn you, the words of a dead man' (p. 1). Cloistered as he is in the 'ancient walls' (p. 2) of his Oxbridge college, Bill's concern with the past overtakes his present concerns.

Bill's interest in the past counteracts his mother's lack of interest in her family history. Bill's mother lives for the present and considers a concern with either posterity or anteriority as 'an avoidance of the central issue of life, which was to wring the most out of the present' (p. 26). This disregard for the past or the future prompts Bill's mother to dispose of the textual remains of the past which she dismisses as 'junk' (p. 36). Recalling the bonfire that she made of her Uncle Ratty's papers, Bill laments the loss of 'All that research. All that *evidence*' and what could have easily been the loss of Matthew's Notebooks (p. 36). The terms in which he figures this hypothetical loss reveal the vital connection between the textual remains and the past they evoke; Bill asserts that 'With my own ignorant hands I might have tossed Matthew on to the pyre' (p. 36). That Matthew's Notebooks survived at all is the result of pure chance and, as Bill ponders, 'who knows if some other, unknown manuscript was not casually cremated' by his mother (p. 36). The casual disregard Bill's mother displays towards the textual remains of the past reveals the extent to which our knowledge of the past is subject to the caprices of the present.

It is only in the final stages of cancer that Bill's mother decides to share the story of her family with Bill. Yet in telling this story she constructs an over-arching narrative that subsumes all the individual figures, as well as their hopes, dreams and desires. According to Bill's mother, the history of her family is that of a series of disasters prompted by 'the desire to cheat death by the vain quest for distinction' (p. 127). She considers the desire for distinction, for an afterlife beyond your own historical moment, as something which particularly afflicts the men in her family. Bill's engagement with his ancestor's Notebooks seeks to recuperate Matthew's life from the family narrative that his mother has constructed. Matthew's Notebooks, which narrate his spiritual crisis, do not fit within Bill's mother's account of her family history. As we saw in the previous chapter, the crisis in faith prompted by Darwin's theories created a concomitant anxiety in Victorian society about the afterlife. Indeed, Matthew's decision to keep a journal is prompted by the death of his youngest son, Felix. Yet, his Notebooks are more concerned with the idea of origins than with posterity, so he disrupts the genealogical narrative that Bill's mother constructs. Bill's own account equally resists being absorbed into this genealogical grand narrative; for most of his life he was content to remain in the shadows of his wife. The novel opens shortly after Bill's attempted suicide and the personal account which he subsequently writes, and which could be seen as an attempt to establish his identity, is less concerned with posterity, or 'cheating death', than with anteriority.

Bill's engagement with Matthew's Notebooks, then, initially seems concerned to understand them on their own terms, free from the familial narrative imposed by his mother. In this respect, he would seem to be adopting a scholarly, academic approach to the past. Yet, as I suggested, Bill's research into the past is motivated by his present anxieties. He turns to the past in an attempt to escape the present, an attempt which leads to an unhealthy prioritization of the past. Bill muses on how reading the Notebooks brings him closer to Matthew, but this connection comes to seem reminiscent of the vampiric relationship between the present and the past identified in *Possession*. Bill comments that, 'when I open their pages, I open, I touch the pages that he once touched. I occupy, as it were his phantom skin' (p. 46). It would seem, then, that Bill seeks to lose his own identity in that of Matthew Pearce, rather than understanding Matthew on his own terms.

The extent to which Bill's relationship to the past is constructed around his present needs and anxieties is most evident in the way that he uses the present, or rather the more recent past, as a model for understanding the Victorian past. In this respect, then, Bill could be accused of adopting a presentist approach to the past, an approach that, as we have seen, was highly criticized in the National Curriculum History debates of the late 1980s and early 1990s. The most telling instance of this presentist approach is Bill's hypothesis surrounding Elizabeth's remarriage after her divorce from Matthew. Bill interprets this incident in light of his mother's own remarriage to Sam, with whom she was having an affair prior to her husband's death, and suggests that Elizabeth may too have been engaged in extra-marital relations. Through his retrospective approach to the past, Bill has drawn Pearce back into a pre-existing genealogical narrative – not his mother's this time, but his father's. In doing so, he removes the Notebooks, and Matthew's marriage, from their original historical and social context. Yet the novel does not entirely censure such an approach; in fact, there is a suggestion that Bill's approach enables him to explore possibilities that were unthinkable in the original context. Matthew's Notebooks hint at a similar conclusion, but Matthew dismisses these suspicions as 'inadmissible' (p. 183).

Despite this, Bill's attempts to connect with the past ultimately fail since they are motivated primarily by present concerns. Whereas *Possession* ended by privileging the family reader, Maud, the end of *Ever After* sees the Notebooks transferred from Bill to Potter, an academic who specializes in the spiritual crisis of the nineteenth century. Although *Ever After* similarly belongs to the genre of campus fiction, it does not engage in academic satire to the same extent as *Possession* does. This might be in large part due to the specific context of the novel; set in an unidentified Oxbridge college, *Ever After* is more concerned with traditional approaches to scholarship than the contemporary theoretical models that come under attack in Byatt's novel. Yet Bill's academic approach is dismissed as old-fashioned, even within the context of the notoriously old-fashioned Oxbridge community. Bill's teaching of literature encourages students to recognize and appreciate the 'beauty' of works of literature, an approach which removes texts from their historical context, and positions them as 'universal' expressions of beauty.[6]

By contrast, the novel privileges the academic Michael Potter, and ultimately rewards him with the texts of the past because of his commitment to historical materialist research. For instance, Potter points out the importance of identifying which version of Lyell's *Principles of Geology* Pearce had read in order to understand its impact on his thinking. Given neo-Victorian fiction's commitment to historical specificity, it is not surprising that Swift rewards Potter by having Bill hand over the Notebooks at the end of the novel. Potter is not quite the 'ideal' reader that Maud is, however; the narrative reveals many of his less attractive qualities such as his womanizing and his position as a TV academic.

By far the most troubling of Potter's qualities is his seemingly egotistical approach to his academic researches. Provoked by Bill, who disingenuously suggests that he is unaware there are different editions of Lyell's work, Potter bursts out with the preposterous claim that 'The spiritual crisis of the mid-nineteenth century is *my subject*!' (p. 164). Potter's outburst seems to connect him to the egocentric approach of Cropper in *Possession*, yet whereas Cropper's relationship with the past was underpinned by his position as a collector, Potter seeks a purely scholarly connection with the past. Unlike Cropper, Potter does not seek to remove the remains of the past from their original context. His sense of proprietorship over the Notebooks is motivated by his conviction that he is the best person to understand and disseminate the scholarly importance of the manuscripts, rather than a desire to acquire and possess the remains of the past.

Whereas Cropper was obsessed with Ash, even to the point of wearing his jewellery, Potter is less concerned with Pearce the individual than with what his Notebooks reveal about the impact of ideas, specifically Darwin's theories, on an individual. Potter wants to position Pearce and his experiences within a wider historical narrative, to understand him as 'representative' of a wider historical 'condition'. This lack of concern for the living individual who wrote the Notebooks is not entirely desirable in Potter's approach, yet the novel circumvents this difficulty by delaying the transfer of the Notebooks to Potter until the end of the novel. Driven as it is by personal, present concerns, Bill's engagement with the Notebooks recognizes the importance of understanding Matthew as an individual who *lived* in the past: 'You see, it is the personal thing that matters. [...] It is knowing who Matthew Pearce *was*' (p. 49). The incorporation of the Notebooks allows the reader to establish a more personal connection with Matthew, and by extension the Victorian past, than would have been possible in Potter's purely scholarly account.

Through the presentation of various types of readers, both novels provide the reader with multiple models of reading. The readers who are favoured at the end of each novel, however, suggest that for Byatt and Swift a positive relationship to the past is one that combines an intellectual and an emotional approach, one that both respects the historical specificity of the past and its connection to the present. In such readings, the past is not rarefied into something dead and gone that can be put under glass and studied, nor is it co-opted for a personal narrative that only understands the past from its own, present perspective. Rather, the past is returned to its specific historical context while also allowed to have an *afterlife* in the present. In this way, reading becomes a metaphor for the nature of the relationship between the present and the past that is advocated in neo-Victorian fiction, a relationship that recognizes the necessity for a dual approach to the past that is grounded in both the historical specificity of the past and an awareness of the distance between then and now. Reading is more than just a metaphor in these novels, however; it is the means by which these narratives establish a connection between the present and the past. Both *Ever After* and *Possession* enact this sense of the afterlife of the past in the present in their adoption of a dual plot. Moreover, both novels incorporate the textual remains of the nineteenth century into their narratives, thereby opening up an 'active cognitive space' (Ferris, p. 150) for the reader to establish a connection with the past. As well as proposing positive models of reading, then, these novels encourage the reader to participate in a similarly active and positive engagement with the past. Although the nineteenth century is mostly mediated through the twentieth-century characters' readings of its textual remains, both novels incorporate instances in which the nineteenth century is directly resurrected for the reader. The textual remains, then, foster a temporality that is akin to the 'gothic modality' Ferris identified in the antiquarian book projects of the early nineteenth century (p. 148). These instances are always to a greater or lesser degree prompted by an engagement with those textual remains and thus it is the act of reading which guarantees the past an afterlife in the present.

Reading the past to life

The nineteenth-century plot of *Ever After* is mostly mediated to the reader through Matthew's Notebooks. Moreover, although the reader is seemingly permitted direct access to the Notebooks, it becomes increasingly clear that this access is determined by Bill, who selects and interprets the entries presented to the reader. The narrative Bill constructs around the Notebooks frequently contains suppositions, but the uncertainty of the status of these events is voiced in the repetition of phrases such as 'quite possibly' (p. 123). At other points, Bill is even more explicit in drawing attention to the imaginative nature of the events he narrates: 'If that scene ever really took place (I imagine, I invent)' (p. 127).

It is not only that Bill uses his imagination to fill in the gaps in the Notebooks, he also attempts to bring the figures from the past imaginatively to life. At points, Bill slips into something akin to free indirect discourse when imagining the views of Matthew's contemporaries. For instance, the narrative adopts the kind of voice the Rector might be supposed to have had: 'To put it plainly, happiness seemed to have taken away some of the man's bite. Well, well, he could hardly complain of that' (p. 125). Bill's imaginative approach becomes even more apparent when the nineteenth-century figures break free from their textual remains. Midway through the novel, the reader witnesses the encounter between Matthew and his Rector father-in-law that precipitated the breakdown of his marriage. This encounter is seen from the perspective of the Rector's wife, the imagined audience for the dispute. Bill justifies his imaginative approach, remarking that 'If it were not for Matthew's Notebooks, nobody might have known it had happened at all, it might have been as though it never was' (p. 185). Bill's approach, then, seems perilously close to the fictionalization of the past considered characteristic of postmodernist literature. Despite this defence, however, Bill's imaginative reconstructions remain grounded in the known facts of the past. The version of events witnessed by the Rector's wife correlates to the account the reader has already been presented with in Matthew's

Notebooks. Indeed, in positioning the Rector's wife, rather than 'God in the sky' (p. 184), as the observer, Bill remains faithful to Matthew's account, which does not record the Rector's thoughts, or even words, on the occasion. For all that he seems to recognize the limits of the historical imagination, however, Bill pushes the boundaries of imaginative license even further when he presents a dramatized version, in the form of a script, for the Rector and Matthew's exchange. Yet he ultimately abandons this fiction, declaring 'But I don't know, I cannot even invent, what the Rector said' (p. 187).

While this instance, then, seems to promise direct access to the past, it remains firmly grounded in the present of Bill's imagination. Although this might initially seem a positive model of the way in which an imaginative reconstruction of the past should operate within the boundaries of historical knowledge, it is ultimately an example of the failure of Bill's imagination. In this failure of Bill's imagination, *Ever After* suggests that the present and the past remain separated by an unbridgeable gulf. The narratives of Bill and Matthew initially seem to be mirror-images; both accounts are prompted by an encounter with death and both Matthew and Bill struggle to understand their own place within a wider historical narrative: genealogical, in the case of Bill, and Darwinian, in the case of Matthew. Yet despite this similarity, Bill is unable to imaginatively inhabit Matthew's world. For Bill, it is impossible to recapture Matthew's experience of seeing an ichthyosaur; he notes that although he has seen ichthyosaurs 'in museums, in books [...] I look at them and don't feel that much at all' (p. 100). Bill recognizes that there is a world of difference between the 'safe, orderly, artificial' (p. 100) space of the museum and the real world, yet this does not sufficiently account for the differing reactions of the two men. Rather, the difference seems to be to do with their relative positions within history. Thus, while Bill's imaginative approach to the past initially promises direct access to that past, it ultimately fails to move beyond present concerns and belief systems.[7]

By contrast, *Possession* succeeds in resurrecting the nineteenth- century past for its readers because unlike Bill's approach it is not prompted by the imagination but rather by the act of reading. For the most part, the Victorian plot of *Possession* is mediated to the reader through the texts discovered by the twentieth-century characters. Yet, there are three occasions when this is not the case; in these instances it is as if Byatt has resurrected the ghosts of the Victorian characters.

In chapter 15, the narrator presents the reader with direct, unmediated access to Ash and LaMotte on their trip to Yorkshire. Although it is initially unclear whether the opening description of '[t]he man and the woman sat opposite each other in the railway carriage' (p. 273) refers to Ash and LaMotte or Roland and Maud, this is soon resolved by the description of Christabel's dress. The resurrection of Ash and LaMotte in this chapter is achieved through poetry as in the preceding chapters (13 and 14) Maud and Roland trace Ash and LaMotte's trip to Yorkshire through the associations in their poems. The second instance occurs shortly after the death of Randolph Henry Ash, yet it is not Randolph who is allowed a physical materiality but rather his wife, Ellen. Again, the nature of what is presented is initially unclear. It is preceded by an account from Ellen's journal of the night her husband died and is introduced by a subheading marking the date as 'NOVEMBER 27th 1889' (p. 446) in a similar fashion to Ellen's journal entries. The use of the third person and a different font script, however, indicates to the reader that this is a narrative account of the events, rather than a textual account. In both of these instances it is almost as if the Victorian figures had been conjured up by their texts. In adopting the omniscient narrator familiar from Victorian fiction, these instances reveal Byatt's confidence in the ability to access and recreate the past.

The third and final instance in which the Victorian characters are directly resurrected occurs at the very end of the novel. Throughout the novel, the power of the past to erupt in and disturb the present has been repeatedly demonstrated, but this is nowhere more forcefully shown than in the conclusion to the quest for Ash and LaMotte's remains. Despite claiming to have moral and ethical reservations, the academics allow Cropper to carry out his most sinister act of repossessing the past: the exhumation of Ash's grave. With the exception Beatrice Nest, all the academics are motivated by a desire to know the end of the story that was uncovered by those first, unsent letters, and they suspect that the final letter LaMotte sent to Ash, unopened by Ash and buried with him by his wife, will provide the resolution they seek. There is no doubt that the pursuit of the past has overtaken the present for most of the twentieth-century characters and thus the novel seems to be suggesting that knowing the end of the story will allow the past to return to its proper place, in the past. Of course, this does not mean that it should not have a connection to the present, and indeed the revelation of the exhumed letter forges positive connections between the present and the past. Not only is Maud revealed to be a direct descendant of both Ash and LaMotte but some of the funds raised from the sale of the letters will be used to modernize Seal Court, making it more habitable for the present generation of Baileys.

While the conclusion of the twentieth-century narrative seems to reposition the Victorians in the past, *Possession* ends with a Postscript dated 1868 which once again 'disturb[s] the clarity of linear flow' in the novel (Ferris, p. 148). The Postscript fulfils the reader's desire to know the end of the Victorian story by narrating an event for which there was 'no discernible trace' (p. 508). The Postscript initially seems to be a postmodern move in its suggestion that the past remains unknowable. Indeed, it explicitly undercuts the academics' conclusion, based on textual evidence, that Ash had no knowledge of the existence of his daughter, revealing that not only did he know about his daughter, but that he also met her. In narrating these events, the Postscript asserts the reality of the past, a reality that may not be entirely captured in its textual remains. The opening of the Postscript leaves the reader in no doubt as to the status of events: 'Two people met, on a hot May day, and never later mentioned their meeting. This is how it was' (p. 508). As Keen argues, postmodern romances of the archive still present 'strong finishes', 'revealing with a certainty rarely exposed to sceptical questioning *which* truth lies permanently inaccessible, beyond the reach of the fallible questioner' (p. 43).

Despite its disavowal of textual traces, however, the events narrated in the Postscript are prompted by an encounter with the textual remains of the past. The preceding scene, in which all the twentieth-century characters converge in a hotel room to read the letter that had been buried with Ash, can be read as a séance:[8]

> So, in that hotel room, to that strange gathering of disparate seekers and hunters, Christabel LaMotte's letter to Randolph Ash was read aloud, by candlelight, with the wind howling past, and the panes of the windows rattling with the little blows of flying debris as it raced on and on, over the downs. (p. 499)

The effect produced by both the candlelight inside and the storm outside the room evokes a sense of otherworldly powers at work. It transpires that Ash and LaMotte's daughter Maia survived and lived with Christabel's sister, making Maud a direct descendant of both Ash and LaMotte, since Maia was her great-great-great-grandmother. The letter's revelation further enhances the association of this scene with a séance as it is through this event that Maud is able to connect with her dead ancestors. If this scene is understood as a séance, then the appearance of Maia and Ash in the Postscript can be interpreted as an effect of the reading of the letter in which LaMotte tells Ash of their daughter.

Whereas the nineteenth-century scenes in *Ever After* remain grounded in Bill's imagination, *Possession* resurrects the nineteenth-century characters for the reader, suggesting a direct encounter with the past. In *Ever After*, Bill's attempt to imaginatively recreate the past fails because of the gulf between the past and the present; Bill's presentist approach prevents him from occupying the mindset of the Rector and understanding his thought processes. By contrast, *Possession* directly resurrects the nineteenth-century characters for the reader, suggesting that it is possible to establish a living connection with the past, as long as it is grounded in the materiality of the past. As we have seen, this connection is made possible through reading the textual remains of the past.

Conclusion

For many critics, this positive connection between the present and the past is exemplified in *Possession* in the final scene of the twentieth-century plot, which sees the consummation of the growing relationship between Roland and Maud. For example, Keen argues that this scene 'brings Roland, Maud, and through Maud their Victorian counterparts together in bed' so that 'the book romantically celebrates a physical union of present and past, scholar and subject' (p. 42). There is, however, an earlier moment in the novel which can equally be seen as redemptive, as marking the point when the relationship with the past becomes positive for the present. This earlier moment concerns Roland alone and is far more important in terms of the role of reading I have been tracing in this chapter. As I have said, at the start of the novel there is a clear distinction between the twentieth-century readers and the nineteenth-century writers; indeed, there is a sense that the twentieth-century figures are unable to create their own literary texts because of the awesome shadow cast by their nineteenth-century predecessors. Returning to England after the discovery of his and Maud's secret quest, however, Roland takes his first tentative steps towards becoming a writer: 'He was writing lists of words. [...] He had hopes – more, intimations of imminence – of writing poems, but so far had got no further than lists' (p. 431). It is only once he has escaped Ash's narrative, once the secret has been discovered and so taken out of his hands, that Roland is able to realize his poetic ambitions. Although Roland rejects the world of academia in favour of writing, the novel, in typical romance fashion, awards him success in the academic world too with multiple job offers from universities around the globe.

If, as I have suggested, reading serves as both a metaphor for and a means to establish a positive connection between the present and the past, what is the significance of Roland's transition from reader to writer? In the Introduction to her critical work *Passions of the Mind* (1991), Byatt sets out her views on the relationship between reading and writing. Whereas other novelists seek to keep their fictional writing distinct from their critical work, Byatt understands reading and writing as 'points on a circle' (p. xiii). She goes on to explain the interrelationship between reading and writing: 'Greedy reading made me want to write, as if this were the only adequate response to the pleasure and power of books. Writing made me want to read [...]' (p. xiii). For Byatt, then, reading is not a passive process; rather, it involves an active participation with and a response to the written text. As we have seen, *Possession* encourages a similar active engagement with the Victorian past not only through the models of active readership such as Maud and Roland but also by incorporating the nineteenth-century texts for the reader to engage with directly.

This active engagement with the past, and the interrelationship between reading and writing, is most explicit in novels like *Possession* and *Ever After* which incorporate nineteenth-century documents into their narratives. These documents are usually written by the neo-Victorian authors themselves as if they were Victorian texts, and so call into question the status of these texts. However, this interaction between reading and writing is central to the entire genre of neo-Victorian fiction. As I argued in the Introduction, the emergence of neo-Victorian fiction can be understood as in part a response to the dominance of the Victorian novel – both in terms of the cultural presence of specific novels and the extent to which our conception of the novel genre derives from nineteenth-century realist forms. In writing *as if* they were Victorians, neo-Victorian authors seem to collapse the distinction between then and now and appropriate the voices of the past. Yet, as I will explore in the following section, such an approach actually highlights the dual position of neo-Victorian fiction and opens up questions about the status of neo-Victorian fiction and the nature of its relationship to Victorian literature.

Coda: Writing *as* the Victorians

In exploring the process of reading Victorian textual remains, *Possession* and *Ever After* highlight the ways in which the Victorians are read in the contemporary moment. Since the Victorian texts are mostly mediated to the reader through the twentieth-century characters, these novels draw attention to the mediated nature of our engagement with Victorian literature. Consequently, Byatt and Swift prompt the reader to self-consciously reflect upon the genre of neo-Victorian fiction. They raise the question of why we continue to read Victorian and neo-Victorian fictions in the twentieth- and twenty-first centuries. Contemporary culture's interest in Victorian literature is evident in the continual republication of Victorian 'classics', often justified by new introductions or marketed as tie-ins to the numerous screen adaptations of such texts. Despite the over-saturation of the market, the popularity of neo-Victorian fiction suggests that the reading public's appetite for Victorian stories has not yet been satiated. As I suggested in the Introduction, Victorian literature's position on publisher's lists of 'classic' texts indicates one of the reasons that we continue to read Victorian novels; the Victorian novel is considered the exemplar of the novel genre. Consequently, the qualities that are valued in a 'good' novel are invariably those that were valued in Victorian novels: rounded characters, a dramatic plot, and a neat ending. One explanation for the popularity of neo-Victorian fictions is that it revives these features of Victorian fiction. Indeed, the marketing of neo-Victorian fiction emphasizes its connection to Victorian fiction, and often encourages readers to view it as a replica of Victorian fiction. For instance, when Alasdair Gray's *Poor Things* was first published in 1992 it had a gold ribbon stitched into the spine for use as a bookmark. Other neo-Victorian novels are published with images which clearly identify the texts as concerned with the Victorian era, such as the pre-Raphaelite images on the cover of *Possession* and interspersed within *Angels and Insects*. These publishing practices construct a nostalgic relationship between neo-Victorian fiction and the Victorian fictions that they seemingly attempt to imitate.

In a 1994 interview, Jeanette Winterson implicitly dismissed the subgenre of neo-Victorian fiction as derivative: 'If you want to read nineteenth-century novels, there are plenty for you to read, and you may as well read the real thing and not go out and buy a reproduction' (qtd. in Wormald, p. 187).[1] Approaching the issue from the perspective of the neo-Victorian writer, Palliser explains that he was prompted to write his neo-Victorian novel *The Quincunx: The Inheritance of John Huffam* (1989) 'when I caught myself again and again looking along the shelves of bookshops for a new Dickens or Brontë or Hardy or Collins' ('Author's Afterword', p. 1208). Although clearly less critical of neo-Victorian fiction than Winterson, Palliser similarly implies that Victorian literature appeals to readers in a way that contemporary fiction does not. Despite their differing perspectives, both Winterson and Palliser position neo-Victorian literature as a copy, or 'reproduction', of Victorian literature. They imply that the Victorian period was a golden age of literature and that neo-Victorian fiction represents an attempt to revive those lost literary forms.[2]

For all that it critically engages with the contemporary uses of the Victorian past, neo-Victorian fiction can itself be appropriated by the nostalgic impulses which have impelled a return to the Victorian era. In the past decade there has been an increase in the number of neo-Victorian texts being adapted for the big or small screen, including all three novels of Sarah Waters's neo-Victorian trilogy – *Tipping the Velvet* (BBC, 2002), *Fingersmith* (BBC, 2005), and *Affinity* (ITV, 2008) – and both Byatt's *Angels and Insects* (1999) and *Possession* (2002).[3] Interestingly, as neo-Victorian texts are adapted for television and film they become subject to the same marketing principles as Victorian novels, with cover images taken from the contemporary screen adaptations. As we saw in the Introduction, such adaptations often flatten out the complexities of Victorian fiction and remove them from their specific historical circumstances. The constant repetition of the Victorian era, then, has become almost indistinguishable from the more general aestheticization of and nostalgic response to the past.

It is important, however, to maintain a distinction between neo-Victorian fiction and the subsequent television and film adaptations that have appeared. While those adaptations often collapse the distinction between the Victorian and the neo-Victorian, the neo-Victorian texts themselves maintain that distinction through their commitment to historical specificity. Similarly, while neo-Victorian fiction can be appropriated for nostalgic purposes, the texts themselves, as we have seen, do not merely nostalgically revive the Victorian past. Indeed, even those neo-Victorian texts that adopt a nostalgic view towards Victorian literature, recognize the distance between the Victorian and the contemporary moment. They accept that it is not possible, and perhaps not even desirable, to return to the Victorian past. Yet they seek to preserve aspects of the Victorian past in the present, in Byatt's words, 'to keep past literatures alive and singing' (2000, 11). While nostalgia implies a passive replication or imitation of the past, neo-Victorian fictions actively engage with the Victorian past and raise questions about the relevance of Victorian models – literary, historical, and moral – for contemporary society.[4]

Neo-Victorian fictions also encourage an active engagement with Victorian literature on the part of their readers. This is most obvious in the intertextual relationships neo-Victorian fictions establish with Victorian literature. Almost all neo-Victorian texts incorporate either direct or indirect references to Victorian texts, and thus implicitly encourage readers to identify them. Reviewers of neo-Victorian texts often delight in identifying such intertextual allusions and implicitly suggest that neo-Victorian fictions privilege those readers who can recognize all of the Victorian references. Such an approach reduces neo-Victorian fiction to a 'puzzle' constructed by the author to tease and please the reader. As with Palliser's and Winterson's comments on the genre, in focusing on identifying the 'original' sources for the neo-Victorian texts, this approach implicitly constructs a hierarchy in which Victorian novels are valued over neo-Victorian novels. Moreover, it suggests that the relationship between Victorian and neo-Victorian fiction is one-way, that Victorian fiction is the original form, which neo-Victorian fiction can only nostalgically hark back to. While neo-Victorian authors and readers undoubtedly take pleasure in such intertextual play, the engagement with Victorian literary narratives in neo-Victorian fiction extends beyond merely playful references and allusions.

In the neo-Victorian texts discussed in this book, the concern with Victorian literary narratives is inextricably related to the interest in historical narratives. As we have seen, these neo-Victorian texts centre on questions of historical narrative: both how the Victorians narrated the past, and how the Victorian past is narrated in the present. Given that the contemporary perception of the Victorian era is in large part derived from its fictional narratives, and their television and film adaptations, this concern with historical narrative inevitably extends to include Victorian literary narratives. Moreover, the engagement with Victorian literary narratives remains grounded in a commitment to historical specificity as neo-Victorian texts explore the relationship between Victorian narrative forms and their historical conditions. Neo-Victorian authors remain acutely aware of the historical distance between the Victorians and us. Thus, while neo-Victorian fictions recognize the value of Victorian literature and Victorian literary forms, they do not prioritize them over contemporary narrative forms or nostalgically revive those earlier forms. As a result of its commitment to the historical specificity of both the Victorian and contemporary moment, neo-Victorian fiction moves beyond a passive engagement with Victorian literary forms to an active engagement that involves the adoption and transformation of the Victorian models.

Quoting Victorian texts

The most obvious, and seemingly most passive, mode of engaging with Victorian literature is the actual incorporation of Victorian texts within neo-Victorian fictions. While considerable time and attention has been devoted to identifying intertextual allusions in neo-Victorian fiction, less attention has been given to the processes and purposes of intertextuality in neo-Victorian fictions. Writing specifically about A. S. Byatt's neo-Victorian texts, Hilary M. Schor proposes the idea of 'ghostwriting' to understand the relationship between Victorian and neo-Victorian texts. She suggests that Byatt interprets this in a 'double sense': 'first, that of the "borrowings" ("writing like ...") that seem to approach the postmodern forms of pastiche, and second, a ghostwriting that is speaking with the dead, not so much as writers but as mouldering bodies, decaying forms' (p. 237). This second form of ghostwriting was explored in Chapter 3, which dealt with spiritualism in neo-Victorian fiction. Here, I am more concerned with the first form of ghostwriting; however, Schor conflates two distinct textual practices within this category of ghostwriting: 'writing like ...' and 'borrowings'. Whereas the process of 'writing like ...' involves the imitation of the style of a previous author or literary form, the technique of 'borrowings' refers to the incorporation of another's text into one's own, a process often designated as intertextuality. Although many neo-Victorian fictions adopt both approaches in their engagement with Victorian texts, it is important to maintain a distinction between these two methods of incorporating Victorian literary forms.

Julian Barnes's *Arthur & George* incorporates various Victorian texts into his novel; interestingly, though, those texts are primarily not literary texts but rather newspapers, government reports, and parliamentary proceedings. The incorporation of such factual texts is clearly part of Barnes's commitment to historical specificity in his neo-Victorian novel. In his 'Author's note', Barnes attests to the historical veracity of the Victorian texts incorporated into his novel, claiming that, with the exception of the letters between Jean Leckie and Arthur, *'all letters quoted, whether signed or anonymous, are authentic'* (p. 505). While the factual accounts of the events are taken from real, historical sources, then, the personal texts of the letters between Jean and Arthur are invented by the neo-Victorian author, and so are more properly pseudo-Victorian texts, a category which will be examined more fully later in this Coda. By restricting his imagination to the personal and emotional aspects of the past, Barnes highlights the frequency with which such elements are excluded from the factual accounts of the past.

The inclusion of historical documents can serve to authenticate the fictional world, especially if ascribed to recognizable Victorian figures. Most of the texts Barnes incorporates, however, are either not written by known Victorian figures or, as is the case with the malicious letters written to the Edalji family, anonymous. Yet these texts still work to authenticate the fictional world; since the author of these documents was never identified, Barnes remains true to the historical context of his novel. The strategy of using Victorian texts to authenticate the neo-Victorian world is also adopted by Byatt. In *Possession*, Byatt incorporates texts ascribed to Crabb Robinson, the leading diarist of the nineteenth century, and Swinburne, an eminent Victorian critic. While one of the Crabb Robinson diary entries is verifiable, the other two are clearly imitations written by Byatt since they mention her fictional Victorian poets Ash and LaMotte.[5] In transgressing the boundaries between historical and fictional characters, Byatt initially seems to be rejecting the commitment to historical specificity that I have argued is central to neo-Victorian fiction. Yet Byatt's use of Crabb Robinson is grounded in his historical position as a prominent figure in the Victorian literary scene who frequently held breakfasts for writers and artists. Given that Byatt's fictional Victorian poets are grounded in historical reality, it makes sense that the people they interact with should be taken from the historical world of the Victorian era.

Unlike Barnes's novel, which incorporates non-literary texts, Byatt's 'The Conjugial Angel' incorporates sections from Tennyson's *In Memoriam*. Moreover, where the incorporation of Victorian texts in

Arthur & George and *Possession* was part of the historical context of the novels, 'The Conjugial Angel' establishes a dialogue with Tennyson's poem and, in doing so, transforms it. The process of selection and the context in which the extracts from Tennyson's poem are reproduced distinguishes the *In Memoriam* of Byatt's novella from the canonized version. In this sense, Byatt questions the notion of an 'original' text by highlighting the extent to which our knowledge of *In Memoriam* is derived from partial readings of the text, such as are commonly provided in anthologies. Although Byatt implicitly rejects the privileging of the Victorian original, this does not mean that she prioritizes her own neo-Victorian text over the Victorian text. 'The Conjugial Angel' should not be understood as correcting or improving on Tennyson's poem, but rather as responding to it from within a new context.

One reviewer, Kathryn Hughes, argues that the incorporation of the extracts from *In Memoriam* contributes to the novella's treatment of the relationship between Alfred Tennyson and Arthur Hallam. She states that 'The Conjugial Angel' is 'an attempt to sort out [...] whether Tennyson and his friend Arthur Hallam were actually at it', a process which she says is assisted by Byatt's incorporation of 'the relevant ambiguous stanzas from "In Memoriam"' (p. 49). Hughes's account implicitly prioritizes Byatt's neo-Victorian text, suggesting that it resolves the unanswered issues of Tennyson's poem. Her account, however, depends upon a reductive reading of both *In Memoriam* and 'The Conjugial Angel' which foregrounds the sexual aspects of both texts. Moreover, while Hughes's interpretation is permitted by some of the extracts from *In Memoriam* in the novella, her account does not apply to all the lyrics incorporated into 'The Conjugial Angel'; her interpretation is a selective reconstruction of the incorporated lyrics to coincide with her pre-determined interpretation of both *In Memoriam* and 'The Conjugial Angel'. The incorporation of the 'borrowed' lyrics from Tennyson's poem is more correctly understood as part of the novella's engagement with spiritualism as the lyrics and the novella are concerned with the after-life, both of Hallam and those left behind. The poem's contribution to the spiritualist aspect of the novella is explicitly foregrounded in the observation that 'The spirits often speak to us through that poem' (p. 204). The spirits' use of *In Memoriam* reveals an affinity with Byatt's own process; as we saw in Chapter 3, 'The Conjugial Angel' is explicitly concerned with literature's power to resurrect the voices of the past.

The incorporation of actual Victorian texts within neo-Victorian fictions replicates at a narrative level these texts' engagement with Victorian fiction. The quotation of a text within a different context always transforms the original text and so the intertextual version is never merely a direct copy of the 'original'. Thus, Victorian texts are never simply transposed into the neo-Victorian texts but rather are transformed by their new context. Similarly, neo-Victorian fictions do not merely replicate Victorian narrative modes, but rather transform them.

Rewriting Victorian texts

The transformation of Victorian narratives is most obvious in those novels that respond to a specific Victorian text. In her definition of neo-Victorian fiction, Dana Shiller identified one of the possible strategies of neo-Victorian fiction as the 'imitat[ion] of Victorian literary conventions', which she suggested could be achieved 'either by creating altogether new stories or by reimagining specific Victorian novels from a new angle' (p. 1). Carey's *Jack Maggs* and Byatt's 'The Conjugial Angel' both re-imagine 'classic' Victorian texts, Charles Dickens's *Great Expectations* and Tennyson's *In Memoriam* respectively. Both authors could be said to have a political purpose in responding to these canonical Victorian texts; while Carey rewrites Dickens's novel from the perspective of the post-colonial subject, the convict Magwitch, Byatt's novella provides a space for Emily Jesse to counter the appropriation of her life and grief in her brother Tennyson's poem. Although both texts have an underlying political purpose, their narrative approaches differ greatly. Carey's novel takes the original premise of Dickens's plot but rewrites it to narrate it from Magwitch's perspective. The transformation of the original novel that ensues is most evident in the alteration of the protagonists' names in Carey's text. *Jack Maggs* highlights the absences in Dickens's canonical novel, and opens it up to new subjectivities. In presenting a new perspective on Dickens's novel, Carey implicitly confirms the role of Victorian literature in the formation of 'English' identity, something which clearly has important consequences for the novel's post-colonial author and protagonist.[6] Byatt's novel adopts a different approach in that it provides a narrative alternative to Tennyson's poem *In Memoriam*. As discussed in Chapter 3, Tennyson's poem ventriloquizes the grief of his sister, Emily Jesse, and traps her in the role of grieving widow, thus denying her a life after Arthur Hallam. Byatt's 'The Conjugial Angel' does not so much rewrite *In Memoriam*, as provide the afterlife for Emily Jesse that is denied in Tennyson's poem. The séances in 'The Conjugial Angel' provide an opportunity for Emily to confront the ghost of Hallam and to oppose the appropriation of her desires by the male figures in her life. Whereas Carey transforms the characters from Dickens's novel, then, Byatt incorporates the 'original' historical figures into her novella. Interestingly, both Byatt's and Carey's texts incorporate the authors of the Victorian novels they transform. In *Jack Maggs*, Carey fictionalizes Dickens in the figure of Tobias Oates, while in 'The Conjugial Angel' Byatt incorporates the ghostly presence of Tennyson. In both texts, the presence of these author figures is connected to the engagement with the historical narratives of biography and spiritualism respectively.

James Wilson's *The Dark Clue* similarly responds to an individual Victorian text, but whereas Byatt and Carey reimagined classic Victorian texts, Wilson explicitly positions his novel as a sequel to Wilkie Collins's *The Woman in White*. In writing a sequel to a Victorian novel, Wilson provides an account of the lives of Collins's protagonists after the pages of *The Woman in White* close; his engagement with Collins's Victorian text, therefore, clearly connects to his concern with Victorian biographical narratives. In his introduction to Collins's novel, John Sutherland suggests a connection between Collins's life and his fiction: 'Shortly after the success of *The Woman in White*, and the financial ease it brought, he set up a *ménage à trois* of the kind hinted at in the last pages of the novel' (p. ix). As I suggested in Chapter 1, Wilson's novel takes up this hint and explores the consequences of the unusual living arrangements of Walter, his wife Laura, and her half-sister Marian. Tracing Marian's gradual awareness of her true feelings for Walter, and Walter's sexual deviance which culminates in him raping Marian in her own bed, Wilson clearly takes Collins's characters in directions that would have been denied to the Victorian novelist.

Although the sexual content is more explicit in *The Dark Clue*, in treating fictional characters as if they had an existence beyond the confines of the novel, Wilson adopts a view that seems to have been shared by many contemporary readers of *The Woman in White*. As Sutherland remarks, one such reader 'took the liberty of writing to Wilkie Collins asking the name of the original [of Marian Halcombe], so he could present his proposals' (p. vii). The impulse of writing sequels, or reimaginings, of Victorian novels seems to stem from an assumption that characters in Victorian fiction are, in some way, more 'real' than characters in contemporary, and particularly postmodern, fiction. As we saw in the Introduction, such an assumption positions the literature of the Victorian period as both better and, implicitly, more simplistic than contemporary fiction. While the conventions of realism do in some sense require more realistic, rounded characters than those of much postmodern fiction, the frequency with which Victorian figures, both fictional characters and historical Victorians, are revived in neo-Victorian fictions is perhaps more a result of the extent to which our contemporary perception of the Victorian era is influenced by the stories and images of individual Victorians.

In responding to Collins's *The Woman in White*, Wilson's *The Dark Clue* engages not only with an individual text, but also with an entire subgenre of Victorian fiction. Collins's novel is widely agreed to be the first sensation novel, a genre of fiction which itself became a sensation in the 1860s. Subtitled *A novel of suspense*, however, Wilson's novel suggests a divergence from the conventions of the Victorian 'original'. According to an article in *The Quarterly Review* in 1863, one of the key features of sensation fiction is the story's proximity to the reader, on which, the author claimed, its effectiveness depends. The author, H. L. Mansel, demonstrates this point through an analogy with a mine:

> It is necessary to be near a mine to be blown up by its explosion; and a tale which aims at electrifying the nerves of the reader is never thoroughly effective unless the scene be laid in our own days and among the people we are in the habit of meeting. ('Sensation Novels', pp. 488-9)

In returning to the Victorian era for the setting of his novel, Wilson clearly diverges from the conventions of sensation fiction. This decision can be read as a comment on the discontinuities between the Victorian era and our own time – given the permissive nature of contemporary society, it has become harder to shock people. Wilson, then, is perhaps suggesting that in order to experience the shock necessary for sensation fiction, we need to return to the Victorian context. This explanation nostalgically positions the Victorian era as a simpler time while simultaneously implying that the contemporary era is more liberated, or sophisticated as the case may be, in its attitudes.

Wilson's engagement with sensation fiction, however, is not merely part of a nostalgic desire for the lost stabilities of the Victorian era. Nor is his transgression of the genre conventions solely part of an attempt to 'sex up' the Victorians. Rather, his adoption, and transformation, of the sensation genre is connected to neo-Victorian fiction's concern with historical narratives. The transgression of the boundaries of decorum that sensation fiction represents recalls the opposition between truth and decency that, as we saw in Chapter 1, was a central concern for Victorian biographical narratives. As we saw, these concerns are dramatized in the structure of Wilson's novel, which is narrated through the letters and diaries of the main characters. Using such personal texts, Wilson explores the ethical dimensions of biographical narratives that sought to reveal their subjects through incorporating documentary evidence which exposed their innermost thoughts and feelings. Sensation fiction is similarly interested in exposing the disjunction between the public persona and private desires of individuals. Thus, in transforming the boundaries of sensation fiction, Wilson reveals the extent to which Victorian narratives, both fictional and biographical, were determined by ideas of decency and propriety.

Imitating Victorian realism

Although the examples discussed thus far have revealed several different strategies neo-Victorian authors adopt to engage with Victorian literature, they have all involved responses to specific Victorian texts. While such direct engagement is perhaps more obvious, neo-Victorian fictions also engage with Victorian literature in indirect ways, most frequently through the adoption of realist narrative techniques. Despite its pretensions to naturalism, realism has long been accepted as a set of fictional conventions which came to prominence at a particular point in the history of the novel, namely the Victorian era. Yet the extent to which the realist mode dominates perceptions of the novel genre elides the historical formulation of those conventions in the popular imagination. As I suggested earlier, labelling Victorian novels as 'good reads' removes those conventions from their specific historical context. As part of the commitment to historical specificity, neo-Victorian fictions seek to restore the relationship between literary narratives and historical conditions. Consequently, they do not merely transpose Victorian conventions into the present moment, but rather raise questions about the relevance of such conventions for contemporary narratives.

Moreover, neo-Victorian fiction's engagement with Victorian realism is intimately connected to its concern with historical narratives because the assumptions of realism are shared by historiography. The position of the historian resembles that of the realist narrator: both occupy a point in the future beyond the events they narrate; both strive to remove their personality from the narrative to become, in Elizabeth Deeds Ermarth's term, 'nobody' (p. 65); and both accept the necessity of imposing closure on their account. Harry Shaw implicitly associates realism with history in his assertion that 'the defining mark [...] is that it can be placed in a determinate positive relationship with historicism [...]. It responds to similar problems with similar tactics' (p. 6). While there have been many challenges to the hegemony of realism within the realm of fiction, this experimentation has not been matched in the sphere of historiography, where realism remains the dominant mode of narration. As Hayden White remarks, 'It is almost as if the historians believed that the *sole possible form* of historical narrative was that used in the English novel as it had developed by the late nineteenth century' (pp. 43–4). In adopting realist narrative modes, neo-Victorian fictions similarly establish a 'positive relationship with historicism'. The realist narrative voice allows neo-Victorian fictions to confidently assert the reality of the past they narrate, as in the opening to the Postscript in Byatt's *Possession* which declares 'This is how it was' (p. 508).

The presence of realist techniques is most apparent in those neo-Victorian novels that eschew a twentieth-century frame and adopt a third-person narrator. Although not all Victorian novels adopt this narrative voice, it holds sway in the popular imagination as one of the most distinctive features of Victorian fiction. Not surprisingly, then, neo-Victorian fiction frequently stages its engagement with Victorian literary narratives through the adoption of such a narrative voice. In the popular perception, Victorian novels are distinguished by the adoption of an omniscient narrator, an all-knowing figure in whom the reader can have complete confidence. Unlike the partial and unreliable narratives of much postmodern fiction, then, Victorian novels encourage the reader to accept the narrator's perspective as the truth. The reader's confidence in the narrative is enhanced by the fact that the narrator is a disembodied presence in the novel who is, therefore, assumed to be providing an objective, historical account of events. This description hints at one of the reasons why contemporary novelists might chose to revive the Victorian narrative voice. As I suggested in the Introduction, the popularity of Victorian narrative forms in contemporary culture can be understood as part of a backlash against postmodernism. Such accounts position Victorian literature as more entertaining because more simplistic than the self-reflexive questioning of postmodern fiction. Yet I have argued throughout this book that neo-Victorian fiction cannot be simply reduced to postmodern categories; neither, however, can it be understood as a naively nostalgic reproduction of Victorian literary forms. Rather, neo-Victorian fiction's engagement with Victorian realism is intimately connected to its dual approach to the Victorian past. This engagement, therefore, is staged as a two-step process of adoption and transformation.

Although drawing on the genre of detective fiction, Julian Barnes's *Arthur & George* adopts the convention of the Victorian realist narrator.

Interleaving episodes from Arthur's and George's life, the narrator transgresses the boundaries of time and space, especially in the early episodes before the two protagonists have met.[7] As we saw in Chapter 2, while Barnes adopts the past tense for the early 'Arthur' episodes, the early 'George' episodes are narrated in the present tense. This difference in narrative technique can be accounted for by the differing positions of Arthur and George in the cultural perception of the Victorian era. Since George is a relatively unknown Victorian figure, Barnes has greater license to invent and bring this figure to life.

According to the neo-Victorian author Charles Palliser, Victorian realism depends on an 'implied contract' between the reader and the author: 'This contract assumes that everything to do with both plot and motivation is eventually explained in full by a narrator or author who is completely trustworthy – however much the reader might have been baffled and teased along the way' ('Author's Afterword', pp. 1203, 1204). The narrator of *Arthur & George* appears to breach this implied contract by withholding the identities of the novel's protagonists. As I suggested in Chapter 2, this suppression of information connects the novel to detective fiction since it encourages the reader to play detective and identify the protagonists. While Arthur's identity is easily guessed by the clues provided in the opening sections of the novel, George's identity is more mysterious. It is only when Sergeant Upton requires the young George to officially declare his full name that the character is identified for the reader. Although this will probably not prompt recognition, since George Edalji is a relatively unknown figure from Victorian history, the revelation of his surname provides the reader with the first suggestion that George is Indian. Up until this point, the narrator has artfully concealed any details which would have made this clear.

In teasing the reader in this way, Barnes raises questions about the narrator's reliability. The suppression of such information, however, is not a postmodern game, but rather a consequence of the novel's position as a detective novel and its desire to keep the reader in suspense. While this impulse might appear to position the detective novel in opposition to the realist novel of the Victorian era, there are actually many similarities in narrative technique. As shown in Chapter 2, detective fiction's obsession with knowing the world is closely allied to the realist project's attempt to fully represent the world to the reader. Indeed, the figure of the detective performs a similar function to that of the omniscient narrator as it is the detective who elucidates the connections between seemingly random characters and events to present a coherent and contained world to the reader. Moreover, both detective and realist fiction suggest that the world is ultimately knowable, if only for particularly gifted individuals. In detective fiction, this position is taken up by the detective figure but in realist fiction it is the omniscient narrator who has the superior knowledge and understanding necessary to make the events of the novel comprehensible to the reader.

The realist narrator of *Arthur & George* appears to be just such a gifted individual as he has access not only to the histories and emotions of the protagonists, but also to events for which there are no witnesses. The first 'George & Arthur' episode does not, as might be expected, tell of the initial meeting between George and Arthur, but rather narrates the first incident of horse-maiming which, through a long sequence of events, eventually brings the protagonists together. This event, we are told, takes place when '[h]umans were sleeping and the birds had not yet woken' (p. 101). The narrator then proceeds to narrate how an individual man approaches, soothes, and eventually kills the colliery pony. Despite seemingly occupying a position of omniscience, the narrator never identifies the figure in the dark. In part, this derives from the novel's position as a detective fiction since detective fiction involves the reader in the process of detection and so rarely reveals the identity of the criminal before the closing pages. But it is more a result of the novel's commitment to historical specificity since the crime was never solved, and the identity of the 'Great Wyrley ripper' was never ascertained.

Barnes's decision to adopt the realist narrator of Victorian fiction has implications for the novel's exploration of the distinction between belief and knowledge. This opposition is most forcefully expressed by Arthur who, at the end of his initial meeting with George, declares, 'No, I do not think you are innocent. No, I do not believe you are innocent. I *know* you are innocent' (p. 306). Although there is some empirical evidence, specifically George's visual impairment, Arthur's confident assertion seems to derive as much from having met George 'in person' (p. 306). Barnes, then, seems to be suggesting that it is possible to know and understand the past through an emotional response to the individuals in the past, as long as that approach is also grounded in the real, historical circumstances of the past. This confidence in the possibility of accessing the past is replicated at a narrative level. Unlike much postmodern historical fiction, which questions the possibility of accessing the past, neo-Victorian fiction suggests that it is possible to narrate the past. Although neo-Victorian fictions explore various ways of narrating the past, and indeed revive the Victorian era through a wide array of narrative strategies, they share both a confident belief in the possibility of accessing the past and the sense of a responsibility to revive the past in the present. Whereas much postmodern historical fiction plays with and fictionalizes the past it revives, the resurrection of the past in neo-Victorian fiction remains grounded in the historical specificity of the Victorian era. By adopting a realist narrative voice, neo-Victorian fictions ground their imaginative reconstruction of the Victorian past in the historically specific forms of Victorian fiction. Neo-Victorian fiction, then, balances an imaginative and emotional response to the past with a commitment to the historical referent. Similarly, neo-Victorian fiction balances a concern with the fictional narratives of the Victorians with an engagement with Victorian historical narratives. Indeed, these two elements are interrelated as neo-Victorian fiction's engagement with Victorian realism draws out the connection between this literary form and the historical conditions of the Victorian era.

Byatt's 'The Conjugial Angel' similarly imitates Victorian literary forms in its adoption of a realist narrator. As I suggested in Chapter 3, the position of the narrator in this novella connects to Byatt's exploration of the relationship between scepticism and belief towards spiritualism in the nineteenth century. The narrator of 'The Conjugial Angel' appears to lack the privileged access to events and characters which would permit a definitive conclusion on the status of the spiritual events in the novella. The opening description of the medium figures Lilias and Sophy plants doubts in the reader's mind, doubts which are never unequivocally confirmed or denied. The narrator, then, appears to lack the objective omniscience considered characteristic of the Victorian realist narrator. The omniscient narrator of Victorian realist fiction is usually figured as a superhuman figure, transcending the boundaries of time and space and thus occupying a privileged position above and beyond human concerns. Taking a different approach, Ermarth claims that the Victorian realist narrator is 'nobody', neither individual nor corporeal, but rather 'a collective result, a specifier of consensus' (pp. 65–6). Yet the narrator of Victorian realist fiction often has a much more corporeal presence than Ermarth's account allows. Byatt herself seems to argue against such a disembodiment of the realist narrator; in her Introduction to *Passions of the Mind*, which discusses the differences between the narrators of Victorian and 'postmodern' fiction and the corresponding levels of freedom they permit in the reader, Byatt refers to Eliot's 'measured exposition and solidly sensible embodiment' (p. xvi). Moreover, Byatt incorporates the real, if ghostly, presence of Tennyson into the novella.[8] The narrator's scepticism concerning Lilias's and Sophie's spiritualist powers, therefore, does not indicate a failure or criticism of realism. Rather, the narrator's oscillation between scepticism and belief reflects the conflicting responses towards spiritual-ism in the nineteenth century. Consequently, Byatt's novella reminds the reader that the narrative voice of Victorian realist fiction is not a disembodied voice which transcends time and space, but rather remains grounded in the historical conditions within which it emerged.

As we saw in Chapter 1, Janice Galloway's adoption of the omnis-cient realist narrator in *Clara* is part of neo-Victorian fiction's commit-ment to reviving the Victorian past; it provides a way of bringing the past to life in the present. *Clara* draws on the Victorian conventions of the *Bildungsroman*, yet rather than adopting the autobiographical first-person that is favoured in such Victorian examples of the genre as *Great Expectations* and *Jane Eyre*, Galloway's novel adopts a third-person narrator. In adopting such a narrative voice, Galloway promises direct access to Clara's thoughts and feelings, elements that are omitted in the textual accounts of the past. As I argued in Chapter 1, Galloway's narra-tive technique of interleaving textual accounts with direct narration is part of the novel's exploration of biographical narratives; it highlights the extent to which emotional responses to the past are overlooked in textual accounts.

The conflict between Clara's account of events and the novel's narrative account centres on the role of memory in constructing nar-ratives of the past. For instance, Clara's recollection of a farewell con-cert reveals that her own account of her life is prone to the fallacies of memory; the narrator comments: 'Had [Joachim] really played for them? and on the same violin he would use all his life? Her diary says so, but Clara can't recall' (p. 280). Such questioning of the relation-ship between the memory and reality of the past is common among postmodern historical fictions. Yet as a neo-Victorian novel, *Clara*, like *Arthur & George*, remains confident about the possibility of accessing the reality of the past. This confidence is conveyed to the reader through the realist narrator. While Clara's memory seems untrustworthy, the omniscient narrator's account confirms that Joachim had indeed 'played' at the farewell concert (p. 280). The omniscient narrator, then, appears to have privileged access to the past which is also extended to the readers of neo-Victorian fiction.

Transforming Victorian realism

Although they adopt Victorian literary conventions, neo-Victorian authors remain aware of their own position within contemporary society which prevents a naive collapsing of the distance between the

Victorians and us. Interestingly, neo-Victorian fiction's commitment to the specificity of the Victorian referent can actually serve to highlight the distance between the moment in which the novel takes place and the moment in which it is read. Neo-Victorian fictions are frequently concerned to establish a very precise historical location, rather than presenting a stereotypical and generalized image of the Victorian era. For instance, the opening scene of Carey's *Jack Maggs* identifies the precise historical location for the reader, with the narrator providing not only the year but also the day and time of Maggs's arrival in London. Set in April 1837, the novel takes place at the very cusp of the Victorian era, in the months before Queen Victoria ascended to the throne. It is not merely that the historical location is precisely identified for the reader, however; the narrator also highlights the distance between the moment of narration and the moment of reading. Opening with Maggs's arrival in London, the narrator notes how much London has changed since Maggs departed for the colonies. Maggs's outsider status connects to the position of the contemporary reader and enables Carey to describe the nineteenth century and provide a sense of its newness for both Maggs and the reader. In this way, the narrator paints a vivid image of the London in which the novel is set, the London of 1837. Such attention to historical detail would have been unnecessary for a Victorian reader since the London in the pages of the novel would have been recognizable to them from their own experience. Thus, while historical details can authenticate the Victorian world created in neo-Victorian fictions, they can also highlight the distance between the Victorian past and contemporary present. Interestingly, then, the very commitment to the historical specificity of the Victorian era in neo-Victorian fiction highlights their position as neo-Victorian novels and prevents a passive replication of Victorian literary forms.

Neo-Victorian fictions also draw attention to the contemporary moment of reading through the incorporation of twentieth-century attitudes. In the case of Barnes's *Arthur & George*, this contemporary perspective only comes through occasionally, but it is there. For instance, the opening discussion of George's lack of a first memory suggests that the explanation for this lack is 'a question for a branch of psychological science which has not yet been devised' (p. 4). Contemporary readers of *Arthur & George* clearly understand this as a reference to the field of psychoanalysis which emerged with Freud in the early part of the twentieth century. In making this observation Barnes draws the reader's attention to the contemporary perspective from which the novel is written and read. Yet in refusing to provide a Freudian account for this lack he avoids suggesting that the contemporary moment provides a better way to understand the Victorian past. Rather, Barnes remains faithful to the historical context of the novel and suggests that the Victorian era needs to be understood within its own historical moment.

In Byatt's 'The Conjugial Angel', the narrative voice is explicitly connected to its historical location. The use of long, complicated sentences, peppered with subordinate clauses, is perhaps the most overt way in which Byatt emulates the style of nineteenth-century novelists, or rather what, in the popular imagination, has come to be thought of as the style of nineteenth-century novelists. Despite adopting a nineteenth-century narrative perspective and style, 'The Conjugial Angel' incorporates elements which seem more akin to modern sensibilities. For instance, the description of Emily Jesse's dog, Pug, displays a frankness concerning bodily functions that would not have been considered decent in Victorian fiction: 'Pug [...] tended to lie snoozing on the couch, occasionally even snoring, or emitting other wet, explosive animal noises at the most sensitive moments' (p. 172). Yet, while the subject matter may have been deemed inappropriate for a Victorian novel, Byatt adopts overly euphemistic terms to express it. The description of Pug's flatulence, then, is given in the language of Victorian middle-class respectability rather than adopting the more direct tone of contemporary fiction.[9]

Galloway's *Clara*, Carey's *Jack Maggs*, and Wilson's *The Dark Clue* similarly incorporate narrative descriptions of privates acts and desires that would have been elided in Victorian fictional accounts. As discussed in Chapter 1, the incorporation of such details is part of these novels' exploration of the tension between truth and decency in Victorian biographical narratives. Yet they can also be seen as part of the eroticization of the Victorians that occurs in many contemporary depictions of the era. Such instances, then, hold shock value for the reader. In transgressing the boundaries of what is considered acceptable in Victorian fiction, these neo-Victorian fictions implicitly mock the nostalgic view of the Victorian era as a simpler and more honest way of life. By focusing on sexually deviant activities, Wilson and Carey reveal the underside of nineteenth-century society and thus undermine the nostalgic ideal of the Victorian era as a time of great values and civic virtue, an ideal that as we saw in the Introduction underpinned Thatcher's political appropriation of 'Victorian Values' in the early 1980s. The incorporation of such elements, however, is also part of the dual approach of neo-Victorian fiction. Aware of the historical specificity of both the Victorian era in which it is set and the contemporary moment in which it is written, neo-Victorian fiction requires a transformation of Victorian narrative conventions and approaches.

One of the ways in which neo-Victorian fictions transform Victorian narrative approaches is to incorporate contemporary political perspectives. This is perhaps most apparent in Carey's *Jack Maggs* which opens up the gaps and silences of Dickens's *Great Expectations* to present a post-colonial perspective on the Victorian classic. Carey alters many aspects of the Victorian 'original' and while many of the altered details might seem insignificant they actually contribute to the post-colonial perspective Carey brings to bear on Dickens's classic novel. In *Great Expectations*, Pip assists the convict Magwitch in secret and when he later comes into a fortune he is unaware of the true identity of his benefactor. By contrast, in Carey's novel Phipps shows kindness to Maggs in full view of the police constables who are taking him into custody and is aware that Maggs is his benefactor, even to the point of corresponding with him. In revising this plot point, Carey suggests that Pip always knew who his benefactor was in *Great Expectations* but that he chose not to believe it because the English seek to avoid admitting their dependence on the colonies. As a neo-Victorian novel, then, *Jack Maggs* does not naively adopt, but rather transforms its Victorian models.

As I have said, the transformation of Victorian narrative modes is part of the dual approach of neo-Victorian fiction, part of its recognition of the historical distance between the Victorian past in which it is set and the contemporary moment in which it is written. The positioning of Victorian novels as classics and the frequency with which such texts are reproduced on television and film screens suggests that such novels transcend social and historical conditions. By incorporating elements that would not have been included in Victorian literature, these neo-Victorian novels draw attention to the ways in which Victorian literary forms were affected by their historical context. While realist narratives purport to provide a complete, naturalistic image of the real world, that image is governed by Victorian ideas of what was considered decent and appropriate for fictional narratives to discuss. Given that realism is frequently removed from its historical context and lauded as the preferred novelistic mode, this restoration of the historical context is particularly important. In revealing realism's historical limits, however, neo-Victorian fictions do not imply that contemporary narrative modes have improved upon or surpassed those models. They do not simply reject Victorian novels but rather acknowledge the continuities between Victorian and contemporary narrative forms and explore creative possibilities for combining them.

Writing pseudo-Victorian texts

The creative possibilities of neo-Victorian fiction are perhaps most apparent in those novels that create their own Victorian texts. This process is akin to the notion of ghost-writing proposed by Schor, yet as we saw, her category conflated the approaches of 'borrowing' and 'writing like ...'. In order to distinguish between these two approaches, then, I adopt the term pseudo-Victorian to refer to those texts that are written by a neo-Victorian author and, for the most part, ascribed to fictional Victorians. In adopting the term pseudo-Victorian, I do not mean to imply a negative judgement of the texts; rather, I use this term because neo-Victorian fiction's commitment to historical specificity necessitates a distinction between actual Victorian texts, which as we have seen are often incorporated into neo-Victorian fiction, and those texts which are created by the neo-Victorian authors themselves. Since these texts are ascribed to the Victorian characters in the novel, they clearly aim at a certain level of authenticity; they seek to pass as Victorian texts. Such pseudo-Victorian texts, then, initially appear to collapse the distance between the Victorians and us, and thus undermine the commitment to historical specificity that I argue is fundamental to neo-Victorian fiction. Yet, these pseudo-Victorian texts remain grounded in the historical reality of the Victorian era: they are based on Victorian models, as indeed are the Victorian characters who supposedly author them.

It is this grounding in historical reality that prevents these texts from being dismissed as part of the postmodern form of pastiche.[10] According to Jameson, postmodern pastiche is 'the imitation of a peculiar or unique, idiosyncratic style, the wearing of a linguistic mask, speech in a dead language' (p. 17). He claims that pastiche is 'blank parody' since it operates 'without any of parody's ulterior motives, amputated of the satiric impulse, devoid of laughter and of any conviction that alongside the abnormal tongue you have momentarily borrowed, some healthy linguistic normality still exists' (p. 17). For Jameson, then, pastiche is parody dislocated from any political or satirical intent, leaving only a 'linguistic mask' that is divorced from its historical referent. In light of neo-Victorian fiction's commitment to the historical referent of the Victorian era, the concept of pastiche is clearly inadequate for understanding the approach of its authors writing *as* Victorians. While Jameson claims that postmodern pastiche replicates the styles of the past, the imitation of Victorian narrative modes in neo-Victorian fiction is always grounded in a commitment to the historical reality of the

Victorian past. Indeed, in adopting pastiche as a literary technique, neo-Victorian authors are in fact reviving a Victorian literary form.[11]

In place of the categories of pastiche or parody, I understand this process as a form of ventriloquism. Ventriloquism involves both 'speaking like' and 'speaking as' a Victorian; it can take the form of both impersonating a voice and 'throwing' your voice so it appears to come from somewhere else. As Williamson notes, 'Ventriloquism is certainly a means of resurrecting and establishing continuity with the Victorian past as a living, breathing presence, and not as an obstinately moribund form' (pp. 120–1). Thus, while 'speaking like' a Victorian could result in a surface imitation of Victorian narrative forms, 'speaking as' a Victorian requires an understanding of the historical conditions to which those forms are responding.[12]

Most of the neo-Victorian novels discussed in this book adopt the process of ventriloquism and incorporate pseudo-Victorian texts into their narratives. As we have seen, Barnes creates the letters between Jean and Arthur for his novel *Arthur & George* and *Jack Maggs* incorporates letters written by Maggs as well as an excerpt from the novel Tobias Oates is writing. Other novels, such as *Affinity* and *The Dark Clue*, are wholly narrated through such pseudo-Victorian texts as the letters and diaries of the principal characters. This process, however, is most obvious in novels which centre around the textual remains of the nineteenth century, such as *Possession* and *Ever After*. In both of these novels, the process of ventriloquism involves creating fictional Victorians for the pseudo-Victorian texts incorporated into the narrative. While the nineteenth-century protagonists of these novels are fictional creations, they are clearly based on historical models. In the case of *Possession*, reviewers and critics have had fun identifying the various historical models for the nineteenth-century poets Ash and LaMotte. Most reviewers concur that LaMotte is based on Christina Rossetti and Emily Dickinson[13], although Kelly proposes a more composite portrait including elements of Elizabeth Barrett Browning, George Eliot and the Brontë sisters (p. 80). Ash is most frequently thought to be based on Robert Browning and Alfred Lord Tennyson.[14] Although not based on a direct model, the spiritual crisis of *Ever After's* Matthew Pearce is reminiscent of the experiences of many Victorian figures. Specifically, his generational disputes with his clergyman father-in-law recall Edmund Gosse's experiences, as documented in *Father and Son* (1907). Interestingly, A. S. Byatt's novella 'Morpho Eugenia,' which was published in the same year as Swift's novel, sets up a similar conflict between the naturalist William Adamson and his clergyman father-in-law Harald Alabaster.[15]

Despite the frequency with which neo-Victorian novels ventriloquize Victorian texts, Byatt's *Possession* remains the most famous example, both because of the range of pseudo-Victorian texts that are incorporated and the publication history surrounding the novel. As I explained in *The Fiction of A. S. Byatt* (2008), 'Byatt struggled to find a publisher in America until Susan Kamil of Turtle Bay offered to publish [*Possession*], providing the author made significant changes, mostly involving cutting the nineteenth-century letters and poems.' Byatt refused, however, and 'the book remained unpublished in America until it had proved its worth with its British sales' (p. 3). Moreover, Byatt's *Possession* is distinctive for another reason: the pseudo-Victorian texts that she creates do not imitate the biographical or novelistic genres of the Victorian era, but rather Victorian poetry. Despite the importance of Victorian poets and poetry in their own day, the Victorian era has come to be thought of as the age of the novel. Byatt's decision to write pseudo-Victorian poetry, therefore, is particularly interesting. In imitating Victorian poetry Byatt could be seen as challenging the narrow perception that the literary accomplishments of the Victorian era are confined to the novel genre. Paradoxically, though, by incorporating this pseudo-Victorian poetry into a neo-Victorian novel, Byatt confirms the dominance of the novel in contemporary perceptions of Victorian literature.

In spite of this, my discussion is going to focus on Byatt's ventriloquism of Victorian poetry through an analysis of the pseudo-Victorian texts ascribed to Ash. While numerous critics have identified the resemblance between Browning and Ash few have gone so far as to identify the sources of Ash's poems in Browning's own work. Ash's use of the dramatic monologue can be seen as a ventriloquism of the form perfected by Browning, and, indeed, the majority of Ash's poems have intertextual links to Browning's poems. For instance, Ash's naturalist poem 'Swammerdam' echoes Browning's 'An Epistle Containing the Strange Medical Experience of Karshish, the Arab Physician' since the protagonists share an interest in collecting specimens of the natural world. Moreover, 'Karshish' could also be a source for Ash's 'Lazarus' as Karshish hears and assesses the story of Lazarus. The intertextual connections between Browning's poetry and Ash's are highlighted by the inclusion of an extract from Browning's 'Mr Sludge, the Medium' as an epigraph to *Possession*.[16]

Byatt's ventriloquism of Browning's poetry, however, is more than just an intertextual game; it is connected to the novel's exploration of Victorian subjects, particularly its concern with spiritualism, as well as the wider dual approach of neo-Victorian fiction. Byatt's commitment to the historical specificity of the Victorian era positions Browning's poetry within its original historical context, yet her awareness of the distance between the Victorian and contemporary moments requires a transformation of his poetic forms.[17] This transformation is most important in Ash's poem 'Mummy Possest', which ventriloquizes Browning's 'Mr Sludge, the Medium'.[18] Browning's poem constructs an opposition between the speaker, a medium, and a sceptical observer who has caught the medium practising a deception. Ash's poem also adopts a medium as the speaker and, although an apprentice rather than an observer, the addressee adopts a similar stance towards the medium's deceptions as that of Browning's addressee. The two medium figures, furthermore, adopt a similar justification for their 'arts'. Mr. Sludge aligns his trickery with art claiming it is 'Really mere novel writing of a sort, / Acting, or improvising, make-believe, / Surely not downright cheating' (l.427–9). The speaker of 'Mummy Possest' similarly justifies her use of tricks saying 'You call these spirit *mises en scène* a lie. / I call it artfulness, or simply Art' (pp. 408–9; l.151–2), which is then extended to the claim that 'A Tale, a Story, that may hide a Truth' (pp. 409; l.153). Again this echoes Mr Sludge's declaration that 'I'm ready to believe my very self – / that every cheat's inspired, and every lie / Quick with a germ of truth' (l.1323–5).

Ash's poem diverges from its model, however, in the reversal of the gender-coding of Browning's poem. The medium figure in 'Mr Sludge' is clearly a male, and is thought to be based on the historical figure D. D. Home who was renowned as a medium in both America and Britain during the mid- to late-nineteenth century. Browning's poem reflects the real importance of Home in the spiritualist movement but it also reveals the implicit gender-coding of Victorian Britain which confined women to the private and domestic sphere. Contrary to this, recent feminist scholarship has highlighted the key role that women played in nineteenth-century spiritualism. In particular Alex Owen's book *The Darkened Room* argues that the Victorian conception of women as weak and passive became partially empowering within the realm of spiritualism. Byatt's response to Browning's poem takes such contemporary scholarship into account in its depiction of a female medium. In reversing the gender-coding of Browning's text, Byatt highlights the historical situation of Victorian spiritualism and the prominent role that, as we saw in Chapter 3, women often played. Yet Byatt also highlights her own position as a contemporary author aware of feminist scholarship and approaches to the Victorian past. As I argue elsewhere, *Possession* further transforms its Victorian models in its expansion of the possibilities available for female characters: whereas LaMotte's historical position prevents her from reconciling the conflicting demands of art and motherhood, Maud's position at the end of the novel suggests that a such a reconciliation is possible in the present.[19] As I have reiterated throughout this Coda, however, this does not imply a privileging of the twentieth century over the Victorian era; rather, it is a recognition that Victorian and neo-Victorian narrative forms respond to different historical circumstances.

It is this recognition of the historical distance between the Victorians and us that prevents neo-Victorian authors from naively replicating Victorian literary forms. Rather than an outright rejection, however, neo-Victorian authors value Victorian forms and seek to establish connections between the Victorian past and the contemporary moment, while also recognizing the discontinuities between the present and the past. Regardless of the technique, then, the incorporation of Victorian literary models into neo-Victorian fiction always involves a two-step process of adoption and transformation. Yet neo-Victorian fictions do not privilege one historical time-frame over another; rather they allow both to co-exist within their own historically specific context. Wendy Lesser's review of *Arthur & George* concludes that in Barnes's novel '[i]t is as if two realities coexist at once [... yet] [n]either reality trumps the other, and neither obliterates the other'. As we saw in Chapter 4, although Byatt's *Possession* is often judged to prioritize the Victorian past over the present, the dual plot of the novel actually reveals the importance of establishing an active engagement with the past which, in this case, acknowledges the interaction between reading and writing.

The co-existence of two realities, or two time periods, is a consequence of these novels' position as historical fictions. Throughout this book, I have sought to re-establish neo-Victorian fiction's relationship to historical fiction and thus understand its dual approach to the past. Yet, I have also argued that neo-Victorian fiction's commitment to the historical specificity of the Victorian era determines all aspects of the genre, and particularly its position as historical fiction. Neo-Victorian fictions explore the possibility of narrating the past through an examination of various Victorian forms of historical narratives. For instance, as we saw in Chapter 1, the Victorian forms of *Bildungsroman* and 'Life and Letters' biography shape the presentation of Victorian individuals in neo-Victorian biographical novels. The connections to Victorian literary narratives that have been traced here have further revealed neo-Victorian fiction's concern with historical narratives. Neo-Victorian fictions explicitly understand those literary forms within their historically specific context. Moreover, since the Victorian form of realism has remained the dominant mode of narration for historiography, in engaging with realist conventions, neo-Victorian fictions implicitly question the way in which history is narrated. Neo-Victorian fiction, then, not only provides a narrative account of the Victorian era but also explores the ways in which the Victorians have been narrated in the present.

In his essay for *Neo-Victorian Studies*, Mark Llewellyn suggests that neo-Victorian fiction's engagement with Victorian literature moves beyond passively imitating or echoing previous Victorian texts: 'This is not contemporary literature as a substitute for the nineteenth century but as a mediator into the experience of reading the "real" thing; after all, neo-Victorian texts are, in the main, processes of writing that act out the results of reading the Victorians and their literary productions' (2008, p. 168). He further suggests that the function of neo-Victorian fiction lies in its ability to 'help us think through the ways in which we teach, research and publish on the Victorians themselves' (2008, p. 165). Although neo-Victorian fiction does open up new ways into the Victorian past and its literature, it is also undeniably a response to its own historical moment.

My approach in this book has sought to respect and mimic the dual approach of neo-Victorian fiction. In drawing out the connections between the fictional texts and specific Victorian forms of historical narrative, I have positioned neo-Victorian fiction within its Victorian context. Yet I have also understood neo-Victorian fiction as emerging out of the cultural situation of the twentieth and twenty-first centuries, examining its engagement with both the wider contemporary fascination with the Victorians and the role of history in contemporary culture. Consequently, my analysis has not valued one historical context over another; rather, I have sought to understand how neo-Victorian fiction responds to the Victorian past and its role in the present by adopting and transforming its historical and literary narratives. In an interview with Jonathan Noakes, A. S. Byatt captured neo-Victorian fiction's paradoxical position in relation to the present and the past: 'I believe that both *Possession* and *Angels and Insects* are modern novels, written by a modern novelist, who is *not* trying to recreate the atmosphere of a Victorian novel, but only to hear the rhythms of one' (p. 28). Throughout this book, I have attempted to understand neo-Victorian fiction as a contemporary genre while also exploring the Victorian rhythms that underlie it.

Notes

Introduction: Writing the Victorians

1. As Sarah Waters pointed out in an interview with Abigail Dennis, however, the Victorians have not been continuously popular since the mid-twentieth century. Talking specifically about attitudes towards Victorian houses in the 1970s, Waters says 'it was *so* unfashionable' (p. 47). For a fuller account of the changing position of the Victorians in the twentieth century, see the introductions to J. B. Bullen's *Writing and Victorianism* (1997), Miles Taylor and Michael Wolff's *The Victorians Since 1901: Histories, Representations and Revisions* (2004), and Simon Joyce's *The Victorians in the Rearview Mirror* (2007).
2. Andrea Kirchknopf addresses this issue, writing that 'the newness of a movement that has been in vogue for almost 50 years [...] deserves further periodisation, however useful it proves to call it (still) new' (p. 63). Cheryl A. Wilson's essay '(Neo-)Victorian Fatigue: Getting Tired of the Victorians in Conrad's *The Secret Agent*' persuasively argues for Conrad's Modernist text to be understood as a neo-Victorian novel.
3. Information from http://www.themanbookerprize.com/.
4. Kohlke points out that the cover images of previous critical studies of neo-Victorian fiction often omit the modern or contemporary subject (p. 13).
5. A number of recent critical texts adopt this term in their titles: see Arias (2008); Dennis (2008) Gamble (2009); Llewellyn (2009); Voigts-Virchow (2009); Arias and Pulham (2010) and Hadley (forthcoming).
6. Although this book focuses on neo-Victorian fiction, the literary revival of the Victorians has also spread into poetry, in Margaret Atwood's *The Journals of Susanna Moodie* (1970) and Anthony Thwaite's *Victorian Voices* (1980), and drama, in Caryl Churchill's *Cloud Nine* (1979) and Tom Stoppard's *Arcadia* (1993).
7. This latter approach is particularly noticeable in the number of chapters on neo-Victorian fiction which appear at the end of texts on Victorian fiction. See Kate Flint, 'Plotting the Victorians: Narrative, Post-Modernism, and Contemporary Fiction' (1997); Robin Gilmour, 'Using the Victorians: the Victorian Age in Contemporary Fiction' (2000); and Anne Humphreys, 'The Afterlife of the Victorian Novel: Novels about Novels' (2002).
8. The University of Exeter's 2007 conference 'Neo-Victorianism: The Politics and Aesthetics of Appropriation', the subsequent double special issue of *LIT: Literature Interpretation Theory* (Vol. 20, 1&2), and the establishment of the online journal *Neo-Victorian Studies* in 2008 are part of this new critical approach towards neo-Victorian fiction.
9. Llewellyn notes that neo-Victorian fiction 'does present a very distinct case in the broader genre of historical fiction', pointing out that it is the only subgenre of historical fiction to be given the prefix 'neo-' (2009, p. 42).

10. There have also been several neo-Victorian texts that have depicted cross-dressing heroines, such as Sarah Waters's *Tipping the Velvet* and Patricia Duncker's *James Miranda Barry* (1999). For a discussion of cross-dressing in neo-Victorian fiction, see Sarah Gamble, '"You cannot impersonate what you are": Questions of Authenticity in the Neo-Victorian Novel' (2009).

11. Caryl Churchill's *Cloud Nine* explicitly dramatizes this idea that the Victorians are our grandparents. Although the play's two acts are set in the nineteenth and twentieth centuries respectively, many of the characters from the first act reappear in the second, revealing the connections and disconnections between the Victorian era and the late 1970s.

12. While Bullen accepts that the Victorians no longer occupy the position of oedipal parents, his account suggests that the Victorians occupy a closer family relationship to us than grandparents: 'Paradoxically, as the ageing Victorian grandparents moved yet another generation away, they began once again to change their family likeness. Within the last 15 years [...] the Victorians began to look more like our elder brothers and sisters than our great-grandparents' (p. 3).

13. Arias and Pulham similarly claim that '[t]he spectral presence of the Victorian past is all around us: it exists in the municipal buildings of our major cities, it is visible in our education system, it informs the legacy of immigration, it underpins cultural tourism, it is ever-present in popular culture in fashion, film and television adaptations, and is evident in the "Classics" section of every bookshop in the country where major novels by Dickens, the Brontës, George Eliot, and Thomas Hardy are always to be found' (p. xi).

14. See Green-Lewis (1996) p. 45.

15. In her earlier book *Framing the Victorians* (1996), Green-Lewis acknowledged that 'the canon [of Victorian images] we affirm [...] is our creation, shaped by the desire to preserve images that correspond to our own versions of what we think we have lost' (p. 16).

16. As Stefan Collini observes, 'in so far as they bear any relation to the actualities of Victorian attitudes, [Thatcher's "Victorian values"] call up those attitudes that were given political expression by the Liberal rather than the Tory Party' (p. 107). On the disjunction between Thatcher's and Victorian attitudes towards the welfare state, see also Joyce (p. 14).

17. For a discussion of the heritage industry in Britain in the 1980s, see Hewison (1987) and Wright (1985).

18. In the introduction to their collection *Victorian Afterlife*, John Kucich and Dianne F. Sadoff incorporate discussions of Austen adaptations into their examination of neo-Victorian culture. Similarly, Joyce's chapter on heritage cinema discusses films based on Regency and *fin de siècle* texts. Indeed, this conflation of the 'long nineteenth century' with the Victorian is evident throughout Joyce's book, which features more references to Forster and his works than to Dickens. One of the most interesting examples of this elision of historical boundaries is the recent Hollywood version of *Pride & Prejudice* (2005), which seems closer to an adaptation of Emily Brontë's early Victorian novel *Wuthering Heights* (1847) than Jane Austen's Regency novel *Pride and Prejudice* (1813).

19. This association is yet another example of the Victorians being taken out of their historical context. As Cora Kaplan notes, in the 'early years of the

swinging sixties', the term *Victorian* was applied to 'all repressive attitudes towards sex, whatever their actual national or historic origins' (p. 85).

20. Nisaa (Scotland) commenting on episode 2 and Melloyd (Uxbridge) commenting on episode 3. http://www.bbc.co.uk/drama/northandsouth/.

21. Claire Graham (Glasgow) on Episode 1. http://www.bbc.co.uk/drama/janeeyre/yourreviews_episode1.shtml.

22. As Bullen notes, Victorian fiction was not always so highly valued: 'as late as 1948 F. R. Leavis omitted most Victorian novelists from his authoritative "great tradition"' (p. 2).

23. Voigts-Virchow agrees that 'Many neo-Victorian novelists revert to the Victorian age as the glory day of the novel and of reading' (p. 113). Referring specifically to the idea that Victorian novels provide neat endings, however, Llewellyn reminds us of the distinction between what Victorian novels actually do and the popular (mis)perception of them (2009, p. 32).

24. This approach resembles the desire to render the Victorians both strange and familiar, and indeed Llewellyn seems to recognize this paradox in his assessment of the appeal of neo-Victorian fictions: 'the aesthetic decision to read and engage with a neo-Victorian novel is often prompted by a desire to have Victorian length, plot, and character but without the "difficulties" of Victorian language and circumlocution concerning issues of the body and sexuality' (2009, p. 33).

25. In her review of the book for *New Statesman*, Kathryn Hughes criticizes Sweet's approach of 'grab[bing] examples of apparently un-Victorian Victorians without worrying too much about detail or context' which, she claims, 'leads him to make some pretty strange (and sometimes completely wrong) assertions' (2001, pp. 51–2).

26. As Kaplan notes, the series 'endlessly praise[s] [the] invention and enterprise' of the Victorian era (p. 6). Although the BBC have also done such series as *What the Romans Did for Us*, the over-arching narrative there is one of discontinuity rather than continuity.

27. Waters made a similar point in a panel discussion at the Edinburgh International Book Festival in 2002, saying '[i]t is the mix of the familiar and the utterly strange that draws me to the nineteenth century'.

28. See the discussion of endings in Chapter 2.

29. Kirchknopf similarly suggests that while '[t]erms like *historical novel* or *historiographic metafiction* prove necessary in a generic sense, [...] they do not specify the age that is being refashioned' (p. 66).

30. See National Curriculum History Working Group, *Final Report* (1990).

31. One of the Core Study units for Key Stage 3 reflects these concerns in its very title: 'Expansion, trade and industry: Britain 1750 to 1900' (History Working Group, p. 46).

32. In comments on my conference paper 'The History Debate: Thatcher and The Victorians', Paul Young pointed out that the call for a return to traditional history 'rehearses uncritically' the position expounded by Mr Gradgrind.

33. As we saw earlier, Margaret Thatcher was herself guilty of this approach in her elevation of 'Victorian values' to timeless values.

34. Barry Unsworth's *Losing Nelson* (1999) is an example of a postmodern novel that engages with the forms and practices of biography.

35. On the historian as detective see Ray B. Browne and Lawrence A. Kreiser Jr., (eds), *The Detective as Historian: History and Art in Historical Crime Fiction* (2002).
36. On the medium as a figure for the historical novelist, see Diana Wallace's *The Woman's Historical Novel: British Women Writers, 1900–2000* (2005), especially chapter 9.

1   Narrating the Victorians

1. See Matthew Sweet, 'Introduction', *Inventing the Victorians* (2001).
2. See 'Churchill voted greatest Briton'.
3. Information on the James Tait Black Memorial Prize is taken from http://www.englit.ed.ac.uk/jtbinf.htm.
4. Rodrick, 'Empathetic Reading Experiences of Nineteenth-Century Novels'. Llewellyn argues that there is a 'critical return to the sphere of the affective' in both neo-Victorian fiction and Victorian studies (2008, p. 182). Rebecca Onion's article 'Reclaiming the Machine: An Introductory Look at Steampunk in Everyday Practice' suggests that steampunk is similarly fuelled by the affective appeal of the Victorian era.
5. This impulse to revive characters from Victorian fiction can be traced back to Jean Rhys's *Wide Sargasso Sea* (1966), which provided the 'back story' for the Bertha Mason character in Charlotte Brontë's *Jane Eyre* (1847).
6. Simon Joyce points out that while *Great Expectations* is clearly an important intertext, Maggs's 'story begins [...] as a version of Oliver Twist's' (p. 160).
7. See Alan Shelston, 'Introduction', *The Life of Charlotte Brontë*, pp. 29–31.
8. See also the discussion on the relationship between photography and history in the Introduction.
9. Nancy Armstrong explicitly connects photography's indexical function to the role of literary realism: 'As Victorian photography established the categories of identity – race, class, gender, nation, and so forth – in terms of which virtually all other peoples of the world could be classified, literary realism showed readers how to play the game of modern identity from the position of observers' (p. 26). On the relationship between photography and realism, see also Jennifer Green-Lewis, *Framing the Victorians: Photography and the Culture of Realism* (1996).
10. In an anonymous article for *Once a Week* in 1863, Andrew Wynter similarly notes the advantages and disadvantages of photography over drawing: 'although the sun is a better draughtsman than any human hand, yet there are certain drawbacks' (p. 150). Interestingly, the author suggests that those drawbacks stem from the situation rather than the process of photography; a photograph fails to capture expression, not because of any limitation in the photographic process but rather because 'the first thing [the sitter] does is to make up a face' (p. 150).
11. For a more detailed discussion of the ways in which photography influences neo-Victorian fiction see Arias (2008) and Mitchell (2008).
12. I am indebted to the anonymous reviewer for pointing out this probable meaning of the letter 'F'.
13. Again, thanks are due to the anonymous reviewer, who reminded me of the sensuality depicted in Christina Rossetti's 'Goblin Market' (1862). While the

sexual undercurrent is clear, the poem adopts the metaphor of ripened fruit for sexual desire and thus the physical residue of Lizzie's encounter with the goblins is euphemistically described as 'the drip/ Of juice that syruped all her face' (l. 433–4). Bullen hints at the problems of reading 'Goblin Market' from our 'post-Freudian' perspective: 'To us it oozes the juices of succulent sexuality [...] we have no way of telling how it fell on those innocent ears of the first audience. Or were they so innocent?' (p. 9).

14. Interestingly, Matthew Beaumont's review of *The Dark Clue* suggests that 'paradoxically, there is something a little too sensational about its characterization and its plot' (p. 22).
15. See Sharon Aronofsky Weltman's 'Victorians on Broadway at the Present Time: John Ruskin's Life on Stage' (2002).
16. Kirchknopf claims that 'anxiety concerning problems of texts' temporality and authenticity in chains of adaptation or appropriation reveals itself in [...] frequently used terms like *prequel, sequel* or *aftering,*' (p. 72). For a fuller discussion of the issues of originality and authenticity in neo-Victorian fiction, see the Coda.

2 Detecting the Victorians

1. On the historian as detective see Ray B. Browne and Lawrence A. Kreiser Jr., (eds), *The Detective as Historian: History and Art in Historical Crime Fiction* (2002).
2. Robert Ashley acknowledges that '[m]ost authorities classify [*The Woman in White*] as a mystery rather than as a detective novel, but its resemblance to the latter type is sufficiently strong to justify its classification as a borderline case' (p. 51).
3. See also John Sutherland's Introduction to the novel, which highlights this analogy in the claim that '[t]he novel's technique is forensic, not historical' (p. xv).
4. Drabble suggests that 'English writers followed [Poe] in creating detectives who were remote from the common herd, creatures of pure ratiocination, emotional hermits [...]' (p. 276).
5. As Knight observes, '[Holmes] has a knowledge of what certain phenomena *will* mean, and is practising deduction, that is drawing from a set of existent theories to explain new events' (p. 86).
6. Information taken from www.met.police.uk/history.
7. As Drabble notes, 'Private detectives are now the exception [...]' (p. 277).
8. For instance, the Sir George Rose Act passed in 1812 required parishes to keep separate registers for baptisms, marriages and deaths.
9. See Caplan and Torpey, who argue that 'Registration and documentation of individual identity are essential if persons are to "count" in a world increasingly distant from the face-to-face encounters characteristic of less complex societies' (p. 6).
10. Information taken from www.met.police.uk/history.
11. *Crime Scene Investigation* first aired in 2000 and has proved so popular it has spawned two spin-off shows *CSI: Miami* and *CSI: NY*.
12. Knight argues that 'The steady collection and analysis of data was in itself the basis of nineteenth-century science and a strong feature of other areas of thought – such as Doyle's own beloved history' (p. 79).

13. As we shall see in the next chapter, several neo-Victorian texts explicitly examine the role of spiritualism in connecting the present and the past.
14. In this respect, Dexter's novel adopts a dual plot structure akin to that of A. S. Byatt's *Possession: A Romance* and Graham Swift's *Ever After*, which are discussed in Chapter 4.
15. Although there were instances of the professional detective in nineteenth-century novels, such as Inspector Bucket in Charles Dickens's *Bleak House* (1852–52) and Sergeant Cuff in Wilkie Collins's *The Moonstone* (1868), these were rarely the protagonists of the story.

3   Resurrecting the Victorians

1. In the introduction to their recent collection *Haunting and Spectrality in Neo-Victorian Fiction: Possessing the Past* (2010), Arias and Pulham suggest that 'Victorianism [is] understood as a revenant or a ghostly visitor from the past' (p. xv).
2. Susan Rowland's essay, 'Women, Spiritualism and Depth Psychology in Michèle Roberts's Victorian Novel' (2000) first made me aware of this connection.
3. Imelda Whelehan similarly suggests that contemporary women writers return to the Victorian era because they 'are unhappy with the available models of post-Victorian female options enacted in literature, to the point that we prefer to return to the primal scene of emergent "female" identity as found in the classic Victorian texts' (p. 76).
4. In the 'Author's note' to her novel, Roberts identifies an essay by Owen as 'invaluable,' while Byatt cites Owen's book as revealing how 'Being a medium was one way in which a Victorian woman could have a career' ('Angels and Insects').
5. See also Diana Basham, *The Trial of Woman: Feminism and the Occult Sciences in Victorian Literature and Society* (1992).
6. Rowland persuasively argues that Roberts's novel 'seeks the mothers of depth psychology [...] in the nineteenth-century women engaged in spiritualism' (p. 211).
7. As Green-Lewis notes 'Early subjects for the camera were corpses, frequently of children, who were represented as sleeping, or (with some careful cutting and pasting) as angels in clouds above their parents' heads' (1996, p. 45).
8. Rosario Arias's article, '(Spirit) Photography and the Past in the Neo-Victorian Novel' (2009), uses the paradoxical position of nineteenth-century photography to explore the relationship between the present and the past in neo-Victorian fictions.
9. See Owen, p. xiv.
10. Similarly, in an anonymous contribution to *The Cornhill Magazine* in 1863, Fitzjames Stephen wrote that 'Believers in ghosts affect to derive their belief from experience. In truth, their belief is antecedent to their experience' (p. 707).
11. Both Mark Llewellyn (2005) and Lucie Armitt and Sarah Gamble (2006) draw attention to the influence of Foucault in *Affinity*.

12. See Owen, p. 25.
13. This is not to say that Waters does not use historical sources; indeed, Llewellyn identifies Henry Mayhew's *The Criminal Prisons of London and Scenes of Prison Life* (1862) as 'one of Waters' key resources' (2004, p. 204).
14. Elsewhere, Llewellyn has discussed how spiritualism and mediumship opens up 'metafictional possibilities for writers to provide a subtle commentary on their own practice in conjuring up or summoning the Victorians in contemporary fiction' (2010, p. 41).
15. For a discussion of William Crookes as a model for William Preston, see Rowland (2000).
16. Rowland's essay first drew my attention to this possible historical identity of the fictional Hat.
17. Llewellyn suggests that Margaret's resistance to the past, both here and elsewhere in her diary, can be read as 'a kind of ironic comment on the escapist impulse to both write and read historical fiction' (2007, p. 200).
18. Similarly, King suggests that Sophy is 'telepathically linked' to Tennyson in the novella (p. 112).
19. Sarah Falcus similarly argues that Roberts's novel 'suggests an approach to history that is not strictly linear, as the women of the text are linked through history and across geography by voice, visuals and even colour associations [...]' (p. 143). See also Agnieszka Golda-Derejczyk's essay 'Repetition and Eternity: The Spectral and Textual Continuity in Michèle Roberts's *In the Red Kitchen*' (2010).

4 Reading the Victorians

1. Other neo-Victorian novels that adopt a dual plot include Colin Dexter's *The Wench is Dead* (1989) and Michèle Roberts's *In the Red Kitchen* (1990), which are examined in Chapters 2 and 3 respectively. Michèle Roberts's *The Mistressclass* (2003) also incorporates two time-frames, but there the nineteenth- and twentieth-century plots remain separate.
2. Maud Bailey's comment that 'the classic detective story arose with the classic adultery novel – everyone wanted to know who was the Father, what was the origin, what is the secret?', indicates *Possession*'s affinity with the detective genre (p. 238).
3. Mary Hawthorne's review of Byatt's *Angels and Insects* for *The New Yorker* opens with a discussion of *Possession*, in which she identifies a 'deep sense of mourning' that belongs as much to Byatt as to her creation, Roland (98).
4. See also Burgass (2002) p. 27.
5. Interestingly, Byatt claims that LaMotte's 'Melusine' was 'written to conform with a feminist interpretation of the imaginary poem – an interpretation I had in fact written before writing the text itself' (*On Histories*, 47). In making LaMotte's poetry fit with critical readings Byatt reverses the usual practice of criticism, which exists in a vampiric relationship to the poetic texts they purport to explain, sucking the life and energy out of them and reducing their complexities to a single preoccupation.

6. Such an approach betrays similar assumptions to the empathy approach to history, which assumes the existence of a shared set of values that transcend historical conditions.
7. See Shuttleworth (1998) for a discussion of Darwin in neo-Victorian fiction.
8. See Hadley (2003).

Coda: Writing *as* the Victorians

1. Although she considers contemporary neo-Victorian fiction as a 'reproduction' of the Victorian original, Winterson criticizes the 'rigid proprieties' of Victorian fiction (Wormald, p. 186). See also Gamble, p. 131.
2. Arias and Pulham suggest that neo-Victorian fiction is 'a ghostly visitor from the past that infiltrates our present' and, consequently, 'calls the contemporary novel's life into question' (p. xv).
3. Although Philip Haas's film bears the name *Angels and Insects*, it actually only adapts the novella 'Morpho Eugenia'.
4. As we saw in the previous chapter, the models of reading that are prioritized in Byatt's and Swift's novels are those that actively engage with the past. Indeed, Palliser's own neo-Victorian novels, *The Quincunx* and *The Unburied* (1999), are much more actively engaged with Victorian literature than his remark about writing a 'new Dickens' suggests.
5. In *Possession*, Byatt directly quotes Robinson's diary entry for February 16th 1859 (p. 24). See Sadler (1869), pp. 463–4.
6. Writing about the reappearance of the Victorian novel series, Kirchknopf similarly notes that 'nineteenth-century literary conventions and the canon are reinforced at the same time as they are deconstructed' (p. 73).
7. The multiple endings of John Fowles's *The French Lieutenant's Woman* (1969) parodies the Victorian narrator's ability to transgress the boundaries of time and space. At the end of the penultimate chapter, the author figure winds his watch back a quarter of an hour, allowing an alternative ending to play out. See Hadley (forthcoming).
8. *Possession* similarly incorporates the real, corporeal presence of Victorian authors, even though they are fictional Victorians.
9. See Glendinning, p. 45.
10. As we saw, Schor conflates the process of 'writing like ...' with the postmodern form of pastiche (p. 237).
11. Thanks to the anonymous reviewer of the manuscript, who pointed out that pastiche is a Victorian form.
12. In her interview with Abigail Dennis, Waters suggests that writing historical fiction involves 'mak[ing] the leap into a slightly different mentality and a different cultural landscape' (p. 48). Interestingly, she remarks shortly afterwards that she decided to move away from the Victorian era in her fiction because of the 'danger of pastiching [herself ...], as well as pastiching Wilkie Collins and Dickens and stuff' (p. 50).
13. See Parini, p. 11; Yelin, p. 38; and Burgass, p. 52.
14. See for instance Yelin, p. 38; and Parini, p. 11.
15. As Shuttleworth notes, 'the story has been told many times before, not least in the Victorian age itself' (p. 254).

16. Browning, 'Mr Sludge, the Medium' (1991). All subsequent line references will appear parenthetically in the text.
17. Shuttleworth's assessment of Byatt's pseudo-Victorian poetry similarly reveals the commitment to historical specificity: 'Although I would not wish to claim that these poems have the force of the original models, they could only have been created by the precise attention to history which Jameson claims is lacking in our post-modern age' (p. 266).
18. Kelly describes Ash's poetry as 'Browningesque' and identifies 'Mummy Possest' as a 'reply' to Browning's 'Mr Sludge' (p. 92).
19. See Hadley (forthcoming).

Bibliography

Neo-Victorian texts

Ackroyd, Peter. *Dickens*. London: Vintage, 1990.

Affinity. dir. Tim Fywell. Screenplay by Andrew Davies. Independent Television (ITV), 2008.

Angels and Insects. dir. Philip Haas. Screenplay by Brenda Haas. MGM Home Entertainment, 1999. DVD.

Atwood, Margaret. *The Journals of Susanna Moodie: Poems by Margaret Atwood*. Oxford: Oxford University Press, 1970.

Atwood, Margaret. *Alias Grace*. New York: Anchor, 1997.

Barnes, Julian. *Arthur & George*. 2005. London: Vintage, 2006.

Byatt, A. S. *Possession: A Romance*. 1990. London: Vintage, 1991.

Byatt, A. S. 'The Conjugial Angel.' *Angels and Insects*. London: Chatto & Windus, 1992.

Byatt, A. S. 'Morpho Eugenia.' *Angels and Insects*. London: Chatto & Windus, 1992.

Byatt, A. S. *The Biographer's Tale*. Chatto & Windus, 2000. London: Vintage, 2001.

Carey, Peter. *Jack Maggs*. London: Faber, 1997.

Churchill, Caryl. *Cloud Nine*. New York: Theatre Communications Group, 1995.

Creation. dir. Jon Amiel. D Films, 2009.

Dexter, Colin. *The Wench is Dead*. 1989. London: Pan Books, 2007.

Duncker, Patricia. *James Miranda Barry*. London: Serpent's Tail, 1999.

Farrell, J. G. *The Siege of Krishnapur*. 1973. Introd. Pankaj Misha. New York: The New York Review Book, 2004.

Fingersmith. dir Aisling Walsh. Screenplay by Peter Ransley. British Broadcasting Corporation, 2005.

Fowles, John. *The French Lieutenant's Woman*. 1969. London: Pan, 1987.

The French Lieutenant's Woman. dir. Karel Reisz. Screenplay by Harold Pinter. United Artists, 1981.

Galloway, Janice. *Clara*. 2002. London: Vintage, 2003.

Gray Alasdair. *Poor Things*. 1992. London: Penguin, 1993.

Kneale, Matthew. *English Passengers: A Novel*. New York: Anchor Books, 2001.

Mrs Brown. dir John Madden. Buena Vista International, 1997.

Palliser, Charles. *The Quincunx: The Inheritance of John Huffam*. 1989. London: Penguin, 1990.

Palliser, Charles. *The Unburied*. 1999. London: Phoenix-Orion, 2000.

Pearce, Philippa. *Tom's Midnight Garden*. 1958. London: Open University Press, 1970.

Possession. dir. Neil LaBute. Screenplay by David Henry Hwang. Warner Bros.-Focus Features, 2002.

Rhys, Jean. *Wide Sargasso Sea*. 1966. Harmondsworth: Penguin, 1968.

Roberts, Michèle. *In the Red Kitchen*. 1990. London: Minerva, 1991.
Roberts, Michèle. *The Mistressclass*. 2003. London: Virago Press, 2007.
Stoppard, Tom. *Arcadia*. London: Faber & Faber, 1993.
Swift, Graham. *Ever After*. London: Picador-Macmillan, 1992.
Thwaite, Anthony. *Victorian Voices*. Oxford: Oxford University Press, 1980.
Tipping the Velvet. dir. Geoffrey Sax. Screenplay by Andrew Davies. British Broadcasting Corporation, 2002.
Waters, Sarah. *Tipping the Velvet*. London: Virago, 1998.
Waters, Sarah. *Affinity*. London: Virago, 1999.
Waters, Sarah. *Fingersmith*. 2002. London: Virago, 2003.
Wilson, James. *The Dark Clue: A Novel of Suspense*. London: Faber, 2001.
The Young Victoria. dir. Jean-Marc Vallée. Momentum Pictures, 2009.

Other primary sources

Arkin, Anat. 'Past Masters in Rebellion.' *The Sunday Times*. 31 Jan 1988: B7.
Austen, Jane. *Pride and Prejudice*. 1813. Ed. Vivian Jones. London: Penguin, 2002.
[Ayton, W. E.] 'Spiritual Manifestations.' *Blackwood's Edinburgh Magazine* 73 (May 1853): 629–46.
Barker, Pat. *Regeneration*. London: Plume, 1993.
Barker, Pat. *The Eye in the Door*. London: Plume, 1995.
Barker, Pat. *The Ghost Road*. London: Plume, 1996.
Bleak House. dir. Justin Chadwick and Susanna White. Screenplay by Andrew Davies. British Broadcasting Corporation, 2005. DVD.
'The British Museum.' *The New Monthly Magazine* 89 (1850): 197–205.
Brontë, Charlotte. *Jane Eyre*. 1847. London: Vintage, 2009.
Brontë, Emily. *Wuthering Heights*. 1847. Ed. Pauline Nestor. London: Penguin, 2002.
Browning, Robert. 'Mr Sludge, the Medium.' *Dramatic Monologues*. Selected and Introd. A. S. Byatt, Illus. Richard Shirley Smith. London: Folio Society, 1991. 206–52.
Carlyle, Thomas. 'Biography.' 1832. *Selected Essays*. Introd. Ian Campbell. London: Dent, 1972. 64–79.
Carlyle, Thomas. 'Boswell's Life of Johnson.' 1832. *Selected Essays*. Introd. Ian Campbell. London: Dent, 1972. 1–64.
'Churchill voted greatest Briton.' *BBC News World Edition*. 24 Nov. 2002. http://news.bbc.co.uk/2/hi/entertainment/2509465.stm.
Collins, Wilkie. *The Woman in White*. 1860. Ed. and Introd. John Sutherland. Oxford: Oxford University Press, 1996.
Collins, Wilkie. *The Moonstone*. 1868. Ed. J. I. M. Stewart. Harmondsworth: Penguin, 1966.
Conan Doyle, Arthur. 'The Adventure of the Blue Carbuncle.' 1892. *The Adventures of Sherlock Holmes*. Ed. Richard Lancelyn Green. Oxford: Oxford University Press, 2008. 149–70.
Cranford. dir. Simon Curtis and Steve Hudson. Written by Sue Birtwistle, Susie Conklin, and Heidi Thomas. British Broadcasting Corporation, 2007. DVD.
CSI: Crime Scene Investigation. CBS Productions. 2000– . Television.

Daniel Deronda. dir. Tom Hooper. Screenplay by Andrew Davies. British Broadcasting Corporation, 2002. DVD.

Darwin, Charles. *On the Origin of Species. A Facsimile of the first Edition.* London: John Murray, 1859. Introd. Ernst Mayr. Cambridge, MA: Harvard University Press, 1964.

Dickens, Charles. *Oliver Twist.* 1838. Ed. Philip Horne. London: Penguin, 2003.

Dickens, Charles. *David Copperfield.* 1850. Ed. Jeremy Tambling. London: Penguin, 2004.

Dickens, Charles. *Bleak House.* 1852–53. Ed. and Introd. Nicola Bradbury. Harmondsworth: Penguin, 1996.

Dickens, Charles. *Hard Times.* 1854. Ed. and Introd. Kate Flint. London: Penguin, 1995.

Dickens, Charles. *Great Expectations.* 1860–61. Ed. and Notes Margaret Cardwell. Introd. Robert Douglas-Fairhurst. Oxford: Oxford University Press, 2008.

[Douglas, R. K.]. 'The British Museum and the People who go there.' *Blackwood's Edinburgh Magazine* 144 (Aug. 1888): 196–217.

Eastlake, Elizabeth. 'Photography.' *Quarterly Review* 101 (Apr. 1857): 442–68.

Eco, Umberto. *The Name of the Rose.* 1980. Trans. William Weaver. 1983. London: Vintage, 1998.

Eliot, George. *Romola.* 1862–3. Ed. and Introd. Dorothea Barrett. Harmondsworth: Penguin, 1996.

Eliot, George. *Middlemarch: A Study of Provincial Life.* 1871–72. Ed. and Introd. Rosemary Ashton. Harmondsworth: Penguin, 1994.

Froude, J. A. ed. *Letters and Memorials of Jane Welsh Carlyle.* New York: C. Scribner's Sons, 1883.

Gaskell, Elizabeth. *The Life of Charlotte Brontë.* 1857. Ed. Alan Shelston. London: Penguin, 1985.

Glen, William Cunningham. *The Metropolitan Interments Act, 1850, with Introduction, Notes, and Appendix.* London: Shaw & Sons, 1850. *Google Books.* Web. 15 May 2009.

Gosse, Edmund. *Father and Son.* 1907. Ed. Michael Newton. Oxford: Oxford University Press, 2004.

Gregory, Philippa. *The Queen's Fool: A Novel.* New York: Touchstone, 2004.

Hardy, Thomas. *Tess of the D'Urbervilles.* 1891. Oxford: Oxford University Press, 2008.

Harrison, Frederic. 'A Few Words About the Nineteenth Century.' 1882. *The Choice of Books and Other Literary Pieces.* London: Macmillan, 1886. 417–47.

Hart-Davis, Adam. *What the Victorians Did for Us.* London: Headline Book Publishing Ltd, 2002.

He Knew He Was Right. dir Tom Vaughn. Screenplay by Andrew Davies. British Broadcasting Corporation, 2004. DVD.

'History of the Metropolitan Police Force.' Web. 24 June 2009. http://www.met.police.uk/history/.

'The James Tait Black Memorial Prizes for Biography and Fiction.' The University of Edinburgh. Web. 15 July 2009. http://www.englit.ed.ac.uk/jtbinf.htm.

Jane Eyre. dir. Susanna White. Screenplay by Sandy Welch. British Broadcasting Corporation, 2006. DVD.

'Jane Eyre.' BBC. Web. 18 August 2006. http://www.bbc.co.uk/drama/janeeyre/yourreviews_episode1.shtml.

Lark Rise to Candleford. British Broadcasting Corporation, 2008—. Television.

Lewes, George Henry. 'Historical Romance.' *The Westminster Review* XLV (1846): 34–55.

Little Dorrit. Screenplay by Andrew Davies. British Broadcasting Corporation, 2008. DVD.

Lyell, Charles. *The Principles of Geology: Being an Attempt to Explain the former Changes of the Earth's Surface, by Reference to Causes Now in Operation.* 3 vols. London: J. Murray, 1830–33.

The Man Booker Prizes. Web. 26 Feb 2010. http://www.themanbookerprize.com/.

[Mansel, H. L]. 'Modern Spiritualism.' *The Quarterly Review* 114 (1863): 179–210.

[Mansel, H. L.]. 'Sensation Novels.' *The Quarterly Review* 113 (1863): 481–514.

[Mansfield, Horatio]. 'The Biographical Mania.' *Tait's Magazine* 21 (1854): 16–23.

'Michel Faber, Sarah Waters and Matthew Sweet on the Victorians.' Edinburgh International Book Festival. Charlotte Square Gardens, Edinburgh. 14 Aug. 2002.

Morrison, Toni. *Beloved.* 1987. London: Vintage, 1997.

National Curriculum History Working Group. *Final Report.* London: HMSO, The Department of Education & Science and the Welsh Office, 1990.

Norris, William. 'Sex through the ages ...' *Times Higher Educational Supplement.* 22 Jan 1988: 10.

'North and South.' BBC. Web. 18 August 2006. http://www.bbc.co.uk/drama/northandsouth/.

North and South. dir. Brian Percival. Adapt. Sandy Welch. 4 episodes. BBC1. 14 Nov.–5 Dec. 2004.

Oliver Twist. dir. Coky Giedroyc. Screenplay by Sarah Phelps. British Broadcasting Corporation, 2007. DVD.

Pride and Prejudice. dir. Joe Wright. Screenplay by Deborah Moggach. Studio Canal, 2005.

Ranke, Leopold von. 'On the Character of Historical Science. (A Manuscript of the 1830s).' Trans. Wilma A. Iggers. Leopold von Ranke, *The Theory and Practice of History.* Eds. and Introd. Georg G. Iggers and Konrad von Moltke. Indianapolis and New York: Bobbs-Merrill, 1973. 33–46.

Rendell, Ruth. *From Doom to Death.* 1964. Minnesota: Fawcett Publications, 1988.

Rodrick, Anne B. 'Empathetic Reading Experiences of Nineteenth-Century Novels.' online posting. 15 Nov. 2004. Victoria. 16 Feb. 2005. https://listserv.indiana.edu/cgi-bin/wa-iub.exe?A2=ind0411c&L=victoria&T=0&F=&S=&P=1130

'Romance of the World's News.' *Penny Illustrated Paper.* 31 Aug. 1912: 261.

Rossetti, Christina. G. 'Goblin Market.' 1862. *The Penguin Book of Victorian Verse.* Ed. and introd. Daniel Karlin. London: Penguin, 1998. 473–88.

'The Royal Commission on Historical Manuscripts.' *Scribner's Monthly* 6 (1873): 629–33.

Sadler, Thomas, ed. *Diary, Reminiscences, and Correspondence of Henry Crabb Robinson.* 3 Vols. London: Macmillan & Co, 1869.

'A Sherlock Holmes in Real Life.' *Penny Illustrated Paper.* 7 Sept. 1912: 296.

Smiles, Samuel. *Self help; with illustrations of conduct and perseverance.* 1859. Abr. George Bull. Introd. Sir Keith Joseph. Harmondsworth: Penguin, 1986.

Sofer, Anne. 'Identity Crisis.' *Times Educational Supplement* 22 Apr. 1988: 128.

[Stephen, Fitzjames]. 'Spiritualism.' *The Cornhill Magazine* 7 (1863): 706–19.

Stone, Norman. 'Put Nuts and Bolts Back Into History.' *The Sunday Times* 13 Mar. 1988: B8.

Strachey, Lytton. *Eminent Victorians*. 1918. Introd. Michael Holroyd. London: Penguin, 1986.

Tennyson, Alfred. *In Memoriam*. 1850. Ed. Susan Shatto and Marion Shaw. Oxford: Clarendon, 1982.

Tess of the D'Ubervilles. dir. David Blair. Screenplay by David Nicholls. British Broadcasting Corporation, 2008.

Thatcher, Margaret. Interview for London Weekend Television *Weekend World*. 10 Downing Street. 16 Jan. 1983. *Margaret Thatcher Foundation*. Web. 11 Jan 2005. http://www.margaretthatcher.org/speeches/displaydocument.asp?docid=105087.

Thatcher, Margaret. Speech to the Glasgow Chamber of Commerce (bicentenary). Holiday Inn, Glasgow. 28 Jan. 1983. *Margaret Thatcher Foundation*. Web. 11 Jan 2005. http://www.margaretthatcher.org/Speeches/displaydocument.asp?docid=105244&doctype=1.

Thatcher, Margaret. Radio Interview for IRN *The Decision Markers*. 15 Apr. 1983. *Margaret Thatcher Foundation*. Web. 11 Jan 2005 http://www.margaretthatcher.org/speeches/displaydocument.asp?docid=105291.

Thatcher, Margaret. Prime Minister's Question Time. House of Commons. 29 Mar. 1990. *Margaret Thatcher Foundation*. Web. 11 Jan 2005. http://www.margaretthatcher.org/search/displaydocument.asp?docid=108048&doctype=1.

Tytler, David. 'Teaching Methods Attacked.' *The Times* 3 Jan. 1989: 4b.

Unsworth, Barry. *Losing Nelson*. 1999. London: Penguin, 2000.

What the Romans Did for Us. Narr. Adam Hart-Davis. British Broadcasting Corporation. 2000.

What the Victorians Did for Us. Narr. Adam Hart-Davis. British Broadcasting Corporation, 3 Sept.–22 Oct. 2001.

'Who we were – or might be.' *Times Educational Supplement*. 22 June 1990: 17.

Secondary criticism

Adams, Ann Marie. 'Reader, I Memorialized Him: A. S. Byatt's Representation of Alfred Lord Tennyson in "The Conjugial Angel".' *Lit: Literature Interpretation Theory* 19.1 (2008): 26–46.

Altick, Richard D. *Lives and Letters: A History of Literary Biography in England and America*. New York: Alfred A. Knopf, 1969.

Amigoni, David. *Victorian Biography: Intellectuals and the Ordering of Discourse*. New York and London: Harvester Wheatsheaf, 1993.

Arias, Rosario. '(Spirit) Photography and the Past in the Neo-Victorian Novel.' *Lit: Literature Interpretation Theory* 19.1 (2008): 92–107.

Arias, Rosario and Patricia Pulham. Introduction. *Haunting and Spectrality in Neo-Victorian Fiction: Possessing the Past*. Eds. Rosario Arias and Patricia Pulham, Basingstoke: Palgrave Macmillan, 2010. xi–xxvi.

Arias, Rosario and Patricia Pulham, eds. *Haunting and Spectrality in Neo-Victorian Fiction: Possessing the Past*. Basingstoke: Palgrave Macmillan, 2010.

Armitt, Lucie and Sarah Gamble. 'The Haunted Geometries of Sarah Waters's *Affinity*.' *Textual Practice* 20.1: 141–59.

Armstrong, Nancy. *Fiction in the Age of Photography: The Legacy of British Realism.* London and Cambridge, MA: Harvard University Press, 1999.

Ashley, Robert P. 'Wilkie Collins and the Detective Story.' *Nineteenth-Century Fiction* 6 (1951): 47–60.

Ayto, John and John Simpson, eds. *The Oxford Dictionary of Modern Slang.* Oxford and New York: Oxford University Press, 1992.

Bann, Stephen. *The Clothing of Clio: A Study of the Representation of History in Nineteenth-Century Britain and France.* Cambridge: Cambridge University Press, 1984.

Barthes, Roland. *Camera Lucida: Reflections on Photography.* Trans. Richard Howard. London: Jonathan Cape, 1982.

Basham, Diana. *The Trial of Woman: Feminism and the Occult Sciences in Victorian Literature and Society.* London: Macmillan, 1992.

Beaumont, Matthew. 'A Brothel in Wapping.' Rev. of *The Dark Clue*, by James Wilson. *The Times Literary Supplement* 27 Apr. 2001: 22.

Benjamin, Walter. 'The Paris of the Second Empire in Baudelaire.' 1938. *The Writer of Modern Life: Essays on Charles Baudelaire.* Ed. Michael William Jennings. Harvard: Harvard University Press, 2006.

Bowen, John. 'The Historical Novel.' *A Companion to the Victorian Novel.* Eds. Patrick Brantlinger and William B. Thesing. Oxford: Blackwell, 2002. 244–59.

Broughton, Trev. 'The Froude–Carlyle Embroilment: Married Life as a Literary Problem.' *Victorian Studies* 38 (1995): 551–85.

Browne, Ray B. and Lawrence A. Kreiser Jr., eds. *The Detective as Historian: History and Art in Historical Crime Fiction.* Preface Robin W. Winks. Bowling Green, Ohio: Bowling Green State University Popular Press, 2002.

Bullen, J. B. Introduction. *Writing and Victorianism.* Ed. J. B. Bullen. London and New York: Longman, 1997. 1–13.

Burgass, Catherine. *A. S. Byatt's Possession: A Reader's Guide.* London: Continuum, 2002.

Byatt, A. S. 'Angels and Insects.' Web. 17 Jan 2003. http://www.asbyatt.com/anglInsct.htm.

Byatt, A. S. *On Histories and Stories: Selected Essays.* London: Chatto and Windus, 2000.

Byatt, A. S. *Passions of the Mind: Selected Writings.* London: Chatto & Windus, 1991.

Caplan, Jane and John Torpey. Introduction. *Documenting Individual Identity: The Development of State Practices in the Modern World.* Eds. Jane Caplan and John Torpey. Princeton: Princeton University Press, 2001. 1–12.

Clayton, Jay. *Charles Dickens in Cyberspace: The Afterlife of the Nineteenth Century in Postmodern Culture.* Oxford: Oxford University Press, 2003.

Collini, Stefan. 'Victorian Values: From the Clapham Set to the Clapham Omnibus.' *English Pasts: Essays in History and Culture.* Oxford: Oxford University Press, 1999. 103–15.

Culler, A. Dwight. *The Victorian Mirror of History.* New Haven and London: Yale University Press, 1985.

Day, Gary, ed. *Varieties of Victorianism: The Uses of a Past.* Basingstoke: Macmillan – now Palgrave Macmillan, 1998.

Dennis, Abigail. '"Ladies in Peril": Sarah Waters on neo-Victorian narrative celebrations and why she stopped writing about the Victorian era.' *Neo-Victorian Studies* 1.1 (2008): 41–52. http://www.neovictorianstudies.com/.

Drabble, Margaret. 'Detective Fiction.' *The Oxford Companion to English Literature*. 6th edn. Oxford: Oxford University Press, 2000.

Ermarth, Elizabeth Deeds. *Realism and Consensus in the English Novel: Time, Space and Narrative*. Edinburgh: Edinburgh University Press, 1998.

Falcus, Sarah. 'Michèle Roberts: Histories and Herstories in *In the Red Kitchen, Fair Exchange*, and *The Looking Glass*'. *Metafiction and Metahistory in Contemporary Women's Writing*. Eds. Ann Heilmann and Mark Llewellyn. Basingstoke: Palgrave Macmillan, 2007. 133–46.

Ferris, Ina. 'Printing the Past: Walter Scott's Bannatyne Club and the Antiquarian Document.' *Romanticism* 11.2 (2005): 143–60.

Fleishman, Avrom. *The English Historical Novel: Walter Scott to Virginia Woolf*. London: The Johns Hopkins Press, 1971.

Flint, Kate. 'Plotting the Victorians: Narrative, Post-Modernism, and Contemporary Fiction.' *Writing and Victorianism*. Ed. J. B. Bullen. London and New York: Longman, 1997. 286–305.

Foucault, Michel. *The History of Sexuality Volume I: An Introduction*. 1976. Trans. Robert Hurley. Harmondsworth: Penguin, 1979.

Frank, Lawrence. *Victorian Detective Fiction and the Nature of Evidence: The Scientific Investigations of Poe, Dickens, and Doyle*. Basingstoke: Palgrave Macmillan, 2003.

Gamble, Sarah. '"You cannot impersonate what you are": Questions of Authenticity in the Neo-Victorian Novel.' *Lit: Literature Interpretation Theory* 20.1 (2009): 126–40.

Gilmour, Robin. 'Using the Victorians: the Victorian Age in Contemporary Fiction.' *Rereading Victorian Fiction*. Eds. Alice Jenkins and Juliet John. Basingstoke: Macmillan – now Palgrave Macmillan, 2000. 189–200.

Gilmartin, Sophie. *Ancestry and Narrative in Nineteenth-Century British Literature: Blood Relations from Edgeworth to Hardy*. Cambridge: Cambridge University Press, 1998.

Glendinning, Victoria. 'Angels and ministers of graciousness.' Rev. of *Angels and Insects*, by A. S. Byatt. *The Times*, Saturday Review, 7 Nov 1992: 45.

Golda-Derejczyk, Agnieszka. 'Repetition and Eternity: The Spectral and Textual Continuity in Michèle Roberts's *In the Red Kitchen*.' *Haunting and Spectrality in Neo-Victorian Fiction: Possessing the Past*. Eds. Rosario Arias and Patricia Pulham, Basingstoke: Palgrave Macmillan, 2010. 45–57.

Green-Lewis, Jennifer. *Framing the Victorians: Photography and the Culture of Realism*. Ithaca and London: Cornell University Press, 1996.

Green-Lewis, Jennifer. 'At Home in the Nineteenth Century: Photography, Nostalgia, and the Will to Authenticity.' *Victorian Afterlife: Postmodern Culture Rewrites the Nineteenth Century*. Eds. John Kucich and Dianne F. Sadoff. Minneapolis: University of Minnesota Press, 2000. 29–48.

Grossgrovel, David. I. *Mystery and its Fictions: From Oedipus to Agatha Christie*. Baltimore, MD: The Johns Hopkins University Press, 1979.

Gutleben, Christian. *Nostalgic Postmodernism: The Victorian Tradition and the Contemporary British Novel*. Amsterdam and New York: Rodopi, 2001.

Hadley, Louisa. 'Spectres of the Past: A. S. Byatt's Victorian Ghost Stories.' *Ghosts of the Victorian*. Eds. David E. Latané and Elisabeth Gruner. Spec. Issue of *Victorians Institute Journal* 31 (2003): 85–99.

Hadley, Louisa. 'The History Debate: Thatcher and The Victorians.' 'Neo-Victorianism: The Politics and Aesthetics of Appropriation.' University of Exeter, Exeter. 10–12 Sept. 2007.

Hadley, Louisa. *The Fiction of A. S. Byatt*. Basingstoke: Palgrave Macmillan, 2008.

Hadley, Louisa. 'Feminine Endings: Neo-Victorian Transformations of the Victorian.' *Victorian Transformations: Genre, Nationalism, and Desire in Nineteenth-Century Literature*. Ed. Bianca Tredennick. Ashgate (Forthcoming).

Hawthorne, Mary. 'Winged Victoriana.' Rev. of *Angels and Insects*, by A. S. Byatt. *The New Yorker* 21 June 1993: 98.

Hewison, Robert. *The Heritage Industry: Britain in a Climate of Decline*. London: Methuen, 1987.

Higson, Andrew. 'Re-presenting the National Past: Nostalgia and Pastiche in the Heritage Film.' *British Cinema and Thatcherism: Fires Were Started*. Ed. Lester Friedman. London: University of Central London Press, 1993. 109–29.

Holmes, Frederick M. *The Historical Imagination: Postmodernism and the Treatment of the Past in Contemporary British Fiction*. Victoria: University of Victoria, 1997.

Hughes, Kathryn. 'Repossession.' Rev. of *Angels and Insects*, by A. S. Byatt. *New Statesman* 6 Nov. 1992: 49–52.

Hughes, Kathryn. 'Dumb, dumber, dumbest.' Rev. of *Inventing the Victorians*, by Matthew Sweet. *New Statesman* 5 Nov. 2001: 51–2.

Humphreys, Anne. 'The Afterlife of the Victorian Novel: Novels about Novels.' *A Companion to the Victorian Novel*. Eds. Patrick Brantlinger and William B. Thesing. Oxford: Blackwell, 2002. 442–57.

Hutcheon, Linda. *A Poetics of Postmodernism: History, Theory, Fiction*. London: Routledge, 1988.

Hutcheon, Linda. 'Circling the Downspout of Empire.' 1989. *Past the Last Post: Theorizing Post-Colonialism and Post-Modernism*. Ed. I. Adam and H. Tiffin. London: Harvester Wheatsheaf, 1991. 167–89.

Iggers, Georg G. and Konrad von Moltke. Introduction. *The Theory and Practice of History*. By Leopold von Ranke. Eds. Georg G. Iggers and Konrad von Moltke. Indianapolis and New York: Bobbs-Merrill, 1973.

Jameson, Fredric. *Postmodernism, or, The Cultural Logic of Late Capitalism*. 1991. London: Verso, 1993.

Janik, Del Ivan. 'No End of History: Evidence from the Contemporary English Novel.' *Twentieth Century Literature* 41.2 (1995): 160–89.

Joyce, Simon. *The Victorians in the Rearview Mirror*. Athens: Ohio University Press, 2007.

Kaplan, Cora. *Victoriana: Histories, Fictions, Criticism*. Edinburgh: Edinburgh University Press, 2007.

Keen, Suzanne. *Romances of the Archive in Contemporary British Fiction*. 2001. London, Toronto: University of Toronto Press. 2003.

Keener, John F. *Biography and the Postmodern Historical Novel*. New York: Edwin Mellen, 2001.

Kelly, Kathleen Coyne. *A. S. Byatt*. London: Prentice Hall, 1996.

Keyman, Martin. *From Bow Street to Baker Street: Mystery, Detection and Narrative*. New York: St. Martin's Press – now Palgrave Macmillan, 1992.

King, Jeanette. *The Victorian Woman Question in Contemporary Feminist Fiction*. Basingstoke, Palgrave Macmillan, 2005.

Kirchknopf, Andrea. '(Re-)Workings of Nineteenth-Century Fiction: Definitions, Terminology, Contexts.' *Neo-Victorian Studies* 1.1 (2008): 53–80. http://www.neovictorianstudies.com/

Knight, Stephen. *Form and Ideology in Crime Fiction*. London and Basingstoke: Macmillan – now Palgrave Macmillan, 1980.

Kohlke, Marie-Luise. 'Introduction: Speculations in and on the Neo-Victorian Encounter'. *Neo-Victorian Studies* 1.1 (2008): 1–18. http://www.neovictorian-studies.com/

Kreuger, Christine L., ed. *Functions of Victorian Culture at the Present Time*. Athens: Ohio University Press, 2002.

Kucich, John and Dianne F. Sadoff. 'Introduction: Histories of the Present.' *Victorian Afterlife: Postmodern Culture Rewrites the Nineteenth Century*. Eds. John Kucich and Dianne F. Sadoff. London: University of Minnesota Press, 2000. ix–xxx.

Lesser, Wendy. 'The Strange Case of Julian Barnes: How an author transcended his sources and unleashed magical powers.' *Slate* Posted Tuesday, Jan. 3, 2006. http://www.slate.com/id/2133506/.

Levine, George. *The Boundaries of Fiction: Carlyle, Macaulay, Newman*. Princeton, N J: Princeton University Press, 1968.

Llewellyn, Mark. '"Queer? I should say it is criminal!": Sarah Waters' *Affinity* (1999).' *Journal of Gender Studies* 12.3 (2004): 203–14.

Llewellyn, Mark. 'Breaking the Mould? Sarah Waters and the Politics of Genre.' *Metafiction and Metahistory in Contemporary Women's Writing*. Eds. Ann Heilmann and Mark Llewellyn. Basingstoke: Palgrave Macmillan, 2007. 195–210.

Llewellyn, Mark. 'What is Neo-Victorian Studies?' *Neo-Victorian Studies* 1.1 (2008): 164–85. http://www.neovictorianstudies.com/.

Llewellyn, Mark. 'Neo-Victorianism: On the Ethics and Aesthetics of Appropriation.' *Lit: Literature Interpretation Theory* 20.1 (2009): 27–44.

Llewellyn, Mark. 'Spectrality, S(p)ecularity, and Textuality: Or, Some Reflections in the Glass.' *Haunting and Spectrality in Neo-Victorian Fiction: Possessing the Past*. Eds. Rosario Arias and Patricia Pulham. Basingstoke: Palgrave Macmillan, 2010. 23–42.

Lukács, Georg. *The Historical Novel*. 1937. Trans. Hannah and Stanley Mitchell. London: Merlin, 1962.

McCracken, Scott. *Pulp: Reading Popular Fiction*. Manchester and New York: Manchester University Press, 1998.

McHale, Brian. *Postmodernist Fiction*. London: Routledge, 1996.

Mitchell, Kate. 'Ghostly Histories and Embodied Memories: Photography, Spectrality and Historical Fiction in *Afterimage* and *Sixty Lights*.' *Neo-Victorian Studies* 1.1 (2008): 81–109. http://www.neovictorianstudies.com/.

Moore, R. Laurence. 'The Spiritualist Medium: A Study of Female Professionalism in Victorian America.' *American Quarterly* 27.2 (1975): 200–21.

Morley, John. *Death, Heaven and the Victorians*. London: Studio Vista, 1971.

Newman, Jenny. Interview with Michèle Roberts. *Contemporary British and Irish Fiction: An Introduction Through Interviews*. Eds. Sharon Monteith, Jenny Newman and Pat Wheeler. London: Arnold, 2004. 119–34.

Noakes, Jonathan. 'Interview with A. S. Byatt.' *A. S. Byatt: Possession: A Romance, Angels and Insects, A Whistling Woman*. Eds. Jonathan Noakes and Margaret Reynolds, with Gillian Alban. London: Vintage, 2003. 11–32.

O'Gorman, Francis. 'Salley Vickers, Venice, and the Victorians.' *Haunting and Spectrality in Neo-Victorian Fiction: Possessing the Past*. Eds. Rosario Arias and Patricia Pulham. Basingstoke: Palgrave Macmillan, 2010. 3–22.

Onion, Rebecca. 'Reclaiming the Machine: An Introductory Look at Steampunk in Everyday Practice.' *Neo-Victorian Studies* 1.1 (2008): 138–63. http://www.neovictorianstudies.com/.

Owen, Alex. *The Darkened Room: Women, Power and Spiritualism in Late Victorian England*. London: Virago, 1989.

Palliser, Charles. 'Author's Afterword.' *The Quincunx: The Inheritance of John Huffam*. 1989. London: Penguin, 1990. 1203–21.

Parini, Jay. 'Unearthing the Secret Lover.' *New York Times* 21 Oct. 1990: 9+.

Richards, Thomas. *The Imperial Archive: Knowledge and the Fantasy of Empire*. London: Verso, 1993.

Rowland, Susan. 'Women, Spiritualism and Depth Psychology in Michèle Roberts's Victorian Novel.' *Rereading Victorian Fiction*. Eds. Alice Jenkins and Juliet John. Basingstoke: Macmillan – now Palgrave Macmillan, 2000.

Samuel, Raphael. 'Mrs Thatcher's Return to Victorian Values.' *Victorian Values: Joint Symposium of the Royal Society of Edinburgh and the British Academy, December 1990*. Ed. T. C. Smout. Oxford: Oxford University Press, 1992. 9–29.

Schor, Hilary M. 'Sorting, Morphing, and Mourning: A. S. Byatt Ghostwrites Victorian Fiction.' *Victorian Afterlife: Postmodern Culture Rewrites the Nineteenth Century*. Eds. John Kucich and Dianne F. Sadoff. Minneapolis and London: University of Minnesota Press, 2000. 234–51.

Shaw, Harry. *Narrating Reality: Austen, Scott, Eliot*. Ithaca and London: Cornell University Press, 1999.

Shelston, Alan. Introduction. *The Life of Charlotte Brontë*, by Elizabeth Gaskell. 1857. London: Penguin, 1985. 9–37.

Shiller, Dana. 'Neo-Victorian Fiction: Reinventing the Victorians.' Diss. University of Washington, 1995.

Shiller, Dana. 'The Redemptive Past in the Neo-Victorian Novel.' *Studies in the Novel* 29.4 (1997): 538–60.

Shuttleworth, Sally. 'Natural History: The Retro-Victorian Novel.' *The Third Culture: Literature and Science*. Ed. Elinor S. Shaffer. New York: W. de Gruyter, 1998. 253–68.

Spooner, Catherine. '"Spiritual Garments": Fashioning the Victorian Séance in Sarah Waters' *Affinity*.' *Styling Texts: Dress and Fashion in Literature*. Eds. Cynthia Kuhn and Cindy Carlson. New York: Cambria Press, 2007.

Stewart, Susan. *On Longing: Narratives of the Miniature, the Gigantic, the Souvenir, the Collection*. Durham: Duke University Press, 1993.

Sutherland, John. Introduction. *The Woman in White*. By Wilkie Collins. Oxford: Oxford University Press, 1996. vi–xxiii.

Sweet, Matthew. *Inventing the Victorians*. London: Faber & Faber, 2001.

Taylor, Miles and Michael Wolff, eds. *The Victorians Since 1901: Histories, Representations and Revisions*. Manchester and New York: Manchester University Press, 2004.

Todorov, Tzvetan. 'The Typology of Detective Fiction.' *The Poetics of Prose*. 1971. Trans. Richard Howard. Ithaca, NY: Cornell University Press, 1984.

Voigts-Virchow, Eckart. 'In-yer-Victorian-face: A Subcultural Hermeneutics of Neo-Victorianism.' *Lit: Literature Interpretation Theory* 20.1 (2009): 108–25.

Wachtel, Eleanor. '"We Really Can Make Ourselves Up": An Interview With Peter Carey.' *Australian and New Zealand Studies in Canada* 9 (1993): 103–05.

Wallace, Diana. *The Woman's Historical Novel: British Women Writers, 1900–2000*. Basingstoke: Palgrave Macmillan, 2005.

Weltman, Sharon Aronofsky. 'Victorians on Broadway at the Present Time: John Ruskin's Life on Stage.' *Functions of Victorian Culture at the Present Time*. Ed. Christine L. Kreuger. Athens: Ohio University Press, 2002. 79–94.

Wheeler, Michael. *Death and the Future Life in Victorian Literature and Theology*. Cambridge: Cambridge University Press, 1990.

Whelehan, Imelda. 'The New Angels in the House?: Feminists as New Victorians.' *Lit: Literature Interpretation Theory* 20.1 (2009): 65–78.

White, Hayden. 'The Burden of History.' *Tropics of Discourse: Essays in Cultural Criticism*. Baltimore: The Johns Hopkins University Press, 1985. 27–50.

Williamson, Andrew. '"The Dead Man Touch'd Me From the Past": Reading as Mourning, Mourning as Reading in A. S. Byatt's "The Conjugial Angel".' *Neo-Victorian Studies* 1.1 (2008): 110–37. http://www.neovictorianstudies.com/.

Wilson, Cheryl A. '(Neo-)Victorian Fatigue: Getting Tired of the Victorians in Conrad's *The Secret Agent*.' *Neo-Victorian Studies* 1.1 (2008): 19–40. http://www.neovictorianstudies.com/.

Wormald, Mark. 'Prior Knowledge: Sarah Waters and the Victorians.' *British Fiction Today*. Eds. Philip Tew and Rod Mengham. London: Continuum, 2006. 186–97.

Wright, Patrick. *On Living in an Old Country: The National Past in Contemporary Britain*. London, New York: Verso, 1985.

Wrigley, E. A., ed. *Nineteenth-Century Society: Essays in the Use of Quantitative Methods for the Study of Social Data*. Cambridge: Cambridge University Press, 1972.

[Wynter, Andrew]. 'Photographic Portraiture.' *Once a Week*. 31 Jan 1863. Vol. 8 (1862–3): 148–50.

Yelin, Louise. 'Cultural Cartography: A. S. Byatt's *Possession* and the Politics of Victorian Studies.' *Victorian Newsletter* 81 (Spring 1992): 38–41.

Young, Hugo. 'Rough Justice for a leader born to battle.' Rpt. in *The Thatcher Legacy: Right to the End*. Eds. H. Birch, Q. McDermott, and M. McNay. *The Guardian* Collection No. 3. London: Guardian Newspapers. n.d. 5–6, 8.

Index

Mansfield, Horatio 23, 34–8, 48, 51, 53, 57
 'The Biographical Mania' 23, 34–8, 51
Mayhew, Henry 38, 56, 171fn13
McCracken, Scott 63, 66
medium 94, 95
 in *Affinity* 4, 28, 85, 98, 99–100, 104–5, 106–7, 110–11, 112–13
 in 'The Conjugial Angel' 28, 85, 100–3
 figure for historical novelist 28, 85, 89–90, 96–7, 98, 105–7, 110–11, 116, 171fn14
 gender 87–8, 89–90, 91–2, 96–7, 101, 162, 170fn2
 historical mediums 86, 91–2, 108
 in *In the Red Kitchen* 28, 85, 86, 97–9, 101, 103–4, 108, 114–15
 in *Possession* 162
 see also ghosts, Owen, Alex, spiritualism, Wallace, Diana
mesmerism 41, 45, 51–2
Metropolitan Police Force 38, 64, 65, 66
modernism 15, 60, 62
modernists 1, 5, 165fn2
 reaction to Victorians 1, 7, 83
Mrs Brown 30–1, 32

National Curriculum 24, 25, 73–4, 119, 132
 presentism 26, 122, 132
 Thatcher, Margaret on 25, 119
 see also empathy, history
neo-Victorian fiction
 Affinity 4, 27, 28, 85, 86, 88–9, 90, 96, 97, 98, 99–100, 104–5, 106–8, 110, 111–12, 160, 170fn11, 171fn13
 Alias Grace 2, 4
 Arthur & George 2, 4, 15, 27, 59, 60, 63, 67, 68–9, 70, 71, 72, 76–9, 80–1, 84, 145, 146, 151–4, 155, 156–7, 160, 163
 Clara 4, 15, 27, 32, 38, 39–40, 41, 43, 45, 46–7, 49, 50–1, 53, 54, 56–7, 58, 155, 157

'The Conjugial Angel' 4, 27, 28, 85–6, 87, 88, 96, 97, 100–3, 106, 109–10, 111, 112–13, 145–6, 147–8, 154–5, 157
The Dark Clue 4, 5, 27, 32, 38–9, 42–3, 44, 46, 47–9, 53, 55–6, 58, 148–50, 157, 160, 169fn14
English Passengers 2
Fingersmith 2, 4, 88
The French Lieutenant's Woman 2, 172fn7
 as historical fiction 5, 14, 15–19, 23, 28–9, 55–7, 89, 106–11, 112, 153–4, 155, 163–4, 165fn9, 167fn29, 171fn17, 172fn12
In the Red Kitchen 4, 15, 27, 28, 85, 86–7, 88, 90, 96, 97–9, 100, 101, 103–4, 108–9, 110, 111, 113–15, 116, 170fn4, 170fn6, 171fn19, 171fn1
Jack Maggs 4, 5, 15, 27, 32, 38, 39, 40–1, 43–4, 45, 47, 49, 51–3, 56, 57, 58, 147–8, 156, 157, 158, 160
James Miranda Barry 166fn10
The Journals of Susanna Moodie 165fn6
'Morpho Eugenia' 160, 172fn3
 and nostalgia 32, 33, 112, 114, 119, 142, 143, 144, 149, 151, 157
Possession: A Romance 2, 4, 12, 15, 27, 59, 74, 85, 93, 97, 117, 118, 119–20, 123–6, 127–30, 132–3, 134–5, 136–40, 141, 142, 145–6, 151, 160, 161–3, 164, 170fn14, 171fn2, 171fn3, 171fn5, 172fn4, 172fn5, 172fn8
 and postmodernism 3, 5, 15, 18–19, 21, 38–9, 68, 89–90, 119, 138, 152, 153–4, 159
 and realism 150–5, 158, 164
 and sex 46–8, 54, 55, 107, 108, 109, 146, 148, 149, 157, 167fn24
The Siege of Krishnapur 4
 and Thatcher 3, 6, 14, 23–4, 83, 157
Tipping the Velvet 4, 88, 166fn10